Praise for *The Ballerinas*

"The ways in which women torture [W9-BBX-603] ~~creative~~
dreams make for enthralling fictional ~~...~~. This terrain proves irresisti-
ble in *The Ballerinas*, a debut novel set in the hothouse atmosphere of the
Paris Opera Ballet academy as three students grow up, compete, forge
friendships, and embark on a trail of destruction. . . . Kapelke-Dale has
thought through the larger picture and examined how trauma and asym-
metries of power derail so many dancers." —*The New York Times*

"This highly readable, dramatic look behind the curtains is an unqualified
success." —*Booklist*

"Deliciously observed emotional tangles." —*Library Journal*

"Deftly uses the professional dance setting to explore the complexities of
female friendships and the lingering impacts of ballet's patriarchal culture
as it hurtles toward the bloody conclusion promised on the first pages."
—*Dance Magazine*

"Engrossing, deft, and insightful . . . I loved *The Ballerinas*—from its
provocative opening pages, to its blistering climax, to its exactly right final
scenes." —Cathy Marie Buchanan, *New York Times*
bestselling author of *The Painted Girls*

"Deftly constructed and crackling with tension, *The Ballerinas* is a stunner
of a novel, with electric prose and careful observations on loyalty, ambi-
tion, power, and rage within the crucible of intense female friendships.
I tore through this unforgettable thriller."
—Andrea Bartz, *New York Times* bestselling author of
We Were Never Here

"Wonderfully atmospheric, *The Ballerinas* is a twirling dream of a story."
—Araminta Hall, author of *Our Kind of Cruelty*

ALSO BY RACHEL KAPELKE-DALE

Graduates in Wonderland:
The International Misadventures of Two (Almost) Adults
(with Jessica Pan)

THE BALLERINAS

A NOVEL

RACHEL KAPELKE-DALE

ST. MARTIN'S GRIFFIN
NEW YORK

Published in the United States by St. Martin's Griffin, an imprint of St. Martin's Publishing Group

THE BALLERINAS. Copyright © 2021 by Rachel Kapelke-Dale. All rights reserved. Printed in the United States of America. For information, address St. Martin's Publishing Group, 120 Broadway, New York, NY 10271.

www.stmartins.com

Designed by Devan Norman

The Library of Congress has cataloged the hardcover edition as follows:

Names: Kapelke-Dale, Rachel, author.
Title: The ballerinas : a novel / Rachel Kapelke-Dale.
Description: First edition. | New York : St. Martin's Press, 2021. |
    Identifiers: LCCN 2021027556 | ISBN 9781250274236 (hardcover) |
    ISBN 9781250281166 (Canadian) | ISBN 9781250274243 (ebook)
    Classification: LCC PS3611.A64 B35 2021 | DDC 813/.6—dc23
    LC record available at https://lccn.loc.gov/2021027556

ISBN 978-1-250-81011-3 (trade paperback)

Our books may be purchased in bulk for promotional, educational, or business use. Please contact your local bookseller or the Macmillan Corporate and Premium Sales Department at 1-800-221-7945, extension 5442, or by email at MacmillanSpecialMarkets@macmillan.com.

First St. Martin's Griffin Edition: 2022

10 9 8 7 6 5 4 3 2 1

FOR JESS

You don't understand the humiliation of it—
to be tricked out of the single assumption which makes our existence viable—
that somebody is *watching*.

—TOM STOPPARD,
ROSENCRANTZ AND GUILDENSTERN ARE DEAD

THE
BALLERINAS

You start out as potential energy and then you fall.

Before Nathalie emailed and offered to take me back, before I killed anyone, I saw variations of the same quotation everywhere: *Paris is always a good idea*. On mugs, on throw pillows, on Instagram. Always attributed to Audrey Hepburn, always in pink. I couldn't escape it; everywhere I went, there were those fucking words. At the time, they seemed like a sign that I should do it. I should go home. When I'd lived in Paris, I'd never had starry-eyed notions about what the city was, but I was perfectly ready to buy into them if they meant I could come back. Paris is always a good idea? Great. Bring on the macarons, the endless wine, the strolls along the Seine.

But the truth is, I didn't know what Paris was like for most people.

When you're the best at something, your world is small—your life is small. And for a few years, I was one of the best dancers on the planet. I was a member of the Paris Opera Ballet. I'd never thought about the city as extending beyond my tiny sphere of influence, which meant that Paris was small for me, too.

Paris was my birthplace, my home for the first twenty-three years of my life. It was where I had my first kiss, where I met my two best friends, where I danced in sixty-four performances of *Swan Lake*, forty-three *Nutcrackers*, twenty-six *La Sylphides*. Where my mother wrenched my three-year-old hand and ground it, smarting, against the wood of the barre.

"It's like church, okay? You know how you have to stay quiet and still during church? Just pretend like you're there." She took hold of my thigh, twisting it so my knee faced out, ninety degrees to the side. Then she took the other and did the same, so that my heels were touching. "There. That's first position."

"It's like . . . church?"

"I mean, you're not in charge of anything, all right? The only thing you're in charge of is your own body."

You start out as whole and then you break.

Now, of course, it's a totally different story. I still see that quote all over the place and it sends needles of rage shooting through my bloodstream. If I'm in a good mood, it irritates me; if I'm in a bad one, it makes me want to grab Audrey Hepburn by her bony shoulders and shake her until her teeth rattle.

Always a good idea? Paris is nothing more than an empty stage. It's only as good or bad as the people in it, and the willful naivete of that statement turns my stomach. I don't see what good it does to mythologize a city. Sure, it's pretty. But how much is *pretty* worth? Paris is also a place where the government massacred its citizens: lining them up against the wall of the cemetery, throwing their bodies into a huge communal trench. Paris is a place where, under siege one freezing winter, the citizens ate every animal in the zoo. Paris is a place that transported more than ten thousand children to death camps.

Audrey did get one thing right, though. Paris is, more than anything else, an idea.

Maybe, in the end, the romantics dreaming about Paris see the same thing in the city that I do: that empty stage. A place where the rough edges are sloughed off behind the scenes, where the pain disappears behind pale pink smiles and satin, where the stage lights erase all shadows as they illuminate you with an otherworldly glow.

But you start out as perfect and you become something else.

CHAPTER 1

Margaux stumbled into my dorm room, groaning as she fell back against the wall. "I hate the yellow."

"You *love* the yellow."

She scanned my body. "It's not fair. You're so pale, you look great in pastels. So basically, you'll be there looking perfect until we graduate, and I'll be over here looking like—like—"

Like she had the stomach flu. But even at thirteen, I knew better than to finish the thought for her. Every year, we had a new leotard color, and every year, it was a pastel that washed her out. With her brown hair and hazel eyes, her warm beauty looked better in anything else: reds, golds, oranges. She was a *Summer*, one of our magazines had told us the previous year. With my black hair and blue eyes, I was a classic *Winter*.

"You'll get to wear white in a couple of years."

But we both knew it wasn't as easy as just waiting. About a quarter of our class disappeared each year after exams. Those final summer days were both exhilarating and heartbreaking as girls—friends—sobbed outside the gates where the school posted our results. We hugged them. We patted their backs. And all the time, our insides were soaring because it wasn't us. We were still the right shape and size, still good enough.

I threw down my brush with frustration. "Will you do my hair?"

Margaux came over and started scraping the thin black strands into a bun, then let it fall as she grabbed a bottle of hair gel. My hair was too fine to stay up all day without it, and none of us had time between classes to dart back to the dorms. Margaux's hair never fell out of its bun.

We headed down to the studio together. Ready to see who was there, ready to dismiss them as temporary. Four of our classmates had been thrown out the previous June. The school didn't have to keep the classes the same size, but they nearly always did, taking students who'd auditioned to fill the empty spaces. This would be the last year that anybody was added to our class, though, because the school didn't take anybody older than thirteen. Past that point, it was too late; the Paris Opera Ballet style, that famous POB touch, would never be natural to them.

"Only three new girls," Margaux whispered as I opened the studio door.

"Yeah," I said grimly. "But if they're any good, three's enough." Enough to jeopardize everything we'd worked for, to push us from the top of the class into the great mass of mediocrities.

There's a compact between the company, the Paris Opera Ballet, and the academy. Around 150 dancers in the company and perhaps ten have trained anywhere else. But those are always midcareer artists, foreigners. The school trains the vast majority of POB dancers from the youngest possible age, then we join their elite ranks.

Maybe we join them. Maybe *some of us* will. POB takes ten times more students than it can ever accept into the company, in the hopes that just one will yield the desired results. Which means attending the school is necessary if you want to join the company—but it's not enough.

Even at thirteen years old, each and every one of us was sure we would be among the chosen. But we kept a hunter's watch on the competition anyway. We entered the studio with wary eyes and curtsied to the teacher, Marie-Cécile. There were Aurélie and Mathilde, Corinne and Talitha. Some new girl with an overbite so severe that they'd never let her into the company if she didn't get serious dental work done, fast. POB likes them pretty. A mousy girl, on the small side, staring down at her legs as she stretched, unwilling to look back at us.

And then there was Lindsay.

Twelve, thirteen. It's the age when everyone's just legs and eyes, and her wary gaze landed on ours. Beautiful, I thought. It was the first time I'd ever consciously thought that about somebody my age. It was also the first time I recognized that someone was unequivocally prettier than I was. Lindsay had so much hair that her blond bun looked like it was containing an explosion; enormous blue eyes; velvety rose-petal skin.

Class began. She seemed good at barre work, but you can't tell anything until you get into the center. It's too hard to really watch someone else at the barre: you're all lined up and you flip around to work both sides for each combination, the exercises of strung-together warm-up steps. I could actually study her technique only half the time.

I heard my mother's voice. *Focusing on others won't get you anywhere. Focus on yourself.*

But Lindsay was all I could see.

She took a place at the front of the class; she wasn't ducking out from Marie-Cécile's gaze just because she was new. Running through the sequences of steps, she had an easy grace. Unlike Mathilde and Talitha, she made it through even the hardest combinations without losing her breath. But it wasn't until adagio that I saw how good her extension was: she could raise her leg within inches of her head with a pure, steady strength.

She was better than any of us. Better than either me or Margaux, who consistently ranked first and second in our class.

Then we changed our shoes for pointe work and I saw we wouldn't have to worry.

"Ladies," Marie-Cécile called, clapping her hands. "Back to the barre, please."

We'd been *en pointe* for only a year by then, but we all had our routines down flat. Bandages around the toes—no, I prefer medical tape—put a blister pad there for prevention, but only after you have the callus—coat it all with lambswool. But Lindsay hadn't mastered it yet. Piles of fluffy wool and American Band-Aid wrappers around her, she sat there frantically trying to stuff her toes into shoes that were just too small for all the shit she was trying to put in there.

"Stop dawdling, Miss Price."

Lindsay looked up, eyes wide, as Marie-Cécile put her hands on her hips; Margaux and I exchanged glances. It was never good when Marie-Cécile called you out directly. That posture was the only warning sign you ever got before she really lost it.

We all watched as Lindsay tried to shove the overstuffed shoe onto her foot, to pull the back of it up over her heel. As it dangled uselessly off of her toes, she glanced up again.

"Well," Marie-Cécile said. "Perhaps we should all come back in half an hour, once you're ready?"

The giggle broke through the eight of us like a wave. And there: there it was. The first time we really saw Lindsay. Glowering up at us all—her gaze frantic, still, but hateful now, too.

She threw her shoe across the room, where it bounced off of the mirror with a satin thump.

"Miss Price," Marie-Cécile said, "you will leave my class immediately. You may come back when you can act like a lady."

Lindsay stared at her, unblinking. Then she stood up, a slight smile on her face, and sauntered out, leaving her shoes and that pile of detritus in her wake.

"She'll be out of here in a week," I said under my breath to Margaux in the stunned silence.

But I stayed late anyway, throwing myself around the studio until long into the night.

— *September 2018* —

You can't see the city from inside the studio. When the dancers take company class, they are in Paris but not of it. With the frosted-glass windows vaulted high above their heads, they can't even see the sky. Instead, they watch themselves. In the studio mirrors, their bodies become architecture; their movements, traffic. They are the only citizens of their private city, borders closed off long ago.

For so long, that city had been mine. Through the hallway window, Nathalie, the artistic director, looked out at me, tapping her watch; company class was running long. I nodded, smiled. Turned away from the studio as the herd of pale-faced dancers craned their necks to see which luminary had commanded her attention. After a second of squinting at me, they all looked away.

I didn't blame them. So few people were left who could recognize me; I'd been gone for so long, but their lives had continued to unspool without me there. Every single one of their days has looked the same for decades and will continue to until they're either forty-two and forced to retire or too broken to go on. Class, fittings, rehearsal, performance. They get the schedule; they follow the schedule. Throw in a banana or a yogurt when they find the time. Sleep when they can, wake when they have to. Do it all over again.

My mother's portrait glittered at me from its prime position in the hallway, directly across from the studio door. ISABELLE DURAND, ÉTOILE, 1970–1987. Not the years she'd been alive, 1945–2004; not the years she'd been with the company, 1964–1987. Just her best years, her time as a star, immortalized forever. Star, *étoile*, is a rank that only Paris Opera Ballet has. The hierarchy of other companies tops out with principal dancers, but POB recognizes that certain dancers deserve something higher. Dancers like her.

I hadn't ever really examined this image of her before; the photographer had caught her in the middle of a *grand jeté*, legs flung apart, her long tutu suspended over them. Something classical, then: *La Sylphide* or *Coppélia*. Back before I was born, back when her rank of star had been earned. Not after the great accident of my birth had occurred, not after she'd taken that year away from the company—that year she could never get back. On her return, they'd kept the rank, sure. But it had been rather grudgingly maintained out of tradition and whatever sense of duty an institution could feel until her retirement four years later.

Here she was in her prime. Young. Perfect. Clutching the air.

This is the promise we dancers make to each other: the world might not remember you, but other ballerinas always will.

In the studio, the music ended. The dancers began to file out into the hall, an endless string of interchangeable twenty-somethings. I pretended to be absorbed in the photograph until a cold hand wrapped around my wrist.

"Delphine," Nathalie said, her long red hair tickling my forearm.

"Hello." The crowd around us drowned out my thin voice. I was back in triumph, I reminded myself. I wasn't one of her little dancers. I'd turned out to be so much more. I cleared my throat. "Hi!"

She tilted her head toward the stairs. "My office."

The dancers had thrown open the door to the dressing room, and the smell of salt and earth wafted heavy into the halls. You'd think that the showers would get rid of the sweat, but the scent is too strong and instead it just rises with the steam, wrapping itself around us.

When I looked back, Nathalie was already halfway down the corridor. Turning toward me, she raised a pale eyebrow.

"Well?" Nathalie said. "Are you coming, or what?"

Back when I was in the company, the older dancers were our priests. We watched them to learn what to do—what to wear to class, which superstitions to follow. We watched them to learn what *not* to do—which people we had to suck up to, whom we could safely ignore. But the thing was, we were their replacements. We could see it clearly in Nathalie

Dorival's face. Twenty-three years older than us, she was already a star by the time we joined the company. Later retired, now artistic director, forever the unreachable older sister who just couldn't be bothered with us.

Until she had to be.

In her office that smelled of lilies and candle wax, I sat on the edge of the ivory couch and watched Antoine, her assistant, bring in a tray with a teapot, loose-leaf tea, strainers. Behind her tank of a desk, Nathalie steepled her fingers. Waiting.

The sweat rolled into the small of my back as I mimicked her smile back to her.

"So," she said, contracting her fingers and relaxing them, slapping her palms onto her thighs. "Where's the cast list?"

I twisted my hands together. She'd always moved fast. "I haven't written anything down yet."

Nathalie laughed, tucked an invisible strand of red hair behind her ear. "But surely you have some ideas. Nothing serious, Delphine! Let's just talk."

I batted away the mounting anxiety and reminded myself: I'm good at my job. I've seen the faces of the audience as they watch my work. And I love this project.

From the moment I'd landed in St. Petersburg thirteen years ago, the Romanovs' wedding-cake palaces beneath the Technicolor skies had fascinated me. Again and again, I'd tried to get the ballet made: the story of the country's last tsarina, a foreign princess brought by love to a country that would eventually turn against her. Her obsession with Rasputin, the wild-bearded mystical healer. Her despair over her only son, her husband's sole heir, his hemophilia. And, finally, her bloody death at the hands of the revolutionaries.

How many times had I proposed it to the Mariinsky? Every time, Olga shut me down, saying it was not my story to tell.

Yet it was a project that Nathalie had desperately wanted. Barely a day after I'd finally pounded out my meanderingly tentative suggestion to her in an email, we were on the phone, planning my great return to the Palais Garnier. *It's a story about love*, I'd written to her, *but it's not a love story. It's about how you think love can save you and yet it never, ever does.*

I took a breath so deep, the air scratched the bottom of my lungs.

"Here's what I'm thinking. For Rasputin"—I bent forward—"I'd really like to see Jock Gerard in the part."

Her fingers rolled against the arm of her chair. "I see him more as a fairy-tale prince than as a mad priest."

Jock was actually *Jacques*, but his name was bastardized by the Americans the same way his dancing was during the summer he spent at the School of American Ballet in New York City. The management at POB hadn't approved of him going to New York in the first place, not at all, but his mother had put up such a fuss that they'd allowed it in the end. When he returned in the fall, more virtuosic than ever—what were they going to do, not take him back? Truly good male dancers are like gold dust.

He carried that nickname, *Jock*, around like a badge of honor. Now everyone, including Nathalie, called him that. He was even listed as *Jock Gerard* in our programs. *Jacques* had become nothing more than some boy I used to know.

"Well. Sure. But I think it's the perfect opportunity to expand his range. He's been a star, now—what, two years?" I was such a fucking liar. I knew it had been three. "I think this could push his limits. Open him up to a greater variety of parts. Besides, there's always been a . . . virtuosic quality about him that I like. That I think I could use."

A body onstage. It was strange to talk about him like that, when he'd always been more than that to me. He'd been the one who'd snuck into the girls' dormitory to get me whenever he found a new Balanchine clip online. The one who burned me CDs, leaving them unlabeled and unpackaged in my mailbox, identifiable only by his signature combination of Noir Désir, Serge Gainsbourg, and Stravinsky. The one whose bright blue eyes caught mine across the auditorium for a shared smile as Marie-Cécile rhapsodized about Paris Opera Ballet's *unique place in the world*.

"I don't know, Delphine. I'd really like to see someone . . . fresher in that role. Someone up-and-coming, less expected? He'd be the perfect Tsar, though. Almost a cameo, yes?"

I hadn't anticipated pushback on this. After all, she'd chosen Jock from the masses for the company's greatest honor. Unlike the other ranks—*coryphée*, *sujet*, and *premier danseur*—which are given out during an annual juried competition, only she, the artistic director, can name the stars.

"I was thinking of Claude Berger for that," I said quickly. I was more than ready to offer Nathalie a concession by casting one of her favorites. "It's a larger part, anyway, and more integral to the ballet. Definitely bigger than a cameo—Rasputin is more of an isolated role. The Tsar gets way more stage time."

Nathalie sighed. "Fine. If you want Jock, take him. Workshop with him. I can't guarantee that I won't ask you to change the casting if this thing takes off, though. Who else?"

It was so French, this way of operating. Sprinkling all of my old friends into the cast list. This wasn't how the Russians worked. Involving Jock was admittedly a gift to myself, though it was well within the realm of plausibility as far as Nathalie was concerned. But my second request? There was nothing to do but spit it out. After everything, I owed it to her. To the memory of her. To what she might have been.

"I want Lindsay."

"Lindsay. Lindsay Price?" As though there were any others. Nathalie's green eyes went wide. "You don't. Delphine, trust me. You really don't."

"I do," I said. "As the Tsarina."

Nathalie made a noise that was half laughing, half choking. "She's *ancient*, Delphine. She's thirty-five!"

I'd rehearsed this. I knew what to do. "The tsarina was forty-six when she died," I said. *Younger than you are now.*

"No."

"I know it's a risk. But Lindsay's who I want."

She frowned. "Even apart from the age thing? Impossible. A soloist in a titular role?"

"It's not like she's in the *corps*." She was more than just some extra, after all. "And it's not like we haven't done it before."

Nathalie briefly shut her eyes.

"All right. You want the truth?" Her gaze was direct now, piercing, just a little bit mean. "She can't dance with anybody else. She freezes when anybody touches her."

I couldn't stop the astonishment from passing over my face.

"I think I would have remembered that?" I said.

The pas de deux, a dance for a man and a woman, is the centerpiece of every classical ballet. *Swan Lake, Don Quixote*, even the goddamn *Nutcracker*. You can't escape it. The man grasping the woman, spinning her around, throwing her through the air. You can't have a star who only dances alone. Nobody wants to see that. Even prima ballerinas need men to show them off: there's no version of the ballet that doesn't depend on them.

"She's an abysmal partner," Nathalie added. "She turns into a statue."

Back at the academy, Lindsay had been a great partner. I was convinced that she should have been promoted to principal years ago. Instead of being where she was: forever stuck in the middle of the company, just another smiling face in the great mass of dancers. Featured occasionally in little solos, but otherwise . . . background noise.

But.

For the Tsarina, who'd have to dance extensively with both the Tsar and Rasputin, could I afford to be wrong?

"She was in my Pas de Deux class for years," I said. "She was spectacular."

"Whatever she may have been at seventeen, she is not now," Nathalie said.

I fought to keep myself from wincing. Who among us is? But that wasn't the kind of argument that would win Nathalie over.

"We cast Lindsay, here's what happens," I said, ticking off the points on my fingers. "You give her real motivation to improve her partnering. She gets better. POB finally gets to use the talent it's invested so much in for two decades. And you get another star."

She snorted. "She's five years away from retirement. Seven, max. I'm not falling for it."

"Do you really," I said slowly, "want a company full of dancers with no reason to do anything but the bare minimum from the second they hit thirty? I've looked at the roster, Nathalie. That's a third of them. You want to be the one to tell them they have no hope? Or do you want to be the one to"—I grasped for the corporate word—"to incentivize them to do more than sleepwalk through endless repetitions of *Swan Lake*?"

Nathalie flopped back against her chair, crossing her arms over her chest like a teenager. She was lit brightly by the windows, the stone ornamentation outside hanging over her view of the Louvre and the river beyond.

She was almost there.

"With Jock and Lindsay in these roles," I said, "you could revitalize your entire company."

She was nodding.

I had it.

But then her head froze, tilted to the side like a wolf's.

"I'll give you a month to try her out in the part. *If,*" she said. "If I name the understudy. And believe me, I'm putting in an understudy from the very start." She caught me with that sharp gaze. "Someone *young*, Delphine."

No understudy would normally be cast this early. Not during choreography, not when the piece was still being made. It was a slap in Lindsay's face. It's a huge honor for a dancer to have a ballet "made on" you, created with you in mind. Having an understudy, and a junior one at that, would underline precisely how much management doubted her. Precisely how much they felt they needed to hedge their bets.

Precisely how much they wanted her to know it.

"Can't we wait?" I said—and to my embarrassment, my voice came out whiny. "Give her three months, really see what she can do?" Wait so long that it becomes impossible to envision anyone else in the role?

Nathalie's invisible brows drew together. "It's our three hundred and fiftieth anniversary season. There's too much going on. So no, *we* cannot," she said.

Slowly, I nodded. Even if I couldn't give Lindsay everything—the perfect prize—still, I could give her something that would change her life. Fourteen years after I had ruined it.

"All right," I said. "I'm ready."

CHAPTER 2

When you enter a small, insular school at eight years old, you have no secrets from your friends. Everyone's been there for every success and humiliation you've ever had; any history you have is a shared history. By the time Lindsay arrived, the permutations and combinations of boys and girls were a known fact—far better known than the geography POB kept trying, with limited success, to shove in our heads. Among our canonical texts were that I had spent a week holding Adam's hand when we were twelve; that Lindsay was far more interested in actual grown-up dancers than she was in anybody in the school; that Talitha had an enormous, unrequited crush on Jacques.

Talitha became our code word for desperation; being like her was the worst thing we could imagine. Desperation gives off a subtle but unmistakable odor, and we could sense it on her whenever Jacques was around: the vague performative turn her gestures took, the slipping away to the bathroom to touch up her lip gloss, the way her eyes seemed magnetized to him. Becoming *Talitha* meant that your desires were clear, too clear, to the rest of the world. It meant that they turned you into an object of ridicule.

Always, then, like gymnasts on a balance beam, we walked the line between wanting and not-wanting: we felt our way through it in impromptu strategy sessions.

"Victor, Adam, Paul, Laurent, Gabriel, Edouard, Arthur, Pierre." Beneath her poster of Margot Fonteyn and Rudolf Nureyev, Lindsay shifted her foot in the arch stretcher, trying to make the curves of her feet bend even more, into the perfect banana shape. Technically, we weren't supposed to use them, but Lindsay had never cared much about rules. She twisted her mouth. "Who am I forgetting?"

"Um," I said, pretending to think. "Jacques."

The fact that I wanted Jacques, too, hadn't softened my attitude toward Talitha. If anything, it made me meaner.

Lindsay rolled her eyes and switched feet. "Of course. Jacques. The town bicycle."

"The town what?"

"Everybody gets a ride sooner or later."

I looked down, trying not to show my flushing face.

It was different with me. Or, I thought it was different with me. I couldn't risk it not being different with me. His eyes were the ones that searched for mine. He was the one who found every opportunity to set his thigh against me when we went out to the local café. His fingers were the ones that lingered too long when he passed me a spoon.

But what if I was wrong?

I couldn't risk it—admitting what I wanted and becoming another Talitha.

But I also couldn't stop myself from defending him.

"That probably describes Laurent better than Jacques, don't you think?"

Her eyes got big, and I could tell she had good gossip to share.

"Yeah, but I think he's finally found *the one.*"

"Who?" Unthinkable that I didn't already know. I was the one the other girls turned to for comfort after each argument, every breakup—wrapping a blanket around their shoulders, running to the common room to make them a mug of powdered cocoa. Besides, our class was small enough that I should have known anyway. And yet nobody seemed plausible, as I ran through the list of students.

Of the veterans, Margaux couldn't have been less interested in boys that way. Corinne had a boyfriend outside of the school. Aurélie was a prude and refused to do more than kiss with a closed mouth. Mathilde had broken up with Laurent six months ago. We'd long since categorized the two other new girls as *not a threat* and *um, definitely not a threat.*

"Talitha?" I said.

Lindsay broke into an enormous grin, even white American teeth shining.

"Gabriel."

"Noooo." I wasn't particularly attracted to Laurent—his mouth was so big it was almost comical—but if he stayed single, he could deflect from the person I really liked.

"Yesssss," Lindsay replied, her smile widening.

"So then it's just Pierre, Victor, Adam, Paul, Edouard, and Arthur left?"

"And Jacques," she said. "Don't forget about Jacques."

Blood rushed into my face, and I looked away.

I never forgot about Jacques.

— *September 2018* —

My father left—well, my mother threw him out—when I was five, but I have one memory of us when we were a family. If he'd been involved in the ballet, I would probably remember more; but he was a tax attorney my mother had met when setting up her will, once she'd become a star and actually had money. A whirlwind romance, a marriage six months later: me, a few years after that. He was always in and out of our lives, even when we lived together, visiting the California branch of his law firm. Turned out he was doing a lot more than visiting—he was also finding an American woman and starting another family. I guess once he'd gotten a taste for family life, he found it as intolerable as my mother did to be alone, even for a few weeks at a time.

I have plenty of memories from the breakup, but they're all of Maman: deranged in a way I had never seen before and never saw after. But there's one nice memory in there, hidden like an Easter egg among the muck. The two of them getting ready to go out for the evening: him throwing on a suit and lying back on the bed, just watching her at the dressing table. I must have been observing from the door or maybe on the bed with him, but in my memory, I have a god's-eye view of the ritual. Her steady hand brushing ice-blue shadow over her lids, tracing flared liner over her lash line. The fish face she made as she put on mascara. The way her mouth went taut and relaxed at once as she used a brush to color it in with lipstick, dab by dab. At the very end, a pat with a powder puff and she'd stand up, spraying her perfume into the air and walking into it. The whole time, him just watching her with a look of . . . I don't know what it was. Not impatience, not admiration. Pride, maybe. Ownership.

She did that same routine every time she had a date, but after he left, the magic was gone. It wasn't a religious ceremony anymore; she was just going through the motions.

Since I'd come back, I thought of her every day as I sat at that same dressing table to do my own face. The vacation rental agency had gutted the apartment when I left for St. Petersburg, but they'd kept the nicer pieces of furniture, that table among them. They'd put twin beds in my old bedroom, so it didn't make sense for me to stay in there; but living in my mother's bedroom, even repainted and refurbished, still gave me the feeling of being a little girl playing dress-up. *This is* her room, *I'm going to get in trouble.*

That Sunday morning, I sat at her table and surveyed my face. I'd started with the eyes: shadow and liner and mascara. On to the skin: concealer, foundation, highlighter, blush, and bronzer. The mouth next: lip liner, lipstick. The final touch: powder, setting the mask in place for the day.

In Russia, I would have looked correct. Back in France, though, in the filtered lemon morning light, I looked like I was ready to go onstage.

Worse than that. I looked like an ancient doll.

I was going to be late to meet Lindsay, and I ran into the bathroom, scrubbed it all off of my face with micellar water. Back at the table, I dabbed some concealer under my eyes, slid on a single coat of mascara and a red lip.

I felt naked, exposed. The imperfections—the slightly long nose, the softening along my jaw—seemed to pop out at me. French beauty is about structure, not artifice: it's about the bones. But I made myself hold my gaze, and after a moment, I let myself stand. If it wasn't perfect, well, at least it was appropriate. And besides, I couldn't waste any more precious minutes fixing my face. It was time to change Lindsay's life.

English words echoed in my head as I raced down the Rue des Francs-Bourgeois: *Lindsay, I'm about to give you everything you ever wanted.*

Everything you ever wanted. It was an ugly phrase, much uglier than in French. Sticky words, nasal words. If you turned it into steps, it would look like a series of *grand pliés* in second, followed by a snapping up of one leg to *petit battement.* My hand brushed against something silky, and I looked up to find a strange woman staring at me incredulously. I'd been miming the motions with my hands and touched her; I started to apologize, but she was already gone.

Chastising myself, I slowed behind an older couple craning to look at the stained glass, the hanging lanterns, the castle-like towers. When I was a kid, the road had been bustling with local shoppers darting in to see their tailors and dry cleaners on their lunch breaks. Now, the ancient thoroughfare had been reimagined as an outdoor mall where you could buy scented candles for 160 euros and perfume for three times as much, from shops you could literally find in any big city in the world: Diptyque. Guerlain. Yet the narrow sidewalks were still three deep in slow-moving tourists.

Everything you ever wanted.

I grinned into the window of Kiehl's.

I'd been imagining her shrieks of excitement for months now. It had all built up to this. And as much as I'd wanted to tell her the moment I'd arrived, it had had to wait for my meeting with Nathalie.

After my email announcing my return, Lindsay's replies had pinged into my in-box with virtual screeches, Margaux's following with muted bemusement. We planned to meet at Bar Hemingway three hours after my rescheduled flight finally landed; Lindsay's idea, of course. Classic Lindsay impatience. *What, Linds, you want her to show up with her suitcases?* Margaux had written. *Yup!!!* Lindsay had replied. She couldn't wait to see me, and it sent a burst of warmth through me: they hadn't been able to manage without me. Our life was still there, just waiting for me to step back into it.

Travel exhaustion had amplified the nostalgia as I'd opened the door to the wood-paneled, leathery lounge. From afar, the blonde and brunette sitting in the booth sent a shock of adrenaline to my heart. Thirteen years since we'd seen each other; our monthly emails had been full of excuses. Russia had always been "just crazy right now" for me: another of Dmitri's ballets always premiering, then my own work to consider. They totally understood, they'd written back. Their vacations were "swallowed up so *easily*," by visits to and from their parents, later by their respective spouses. One of these days, we'd finally get back together. One of these days.

How had thirteen years passed without them?

Lindsay spotted me first and the smile bursting across her face took me right back to 2005.

We were together again.

They jumped up. Squealed. I squealed, too. Kissed Margaux's cheeks. Lindsay's. *You're not in St. Petersburg anymore*, I reminded myself. *It's okay to smile.*

Years of their curated self-presentations online had obscured the truth of their bodies. Their public images had become more real to me than they'd ever been, and the changes in how they actually looked popped like those pictures in children's magazines: spot the five differences. Crow's-feet around the eyes, hints of fine lines around the lips, wrinkles high up on Margaux's forehead, grooves between Lindsay's nose and her mouth. A certain tiredness even as they smiled.

"So," Lindsay said—and I knew what was coming: the same thing she always said when there was everything and nothing to say. "How's life?"

I smiled. "Life is—" *Good* felt too strong, given the images of Dmitri still dancing through my mind. But it wasn't *bad*; I was back here, with them. "Long," I said finally, to their laughter.

They were the same and not the same. Even as we ordered, as we talked, things had been almost what I'd expected, but not exactly. Their conversation was peppered with the litany of roles they'd performed, parties they'd been to, tours they'd gone on—a few stints in Tokyo and even a visit to New York. Then their catalog of injuries, rattled off as easily as their roles. I tried to keep my face active, engaged, but I felt it falling slack. I knew all of this from their emails, and anyway, it was about as revealing as reading their CVs. *How do you feel?* I wanted to ask. *Are you tired all the time, too? Do you find it harder and harder to lose a kilo? Are you sometimes irate for no discernible reason?*

And when I left that day, camaraderie dissipating into bone-heavy exhaustion, I knew I hadn't really returned. Not for them.

It had been so long.

I would have to work to weave myself back into our group. The first thing to do was to tell Lindsay the news; I'd sent her a quick text for a Sunday-morning coffee—though as I pulled up her number, I saw with a wince that I hadn't texted her since 2016. Everything else had been in a group chain with Margaux, once we'd all gotten WhatsApp.

MARRIED? OMG Linds, so exciting!

PACS, she'd written back. A French civil union, not a religious ceremony. *For taxes.* Lindsay had never been sentimental about guys; she was always strategizing, and her machinations had finally paid off. In some ways, her life had turned out exactly as she'd planned. Career-wise, not so much.

I was turning from the Rue Vieille du Temple to the passageway leading to the café when the sight of two women sitting in front of a fountain hit me like a punch to the throat.

Margaux was there with Lindsay.

The idea of the two of them spending the last thirteen years together, going everywhere as a pair, gave me a strange, lonely feeling. They'd had a whole life together, a whole separate friendship, in the span of time that I'd been gone.

And yet Margaux and I would always have a different kind of relationship. We had met first, yes. We were also the keeper of each other's deepest secrets. Margaux was the only other person in the world who knew what I'd done.

"Delphine!" Lindsay called as I approached.

"I hope you don't mind me fence-crashing," Margaux said, blowing out a cloud of smoke that hovered like a dirty halo above her head.

"Gate," Lindsay said. "Gate-crashing."

Margaux rolled her eyes as I bent to kiss her cheeks. "We meet every Sunday for brunch anyway. It lets us get the hell away from that place a little. You don't care that I came, do you?"

She was studying me, waiting for my reaction. "Of course not!" I replied brightly.

One of those absurd French brunches was spread across the table. A bit of everything: yogurt, fruit, croissants, tartines, meats and cheeses, lattes and juice and champagne.

Margaux saw me scanning it. "Yeah," she said, shoving half a croissant into her mouth and nodding my way. "I eat now."

It didn't show. Margaux's face still looked like it always had: sharp and angular, like she'd been drawn by a child out of straight lines, down to her triangular eyes. Lindsay's, on the other hand, was all soft curves and delicate turns. I pushed the wrought-iron chair back across the cobblestones and sat down.

"So," Lindsay said. "Your first meeting . . ."

I rummaged in my purse for my Camel Blues, pausing to grab a full champagne flute from Margaux's hand. "Oh. You know. It's Nathalie."

Lindsay's saucer eyes latched on to me. "So, what are you going to be doing?" She propped her head on her hand like a *Vogue* model from the 1920s. *Tell me more.* Not for the first time in my life, I was grateful for her sheer reliability. She was like an algebra equation: for any real input, you get a predictable and defined output.

"*Tsarina*," I said finally, lighting my cigarette. "About the last Romanovs in the years leading up to the First World War." I paused. "And guess who's playing the Tsarina?"

She waited, suspended still for a moment.

Then it came to her and she clasped her palm to her chest, showing the whites of her eyes.

"Me?"

"You." The word came out mixed with smoke and I choked.

"No! Are you kidding? Delphine!" She thrust herself into my arms, but I was coughing still and got ash all over her. She didn't notice. "That's amazing! The lead? The title?" I barely had time to nod before she rattled on, face luminous. "Can you imagine how sick with jealousy everyone else is going to be? We're all so fucking *tired* of the repertory. Every single ballet, it's the same shit. Nathalie's all, *Softer, Lindsay, you're a princess and he's your prince. Go to him, go to him—smile now. Smile more. Smile like you mean it.* This'll give me so much more . . . scope, you know? Wait, what's a Romanov?"

Margaux's face was flushing. "Who else did you cast?" she said quietly. Even through her rambling, Lindsay heard and stopped short, slapping her playfully on the arm.

"Marg, knock it off. I'm sure you'll get something good."

Margaux rolled her eyes.

"I haven't gotten that far yet," I said.

"But . . ." Margaux prompted.

"But I'm thinking, um, Claude for the Tsar, Camille What's-it—you know, that new one?—as Anastasia and Lindsay's understudy, and, um, Jock as Rasputin." The email from Nathalie had come through a few hours after our meeting: *Use Camille as the understudy. Keep the Rasputin scenes to a minimum, though, okay?* Apart from the bizarre not-quite-a-question at the end, I was okay with it. Camille d'Ivoire, this year's prodigy. Fine, whatever. I'd never actually have to use her. And as for that command—it wasn't like the ballet was called *Rasputin* or anything. Still, I'd use Jock exactly as much as I wanted. I was the choreographer, after all. The choice was mine.

Clarity spread over Margaux, who smoothed her face, those high cheekbones, into something like a grin. "Mmm."

Lindsay froze. "Understudy?"

Nathalie's making me. The excuses gathered fast at the back of my throat. *I didn't want to—you're the only one for it—*

But they were all pale imitations of the truth, of the one thing I could never actually say. *You don't get it, Linds. How much of a risk you are.*

The champagne flute came flying out of Margaux's hand, landing with a crash on the ground.

"*Merde,*" Margaux said, staring at her hand as though it had acted without her knowledge.

Lindsay was on her knees immediately, gathering the glass. I pushed back my chair, ready to join her, when she cried out.

"Shit," she muttered, putting a bloodied palm to her mouth.

"You'd better go wash that off. Ask the waiter for a bandage," Margaux said. "Can you imagine clutching the barre like that?"

"Yeah," Lindsay said, standing up so fast that her chair fell. It clanged and echoed against the stones, but she leapt back over it easily, propping it upright. "You're right. Back in a sec."

As Lindsay went inside, we shoveled the rest of the glass into the ashtray and I tried to get back to the mental space of thirteen years ago. It was good to have a friend like Margaux because nobody ever messed with you; because she'd protect you from other people's bitchiness with her own acid-tongued retorts; because she was quick to take revenge on your behalf. It was good to have a friend like Lindsay because it drew guys to your group; because your own stock rose as people saw you with her, especially when she genuinely believed that you were beautiful, too. All of it had been so good. To dance with them. To drink together. To climb over the fences of the Place des Vosges late on a summer night, to laugh together into the dark.

I poured out the rest of the champagne into our glasses and looked up at Margaux. She was glaring.

"You've got to be kidding me with this shit," she said to me in her quick French.

A knot of poison began to burn in my diaphragm. I stared at the shallow late-morning shadows on the tablecloth. Jealousy? But surely she realized why I had to do this. It didn't have anything to do with liking Lindsay better or even thinking she was a better dancer. After all, Margaux was one of the most beautiful dancers I'd ever seen.

"Margaux, I'm so sorry. I'll find something good for you, too. I promise—"

"Oh, fuck off. The ballet? You think I give a shit about that stuff anymore? I'm five years from retirement, Delphine, and believe me: I, for one, know it."

"Then—"

"I know what you're doing and it's not going to work. Promising her the Tsarina was really, really stupid. She's not ready for a role that big."

I'd forgotten how easily Margaux could read me. She just didn't know what she was reading anymore.

I made a face. "She's thirty-five. She's ready."

"You want to play at semantics? Fine, then. She's ready. But she's incapable. She's not good enough. You're going to have to break her all over again. Yeah," she said, narrowing her eyes, daring me. "Just like before."

My throat tightened, and I swallowed.

"It's a part in a ballet, Marg. It's not the end of the world."

But we both knew it could be.

"Just stay out of her career. It's not worth it," she said.

I sighed. "If I can help—it's such a small thing—"

"It's not *such a small thing*, and you know it. Nathalie's up to her neck in this job, and she's got absolutely no time for the older dancers at the moment. Lindsay will be out"—she snapped her fingers—"like *that*. And it's easy for you to come back here like the good fairy bestowing gifts, but I still have to see her every day." She swallowed; there was something wobbly, unsteady, in her face. "Do you get it, Delphine? I live with what we did *every day*. Every fucking day. You live like this for a while, see if it feels so small to you then."

The door swung open and Lindsay was back.

"All better," she proclaimed, coming toward us with the fingers of her hand outspread like a little kid.

"That's great," I said.

We sat for a moment in almost unbearable silence.

"So, how are you doing?" Lindsay asked, her voice ringing loud in the otherwise empty courtyard. "Since . . . well, since Dmitri."

On Sunday mornings, we are French. Not for the first time since I'd left him nearly six months ago, Dmitri's voice came unbidden into my mind. The rest of the week, we were Russian: he cooked blinis and chopped beetroot, made pea soup and salted cucumbers. But on Saturday afternoons, I'd go to the fancy grocery store a few blocks away and buy baguettes, jams, free-range eggs, and cèpes, the tiny savory mushrooms so perfect in omelets. And then I'd wake up and put the coffee on, serving it with warm milk in the bowls we usually used for cereal, before we ate breakfast in bed. Often, especially at the beginning, those mornings had ended with me stripping the bed of its linens after our bodies frantically joined, knocking over the tiny, beautiful jars of apple jam imported from Normandy.

I tried to wrap my mind around my feelings, compress them into an answer to Lindsay's question.

"I don't miss him," I said—and I didn't, but the sound of my voice still rang false. "It's more like—I miss the shape of our life together. I miss knowing that my life *had* a shape. I miss having someone to trust with everything—even though I couldn't, of course, in the end. I guess it's just—I miss someone to be accountable to. I don't think I realized how meaningless life would feel, with nobody paying attention. If that makes any sense."

Lindsay grabbed my hand. Hers was bony and cold. "*We* are," she said. "We're paying attention."

I swallowed.

"Anyway . . ." She pulled back, crossing her arms over her chest. "You should be happy. You're free now! I hate all that checking-in shit, that *accountability*. You can do whatever you want. You're the luckiest person I know."

"I get it," Margaux said. Her low murmur was almost a growl. "I honestly think I'd be dead by now without that."

Lindsay and I stared at her. Lindsay had been with Daniel for years. Her early emails had formed a particular image of him in my mind: a sexy, strong man with an almost worshipful admiration of her. Not a dancer—such a shock, after all these years, that she hadn't ended up with a dancer, but I could almost see her shrug in the email when I asked her what company he was with. *He's not a dancer. I'm the only performer in our relationship.* No matter how much she loved him, though, it didn't surprise me that the bonds of long-term partnership had begun to chafe. Lindsay was at her best when performing for masses of people. One-on-one, though? Once the initial rush of serotonin and dopamine faded, it would take someone truly dedicated to keep her interested, keep her faithful. Keep her.

But Margaux. Margaux had never seemed to need that rush of first love. Never seemed to need much of anything or anyone. When we were younger, she'd disappeared into flings for a month sometimes, maybe two, as we all did. But she never gossiped about them, never kissed and told. Wherever the open, vulnerable part of her lived, the part that was capable of falling in love, she kept it hidden—beneath her mask of sarcasm and her endless string of *fuck thats*. The surprise on Lindsay's face told me that Margaux hadn't changed in all this time. That even now, this shred of vulnerability came as a surprise to her, too.

"In any case, we all need to get together soon. The—the five of us," I said. Five. It had always been *the three of us*, before. "I need to meet these mysterious partners."

"Eech," Lindsay said, making a face. Margaux and I started to laugh, and Lindsay looked at us, wide-eyed. "Who needs them around? We're the best ones, anyway."

As our laughter rose again, I caught a glance of our reflection in the restaurant window. Three girls, giggling and drinking at a table in the Marais, silhouetted by a rose garden, water from the fountain tumbling behind my head, coating our reflection with a shimmery rainbow glow. The three of us together again.

And for a moment, if I didn't look too closely at their eyes, if I didn't look too closely at myself, it felt exactly like thirteen years ago.

Exactly like before.

CHAPTER 3

*P*as de Deux class was like getting your first period: you knew it was coming for years before it arrived; it sounded incredibly unpleasant and impossibly terrifying; and it was entirely necessary. Unlike periods, though, it came for both the boys and the girls, and we were equally petrified. The pas de deux, where the man and the woman dance together, is key to the ballet. To every ballet. But I'd only ever seen it as a finished product before: the stage clearing for the pair to dance, the man showing the woman off, lifting her high above his head, dropping her into perilous dives, spinning her into a series of turns that would be impossible for her to do on her own. I had no idea how we got from where we were, at the school, to that kind of performance.

I did know that I'd have to learn to dance with boys, and their hands had to go everywhere: around my ribs, on my ass, in my inner thighs. After years of dancing entirely alone, at sixteen I'd have to put my body entirely at the mercy of somebody else's. After years of taking Technique class separately, the girls taught primarily by women, the boys by men, it was time to bring us together.

Men, not women, tend to teach these classes. For the girls, partnering is all about what's being done to you, about becoming a better package that can be twirled, thrown into the air, carried from point A to point B. But for the boys, it's entirely different: they have to build their muscles, their endurance, their rhythm. We have to be able to rely on them. If they drop us, it could be career ending—horror stories abounded of women who'd had their bones broken, their spinal cords snapped, their ribs cracked. Which just made it all the more important that the boys knew their shit.

And so, not only was it our first time in class with boys, it was also our first time with a male teacher: Phillippe Condorcet.

Everyone called him Monsieur Condorcet, but he'd always be Phillippe to me. Had been ever since the day I was seven and first saw him sitting shirtless at our kitchen table, my mother's hands on his shoulders. She'd jumped away when I entered the room, but he'd just smiled lazily, like a cat. The scene repeated itself in various permutations over the following year before Phillippe disappeared from our apartment and became just another of POB's stars: an image in the program, a blur onstage. My heart had sped up when I saw his name on our schedules, but I hadn't realized quite how different it would be, seeing him in this context.

And now he was standing in front of us.

He smiled at me, and I winced, tried to turn it into an approximation of a grin. I hadn't realized just how much younger than my mother he was. She was fifty-three, now, but he was forty-two, just retired from the company and transitioning into teaching. Lindsay had grumbled about being guinea pigs for a new teacher, but she shut up once Margaux and I showed her his picture. The sandy hair brushed back from his face, his jaw as square as a Disney prince's.

"The relationship between a man and a woman is at the center of the ballet," he said, his tenor voice somehow calm and booming at the same time. "Sure, we've tried to get around it, and POB—as in so many things—was a pioneer in this area from the beginning." He held up one hand, fingers splayed. "In the mid-nineteenth century, we have Fanny Elssler, who used her sister, Thérèse, as a partner." He held up the other, its mirror image. "And we have the original version of *Coppélia*, where a ballerina performed the role of Franz." He clasped his hands together. "But only when we have the joining of the masculine and the feminine do we truly have something worth watching."

Beside me, Margaux made a disgusted noise at the back of her throat.

"Counterpoint, Mademoiselle Bisset?"

For the first time in our lives, I saw Margaux hesitate. After a moment, Phillippe nodded.

"I thought not. All right. If I could get you to line up, boys here, girls here"—he pointed—"and arrange yourselves by height."

My stomach dropped, contracted. I put myself at the front of the line.

It took me a minute before I could look over to the boys to see who my partner would be—but part of me already knew.

Jacques. We'd had parallel growth spurts the year before, and now, at 165 and 183 centimeters, we were the tallest girl and boy in the class. It was going to be Jacques. How was it possible to want something so much and be so scared of it at the same time?

Phillippe watched us; I felt Lindsay, beside me, watching him. But all I could see was Jacques, moving confidently to the front.

"Pair off," Phillippe commanded. Jacques and I walked side by side to the far left of the room. Hesitantly, I turned toward him. He caught my eye and winked; I quickly looked down, my face on fire.

"Oh, lighten *up*, people!" Phillippe cried. "I'm not going to ask you to touch each other right away. Jesus Christ, you're sixteen, half of you would probably cum on the spot."

We all giggled nervously, but a few of the boys looked slightly haunted.

His voice turned kinder as he went on. "You're scared. That's normal. You're teenagers, you're idiots." Before he could even notice the outrage on our faces, he went on. "Here's what we're going to do. For the next four minutes, I want you to look into each other's eyes. That's all."

A snort from Margaux. She was paired with Gabriel, and you could feel the disinterest rolling off them in waves. He liked boys; she liked girls. This was just another day in class for them.

"All right . . ." Phillippe's eyes flicked to the clock. "Go."

I took a deep breath and turned to Jacques.

His chest was broad, broader than the other boys'. Above the scoop neck of his leotard, a bit of dark hair against his pale skin; just the sight of it made me swallow. His collarbones were just at my eyeline, strong and delicate at the same time—my heart rate was rising, it wasn't fair—

"Hey," Jacques said lightly. "Dolphin. I think we're supposed to be looking at each other?"

Dauphine, Delphine. The words in French are so similar, it amazed me that nobody had ever made the joke before. But my face was frozen, as though my body were protecting me, barring me from noticing yet another reason to like him. I swallowed and tilted my head. Couldn't bring myself to look directly into his eyes. I already *knew* how much I liked his eyes, the bright blue of them. I settled on his nose.

This had to be almost over, right? Four minutes must surely be up by now.

"Hey! Delphine and pretty boy!" Phillippe called, and we turned to see him heading toward us. "Yeah, the two of you." He grabbed my chin with one hand, the other hand on the back of my head. "Look. At. Each. Other."

Suddenly, my eyes were locked on his. The long, dark lashes. The shock of blue beneath them. The cracked-glass pattern of his irises. I'd never been close enough to see them before, and they were like a kaleidoscope, like a broken mirror.

The whites of his eyes, though, were slightly red, bloodshot. Jacques was tired. Had he lain awake last night, worried about the stakes of this class? Worried that for the first time in his life, he would fail?

That was when I realized: he smelled like soap and mints. The boys never smelled good. Neither did the girls. We moved too much, we always smelled just like *bodies*.

He had thought about this moment. He'd been scared, too.

My lungs started to burn and I realized I was holding my breath. But that blue just pulsed at me. Not asking anything, not waiting for anything. Just *there*. I inhaled deep as the warmth of his gaze wrapped itself around the seams of my hips, my lower abdomen. And his eyes turned questioning and I wondered, for a moment, if he could see inside of my head when we looked at each other like that.

If I could have looked away, I would have.

As Phillippe let go of my chin, I let it down, staring at my hands. They were shaking.

I'd felt anxiety, even panic, before auditions, performances. But if my legs trembled during class, it was because of what *I'd* done, choices *I'd* made, to try to become better, stronger. Meanwhile, my feelings for Jacques lived entirely in my head, tucked gently away in a drawer where I could take them out at my leisure and examine them, safe in the comfort that they were invisible to everyone else.

It astonished me that they manifested like this. That they could change what my body did. That they could change *me*.

"All right, kids. Next-level stuff, now. I want you to move. Mirror each other's movements. It doesn't matter who leads, but I want to see you moving together. Four minutes on the clock—go."

I looked over at Margaux, who was starting to do the Charleston as Gabriel stared at her, baffled, before grinning and joining in. Lindsay had called Phillippe over to her and Adam to question him, her head tilted back, lips parted, as she listened to his answer. Fuck, she wanted *Phillippe*? She had every boy in the school lining up to serve her, but it wasn't enough. Jesus fucking Christ, my mother *and* my best friend?

"Let's make this easy," Jacques said, and grabbed my shaking hands. His were so large, they entirely engulfed mine and I stared at the place where we met. I'd always imagined his touch would be smooth, slippery, even— but it wasn't. His hands were rough, calloused. From the weights, probably. That new broadness in his chest had been earned over the last year; the boys now had mandatory weight training. He'd been in the gym four times a week, lying on the bench press, his torso straining as he grunted—

I was yanked out of my head, back into my body, as he pulled my arm gently along in a sweeping motion.

I met his eyes. Those fucking eyes.

"Yeah?" he said.

I nodded.

And then we were moving. Moving together. It was easy to follow him with our hands entwined, the rough and the smooth, as he swooped and pushed, as he pulled. And the whole time, I was still trembling like a rabbit. For the first time in my life, my body was out of my control. It was not just an instrument. Or—if it was—it was one that other people could play. The warmth at the base of my abs was still there but joined this time by a tightness in my throat, a constricting of my chest. My body was mine and not mine. My body was—ours?

Jacques slowed, then stopped. Our hands hung between us, still clasped together.

"Your turn," he said. His voice was low, gravelly—he sounded almost like an adult, and the heat in my core turned liquid. I breathed, trying to spread the feeling throughout my body, dilute it.

And then I lifted our arms. It was enough, with him, to gently pull in a particular direction; he followed easily, even as he let me take the lead. Like him, I swept us along together, painting imaginary pictures in the air, bending and stretching and pushing. After a minute, I twisted around, thinking he'd drop my hand and follow—but he didn't, instead adjusting his grip so that my hand stayed in his, wrapping his arm around me; and then he was behind me, arm against the front of my body, the rest of him separated by an inch or two of air. I could feel the heat coming off him and, just as Phillippe nodded approval at us, I slipped out of his grip, turned back around.

The rest of the class was easier. We went along into more traditional exercises: the boys behind us, dragging us from side to side on our pointes, pulling us back and forth. We had to walk across the studio hand in hand at the end, but it was a ballet walk, not like real walking at all, and the way we held hands was courtly, polite—none of the almost obscene intertwining of fingers Jacques and I had done earlier.

"See?" Phillippe said as we finished. "Nobody died."

While the others gathered their things, I darted over to Lindsay, who was standing, mouth slightly open, as she stared at Phillippe. Margaux had already left with Gabriel, both laughing.

"Whew." I sighed, exaggerating the exhale. "Pretty rough, yeah? Want to sneak off for a smoke?"

"You go on ahead," Lindsay said, not taking her eyes from our teacher's dark brown gaze. "I've just got a few . . . questions."

"Ugh, Linds. Could you not?"

She turned to me. "C'mon, Delphine. Give me this. After all, you got *Jacques* and he's the best partner by far. If I were one fucking centimeter taller—if you two didn't look like a pair of fucking bookends, maybe the rest of us could actually get a chance."

I smiled; I couldn't help it. Most of our class had dark hair, but it was true that ours was darker than most, verging on black. True that our eyes were matched, pale blue. Had other people noticed that? Did they think of us as a pair?

"Do you really think I look like him?"

Lindsay rolled her eyes. "Stop planning your wedding-cake topper. You're missing the fucking point."

But I wasn't, I thought as I left the studio alone. I knew what the fucking point was: the point of all of this. We'd honed ourselves for so many years into something resembling perfection. Developed our strength, our control. And from here, the boys would go on to build more, more, growing their muscles and getting bigger and better and stronger. But for the girls, it was something different. It was about taking our strength and making it pliable, supple, compliant.

And even as the echo of Jacques's touch thrummed through my body, I felt something else, something dark and hard at the base of my spine. That was the real lesson that day, I guess: I'd never belong completely to myself ever again.

— September 2018 —

It's easy to believe that buildings are static, unchanging; harder to accept that your time there is inconsequential in the face of their history. It's even easier with a place like the Palais Garnier, which grasps its heritage around it as greedily as the caped aristocrats we killed off two centuries ago. A few floors beneath the studios were the red-carpeted staircases and the candelabras, the gilded mirrors and the plush seats. The stage that hosted Petipa and Nureyev. Taglioni and Zambelli. My mother and me.

But it wasn't ours anymore.

My dead mother was pinned to the wall and neither of us had spun through these halls in over a decade.

She was an artifact; I was a visitor.

And I knew that if I was going to make anything worth watching on that stage, I had to go back to it.

I came in early the next day, before the dancers arrived for their nine-thirty class, before even the stagehands would be in. In the weeks leading up to the gala that would start the season, the stage had been stripped down to its bones. It was no longer a royal court or a cursed lake or a fairy's kingdom; it was just empty space.

As I wove my way through the sets and ropes and lights, I knew I'd have to start thinking bigger for this ballet. The Garnier, I reminded myself as the familiarity of the black-painted backstage wrapped itself around my heart, has the largest stage in Europe. Bigger even than the Mariinsky's. Which is really saying something, because the Russians don't do anything by half measures—at least on the surface. While the Mariinsky is also all velvet and gilt to the public, everything behind the scenes is chipped paint, worn wood, squeaking floorboards. POB, on the other hand, actually knows how to treat its dancers.

And then I was there. Again.

I was onstage at the Palais Garnier.

I inched downstage, toward the seats. I wasn't used to this darkness, with only the emergency lights and the ghost lights on. It gave me the oddest feeling of having died and come back into a netherworld that was partially my Opéra, partially not.

They'd started renovating the auditorium a few years after I left. I hadn't ever opened the emails from the press office showing the pictures; I'd wanted to keep the memory perfect in my mind. But as I craned my head up at the shadowy ceiling, I realized: the Palais was still itself, only more so. The gold was fresher, brighter even in this half-light. The chandelier glittered, still in the dark. Chagall's dreamy figures floated around it, great splotches of color from where I stood.

I took out my phone, pressed play on the music I'd been listening to on my commute. Jeanne Moreau came on: "Le Tourbillon de la vie." I'd been craving the old French songs since I decided to come back, and this jaunty, simple tune had always thumped me right in the sternum with its mysterious heroine reunited with her lover, so much like my idealized version of myself. Moreau's voice rang out over the stage, tinny and almost ghostly, and I didn't need anything else; I kicked off my shoes and I was moving.

Elle avait des yeux, des yeux d'opale

My feet twitched in quick beats, my arms reaching, flipping—playing. For the first time in years, I was dancing, actually dancing. More than just the approximated shorthand I used as a choreographer. More than just moving someone else's body.

Qui m'fascinaient, qui m'fascinaient . . .

And then I was bouncing across the stage in a series of short, turning leaps. My mind soared, but my body—my body was already running out of breath. I carried my weight differently now, and there was more of it, besides. The last time I was up here, I'd been pure muscle. A cat, ready to pounce. Now I had an extra ten kilos wrapped around my stomach and ass, obscuring who I really was.

This building had been my home.

How had everything changed so much?

I stopped, bending over with my hands on my thighs as I tried to catch my breath, as Serge Gainsbourg's gravelly voice started to autoplay something about too many cigarettes—and as the sound of a single person clapping rang out through the theater.

For a moment, I stood frozen, fear prickling through me.

I fumbled to turn off the music.

"Who's there?" I called, rage snapping irrationally in my chest. "What are you doing here?"

I squinted out at the figure. A man, rising from his seat, features resolving into readability and a strange familiarity as he came closer. Thick light hair brushed back from a wide forehead. A thin mouth, ticking up at one side now as he watched me regain my balance. Dark eyes that probably looked black in photographs. Yet there was a softness to his face, giving him a childishness that began to dissolve my fear.

"I'm sorry," I added weakly. "You just gave me a fright, that's all."

"No, it's my fault," he said, eyes crinkling. "You were so much in your own world that I wanted to see how far you'd get before noticing me. That probably sounds pretty creepy," he added, stopping as he came up to the orchestra pit. He said it in English: *creepy*. There's no real word for *creepy* in French. The closest translation is something more like *terrifying*.

And maybe it was his thick accent on that one English word, but I felt my limbs soften as though my skin were becoming more porous, open to the world.

Did we know each other already? I could tell he wasn't a dancer; he was too short. Why did I recognize him, and why didn't he know me?

"I'm Delphine, by the way," I said.

"Daniel," he said, and I felt a fist close around my heart.

"Lindsay's Daniel?" I said.

He laughed, full and round.

"I'm not sure I'd introduce myself that way, but yeah, okay," he said, leaning against the barrier of the orchestra. "That must make you Lindsay's Delphine."

So here he was, after all these years. The man who'd stolen her heart. The guy who had handled POB's press in 2013 had slowly turned into her husband. *I've never felt anything like this before*, she'd written to me, and I'd rolled my eyes. Lindsay had fallen in love with somebody new every three to four months since we were teenagers. But month after month passed, and the Daniel phase had never dissipated. *He's only got eyes for me. I'd die of shock if he even knew another woman existed. And Delphine, the sex—!* And over the years, he'd emerged in my mind like the world's slowest-developing Polaroid: a sensual man, reliably calm, with an obsession for Lindsay that matched only her own for the ballet.

For a moment, I felt Dmitri's absence stronger than ever. *You had that once*, the voice in my head mocked me. No, I corrected myself. No, I thought I had it. I never really did.

"We were really sorry you couldn't make it," he said. "For the wedding."

"Oh. Yeah, I was really sorry to miss it," I said. "Things were just so crazy in Russia, you know. Congratulations."

"Lindsay missed having you there," he said. I watched his face for some sign of an ulterior motive, but I didn't know him well enough to recognize if it was there.

"What . . . are you doing here?" I asked.

"I dropped Lindsay off this morning. I had a meeting down the street earlier, but my next few hours were free, so I thought I'd see if I could grab her for a coffee after her class." He smiled slightly and held up his iPhone. "In the meantime, I can do my work from pretty much anywhere that has a cell signal. I'm in PR, I'm not sure how much she's told you?" I nodded. "They gave me a security pass back when I was doing some work for the company. Turns out, they don't actually check the date on those things."

It was terribly sweet and probably terribly useless of him. How many women would give their left legs for a husband who'd go out of their way to walk them to work? Not Lindsay. Lindsay wouldn't have given up a limb for anything.

"You know I have her in rehearsal at one," I said with an apologetic wince.

He smiled. "Yeah. She still comes to meet me whenever she has the chance. Well. Less so lately. She was so happy to get the lead in your ballet."

Around him, the auditorium seemed to darken.

"She was always the best of us. I've wanted to put her in a ballet for—well, for years."

Even as I spoke, I couldn't stop looking at all those empty seats. Each one a phantom spectator. Back when I was still in the company, people looked at me when I walked down the street, and I told myself they recognized me from POB. It was stupid; at my very best, I was only a *sujet*, not exactly a celebrity. But when you spend that amount of time onstage, being watched just feels right.

That sensation—everyone is watching, everyone is waiting—had mostly vanished in Russia, but it was back now.

I looked down at my hands, twisted together.

"How long has it been, fifteen years?" he asked.

"Thirteen," I said.

"Well, Delphine. I'll get out of here, let you get back to work. But it's a real pleasure to finally meet you, after all this time. All those stories of the three of you!"

The implication was innocent, yet the words themselves felt ominous; hearing them sent a strange, plunging-elevator sensation swooping through my stomach.

"She always says, *Delphine's the nice one*. I mean, I guess you'd have to be, with Margaux and Lindsay as your friends. But still. You seem like you are. Nice, I mean," he said, laughing.

Of course that's what she'd said. It had been like a refrain at the academy: Lindsay's hot, Margaux's a bitch, Delphine's nice.

"Thanks," I replied half-heartedly.

Nice. In Russia, that's last on the list of national virtues. Smart, now. Smart is good. Smart gets you things. Strong is better. Strong lets you survive. Best of all, though? Powerful.

"We don't think of it as *power* per se," Dmitri said to me once. "We think of it more as *influence*." That was around the time his influence got me my position at the Mariinsky, still a few years before I found out exactly where the limits of my own influence were.

Nice? What is nice, anyway? Nice is about how you make the people around you feel. It's not about you at all; it's about them. I don't know why people always see that in me. I'd have thought that Russia, of all places, would have hammered *nice* out of me.

Besides, I was never all that nice to begin with.

CHAPTER 4

At the academy, the fact of my mother was like a blister about to form: rubbing against my skin, slightly uncomfortable, always carrying the promise of pain. Her legend, as one of Nureyev's last muses, permeated my life there. Her picture still hung in the halls of the company space at the Palais Garnier. The dance critic for Le Monde still compared every new Coppélia to her version. The dancers all stopped me in the hallways of the school, asking me how she was doing. I don't remember a time when I was unaware of her influence.

At home one weekend, ten years old: "Could you do this when *you* were my age?" I asked, pulling my leg straight up to my face.

She barely glanced at me.

"Of course."

She, like me, was double-jointed in the hips. That was what made me better than other girls in the class, the only thing that made me stand out. But when it came to my mother, I could never win; she was always ahead of me. If only I could outdo her in *something*, that would have been enough, even if it was as simple as flexibility. But that was never even an option.

It happened in the studio, too. The teachers—"*Again*, Delphine. I swear, if I didn't know you were Isabelle's daughter . . ." The students—"Do you think your mom could introduce us to Baryshnikov?" And, always, the secret that burned in the back of my mind: I'd been two centimeters too short to qualify for the school in the first place. They'd made an exception, the registrar winking at Maman as she took down my statistics. Two centimeters. So small a difference, the other kids had never spotted that I'd stolen what they'd earned.

But they must have suspected. How could they not, when my limbs shook while theirs held fast? When the jury members from the company whispered furiously every time I came into the studio for our annual reviews? When I consistently placed first or second in the class, despite my all-too-obvious weaknesses?

By the time we were seventeen, though, I was certain I'd won them over. When Aurélie got harshly reprimanded by Marie-Cécile, I was there with a kind word about what a bitch she was. When Mathilde was in danger of failing biology, I let her copy my homework. When Corinne struggled with a fiendish *petit battement* combination, I stayed after class to work through it with her, cutting into the extra hours I regularly put in there on my own.

And then there was Dance History.

I knew my mother would be on the curriculum. There was a lot I still didn't know about the history of dance then, but I was an expert on the subject of my mother. You can't teach the history of ballet without teaching Rudolf Nureyev. And you can't teach Rudolf Nureyev without discussing his muses. There she'd be, with her perfect blend of strength and flexibility. Showing off the ideal, sculpted lines of her body as she floated across the stage. Again, and always—better than me.

We spent January stuck in the seventeenth century with our founder, the inventor of modern ballet, good old Louis XIV. February passed in an eighteenth-century haze of operas and third-act dances. When March came and we'd reached 1875 and the construction of the Palais Garnier, I knew my time was almost up. It had to be April, then. But April was full of the Ballets Russes and their iconic founder, Sergei Diaghilev.

On the last day of the month, as Madame Beaumont turned off the projector, I thought, Maybe we won't even get to Nureyev this semester.

But then she winked. Directly at me.

"You'll all want to make sure to be on time on Monday," she said. "We'll be seeing some familiar faces."

Something unfamiliar pinged through me. It was—excitement? Excitement and pride, snapping like a rubber band against my sternum.

In all of the myths about her talents, surrounding our life like filmy scarves, I couldn't remember ever having actually seen my mother perform. I must have; when I was really small and Stella wasn't available, she'd bring me to the dressing room during her performances and let whatever corps member was around look after me. But I couldn't remember actually watching the stage.

My mother, the legend: I was going to see her dance for the first time.

On Monday morning, I got to class too early and sat alone for a long moment in the white-walled classroom so new it still smelled of paint and plaster. Here was Madame Beaumont, all frizzy hair and smiling, crescent-moon eyes; Lindsay, eyeliner blurred and hair tousled as though she'd come right from Phillippe's bed, which she probably had; Margaux, dropping into her seat with a groan, not yet ready to let the weekend go; the big crowd of boys, who only ever seemed to move as a unified pack. And then class started and Madame Beaumont was telling us all about the Cold War for some reason—oh, because Nureyev was Russian, of course he was, he defected—and then Fonteyn, yes, lots of Margot Fonteyn.

"But she was nineteen years older than he was," Madame said, wheeling out the boxy, oversize television on its trolley. "And so, as she performed less and less, they saved their partnering primarily for the Royal Ballet. Throughout the 1970s and 1980s, particularly on tour, he paired with other, younger dancers. French dancers."

There: the grainy footage, tinged bluish around the edges, and my mother stepped onto the Garnier stage. The white block letters over her— ISABELLE DURAND AS NIKIYA, *LA BAYADÈRE*—sent a shiver through me. A close-up on her face.

As she paused, waiting for the music to start, her eyes darted over the audience. Wide as she licked dry lips, swallowed.

She looked scared.

And beyond that—she looked exactly like me. I almost gasped.

"It's little Isabelle!" one company member had cried when spotting me in the Opéra hallway during *Nutcracker* rehearsals. And I'd just thought: No. I didn't know a whole lot back then, but I knew that much. It was only from far away that the resemblance was apparent, when you looked at our black hair, blue eyes, pale skin. Close up, I was the designer knockoff to her haute couture. My seams were off, my logo wrong.

My mother had been on the cover of *Vogue* twice: March 1974 and May 1976. My mother had modeled for Cartier, her bejeweled hand suspended in the air. My mother had had cameos in films by both François Truffaut and Federico Fellini. She had cheekbones like icebergs and a neck like a swan. She had finely muscled arms and legendary legs.

I had a baby face and soft limbs that trembled if I held them in the air for more than ten seconds.

My mother was the real thing.

But as I saw her on the glowing screen, spotted that flicker of vulnerability—the makeup and the gauzy red costume and the crown and the scarves faded away. She was me, and I was her. It pushed at something in my chest, inflating me with the warmth of it. I couldn't take my eyes off of her. We were the *same*. And she was incandescent.

"Wow," Lindsay said, stringing her arm through mine after class.

"Yeah," Margaux said. "I mean, Jesus fucking Christ, Delphine."

Every word was a gush of air to the pride burning in my chest. I grinned.

As we made our way down the hall, footsteps echoed behind us, speeding up, pounding toward us in the cold white space. And then Jacques was in front of me, breathless.

Lindsay and Margaux dissolved like sugar, Lindsay widening her eyes behind his back as they left, Margaux rolling hers.

"Isabelle Durand? That's your mom?" Jacques said.

How had he not known? Maybe the boys didn't gossip the way the girls did. Maybe they paid less attention to the women stars than the male ones. Maybe he just hadn't ever paid enough attention to *me* to notice. And after all, my mother and I had different last names. Though my mother had shed it like snakeskin, I'd kept my father's name after he'd moved to California with his new family. *Delphine Durand* sounded idiotic, she and I had both agreed.

"Yeah," I said, looking up at him, a solid block of muscle and flesh. Just like in Pas de Deux class, but he was somehow realer here, outside of the studio, in his street clothes. The sharp underside of his jaw. The soft lines of his neck. The faint warmth coming off him in waves.

"That's amazing. You look just like her, you know."

The fire in my chest flared.

"Do you . . ." he muttered, then paused.

"Do I what?" I said, and it came out mean.

And there in the hall, maybe for the first time, I felt like her daughter: I was imperious and regal and—more than what I was. More than I'd ever been before.

"Doyoumaybewanttoseeamoviesometime," he said, low from the back of his throat, staring at a spot somewhere between us on the floor.

I opened my mouth eagerly, then stopped.

What would she do? What would she say?

I tossed my hair over my shoulder. My neck cracked at the unfamiliar movement and he looked up, alarmed at the noise, into my face.

I took a deep breath and smiled the way I'd seen her smile. Slow and measured. Scary.

"Sure," I said. "Why not?"

— *September 2018* —

Ballerinas are like pointe shoes: you have to break them down before they're of any use. Swirl glue around the boxes, the toes, to harden them. Particularly important at POB, where dancers get only seven free pairs a month—which is nothing when a single performance can make a new set unusable. Trim the satin from the tips or embroider them for traction, sew satin ribbons and elastics to the heels. Rip out the insole and cut the shank down to accentuate the curve of the feet. If you're Black or brown, cover them in pancake makeup to match your skin; racially, ballet is an incredibly problematic milieu, and even now, almost no companies make shoes in a "skin tone" that ranges beyond pale pink. Put them on, then spray the damn things with water to mold them to your shape. Each sixty-euro pair lasts about a day, though you can drag out their life span over two or three if you're careful.

Same thing with the dancers. When you're a choreographer, you have to strike the same delicate balance. Be strong to show them you won't take any shit. Avoid letting them offer their own ideas or change the steps. That's not what they're there for. They're bodies, instruments. They're not the song itself. Never end rehearsal early; get every second of work you can out of them. Work them until their muscles shake. Work them until they bleed.

It's what they signed up for, after all.

It was time to show them what I could do.

"Delphine!" a voice cried.

Startled, I looked into the strange golden eyes of Camille, Lindsay's nineteen-year-old understudy. Nathalie's choice.

"I'm sorry," she said quickly. "I didn't mean to surprise you."

"You didn't. What's up?"

We were standing in the middle of the hallway, studio doors on both sides, dancers scurrying around us. Amid it all, there was something eerily watchful about her lion-colored eyes.

"I just wanted to say . . . well, thank you, I guess. This is such a great opportunity for me, you know, and I'm so glad you came back. It's funny, isn't it? Most dancers come from Russia to the West, not the other way around?"

Balanchine. Baryshnikov. Nureyev. She wasn't wrong. I had gone against the grain when I'd moved to St. Petersburg at twenty-three. Did it count if a Russian pulled you back with him, though?

"Anyway, I couldn't believe it when I saw the call sheet. This role! Even as an understudy. I mean, of course I know I'm just an understudy," she said with a giggle. She clearly had no idea that Nathalie had forced the issue. "It's just—the chance of a lifetime!"

Waiting for me to reply, she stood motionless. You never see that with dancers: they have so many nervous tics, the constant motion grates on you. Camille's stillness made her seem glazed, uncanny. Robotic.

"I'm guessing you'll have many other chances before you're done," I said. "You have no idea how long life is. Well. Long, but also short."

Her automaton eyes stared at me for a beat too long, before she smiled. "I guess. Just—thanks!" she said, and trotted off into the studio. The replacement appointed from on high, ready to step in at a moment's notice to erase one of my oldest friends.

And all I could think was: *Lindsay, you better fucking come through for me.*

Camille trotted over to a group of young dancers. She had that quality that made you want to watch her; I'd give Nathalie that much. But that matching getup she was wearing—pale pink shoes, tights, skirt, leotard, sweater—she was like a three-year-old's dream of a ballerina.

For a moment, I couldn't even pick Lindsay out of the crowd. After a decade of relentless academy uniforms, company members become determined to show their individuality in the layers of warm-ups they drape over themselves. Cut out the neck of your favorite sweatshirt, pull on the bright blue leggings that are more hole than weave, dress yourself in black, black, black. It should make each dancer easier to identify, but there's a sameness in the chaos that makes them harder to differentiate.

They all have startlingly similar bodies, after all. A big part of why the thirty-eight of them were in that studio in the first place was because they'd each won a freakish genetic lottery.

A ballerina is a perfect woman. Thin. Beautiful. Invisibly strong.

There are no evolutionary reasons we should look the way we do. If what you want is a good procreator, look anywhere but a ballet company, where you're unlikely to find a period that comes more regularly than one month out of three. What you want is someone round, with wide hips and pendulous breasts; someone ready to take a few months of war or famine in stride and still guarantee the future of the human race. Arms ready to plow a field, knead some bread, comfort a child. Good peasant stock.

Yet somehow, delicate and breakable, we have become the height of feminine perfection.

I mean, *they*. They have.

At the school, instructors train us to dance as a group: faceless, nameless, indistinguishable. In terms of which dancers eventually make it, there's an exponential decline over time. At the end of our studies, the company takes around ten percent of the few remaining dancers as *quadrilles*, apprentices, in training to become *coryphées*, corps members: a mass of identical dancers. Maybe half of those will have a long-term career in the company, as long-term as our careers get. Of those, around ten percent will be promoted beyond the corps to *sujet*, soloist, and dance short, featured parts; ten percent of those will be promoted beyond soloist to *premier danseur*, principal; ten percent of those will be promoted to star.

So, if you're an eight-year-old accepted into the school, there's still a literal one-in-a-million chance that someday you will be a star. Your best bet is to dance exactly like everybody else.

And yet—stars are the ones you think of when you think of ballerinas. They're the ones you come to see.

I cleared my throat. "Okay, guys. Let's get started."

Nobody moved. Nobody even stopped talking. Not even fucking Lindsay.

Actually, one person did. Camille turned her gaze to me.

I was the choreographer. They should have fallen quiet the second I entered the room. According to Jock, Balanchine had commanded absolute silence at New York City Ballet, unwavering respect from the dancers, most of whom were scared even to speak in his presence. Not just scared to speak *to* him—scared to speak *in front of* him.

He never let them wear warm-ups, either.

Jock was still away on vacation for another week; he wasn't there to help me impose order. As eager as I was to see him again, it was a relief to be able to focus on the dance without him around. He had always distracted me too much.

I found a chair, stood on top of it, and clapped my hands together. Margaux caught my eye and winked, a dimple showing. After brunch, she'd sent me a text: *Sorry I lost my shit. The ballet will be great, no matter who you cast.* And now, looking at her, I could almost hear her voice: *Delphine, you've got this.*

"Let's get started!"

Now they were paying attention.

"Okay. So today, I want to go over the first scene. The meeting between Alix and Nicky."

I'd always known where I wanted to start the ballet: when Alix, the future tsarina but currently a minor princess of a tiny German principality, falls in love with Nicky—Nicholas, the future and last tsar of Russia. But it was messy, trying to get the narrative to work. The first time they technically met was when her sister married Nicky's uncle, but she was *eleven*, and he was sixteen. Not a great look for the ballet. So I was fudging history a bit and starting when she was sixteen and came to visit her sister at Tsarskoe Selo, the imperial family's country estate. Sixteen and twenty made for a much more palatable romance.

"The first thing you should know," I said, "is that this is not a love story."

"But the letters—" Camille cut in, then closed her mouth. The entire group looked at her in surprise. I'd given them all copies of *A Lifelong Passion*, the book of love letters and diary excerpts from Alix and Nicky, to read before rehearsal; whether they were surprised that Camille had actually read them (as a group, we'd never been great about homework) or that this little nineteen-year-old was speaking up, I wasn't sure.

"Don't get me wrong, there's love *in* this story. But the story itself is about a woman with enormous potential. A brilliant woman, a funny woman, a loving woman. A woman who makes a choice that takes her thousands of miles from her home, which eventually leads to her tragic death and the end of her husband's bloodline—not to mention the fall of the imperial house of Romanov. And that choice starts here, in this scene, when she falls in love with Nicky." I nodded at Claude, who lifted his hands in an exaggerated shrug, to the group's laughter. *What can you do? She loves me.* "So yes, we play it like a love story. But the entire time, I very much want this sense of impending doom. You understand? Linds, can I get you upstage right, please?"

I hopped down off the chair as Lindsay took her place, shadowed closely by Camille. Lindsay was in a beat-up T-shirt with the neck cut out, the words SIDWELL FRIENDS only just visible, and black tights. She'd been wearing that shirt to class for the past twenty years, elementary school memories echoing into the present, its original significance fading with every year. Behind her, Camille stood like a fucking Disney princess.

"After the entrances, I want a little pas de deux. Linds, Claude—" I showed them what I wanted them to do. They echoed the motions as I explained them, nodding along.

I turned back to the mirrors.

I hit play.

I'd never actually say it, but the part I love most about being a choreographer is pushing the dancers to their limits. Being the one with power for once.

Only dancers really know what it's like to lift, to float, to grind through the infinite combinations of the same positions, day after day, underneath the ticking, appraising eyes of a choreographer or ballet mistress or artistic director.

Every time I work, I watch their pink satin feet and I know. Underneath those shoes, the flesh is exposed, has been rubbed down into multilayered wounds.

Beneath the glossy pink tights, they ache to the marrow of their bones.

Below the crowns and the tutus and the perfection, they're all just quivering messes.

And it's all for me.

Until, of course, they step onto the stage—becoming my agents, my brushstrokes, my tools. Then it's all for the audience. It's all for you.

"Don't they realize," I'd hissed to Margaux during a curtain call after a particularly grisly performance of *Swan Lake* fifteen years ago, "that we're all covered in the most disgusting sores under our shoes?"

She'd plastered her pink grin wide, grabbing my hand as the curtain went up, exposing us once more.

"Of course they know," she said between her teeth. "That's why they like to watch."

And that was what I liked. To hide the suffering with my own brand of perfection.

That's also why I hate it so much when they get it wrong.

With Claude beside her, Lindsay looked exactly like a marionette. All of a sudden, the fire had drained right out of her. Having Camille in the background wasn't doing her any favors, either. As Lindsay made her way mechanically through the movements, there was this younger, fresher version of her two feet away. Without the constraints of a partner, Camille's motions were full of youthful hubris—like the angel in Botticelli's *Cestello Annunciation*, delicate and precocious and yet somehow *knowing*.

In other words, exactly right. And she only made Lindsay look that much more wrong—like a ballerina in a music box.

Was it possible that all this time, I'd been remembering a different Lindsay? A Lindsay trained in the French style but who retained a loose Americanness? An acrobatic Lindsay, driving the rest of us crazy with jealousy? A Lindsay full of grace, innocent and seductive at once?

And then the real Lindsay tipped over.

As a ballerina, you're doing a lot of things at the same time. Leg up, straight, steady, turned out; arm reaching, fingers fluttering, lifted higher; torso up, shoulders back, rolled down; head high, chin up, never forget to smile. If you can't smile, at least keep yourself straight. If you can't keep yourself straight, at least keep your arms high. If you can't keep your arms high—well, at the very least, you can try not to fucking fall.

"That was good, you guys!" I called, halting the music as Lindsay picked herself up. "Just—a little looser this time, yeah?"

Lindsay, breathless, nodded tightly. Behind her, Camille was still, hands on her hips.

"From the beginning, then."

My hands were sweaty, and it took me three tries to start the music again. This was still salvageable. This could still work.

Camille sprang into life, dancing half of the pas de deux better than Claude and Lindsay were doing the real thing. She hit her arabesque perfectly, hovering still in the air.

In front of her, Lindsay wobbled.

They went into the turn series, whipping pirouettes into *fouettés*. Camille danced crisp and clean. Textbook perfect, but with something else animating her, something clever and insouciant.

French dancers are a different species. For thirteen years, I'd worked almost exclusively with Russians. And as wonderful as they'd been onstage, it was like I could hear an accent as they danced; it's in their natures to be performative. We're not about showing off, at POB. We're about precision.

Lindsay and Claude broke apart, circling into a series of leaps. Behind Lindsay, Camille soared through the air. Higher. Longer. Better.

For all their supposed lyricism, the Russian dancers were always stony in rehearsal, like they were made of metal. Dmitri used to scold me about

treating them like machines: "You can't just pop in fifty centimes and expect to get a perfect pirouette."

But here at POB, that's exactly what I expected.

Claude took center stage, whirling into a series of tiny beats. His legs
seemed to blur as he added more, more with each jump. Five. Six. Eight.
Off to the side, Lindsay was trying to hide that she was out of breath, sti-
fling gasps so that only her heaving rib cage gave her away. Camille just
stood there, poised.

French dancers are like violins. Handcrafted, unbelievably beautiful,
their whole bodies joined only by fine slivers of wood. Likely to crack at
any time.

Lindsay and Claude came together again. Moved apart.

Camille stepped forward.

And then, breaking completely with the choreography, Lindsay whipped
her leg up in a *grand battement* and struck Camille directly in the nose
with her foot.

The room stopped. For a moment, we were a tableau: static, frozen.

And then Camille whimpered, falling back, clutching her face as blood
dripped through her fingers; and the world sped into motion again. Dancers ran over to her, encircling her.

Lindsay stumbled back.

Margaux shrieked, then dissolved into laughter.

My head swiveled between Camille and Lindsay and Margaux, unsure
if I was more disturbed by the laughter or the blood.

Accidents happen in rehearsals—they happen all the time. Dancers
turn their ankles, fall over, even hit their heads. And when they do, the
only person they tend to hurt is themselves. This shit, though? This shit
doesn't happen. Dancers earn their livings by getting movements exactly
right. They know what's around them almost instinctually; the best ones
could dance a given sequence blindfolded in a crowded room. An odd elbow in the ribs, sure. A knee in the groin? Sometimes.

A kick in the face? I'd never seen it happen before. Not even in Russia.

"Claude, go get her some ice," I called over the music. "Camille, you
poor thing, here—" I grabbed my sweatshirt from the ground. She blinked
at me, blood painting her face from the bridge of the nose down, as I
pressed it into her hands. "Keep your head back, okay? . . . No, farther."

Lindsay slunk up to the front of the room and stopped the music. The
studio was silent except for Margaux's laughter, which rang off the walls,
bizarre and bright and wrong. A corps member put a hand on Margaux's

back, but she shrugged it off, holding her sides and just laughing and laughing.

As another dancer tended to Camille, I grabbed Lindsay's arm. "Linds, what the fuck were you thinking?" I hissed.

"I couldn't help it. She was just waiting for me to fail."

"She wasn't, though. She was learning the part, Lindsay. It's her job."

Lindsay's face turned pleading. "This is *my part*. You know how long I've waited for a chance like this. And you know as well as I do that by this age, all the young ones are all just lined up behind us. Literally ready to take our place."

I did know. We'd been those girls. And I knew, too, exactly what she was feeling now. What are you supposed to do when you still have a teenager's dreams but you somehow got old?

But I'd never made anyone bleed.

"Besides," Lindsay said, lowering her voice, "don't you just hate her little face? I just hate her little face so much."

A group of nearby corps members looked up, shocked. It's not like English was our secret language. Everyone in the company spoke it; we'd been trained to.

"Just . . ." I trailed off, then addressed the group. "That's all for today, guys. Camille, why don't you head up to the doctor, just to make sure your"—*face isn't broken?*—"just to make sure?"

Camille nodded miserably. The dancers filed out of the studio in twos and threes until I was standing there, alone, my face flushed with guilt.

Because it didn't matter that Lindsay was the one who'd done it. This was my studio, my rehearsal. I might as well have kicked Camille in the face myself.

And the thing was, I would have. I knew exactly what Lindsay meant.

I hated her stupid little face, too.

CHAPTER 5

— May 1999 —

I saw Jacques before he saw me, hovering at the exit to the Franklin D. Roosevelt station. Gray Oxbow shirt, baggy jeans. The same thing he always wore to our academic classes. Just like it was any other day.

Don't you dare treat him like he's special. Lindsay's warning from the night before echoed at me. *Or he'll have all the power.*

I watched the falling daylight thread Jock's dark hair with red. He was so good-looking; there was no way in hell I was pretty enough for him. No matter what Lindsay said about us looking alike.

Less than an hour before, I'd stood at my mother's dressing table, eyeliner firmly in hand. Ever since she'd started seeing Phillippe, Lindsay had been traipsing around the dorms as she got ready for their dates, showing off her conquest like a new purse. *Do you think Phillippe would like me in this? What about that?* I couldn't stand the thought of his hands—those hands that had touched my *mother*—on her body, and she couldn't stand my constant disapproval. *There's no age of consent in France,* she'd finally spat back at me earlier that week. *Just fucking deal with it, okay?*

She was right. There wasn't, back then. And so, I'd come home for the weekend. For the most important weekend of my life.

If Maman had been in the flat, I never would have dared go through her things. But she was in Nice, her hometown, for the weekend (with a man, I thought, though I didn't know who and she hadn't said). I rummaged with abandon through the makeup she'd left scattered in the drawers. Where was the secret ingredient that would turn me into her?

When I finally found the liquid liner, it took a firm grasp to get the ancient bottle open. I could hear my mother laughing at me. With uncertain fingers, I slid the black liquid over my eyelid and checked my work in the mirror. It was halfway to my brow and I sighed, rubbed it off with one of the cotton balls dotting the marble surface, started again.

In the end, I'd gone with a thick coat of mascara and some brown eye shadow. With the spaghetti-strap blue dress and beige platforms, I told myself, eyeliner would seem like I was trying too hard.

I was glad I hadn't worn more as I made my way up the Métro stairs, clutching my skirt hem as the breeze from the train tried to hike it up my thighs. The bright lights would have made me look like a clown. Around Jacques, the neon of the Champs-Elysées blinked and cartwheeled and flashed on screens, casting his skin with a faint golden glow.

He saw me in my leotard every day, but I'd never felt more naked as I approached him. He didn't see me until I came up and tapped him on the shoulder.

Startled, he pulled down the headphones of his Discman, the faint sounds of Noir Désir whining out at us. Stopping the music, he kissed my cheeks, his stubble rough against my skin. Over the past few years, the boys had all claimed to have started shaving, though only a few of them really had to. Jacques was among those with actual facial hair—though he was lazy on the weekends, always letting this faint shadow emerge.

"Hey," I said.

"Dolphin!" He stopped, grinned. "So." He stuck his hands in his pockets, then immediately took them back out so they hung loosely in front of his thighs. "Ready for our American-themed night?"

"American . . . ?"

He blinked his long lashes at me, a lock of hair flopping onto his forehead. "You know . . . the Métro station? Franklin Roosevelt? And the movie, of course."

"*Great Expectations*? But I thought Dickens was English."

"Well, yeah. But the adaptation's American. It wouldn't be so popular, otherwise. There's such an obsession with American culture that—"

He went on talking, but I was so cold I could barely listen. Goose bumps popped up on my arms; I hadn't thought about the cool May breeze when planning my outfit. I swallowed, turning toward the movie theater. It was easier to walk side by side than it had been to look directly at him, but the silence quickly turned unbearable. As he slipped his hand into mine, I flinched.

"Sorry," he said, flexing his hand, letting us fall apart. "Sorry, is that not okay?"

"No," I said, and he shoved his hands into his pockets, head tilted down. "No," I said, reaching over and—not believing my gall—tugging on his left wrist, weaving my fingers with his. "I mean, yes. It's definitely okay." I didn't look at him as I said it but felt his response in the pulse thumping firmly against my skin.

It was strange to walk with our hands swinging between us, the same kind of awkwardness as being in a three-legged race. We'd gotten over that awkwardness in Pas de Deux class months ago, but there was something different about walking down the street; we didn't have the rhythm down yet. His long legs propelled him slightly ahead of me, my arm gently pulled him back. Our clasped skin was a little bit sweaty, but sweaty in a good way.

"So," I said. "You like Noir Désir?" I couldn't stand their grating, pounding noise, but I was alone in that; their latest album had been circulating among the other students for months.

"Sometimes," he said. "I like a lot of things. Old stuff. Classical stuff."

"Yeah?" Unlike my friends, I loved to listen to Charles Trenet and Serge Gainsbourg and Tom Waits mixed in with my Axelle Red and Fiona Apple. But it was something I only ever did on my own, with headphones; that kind of music would get you teased mercilessly. "Like ballet stuff?"

"Sometimes. Like—here, there's one on this mix." He lifted up his headphones and plopped them on my head. The disc whirred and violins began whining discordantly.

I tried not to make a face. "What is this?"

"Stravinsky," he said, screeches half drowning him out. But then he saw my face and laughed. "Here," he said, stopping it and skipping ahead. "How about this?"

Louise Attaque came on.

"Yeah?" he mouthed as the opening chords of my favorite song began to play.

Amour, de longue date qui s'étend, qui s'étend—

I started laughing.

"Yeah," I said.

Around us, the avenue rose up, grand and bright and just slightly too wide to be on a human scale. It was like the boulevard had been built for something larger than us; for elephants, maybe. Hadn't Napoleon used elephants? Or was that someone older? Someone older, I thought, but I'd barely scraped a 10 out of 20 in history last term, the lowest passing grade.

I took off the headphones as the song ended.

"Not too noisy?" he said.

I shook my head, smiling as wide as my face would go. It was all I could do not to giggle.

"Just noisy enough."

"Wait. Stop," Jacques said, squeezing my hand. "Look—" Nodding at the Arc de Triomphe, a kilometer ahead of us down the avenue.

I looked. It was the same old arch as ever. Carved, ornate. Now, *that* was Napoleon. I was almost positive.

I could feel him looking over at me.

"The sky," he said.

I glanced up: muted lavender and electric blue. Shots of fuchsia like blood vessels running through them. Jacques dropped my hand to put a heavy arm around my shoulders; the panorama swirled dizzyingly as the clouds twisted across the sky.

There we were, teenagers pinned in place on this broad stretch of concrete lined with full green trees and flashing lights. There we were, spinning through a universe that was all color and light and triumph.

There we were. And for a moment, it seemed like the only thing tying me to the earth was him.

— *September 2018* —

For a few days, I got away with rehearsing only the corps: after all, the nameless courtiers had to be trained, too. After we'd finished that Thursday, I stayed behind to work through a particularly tricky combination in the second act. I'd already decided that I was going full opera in terms of the music, but it wasn't easy to pull together. For the first act, as Nicky and Alix fall in love, I was using an excerpt from *Tristan und Isolde*; for the third, I knew I wanted to use Puccini's *La Bohème*, subtly bringing class and the wider world into the tragic, yet seemingly inevitable, deaths of the imperial family. But the second act—the Rasputin act—was giving me trouble. It was so clear to me that the music had to be Stravinsky's *Perséphone*—the descent into the Underworld, the interest bordering on obsession, the flirtation with madness—and yet I couldn't seem to make the strange, modern music flow with Alix's nineteenth-century body. The image I had of her just wouldn't contort that way.

Maybe, though—maybe there was something in that itself, as an idea. The inability to keep up with the times, the clinging to an idealized vision of the colonized world that had maybe never even existed in reality. But that made *La Bohème* all wrong for the third act, then—it was too romantic, too beautiful. I'd have to find something new. Something truly shocking, revolutionary.

But that was a problem for a different day. Once I'd realized the rich potential in the Stravinsky, the ideas wouldn't stop coming. Alix would be courtly, composed, as the music broke into jagged, heart-wrenching modernity around her. But as I danced alone in the studio, my faulty body only approximating the true movements, I felt it: somebody was watching me. I knew who it was even before I turned to the door and saw Nathalie's cool green gaze. Because it is always, always, the person you most fear.

"My office," she said, letting the door swing shut behind her.

It was cowardly, but I made myself wait thirty seconds before going after her. What had she heard about Lindsay and Camille? Whatever it was, it wasn't good, and I didn't want her to start railing against me as we walked through the halls together. Far better to be in the safety, the silence, of her office before she could start yelling.

I followed her through her open office door. When Marc LeBon was artistic director, back when my mother was a star, the office had been a haphazard mix of modern art and nineteenth-century prints, random books left open all over the dingy blue-gray carpeting. Now, Nathalie had bathed the room in creamy white, silver picture frames and orchids scattered beneath the ornate windows.

The cleanliness of it made it harder to defend myself. I'd understood how to handle Marc and his chaotic, disorganized mind. Marc had known me since I was six months old and my mother had returned to the company. And though it had rankled at the time—would I ever be an adult to him? Would I ever be anything but a watered-down version of my mother?—I wished more than anything that he were still here.

"We need," Nathalie said finally, making her way over to the chair across from me, "to address what has happened."

How did she know? But that was the wrong question, stupid to even think. The correct one was: *What made me want to believe she wouldn't find out?*

Nathalie's pale eyebrows drew together. "Delphine. What *was* that?"

I tried to swallow, but my mouth was dry.

"It was an accident," I said.

Nathalie's face whipped into fury, and I caught my breath. Clearly, I'd picked the worst of all possible excuses. But what was I supposed to say? After all I'd done to fight for Lindsay, if I admitted in any way that what she'd done had been intentional—

"An *accident*?" she said. "No. Are you kidding me? No. You insist on putting her in one of my ballets, it's your fault when she goes full-on *All About Eve*."

She was right. Lindsay didn't mean to? Of course she meant to. She understood the space around her in a profound way. There was no world in which Lindsay's kick had not been deliberate.

"I will not have this—bullshit—going on in my company. And as for the choreography itself?"

This was exactly where I hadn't wanted the conversation to go. I bit my lip. I'm good at my job, I reminded myself. Also, she couldn't fire me even if I were terrible—I had a contract.

But I'm not terrible.

I'm good at my job.

"As a nineteenth-century ballet goes, fine. All well and good. Inspired, even. You're back in France, perhaps we should understand the natural tendency to fall back into these ancient traditions. And yet as contemporary ballet goes, it's execrable. Overly mannered. Strange. You're not Petipa. You do understand that, no? And as a ballet I have commissioned in the *twenty-first century*, it is unthinkable. You will clean this up, Delphine. This is too absurd for words. I expected so much more of you."

She finished and held my gaze, shrugging impatiently after a moment as I stood gaping at her. *Well?*

I had nothing to say. My face aflame, I looked down at the ground.

"I'm sorry," I muttered. "I'll fix the steps. But this is Lindsay's role. I really think—can't I let her off with a warning or something?"

Nathalie made a frustrated sound at the back of her throat.

"Roles don't *belong* to anyone. And especially not this role. I told you that from the very start, didn't I? That was the whole point of putting Camille in, wasn't it?"

I bit the inside of my cheek. She rolled her eyes.

"Oh, none of you ever listen. Not really. I warned you, Delphine, I really did. *She's useless in a pas de deux.* That's what I said. And it was true."

"I know," I murmured. "I'm sorry. Couldn't we just—just one more chance? With corrections, with extra rehearsals—I really think—"

Nathalie reached over to cup my chin, a gentle gesture that changed as she yanked my head up so I was looking her in the eyes. Her fingers were hot and tight on my skin.

"Not good enough," she said. "How on earth did you make it so far in your career being so nice? She's out. Go tell her."

Tears filled my eyes. I wasn't sad: I was enraged, and even madder at myself for not being able to control my emotions.

Nathalie sighed and dropped my chin. "I'm not a monster." Her tone indicated that she'd had to say it before. "But you work with your friends, you have to pay the price when it goes badly. And I'm not going to run a company in which that kind of behavior is rewarded. Are we clear?"

I nodded. "Can I wait—until after the gala, at least?"

Nathalie paused, then nodded. "Please do. God knows I don't want her acting up any more than you do. But no more than a day or two."

She scanned my face for a moment, and her eyes narrowed. "You seem scared," she said. "Why do you seem scared?"

CHAPTER 6

By the time I was seventeen, I had few memories left of my father. My own personal tragedy was that I couldn't remember his face: it had been more than a decade since I'd seen him, and my mother had removed pictures of him from the apartment right after he'd fucked off to California with his new family. He never included photos, of them or himself, in my February birthday cards. All I ever got was a twenty-dollar bill I had to change at the bank and his bizarrely formal signature: *"Bien à toi, Papa."*

I was left with my own features—and a laughably incomplete under-standing of Mendelian genetics—to paint a portrait of him in my mind: his eyes must have been blue, it was a recessive gene; his mouth must have been small, since I hadn't gotten my mother's full lips; he must have had wide, soft cheeks, since I hadn't gotten my mother's sharp bones.

Though I didn't have my father, I believed I had someone better: Stella. She lived directly across the hall from us and worked at the Jardin des Plantes as an entomologist. Stella found nothing so fascinating as a butter-fly's wings; and in her singsong Swedish accent, every sentence sounded like a fairy tale. But unlike the princesses I read about in books, Stella had brightly dyed punk hair and a wardrobe of vintage Pucci.

Long before I was at the academy, back when my mother was still per-forming, Stella had babysat me after school on Wednesdays and Satur-days. Those were the best nights, as she let me model her accessories in impromptu fashion shows, braided my hair, and showed me Baryshnikov films I was really far too young to watch.

Three weeks after my date with Jacques, I knocked on her door. Her hair was pale green that month, and she immediately wrapped me in her thin arms. "Home for the weekend?"

I shook my head. As one of the few Parisians at the school, I had the option, but home was increasingly dull and dusty compared with the excitements of the dorms.

"Just a few hours," I said. "Do you have time for a coffee?"

"Always, dear," she said, and I followed her into the kitchen.

I'd had my first coffee right here a few years before. I'd been so disappointed when, a week later and flush with my new maturity, I'd ordered a *café crème* with my friends and found that normal coffee was to Stella's coffee what normal people were to Stella. It had been burned, watery, bitter. Only Stella's had that richness, that fullness against your tongue.

"Go ahead, then," she said, nodding to the cabinet. "Pick us some mugs."

There was the entire world before me—as much of the world as Stella had seen. I ♥ NEW YORK. THE FORBIDDEN CITY. CONCORDIA RESEARCH STATION, ANTARCTICA. And, of course, the onion domes of the Church of the Savior on Spilled Blood, Leningrad, bought on a trip behind the Iron Curtain years ago. I took out L.A.'S THE PLACE and the tortoise mug from the Galápagos.

"And how are things at school?"

"Things are good!" My bright voice echoed off of the kitchen walls.

She scanned me with those marble eyes. "Oh, something exciting's happened, then? Let me guess. You beat those friends of yours in some kind of competition?"

I hadn't ever brought Lindsay and Margaux over to meet her. There was school, and then there was everything else. And if my mother's apartment felt like a shrine to her dead life as a star, Stella's apartment was home. A place where the labels that followed me and my friends around school—*the bitch, the hot one, the nice one*—had no meaning, because I was just me.

I laughed. "Stel*la*. We won't even be evaluated until the end of the month, you know that."

She bit her lip. "Well, my dear, if it's not that—I'd say you're in love."

I twisted my feet around the legs of the chair. The past few weeks with Jock—ever since our first, tentative kiss after that movie—had been a revelation. After lights out, he'd sneak into my room with his latest downloads. A video of Peter Martins doing Apollo for New York City Ballet; a bootleg record of Yves Montand at a nightclub; the screechy violins he kept insisting I'd learn to like if I just listened hard enough. It didn't matter to me what he brought, because he brought himself. We mostly just ended up kissing, anyway.

"Of course not," I muttered.

She got to her feet as the kettle began to hiss. "Mm. But I'm guessing this has something to do with why you came home?"

Sometimes, I could have sworn Stella was some kind of good witch. I thought of the packet of birth control pills my mother had given me three months ago, on my seventeenth birthday, shoved into the back of my top dresser drawer. Maman had plunged into a speech that quickly turned into a rant, while I sat there trying to block out the image of my mother having sex. Of course she had sex; a few times a year, a random man would start appearing in our kitchen on weekend mornings, acting like he owned the place before disappearing some short time later—always inevitably followed by weeks of muffled late-night sobs from her room. But in that excruciating exchange, as she'd enumerated each and every reason I was *not* getting pregnant, the reality of sex was impossible to ignore.

Do you know what happens *when you get pregnant, Delphine? Your body just explodes. Every part of you gets swollen: Your breasts. Your vagina. Your feet. You get these veins everywhere—everywhere. You get bleeding gums and soft nails, your nipples get dark, you get these brown patches on your face. And then at the end of all that? Don't forget that when all that's finally over, you have a baby. A baby? It'll ruin your whole life.*

I'd let her litany roll off of me at first. If she knew how entirely irrelevant this was to my life, she wouldn't have wasted the energy. But with every body part she named, it was like she was throwing another boulder into my lap, each rough stone one of the ways in which I had destroyed her.

The whole thing felt like a punishment for crimes I'd had no part in, had never even considered committing.

Well, I was considering it now. The memory of Jacques's hands on my hips sent a shiver through me so sharp that I was glad Stella had turned toward the stove, couldn't see my face.

"Can't I just come say hi?"

"You *could*, but you don't." After shoving the plunger into the French press, she faced me, leaning back against the counter as she waited for the grinds to consolidate. Her face was soft. Kind. "What I mean is that your mother might like to see you a little bit more. That's all."

I wrinkled my nose. "Stella. She's gone completely *unhinged.* Did she tell you what happened the last time we were out together? At the bank?"

Stella shook her head, curly mermaid hair shaking out around her face.

"She was trying to take out a whole lot of cash and the guy wouldn't let her, I don't know why. And then she just started *screaming* at him. She was like, *Do you have any idea how much money I have in here? Mine. My money. Money that I earned.* Mine." My face was all screwed up at the memory. "And then she—" I shuddered. "She *spat* in the teller's face." I put my head in my hands. "It was just—*awful. So* humiliating. She was just so *mad.*"

Stella set the two mugs between us on the table. It was a long time before she said anything.

"Did you ever think," she said slowly, "that maybe she has a lot to be mad about?"

I rolled my eyes.

"At the very least," Stella said, lifting the tortoise mug, "you must admit that some men deserve to be spat on." She hesitated, holding the steaming drink steady in front of her mouth. "You just be sure this young man of yours isn't one of them."

— *September 2018* —

I awoke the next morning to the sound of wheels bumping up old marble stairs. My heartbeat pulsing through my skin, I sprang out of bed and ran into the hallway. *Stella.* Stella was home. As the mustachioed taxi driver shuffled back down the steps, I thrust myself into her arms. All these years away from her had felt like nothing, yet the past three weeks had been unbearable as I'd waited for her to return from Lima.

After a minute, Stella stepped back, her hands on my shoulders as she studied my face.

"You look different," she said finally in her soft, Swedish-tinted voice.

I winced. "Yeah," I said. "Older."

"No." Stella pulled back, waving a hand in dismissal. "No, not that at all. I mean, we're all *older*, dear. Better that than the alternative. No, it's that mask of makeup you were wearing when I saw you in St. Petersburg. You look fresh faced again."

My hand went automatically to my face. To the eyebrows I hadn't had waxed in a month, to the crease I normally Botoxed, just between them. "It just felt—wrong, here, somehow. French beauty and all that."

"Well, I don't know that nationality comes into it. But you look better this way. More yourself."

It was my turn to study her, now. The bright morning light pulsed in from the hallway windows, and her purple hair looked almost electric. The last time I'd seen her, it had been robin's-egg blue and had stayed that way in my memory, frozen in time. I'd liked the blue. It had matched her eyes. The purple was too bright, almost garish—never mind, though. She'd change it again in a few weeks. Maybe I could convince her to dye it back.

But as I scanned her body, all thoughts of her hair went out of my mind.

"Why are you using a cane?" I asked.

She waved her free hand. "My bones are old," she said. "No big deal. I'm getting my hip replaced the first week of October."

Eighty. Stella was eighty now. When I was little, she'd used those same legs to show me the dances from her youth. Those same exact legs had jitterbugged, jived, bopped across the length of her apartment. I'd never been able to match her, even as I got older. Especially as I got older. The more my ballet training sank in, the harder I found it to move my hips when music played, even when that music was Elvis or Jerry Lee Lewis or an anachronistic Bob Seger.

"Here," I said, grabbing her suitcase as she fumbled to get her key in the door.

"Thank you, dear. You can just leave it there for me to deal with later," she said, nodding at her coatrack as we went inside. "I'm dying for some coffee."

The kitchen was smaller than I remembered it. It had always felt enormous to me; I'd been able to stand up straight in the oversize fireplace until I was thirteen. The furniture was the same: a battered wood table and mismatched wicker chairs. The same posters for old museum exhibits (SEE THE WONDERS OF NATURE AT THE JARDIN DES PLANTES!) were still taped on the walls. There were a few new refrigerator magnets—evidence of Stella's globe-trotting ways—but that alone wasn't enough to change the feeling of the room. It must have been St. Petersburg; it throws off your sense of scale.

Stella put the kettle on. Then she stood, watching me closely.

"What's wrong?"

"Surgery, Stella? You should have told me!" Her last email, sent right after her arrival in Lima, had been full of descriptions of jungle beetles and mysterious termites and little else. So like Stella: explain the bugs, forget the life-altering medical news.

She shrugged. "I had more important things on my mind. It's routine, you know. Hip replacements? They do them every day." She flipped the electric kettle off—she never had enough patience to wait for it to turn off automatically—then reached in her tote, pulled out an unmarked brown bag, and opened it.

"Smell," she commanded, holding it under my nose.

"Smells . . . good?" I said.

"Peruvian coffee has less acid, you know—"

"Stella!" I said, flopping down into a chair. "Stop changing the subject. When's the surgery? The tenth, you said?" I pulled my phone out of my pocket.

"The fifth."

I nodded, opening the calendar. The empty dates whizzed by, each one offering infinite possibilities for catastrophe. How could she be alone at a time like this? On the seventeenth, she could try to get out of bed and fall. On the twenty-third, she could slip in the shower and hit her head. On the second—

"Look," I said, adding the surgery and turning my phone off. "I've been wondering. My Nespresso machine's completely messed up—too many tourists messing around with it, I guess. But I'm helpless without my coffee. Would you mind if I came across the hall in the mornings, before work . . ." I trailed off, the excuse sounding flimsier and flimsier with each word.

Stella only nodded, pouring the steaming water over the grinds. "I'd love that, dear. Now, tell me. How is the ballet coming along?"

"Oh." I bit my lip. "Well, remember Lindsay?"

"The crazy American?"

"Lindsay isn't crazy." *Lindsay is very crazy.* "Anyway, I cast her as the lead and—well, she kicked another dancer in the face during rehearsal last week."

"See?" Stella said slyly, popping the lid of the French press over the stewing coffee. "Crazy."

"Look. I really hate it when people call women crazy," I said.

Stella's smile widened. Early as it was, her dark pink lipstick had already started bleeding into the cracks around her mouth.

"We're all crazy, dear. Doesn't matter what's between our legs."

CHAPTER 7

— June 1999 —

The night before his first trip to New York, Jacques waited for me in the copse of trees behind the school. The six weeks he'd be gone infused the evening with significance: we could be entirely different people by the time he got back. I wanted it to be special, to press myself into his brain so that no American girl stood a chance. But while I was getting used to him in the dark, to the feel of his body, as I moved toward him, I had the sense of being all wrong. Should I be going faster or maybe slower? Smiling or serious? In our hundreds of late-night sessions, Lindsay and Margaux and I had discussed everything to do with boys, except what to actually *do* with them. And I still didn't know what to do with myself when he watched me.

In a way, it didn't really matter what I did. I was already here, wasn't I? I was already showing my willingness to come to him. He had all the power; everything else was just details.

"Hi," I said softly.

"Hey," Jacques said, smiling.

And then my hands were around his neck and my mouth was on his. He parted his lips and I was kissing him fiercely. His hands were in my hair, on my back, as though he were trying to touch all of me at once. He ground against me, and every part of me was open, thrumming in time with the heat of his body.

I took his hand in mine and led him back, back.

He followed until I was against a tree, then his body covered mine; I moaned as his hands went to either side of my waist.

"Delphine," he murmured, looking into my half-closed eyes. His lips traced the curve of my neck urgently, then found mine again, biting my bottom lip gently, tongue smoothing out the little pain immediately afterward.

I wasn't thinking, I was only feeling, as the hard length of his body pressed against me—I realized what it was and had to catch my breath, sighing against him.

And for that one moment, it was like we were suspended between his power and my own. Sure, I'd come to him. Sure, I'd shown him that I wanted him. But he wanted me, too. His body was incontrovertible proof of that. *I did that to you*, I wanted to say. *Me. Look what I did.*

And then I was back in my body as his lips went to my earlobe, his hand drifting up and almost lazily grazing the curve of my breast.

I gasped. My leg rose and wrapped around him of its own accord as I fumbled for the bottom of his shirt, lifting it up, up, get it off, over his head. I had to feel his skin on mine, I wanted more—

Your body just explodes.

His hand went down, down, to the bottom of my dress, and then his fingers slid up my thigh, tracing my skin so lightly that I choked back a breath—

You get these veins everywhere—everywhere.

"Jacques," I whispered.

My hands were entwined in his hair, soft and rough at the same time, and his ragged breath was hot on my face.

A baby? It'll ruin your whole life.

Heart hammering, I twisted my face away.

"Jacques. I'm not going to have sex with you," I said.

Jacques pulled back. "Oh," he said. "Okay."

Suddenly, the air against my skin felt very cold. I tugged the top of my dress straight so it covered my breasts.

"I mean, I want to—"

"You don't have to explain." He was already looking for his shirt. I didn't mean we had to stop *everything*. But I didn't know how to say that. *I want something, not everything; a lot, but not all.*

He slipped his shirt over his head. That's how fast it was over.

"I'm sorry," I whispered.

He patted my shoulder. "Don't worry about it," he said.

— September 2018 —

As I left Stella's kitchen, a photograph on the back of her piano caught my eye. I thought it was new, but it was hard to tell—images populated her living room like a miniature village, and she rearranged them every now and then. This one looked like it was from the early 1960s: Stella stood in a flared, cocktail-length white dress, a short veil hovering like a cloud around her head, arm in arm with a dark-haired, dapper, consummate Frenchman: Roger. I remembered her husband only from his last days, shuffling down the hallway, nearly doubled over in pain. He terrified me when I was small—the fact of his body's betrayal, not the man he was. I had never really known him, but my mother assured me he was kind, that there was nothing to be afraid of.

He'd been dead for thirty years, but Stella's young black-and-white eyes, glowing merrily with a smile, had had no idea this would happen. That this aristocratic Frenchman she'd met on an airplane to Morocco, who'd vowed to join his life with hers, would leave her alone for decades.

For the first time in thirteen years, I was alone, too. It felt like I'd had a limb amputated: too light, part of me missing. No matter that I'd hated that part of myself by the end; the part of me that craved Dmitri's approval, that yearned for his validation. No matter that our relationship had been disfigured by his countless betrayals, my perpetual disappointment. Loving him as I did, for the time that I had, still changed me.

It should have felt liberating to be able to eat cereal for dinner or pizza for breakfast. Should have felt like freedom not to be constantly texting: *what time are you getting home, did you remember to pay the gas bill, have you seen my blue sweater from that time we went out with Ilya.* It should have been a relief to be accountable to no one but myself. But instead, it felt like nothing mattered anymore. Like I was skating on top of a thin layer of soap coating the world, looking through the filmy coating at everyone else who was actually alive. I could finish the vodka without anybody yelling at me—but I was still drinking alone.

I had tried to explain this to Margaux and Lindsay at our first brunch together, but I knew they couldn't really understand: they were happily coupled, living their lives with the hectic comfort of their partners. There was room for me, too, but it wasn't like it had been before, when all three of us were frantically dating everyone in sight, disappearing briefly in ecstasy

only to reappear shortly thereafter, deflated but still whole, easily reab-
sorbed into the trio.

Lindsay seemed to recognize that the woman I'd been from twenty-
three to thirty-six had just been gouged out with a dull scalpel. And
though she had more reason than anyone to doubt me, hate me, she
seemed to understand intuitively what I needed from her, which was for
her to be exactly the same bright and giggly girl I'd known when I left.
But Margaux—there was something between us, a splintery wedge. And I
wondered how much of it had to do with my refusal to see her life the way
it was now: with a partner. I'd missed both her wedding and Lindsay's,
but Lindsay had genuinely seemed not to care, despite what Daniel had
said. Margaux had sent a typically curt reply to me when I RSVP'd "with
regrets," and I'd told myself we were fine. But now I was beginning to
suspect that there had been pain beneath her words, a deeper hurt.

How do you skip your best friend's wedding? Simple: you just don't go.
The invitation comes and you grab it eagerly. A fancy envelope! Then you
open it and you feel a warm glow—love, she's found true love. But if your
own partner has been secretly cheating on you for the past decade, if he's
been undermining you professionally for just as long, you feel something
else, too. A wrenching pain in your chest. A feeling that everyone you've
ever loved has found a place at the grown-up table and here you are, still
searching. Still grasping, still alone.

You say you'll go. Of course you'll be there. But the two-hundred-euro
ticket seems impossibly expensive, given that you had to get rid of the mat-
tress he'd been fucking other women on and buy a new one, given the
entire drawer of lingerie you had to replace because he'd seen, touched,
everything in it. And somehow the weeks slip by and then the months,
and then there's no excuse except that you missed your flight: the flight
you'd never actually booked.

It was early enough that Margaux would be at the studio, not so early
that she'd already be in rehearsal. I knew what I had to do. I'd planned to
spend the day poring over archival Romanov footage on my couch, but it
would have to wait. If I was going to get back the friendships I'd discarded,
I had to invest the time. I had to try to fit back into the fabric of Margaux's
days.

On Line 8 to the Opéra, I went over what I knew of Julie, Margaux's
wife. The photos on her Facebook page revealed a round, smiling, shiny
person. She was a baker and owned the family boulangerie; they were
known for star-shaped chocolate-chip muffins.

She's pretty great, Margaux had written. That was Margaux's version of early love's bliss.

I've never seen Margaux like this, Lindsay had emailed. *You can see the hearts in her eyes like she's a fucking cartoon character. And it's so funny when you actually meet Julie—because she's really sweet, she's great, but she's also just kind of* there, *if you know what I mean?*

And so the image had formed: she was the softness to Margaux's sharpness. The idea hurt just a little bit: even though we'd never been romantically involved, *I* had always been the soft to her sharp. Julie now filled the place in Margaux's life that I had left empty.

The September sun pounded on my face as I walked from the Opéra Métro station through the tall gilded gates. The Place de l'Opéra sits at the intersection of five of Haussmann's boulevards. It must be thirty meters across, and it's a bizarre sensation to have so much room in the center of Paris. I've always felt insignificant there, a smudge in the vast stretch of space and people around me.

Now that I was back, it was the only place in the city that reminded me of Russia. Elsewhere, compared with St. Petersburg's oversize grandeur, Paris felt like a dollhouse. St. Petersburg's wedding-cake mansions were an oil painting, Paris's *hôtels particuliers* a watercolor. St. Petersburg's skies were Technicolor, Paris's a muted pastel. Petersburgians were hard, unyielding, while Parisians were—something else.

Scanning my emails on the Métro, I hadn't seen Margaux's name on the rehearsal list for the day, but she was unlikely to have gone all the way home before her performance that evening. I walked past the artists' entrance to the place where the Opéra's stone walls curved into an unlikely nook. And yes: there, cigarette smoke rising around her, sticking to the air like paint in water, was Margaux.

"Marg," I called, and she squinted over at me. "Why haven't you been picking up your phone?"

She shrugged. "If someone needs me enough, they'll text."

I didn't say that I'd sent her three messages and instead rummaged in my purse for my own Camels, lit one. "Do you want to get a coffee or something?"

"That's your emergency?" Her laughter again, that same loose, rumbling laugh. There was something odd about it, but I wasn't entirely sure what. The way her head fell slightly to the side, maybe, as though her muscles wouldn't keep her neck straight? The unrestrained sound of it coming up, deep from her belly? "Fuck. Chill out, Delphine."

A muscle in my jaw twitched, and I made myself drop my shoulders, speak slowly. "It's just—three weeks, I've been back, and we've seen each other—what, twice?"

"I'm married now. I have a full-time job. Twice is a lot. And I see you here every single day."

"Yeah, but not—" I forced myself to take a breath, smile. *I'm married now.* Yes, I'd been right, this was the canker. "I just wanted to hang out, that's all. And actually, I wanted to talk to you about getting together with Julie. I'd love to meet her, you know—I'm dying to. Let's get a coffee and make plans! What are you up to now?"

"I'm having lunch with Julie."

I waited for her to invite me along.

"Ugh, don't do that. Don't make that face. You'll meet her eventually, you know. It's kind of inevitable. But today, right now . . . I like to keep my life separate from my work. Always have," Margaux said, tilting her head back so the smoke blew straight up into the sky.

"Well, then—maybe your Sunday brunches with Lindsay? It sounded like you guys are doing them pretty regularly? Maybe I could . . . and you could bring . . ." But I heard the tone in my voice and let the sentence fade. It was too desperate. Too sad.

"We don't do those anymore."

"Oh."

She shuffled her feet as she ashed her cigarette. "Really. I have a thing most Sunday mornings."

"A thing?"

"Stop taking everything so fucking personally, Delphine. My life's just— you know rehearsal the other day? All that blood?"

I flushed. "Uh, yeah," I said. "That shit show? Yes, I remember it."

"Well, that's what my whole life has felt like lately. It has nothing to do with you."

Before the words could sting, Lindsay's chirping voice bounced off the stone walls. "Look who I found!"

Julie. Here was Julie.

I looked her over. You'd never mistake her for a dancer: too short (yes, we can be too short—though we're rarely over 165 centimeters, we're never under 153 centimeters, either). She had a good twenty kilos on Margaux, much of it in her breasts and hips, softening the edges of her pleasant face. Chestnut hair falling in ringlets. Everything about her was curved, setting off Margaux's angles sharply. She was what I'd expected, but also something more than the image I'd created in my head. There was something hardy, almost steely, about her. I couldn't pinpoint why, but I could have seen her on any street in any city in the world and somehow been reminded of Margaux.

"Hey," Margaux said, kissing her softly on the lips. Julie pulled back, frowning as though she'd tasted something funny.

"Hi, I'm Delphine," I said, making my voice as cheery as Lindsay's had been. "You must be Julie! I can't believe we've never met," I went on. "I was just saying to Margaux that we should really all get together—"

Julie opened her mouth.

"Hon, can I talk to you for a second?" Margaux's urgent eyes turned to Julie.

"Of course—" I said, waving a hand as they walked away. "Sorry. It was great to meet you."

Lindsay wrapped an arm through mine.

"She seems nice," I said.

"Julie? Yeah, Julie's the best."

"I think I made Margaux mad just now. But I really want to get to know Julie," I said. "Speaking of, I finally met Daniel the other day, did he tell you? It made me realize how much I—I want to know these parts of your lives."

She squeezed my arm toward her body.

"You will. It's just—you remember how things are here, Delphine. POB *is* our life. Everything else is just noise. And we're just so glad to have you back that we want to keep you to ourselves as long as we can, yeah?"

I softened. It wasn't completely true for Margaux; I knew there was something wrong there, a sliver in the skin of our friendship. But it was true for Lindsay, and her words were like a warm blanket, wrapping us together.

"I've got an hour until rehearsal. Let's grab a coffee and get into some ballet gossip, just the two of us?" she said. The wind rose up, whipping her blond hair around her head, over her eyes.

The imaginary blanket slipped and fell.

The two of us meant talking about *Tsarina*. *The two of us* meant that I'd have to do the right thing and tell her that she was out. But I'd already spent too much time in stilted conversations with Lindsay, repressing the only thing I wanted to confess to her, the only thing that would ruin our friendship.

And I had until after the gala, didn't I? Nathalie had said.

"You know, I really should get some of this stuff taken care of before tomorrow," I said, my words too quick, all jumbled together.

She shrugged. "Sure. I saw I wasn't on the call list for tomorrow, though, was that—"

"Oh, Nathalie just wanted you for *Swan Lake*, that's all. We'll make do with Camille," I said, the lie burning like acid in my throat.

Lindsay made a face. "Ugh, *her.* Okay. Well, I'll see you—soon, then?"

"Yes!" I said, my accent coming out thick on the vowel. "Soon!"

I turned toward the gate, reminding myself not to look like I was running away. I fumbled with my headphones until the jilted, broken sounds of the Stravinsky from "Rubies" filled my ears. Jock's favorite of Balanchine's *Jewels* ballets, my least favorite; we'd had a playful fight about it once, a lifetime ago.

Even the thought of Jock wasn't enough to shift my focus. The guilt over Lindsay kept rushing through me in waves.

But it wasn't like I'd done anything wrong, I told myself. I'd just spared her a painful conversation—well, postponed it. Sometimes that was the best you could do.

I was the good guy here. Even if I hadn't been before—this time, I would be.

CHAPTER 8

A s Jacques stepped back, I faced the tree to rearrange my clothes. I'd wanted him to undress me—took pleasure in him doing so—and yet the indignity of having him watch me dress myself again seemed too much to bear.

Panic shot through my limbs as I smoothed my skirt down, pulled my top up. Did he think I didn't like him enough? Or anymore? Would he think I was a prude? I didn't want him to argue with me, try to convince me to sleep with him—but shouldn't he have cared more?

I licked my swollen, drying lips and tried to collect my thoughts. There were times when you had to take the lead. Times when *nobody* knew what to say. Maybe I could just say what I was thinking. Actually explain myself. Be an adult about it.

"Hey, Jacques?" I said.

There was no answer. He was already walking away.

I waited until he was inside before returning to the dorm myself, cheeks warm despite the coolness of the evening. I made it back to the girls' hall without running into anybody and found Margaux and Lindsay in Lindsay's room, crouched over her computer. She'd broken off the affair with Phillippe a few days earlier (*He never wants to take me out, he just wants to go back to his place and fuck*) and had been emailing one of POB's newest soloists, an Argentinian import who had guest-taught our Character class a few weeks ago. Normally, Lindsay never fantasized about anybody beneath principal, but Pablo's appearance had drawn a fair amount of press attention: even then, POB was an overwhelmingly white company. All the big ballet companies were.

As ever, Margaux was at her shoulder, reading through everything and stopping her when she got too explicit.

I threw myself onto Lindsay's bed.

"What *happened?*" Lindsay said breathlessly.

I couldn't even answer at first. The dynamic was too strange; I was never the one with the drama. Always, it was Lindsay concocting plans to drop her latest admirer (*I can just ignore his calls, right? He'll get the hint*), Margaux moaning over the lack of any other gay girls at the school (*It doesn't even matter what they* look *like at this point, I fucking swear to God*). And always, me in the role of adviser, one step removed from any real pain.

I tried not to break down into tears as I told them what had happened. I didn't know if tears were even warranted. Maybe he was just being a good guy and trying to give me space. On the other hand, maybe I really had killed every spark of desire he'd ever had for me. I wanted to believe he was just being respectful—but I worried I was just fooling myself.

The words came spilling out of me, faster and faster.

Neither one of them ever lied, though Lindsay had been known to evade the truth. I watched their faces, looking for answers. Margaux had a better read on the boys in our class than Lindsay or I did, because she was never distracted by desire for them. She met my gaze calmly, and the hope budding in my heart burst to life. This wasn't a big deal.

But then I saw Lindsay, biting down on her bottom lip, looking at the floor. She was the one who actually went out with boys.

"Linds?" I said, my voice rough.

She looked over at Margaux, as though asking for help. Margaux tilted her head. *Your turn.*

"I don't know," Lindsay said, and tears filled my eyes. How was it possible to feel so many things at once? Uncertain and excited, hopeful and despairing, ashamed and relieved? She wrapped an arm around me and let me lean against her. "I really don't. If it were anyone else—but Jacques's complicated."

"Do you think he still likes me?" My voice was small; I'd never have asked anyone else.

"Honestly?" Margaux said. "Who knows? He'd be an idiot not to, but then again . . ."

"He *is* an idiot," Lindsay finished. "But you'll have tons of other opportunities. The sun doesn't rise and set with Jacques, you know."

The tears were running down my face now.

"Okay, maybe it feels like it does right now," she amended quickly. "He's not the right person for your first time, though. It's a good thing you didn't sleep with him. In the woods? What was he even thinking?"

"It was just in the moment," I muttered. "I don't think he planned it that way."

"Hmm," Margaux said.

Lindsay bounced up, crossing her legs. "You should be glad! Be proud of yourself. You didn't want to sleep with him, so you didn't."

"But the thing is . . ."

"What is the thing?" Margaux asked, her accent thick.

"I kind of wish that I had. I mean, I have the Pill—" They knew the story already, had rolled with laughter as I'd pantomimed the story of my mother giving it to me. "Maybe I should just start taking it so that next time I'm ready. Just get it over with, you know? If there is a next time."

Lindsay was weighing the pros and cons. I could see the thoughts moving like clockwork behind her eyes.

"No," she said finally. "No. That's the totally wrong attitude to take. Jacques's hot and all, but he's so full of himself. Your first time should be with somebody older. Somebody classy."

Margaux shook her head. "Too hard to arrange. I agree, *not Jacques*, but I think—if what you really want to do is just get it over with . . . what about Victor or someone you actually know?" She held up her hands as I stared at her, wide-eyed. "Or not Victor! But then I think you have to be honest with yourself about whether you really do *just want to get it over with* or if you're just trying to . . ." She trailed off. Get Jacques back. I knew what she meant. We'd been finishing each other's thoughts for almost a decade.

Lindsay made a face. "Who wants to sleep with a seventeen-year-old boy? It should be somebody foreign. Not American. A Brit, maybe. And he should be obsessed with her. And he'll have to be cool and aloof or she'll never go for him—"

"Hey," I cut in mildly. Maybe Jacques seemed cool and aloof to everyone else, yes. But he was different with me. He'd be telling a story about something innocuous and suddenly, these vulnerable details would slip in: how embarrassed he'd been about something, how hopeful he was. The big, scary emotions nobody ever seemed to talk about without shame, he was willing to share with me.

It wasn't his coldness I liked. It was everything else.

Margaux put her hand down on my knee. "The point is, Jacques—he doesn't deserve you."

I rolled my eyes. "That's just something to say."

"Anyway, I do think you should start taking the Pill," Lindsay said. "Then next time, you'll have the choice. You'll be prepared when he gets back from New York."

The world opened up again. There was a possible future with Jacques. All I had to do was wait long enough and I'd see him again, get a read on him, figure out where I'd gone wrong, and correct it.

"What did he do, even, when you said no?" Margaux asked.

"He put his shirt back on. He said something like, *Okay*, I think."

"I'm surprised he listened," Margaux said.

"Really?" I said. "Why?"

She shrugged. "Because he doesn't seem like the type who would stop," she said.

— *September 2018* —

I bolted down the Place de l'Opéra toward the carousel, feeling smaller than ever.

The carousel is a gorgeous art nouveau thing, probably installed around the time the Palais Garnier was built. When I was little, Stella used to take me there when we were waiting for my mother to get out of rehearsal. I loved to see the curtains pulled back around the poles; it had delighted me, how much the carousel felt like a stage.

I cut through the Tuileries. They, at least, never changed. Still the same symmetrical patches of grass, the same view of the Musée d'Orsay's clock tower, the same unexpectedly intimate niches hidden behind ancient, crumbling stone walls and convenient trees.

In front of the carousel, I sat on an empty bench. The day stretched out before me, just like the days had back when we were first in the company. I could have gone up to the flea market or drunk wine along the riverbank or gone to La Perla to try on fancy lingerie. But I'd be doing it alone. My freedom tasted sour. Margaux was with Julie, and Lindsay was unknowingly on the verge of losing—well. *Everything she ever wanted.*

So here I was, again.

If I couldn't use *Tsarina* to make things right with Lindsay, perhaps I could with Margaux. I could give her something special. Not great—even from our early rehearsals, I could tell that part of her, the part that had promised greatness when we were younger, was absent. Split from her body like a shadow. But something meaty. Queen Victoria, maybe.

The more I thought about it, the more Queen Victoria was right for her. Perfect casting: the imperious ruler, regal and cold, hiding every vulnerability behind a carefully constructed façade. And it would work well with the story line, too. The queen was Alix's grandmother but also a close, precious confidante. Maybe her closest friend. And when Alix moved to Russia, to be with her beloved Nicky but also to play her part in the expanding Victorian empire, she'd been surgically removed from the life she'd known, grafted into a strange, brutal new world. She came to Russia as Nicky's bride, but she didn't speak Russian, and she had almost no friends at court, the only stage upon which her life could possibly take place. The people hated her, seeing her as cursed; her marriage had coincided with the death of the previous tsar. So, she'd renounced everything she'd grown up with—only to witness the ascension of her ineffectual husband to a position of great power. A man who was better suited to a life as a country squire than to ruling one-sixth of the world, a man who diligently applied everything he'd been taught about nineteenth-century leadership and yet would still fuck up his country beyond repair as it straddled two centuries. He was all Alix had, this person who meant more to her than anyone and for whom she'd literally given up the entire world.

All she had was her husband—and her letters to her grandmother.

It would be hard to illustrate, but I could do it. Margaux, as Queen Victoria, could dance in Act I, then sit on her throne throughout Acts II and III, upstage behind a semitransparent screen, like a memory. And Lindsay—no, Camille, I corrected myself—Camille could have a lovely solo, dancing for her, trying to reach her, always and irrevocably separated by the screen between them.

I was reaching for my notebook to jot the idea down when I saw a shadow fall over me.

I looked up. A tall, well-built man had appeared at my side. Almond eyes, chiseled lips. The hair swooping, ever so slightly too long, over his forehead.

This man knew he was far too attractive.

"Hey, Dolphin," he said, bending down to kiss my cheeks.

Jock.

With every email he'd sent over the past decade, I'd imagined what it would be like: to come back to the Opéra in triumph, to be waiting at the window outside a studio as he spun about the room. His hair flopping onto his forehead, the delicate muscles of his body propelling him around. He'd come out of a turn sequence and spare a passing glance, breathless, at the dark figure at the glass—his eyes would widen, and he'd come running out, eager and puppyish as ever; and there I would be. Princess Grace, cool and perfect and benevolent.

His jaw was as finely cut as ever. So was his body. The last time I'd seen him, he'd still been halfway between childhood and adulthood, like we all were. There'd been some softness to him. But in the time since, which he'd spent weight training and lifting dancers who, okay, didn't weigh that much but who were almost certainly at least forty-five kilos, that softness had gone. He was rough-hewn now, like the Normandy cliffs, shape carved away by wind and water.

Before I knew it, I was standing, throwing myself into his arms. My body has always had a mind of its own. He picked me up, spun me around, just like the movies. And that boyish enthusiasm washed through me like water. *This* was what I'd missed with Dmitri.

"It's you!" I said. So much for a cool entrance. So much for Princess Grace.

He smiled. "It is. It is me." He gestured to the bench beside me. "May I?"

"Of course," I said, but he was already sitting. He crossed his legs with a lazy grace. "I thought you weren't returning until next week?"

He shrugged. "You know how it is. I have to sneak in my vacation days whenever I can find them. But then I heard you were back—"

"How did you know I was here?" I asked. "Not in Paris—*here*, here." I waved at the carousel.

The left side of his mouth lifted up.

"I come here every day for lunch," he said, pulling out an éclair from the tote bag he so casually wore over his shoulder. I must have looked at the éclair longingly, because he held it to my mouth. Embarrassed, I bit off the end.

"How long have you been back?" he asked.

I'd taken too big a bite and had to remind myself to chew, swallow, before replying.

"Three weeks."

"Over the jet lag?"

I tilted my head as I pulled out my cigarettes, grabbed another. "It's only a one-hour time difference."

He shook his head, impatient with his own stupidity. "And only a three-hour flight," he added.

Had he visited St. Petersburg and not told me? "When were you in Russia?"

"Oh. Ah—" Was he blushing? He reached for my packet of Camel Blues and slid one out. He sat there for a minute with the unlit cigarette sticking out of his mouth until I reached into my pocket, lit my own, then tossed him the lighter. I wanted to hand it to him, to let my fingers linger on his palm, but I felt tremulous, even though my hands were steady.

"I thought I might go this summer. But it didn't work out."

Because I'd come back. I could hear the words as clearly as if he'd said them. It was what I'd been waiting all summer to hear. Waiting—if I was really honest with myself—for the past thirteen years to hear.

"I can't believe you're back," I said instead. "We're already making progress in rehearsals—I know everyone's going to be so excited you're here."

His eyebrows jumped, mouth widening into a smile that matched my own. "I'm in your piece?"

The excitement of telling him—of showing him that I was more than a *sujet*, that I was a choreographer now—flooded through me; at the same time, my stomach lurched.

"Oh—I thought that Nathalie would have told you—"

He shook his head.

"We've all been wondering for weeks what you're going to do. So, what is it?"

"*Tsarina*," I said. "About the last days of the Russian royal family."

The dimple again. "And you want me."

I wished he'd chosen different words.

"Um. Yes. For Rasputin. I do."

Then he was hugging me, his body pressed directly against mine, and I was seventeen again, I was swooning, and I hated myself but there it was.

"Thank you. That means a lot."

That was all?

Of course, it wasn't a big deal for him. He'd been a principal since 2008, a star since 2015. Choreographers fell over themselves to make ballets for him. This was his life.

"Jock, tell me something," I said slowly. "Why did you really leave New York and come back to Paris? I know you said you wanted to expand your repertoire. And I mean, obviously I'm glad you did, but—" I cut myself off. "You seemed so in love with Balanchine's work. I guess I was just surprised."

It's about the music, he'd told me before he left for New York. *With Balanchine, you become it. Here—it's different for you girls. You get to be flowers and animals and dolls and all kinds of things. But as long as I stay in Paris, I'm only the fairy-tale prince. Nothing else.*

He thought for a long moment. "Part of it was that I was named a principal so young, you know?"

I made a sound of false pity. He laughed.

"No, I know how that sounds. But, it's like, there was nowhere to go after that. I was twenty-six and I'd done everything I could ever do. But if I came back to Paris—well, there was always *étoile* to shoot for."

As he had when we were younger, Jock was saying the silent things, the things other dancers feel but never utter out loud.

"It was more than that, too. I'm not sure I have the words for it. It was like—all that music, no characters? I loved it at first, you're right. After a while, though? I started to feel . . . formless. There was no model, nothing to use as a guide. At a certain point, it was like I was losing myself every night. Just—drowning."

I swallowed.

"And then, one Christmas, they put me in *The Nutcracker*—and it was like coming home. Like remembering who I was for the first time since I was a kid."

"The Nutcracker Prince?"

He nodded, a look of mock seriousness on his face. "As you know, I've *always* been a Nutcracker Prince at heart." His face relaxed into a smile. "Anyway. That was when I knew I had to come back. To find myself. To rediscover the joy of dancing."

This was the thing about Jock that Lindsay and Margaux never really got. Yes, he was too handsome for his own good. Yes, he had an insouciance that could too easily cross over into arrogance. But he also had this vulnerability, this openness, that was so hard to find in fellow dancers. After all: we were nothing if not performers.

We sat there together, watching the carousel move around and around until the afternoon shadows began to slant sideways, talking about the people we knew: what they'd been like in the past, what they were doing now.

"Don't you have rehearsal?" I finally said. It was the seventeen-year-old me speaking, worried about his loose relationship with time and his inability to show up anywhere he was expected. And yet he made up for it, always, with these unexpected appearances and the sun-like attention that made you happy to simply bask. No matter how much it made you sweat.

"Yeah. I'll head out soon. But Dolphin? Really? I can't believe you're back," he said. "It's been so long, and then you're just . . . here. It doesn't feel like enough, you know? You deserve parties. At least one party."

"But I've already seen everybody I want to see."

I had to look away from the brightness of his smile.

CHAPTER 9

Margaux's seventeenth birthday fell on a Wednesday. That weekend, my mother went to Nice. My latest theory was that her hometown held a teenage romance that she kept reverting to—given that her parents were long dead, why else would she return so often, never taking me? Her frequent absences suited me and Lindsay and Margaux perfectly, though, and preparations for Margaux's birthday party were well under way. My own secret preparations were, too. I was usually a little lazy about remembering to take the Pill, but I'd been taking it religiously for the past week. Jacques was coming back from New York, and this was my shot.

Margaux, Lindsay, and I went to get the wine together after class. But we didn't think it through, buying twenty bottles out in Nanterre near the school and then lugging them on the Métro over to Saint-Paul.

"Let's get started," Margaux said, flipping the cork out of a bottle of champagne, dribbling it all over the rug before I ran up with three plastic cups.

"Small for me," I said. "It's only five."

She rolled her eyes and poured full glasses. "We deserve a celebration."

By the time the others arrived, my eyeliner was smeared under my eyes from laughing so hard and a faint tangy scent seemed to be following me throughout the apartment. The boys came first in a great booming group; they didn't know enough not to show up first to a party. Margaux followed my gaze with slight disdain.

There. There he was. He seemed more muscular, though obviously he couldn't have put on that much muscle in six weeks. He seemed taller, though surely he couldn't have grown that much in such a short period. He seemed sophisticated and laid-back at the same time, a vague Americanness attached to him that extended far beyond his Abercrombie shirt and soft, dark jeans.

I was not going to approach him. Lindsay had said I should, that he'd be too embarrassed to talk to me. That he'd think *I* assumed he had only one thing on his mind. But there was such a thing as dignity, after all.

The girls came next, in pairs and trios. There was Aurélie, who'd never made it back to the top of the class after an injury the year before. Mathilde, who'd started filling out her leotards more fully; whom all the boys wanted to partner with; who would not be asked back at the end of the year. And Talitha, with her Jacques obsession and her naturally red hair—just like Nathalie Dorival, our favorite company star.

I went into the kitchen—and that's when I saw them. Leaning against the doorway, drink in his hand, his head thrown back laughing. Jacques was talking to Talitha, their faces an inch apart. For the first time, it occurred to me that I was not that different from her and that maybe he'd kissed her, too. Maybe she wasn't as crazy as we'd thought. Maybe there was a legitimate reason for how she acted.

Would it look too desperate to cut in on their conversation? It would look too desperate.

I had to get him alone, to talk to him, to explain that I was ready now. But how could I do that when he was so artfully avoiding me?

People—filler people, I thought, meaning *not Jacques*—kept coming up and talking to me. I was roped into discussion after discussion about Marie-Cécile, about Nathalie's dreamy new husband, Louis, a soloist with smoldering eyes, about the rehearsals for *La Fille mal gardée* we'd sat in on the week before.

When I looked back up, Jacques had disappeared.

I grabbed Lindsay's arm.

"Where's Jacques?"

Her eyes widened.

"I don't know," she said. "Maybe he left?"

But there were circles of pink on her cheeks.

"Marg," I called across the room. She was still a few meters away, moving *so slowly*, when I asked her the same question. As she hesitated, opened her mouth and closed it, I could see she didn't want to tell me the truth either.

I followed her gaze to the hall leading to my bedroom.

And all thoughts of playing it cool, maintaining my power, pretending I didn't care, flew out of my head. I had to talk to him and he was there, in my room, cornered, ready for me. He'd have to listen to what I said. I was at my door in no time at all.

"Delphine, stop—" Lindsay and Margaux were at my heels.

But they were too late. I was already staring at Jacques and Talitha, tangled up in my sheets.

Lindsay steered me to my mother's room before I could even start crying. By the time I was sitting on the floral comforter, looking up at the black-and-white photographs of Maman onstage, I was sobbing so hard that I had to clutch my stomach to stop it.

What an asshole. Such an idiot. You didn't want him anyway—I wasn't sure exactly what Lindsay was saying; it was like English was a radio channel and I was tuned in to the wrong station. All I knew was that her arm was around one side of me, Margaux's on the other, and one of them had brought the box of tissues from the bedside table and was holding one to my face.

"He—*Talitha*—"

"Shh," they said.

They conferred behind my back as I wiped my cheeks.

"We need to get you out of here," Lindsay said a minute later.

Simple, declarative sentences were the only thing I could manage. "I can't leave. It's Margaux's party. And it's my house. Besides, we never said we were excl—exclu—" I was off again.

"Fuck that guy. And fuck the party," Margaux told me. "We're the party. Besides, what's the worst they could do?"

Once they'd repaired my makeup using the hundreds of products they found on my mother's dressing table, we went down the servants' staircase. I was still sniffling, but something about the night air blowing through us kept me from full-blown crying. Lindsay balanced a plate with the remains of the birthday cake on her palms, while Margaux carried four bottles of prosecco. I held the tissue box.

In the Place des Vosges, Lindsay went up over the fence guarding the garden square first, Margaux staying behind to boost me up; then we pulled her over from the other side. I'd never had the place all to myself before. Though it was summer, the night air was chilly, and we huddled together on a bench for warmth.

And then, for hours, we were just there. Together. We sat in front of the playground equipment, staring at the monumental statue of some famous man, Henry IV—or was it Louis XIII?—smoking, drinking prosecco, talking about everything and nothing, but certainly not Jacques, until the sun came up and we could finally go home.

— *September 2018* —

That Friday, I came into Stella's kitchen for my morning coffee to find a pair of impeccably polished beige Ferragamos propped up on my usual chair.

"Stel, these are gorgeous!" I cried, rushing over and holding them up to the light. "But they look brand-new—are you sure you're done with them?" We both wore thirty-sevens, and I'd had a habit of borrowing some of her more beautiful pairs when I was a teenager—pairs that inevitably made their way to my closet permanently at the end of every season.

"Oh, no, you don't," she said, holding up a finger. "Those are classics, dear. A wardrobe staple. I want them back in mint condition, if you please."

I turned them over. The soles were flawless; never been worn. How was she supposed to wear them and use a cane at the same time?

"Back . . . from what?"

She raised her eyebrows like she had when I was a child and being deliberately obstinate. "The gala?"

"Oh, fuck. The gala."

The gala is an annual gathering for high society to watch Paris Opera Ballet dancers parade around onstage for them. The royalty, the movie stars, the politicians, would all arrive to ring in the new season officially.

Tonight.

Stella's face was wide open in bafflement. "Delphine, how did you—you have to start taking responsibility for your life, darling! Did you really forget?"

"Shit," I muttered. "It's okay—I have my dress. But I forgot the hair appointment—and I wanted to get a manicure—"

It wasn't exactly that I'd forgotten—the galas had been a staple of my life for years—but I had always been in them. I'd never actually *attended* one, and the requisite preparations were a foreign land. I was relieved that I wasn't onstage anymore, but I was dreading the obligation to network, having to prove myself in my new role. And more than that: after the gala, I'd have to tell Lindsay she was out of the ballet. It was our last night together with me as the creator and her as the star. After this, I would always and forever be the bitch who'd cut her.

How was I going to survive this evening?

"Hmm," she said, drumming light fingers on the blue-and-white table. "Are you working this morning?"

"This afternoon. Twelve to three."

She clapped her hands together. "All right, then. I'll call Sandrine over to do some semipermanent polish this morning. No, I'm a good customer, she'll come," she said, waving at me as I began to protest. "You. Take a bath. I'll see if Roland can come by around four for the hair. He loves seeing his work in the glossies, I'm sure he'll drop everything. And darling, I *know* you can do your own makeup after all this time."

"Yes—" I said, thinking it through. "As long as I'm out of here by six thirty—"

"What are you waiting for? Go wash! I have calls to make!"

I ran back into my apartment, heels in hand. Find the iron, get the dress pressed, I should never have left it in the bag that long. Run a bath, search for a clutch. The shoes—yes, the shoes were right. I had the lipstick, the foundation—

As I looked in the mirror and detected the dread in my eyes, I told myself: *You've hidden things from Lindsay before. You know what to do.* It was just another performance, after all.

But—never like this before. I had never been the one with all the power. And I was still learning how to wield it.

Do you miss it? Dancers ask me that all the time. A knowing smile and a shake of my head are usually enough to put them off. What they're really asking is, *Why did you fail? Did it break your heart? What's it like on the other side?*

What I don't say is: *I can't help missing it.* It's the same way I miss my childhood. And for me, for any dancer really, they're one and the same. The sense that you have something special, that you *are* something special. That cockiness of the very young or the very talented? It's like armor. Nothing can touch you when you have it.

It's not the same when you choreograph. Nobody knows what you look like, nobody knows your name, nobody cares if (when) your body goes to hell. You're in the audience or, more likely, in the wings. I'd wanted that invisibility, once—by the time I left Paris, I craved it, the way you crave a glass of sweet fruit juice when you're thirsty. My mouth watered with wanting it. But that was before I understood what invisibility meant. Before I knew that once you choose it, it chooses you, too, and you can't ever go back.

Sometimes I think it would have been better a hundred years ago. True, I couldn't have been a choreographer (*A woman? You must be joking*). But I also wouldn't have had to see the people I danced with all over YouTube, prancing across Instagram, pointing and flexing around Facebook, either. I wouldn't have been able to watch them catch the air, glide across the ground, whirl into oblivion. I wouldn't be forced to remember what my body felt like when it was perfect and light, when it did whatever I wanted, when I hadn't yet made any mistakes.

I still have dreams where I'm dancing, where we're still together, the ballet and I, and I wake up in sweaty sheets, going cold and clammy as reality descends in the morning light.

Yes. I miss it.

But it's not the kind of thing you can say.

CHAPTER 10

— November 1999 —

That fall, the three of us had to get serious. We had only a year left at the academy. While I'd always stuck behind after class to keep practicing, Lindsay and Margaux started to join me. But there was only so much time before dinner.

And so, late at night, when the school was dark and we could see only by the watered-down security lamps dotting the halls like spotlights, Lindsay would rap on my door. In order not to wake anybody else, she'd use her fingertips, and it ended up sounding creepy, like a frantic animal was clawing at the wood. Together, we'd go to Margaux's room, and then the three of us would descend the stairs, soft shoed and silent, into the space age atrium, so different from the belle epoque grandeur of the Palais Garnier. Hearts pounding at our own gall, we'd turn down the hall to our favorite studio.

It wasn't our favorite because it was pretty; none of the rooms in the school were pretty, really. They were cold, stark, intended only to be a neutral backdrop for our bodies. It was our favorite because we'd discovered by trial and error that the lights couldn't be seen from outside. This was important, as our first after-hours practice session had ended with Lindsay running smack into a security guard and subsequently getting all her off-campus privileges revoked by Marie-Cécile. It wouldn't have mattered if it was just about missing out on the indifferent cafés we visited, but it also meant she wasn't allowed to go see any performances for the rest of the semester, which had been devastating.

There was something about that studio that appealed to me beyond

the practicalities, though. The school is like a UFO, this strange, newish
white building in a strange, newish area of one of the city's old suburbs.
The silence around us at night could be unsettling, never letting us forget
that we were both in Paris and outside of it at the same time. Being co-
cooned together in that room, where we could focus only on our bodies,
on the music, felt comforting. Cozy.

Lindsay didn't tell on Margaux and me when she got caught. She didn't
even complain about having been unfairly targeted when we'd had the
good luck to get away. But once it occurred to Margaux that the lack of
windows in our studio would work to our advantage, Lindsay got her revenge in the fiendish combinations she made us do.

"Try this," one of us would say, launching into the hardest combination we could think of. Margaux's were always full of enormous leaps
and brutal turns, matching the Pixies and Smashing Pumpkins songs she
chose, playing them at minimum volume, just loud enough for us to hear.
I liked to put on more lyrical music—Fiona Apple, Sarah McLachlan—
and demand crazy stretches, the kind that suited my double-jointedness
perfectly and required a total release of control.

But Lindsay—Lindsay's combinations to Radiohead and Velvet Under-
ground were nearly impossible, with their stops and starts, their subtle
reversals, the momentum that would push you in one direction just as you
had to put all your weight in another.

I loved to watch Lindsay. Margaux was good, very good, but she was
good in the same way I was. We'd had the same training from so early. But
Lindsay, who'd spent her first twelve years in Washington, D.C.—Lindsay
had a ferocity to her dancing that neither of us did. Her placement wasn't
always totally right, and yet you didn't care as she whipped around, leapt
high. She was constantly being corrected—at POB, what they valued
most was the type of precision Margaux and I had ingrained in us, which
meant we took the top places in the class rankings, with Lindsay following
a close third.

But they were blind. Lindsay was the best of us all.

I loved to watch her, and I hated it, too. A lot of people think that
being double-jointed would be a good thing for ballet—and it is, in the
early years. As you get older, though, and particularly at POB, that loose
flexibility becomes less valuable. You need strength, control, and it's
harder to build that up when you haven't had to push yourself into the
splits, when you can pull your leg up by your ear without any apparent
effort. Margaux had that control. But it was more impressive in Lindsay,

who was like a barely contained wildfire. She had these instincts to kick higher, spin more, jump faster, and every single motion was reined in like she was fighting against her own body, like she was pushing against what she could do.

When she was dancing, you couldn't take your eyes off of her.

I never told her how I felt. Envy is an ugly, dark emotion, and the three of us prided ourselves on being collaborative. Those early competitions were part of what made us better than everyone else, maybe even what got us into the company.

Ballet is full of jealousy, but when you're expressing your admiration for another dancer, you say only the small things. You can say, *I wish I could turn like you.* You can say, *I wish I had arms like yours.* You can say, *I wish I could hold my leg like that.*

I loved to watch Lindsay. I longed to dance like her. I wanted to be her.

But that was one thing I would never, ever, say.

— *September 2018* —

As I walked into the Palais Garnier, its candelabras alight around the enormous branching staircase, photographers' flashbulbs began to go off and it occurred to me that I should have brought a date. People were standing in groups, and the groups were made of couples. But whom would I have brought? Stella? Everyone else I knew was a dancer.

One goal, I thought grimly. *Only one. Just don't humiliate yourself.*

I grabbed a flute of champagne from a waiter. I was all right. I could blend in. I might have been ten kilos heavier than the average dancer, but that still left me on the thin side for the average philanthropist. I'd blown the entirety of my very first POB paycheck on a strapless white silk gown from Carven, which—complemented by my mother's diamonds and the crown of black braids encircling my head—at least allowed me to look the part. And at the ballet, that was always what truly mattered.

A hand grabbed my bare arm. Relief rushed through me. "Hello, Daniel," I said, kissing his cheeks.

"Delphine!" he said. He looked dapper in a dark suit. "I've been calling after you since you came in. Didn't you hear me?"

"I can barely hear you now," I said.

We stood there blinking at each other, our conversational topics already exhausted.

"It's nice of you to come support Lindsay," I said.

He smiled. "I come every year," he said. He looked proud. It was the expression I'd felt on my own face at each of Dmitri's premieres. It made me ache—when had anyone ever looked that way because of me?

"Where are you sitting?" I asked.

"Fourth side loge," he said. "Real nosebleed seat. You?"

"Orchestra. You know, because of the publicity."

"Clever of them."

I smiled.

"This must be exciting for you," he said. "Have you ever seen one of these galas before?"

"Oh—no. But I was in them for fourteen years in a row."

The lights blinked their warning. "I'd better start climbing," Daniel said, nodding toward the staircase. I smiled and watched him go, his well-tailored suit just skimming his shoulders.

I felt a dull pang watching him walk away. He was the perfect audience member for Lindsay; the perfect worshipper. I had the very American impulse to say that I appreciated him. *I really like you for her,* I wanted to call after him. *There's something about you that's very calming.*

Instead, I headed to the orchestra and settled into my red velvet seat. *Brace yourself,* I thought. *Here comes the tidal wave of memories.*

Still, the sight of the stage as the curtains opened hit me like a clout to the heart.

Every year, it's the same. It always begins with one little girl, chosen from the youngest class, presented beautifully onstage: opening her arms as she stands, silently welcoming you to the Paris Opera Ballet.

I'd been the wake-up girl my first year. I thought it had meant something, like a promise.

It starts with her and ends with the male stars. In the middle are lines of dancers, walking beautifully downstage, then peeling off into the wings. All the women wear white tutus. All the men are in white tights and shirts. Eventually, the stars come in. It's lines and lines of white until it hurts your eyes.

I began to tear up.

They just walk, but it's so charming, you want to die.

Lindsay and Margaux came in on the same line. They looked just like the others, and I didn't even realize it was them until they were close enough to see their faces. Margaux's expression listless, almost bored. Lindsay transcendent, knowing—well, *believing*—that this was her last year as a *sujet*, that soon she'd be lining up among the principals—then curtsying to the audience alone, as a star.

I remembered that kind of hope all too well. Once, I was one of them. Once, I was part of this. The music seemed to echo it. *Once. Once. Once upon a time.*

I was full-blown crying ten minutes into the procession, even though, really, it was as hypnotic and dull to watch as it was to participate in. I waited until the applause, then wiped my face frantically. I hadn't brought any tissues with me. I hadn't brought a mirror, either. Somehow, I made it through the rest without mascara running directly onto my white dress.

When it finished, I waited until the theater emptied so I could use my phone to look at my makeup. I reapplied my eyeliner and took a deep breath. I felt like I'd spent all day at the beach, that empty, hot, and calm feeling you get only after hours in the sun or a good cry.

And that hadn't even been the hard part.

Fifteen minutes of mingling, I promised myself. *Fifteen more minutes, and then you can leave.*

In the great hall of the Opéra, the crowd gathered for cocktails. It felt like Versailles—but it was mine, the palace I'd grown up in. Twenty-meter ceilings, chandeliers with so many lights they were gathered like bouquets of flowers, every surface and column covered in bronze so that the room was lit with a fierce gold glow. A mural of gods and monsters hung over us, watching us all.

And everywhere, beautiful people in beautiful gowns. At the end of the room, an enormous mirror reflected them back at themselves.

My body began to clench tight like a fist as I saw that many dancers were already there; I'd sat for so long in the theater that they'd already changed out of their costumes and come to grace the audience with their presence. *You have every right to be here,* I reminded myself. *You belong to this place, and it belongs to you. It's in your blood.*

Suddenly, Jock appeared next to me. His hair was damp from the shower he'd taken after his performance, and there were still traces of eyeliner around his eyes. Looking out over the room, he pressed his lips together.

"Miss it?" he said.

"I like what I'm doing now," I said.

Jock's dimple revealed itself.

"I heard about Lindsay freaking out in rehearsal," he said. "I'm sorry that she didn't work out."

I snorted. "Are you?"

When he looked down his eyes were strangely intense.

"I am," he said. "But you *are* taking her out of it, aren't you?"

Yes, but I don't want to. Yes, but not tonight. Yes, but let me hang on to this perfect, golden moment—just a second longer.

"You better not say a word to her. I haven't had the chance to tell her yet."

"You'll have to soon, though, no?"

"Why are you so worried?" Had Nathalie been in his ear?

"I don't know why you're not. It's your name. Your reputation . . ." But his voice trailed off as a bright figure elbowed her way through the crowd toward us.

Lindsay. In a gold gown that clung to her like liquid, picking up the million lights around us, her hair loose and wild around her shoulders. Margaux in dark gray at her side. And behind them, like a shadow, Daniel.

"You guys!" I bent toward them, kissing their cheeks, hands on their slim shoulders. "You were wonderful."

Lindsay smiled broadly as Daniel wrapped an arm around her, but Margaux just rolled her eyes.

"Delphine," she said, "you know better than anyone that this is nothing more than a dog show."

"A dog show?" Jock said it in French, eyebrows drawn together.

"Yes, *Jacques*, a dog show. You know, trotting us out, congratulating us for being such good little specimens," she shot back in her native tongue.

Annoyance flitted across Lindsay's face; even after decades of being educated in French, she still hated it when we fell into it. I don't know what it was, exactly: The idioms? Our accents? She spoke French, good French at that, but I couldn't remember the last time I'd heard her use it to order more than a coffee.

Daniel set a calming hand on her shoulder as he murmured in her ear. I was struck anew by his warm openness, his steady certainty. You couldn't fake that kind of unwavering admiration. In addition to being the perfect spectator, Daniel appeared to be the perfect director, gently guiding her so skillfully that she thought she was doing it all alone.

No dancer would ever have done as much for her.

"Where's Julie?" I asked Margaux, back to English again.

Margaux's mouth twitched. "I made her stop coming years ago. Well, *let* her, really."

"It's interesting, isn't it," Daniel said. "The ballet spouses. Some of us can't stand this place and others can't get enough."

Coyly—I knew I was being coy, even as I did it—I turned a questioning face to Jock, and everyone, Jock included, burst into laughter.

"He only dates dancers," Lindsay said. "Well. He only dates them *now*," she added under her breath. She knew what I knew: that his time in New York had been seasoned with dates with socialites and minor celebrities.

"And never long enough to have these kinds of problems," Margaux said, downing the rest of her champagne.

Jock smirked, and my insides felt like they were collapsing in on themselves. He shrugged good-naturedly. That was the thing about Jock. He had such a good nature.

"So how's the ballet coming?" Daniel asked.

I thought back to rehearsal earlier that week, Jock leaping around the studio. The way he embodied Rasputin's talent, his arrogance, his creepiness. The sly movement of his hips—

"It's going really well!" I said. "I mean"—looking over at Jock—"I think it is?"

He grinned, nodded. "Yeah. It really is."

"At the beginning, you know, I was so fixated on making it the story of the Tsarina. But the more we've been in the studio, the more this fascination she has with Rasputin has really captured me. He's this mystical healer, and he's the only one who seems to be able to stop her son's bleeding—he's got hemophilia—" Daniel's face was a careful blank as he watched me babble, but I could feel Jock's gaze was fixed on me and I couldn't have stopped talking if I'd tried. "So now I'm structuring it more around Rasputin. It's like an ancient Greek tragedy, you know? There's always a curse—and the one thing you want is always the thing that actually leads to your downfall—"

And that was when I registered Lindsay's expression, and I finally shut up. She still thought I was talking about *her* ballet. And here I was, running on and on about minimizing her role, maximizing Jock's.

I let the others take over, Daniel making some meaningless conversation about the food they were serving—was that lobster in the appetizers they were passing around? How could we get a tray of them over here?

And then: across from me, Lindsay caught my eye and winked. She didn't know the true meaning behind my soliloquy, but for now, we were okay, and the knowledge of that rushed through me like the champagne through my blood.

I grabbed her hand.

"I have an idea," I said nodding toward the door. "Bring your glasses."

I swiped a bottle of champagne from behind the bar, then pulled our group of five along in a grown-up game of follow the leader. Dwarfed as we were in the opulent surroundings, it did feel like we were kids again, evading the adults, slipping away.

"Delphine!" Lindsay shrieked as we cut into the back hallways. "Where are we—"

But Margaux's "Shush!" came so sharply and quickly that she just dissolved into giggles, Jock's lower, quieter laughter blending in.

The Mariinsky is ornate, but it has nothing on the Palais Garnier. Behind the stage, there's a golden rehearsal room that we use for warm-ups before performances, once we're in costume. Portraits of dancers from the 1700s and 1800s line the walls, flanked by golden cherubs and butterflies. Elaborate columns stretch up toward an arched ceiling covered in a blue-and-green fresco, where a balcony allows spectators to observe. A century ago, that balcony was reserved for the aristocrats who made mistresses out of the same ballerinas now fixed, as though in amber, on the walls. It had always been one of my favorite places.

Once inside, I lowered myself to the floor, dress spreading around me in pools of white silk. Margaux nodded approvingly, grabbing the champagne from me, ripping off the foil, and sliding the cork out with an impressively quiet pop as the others sat.

"Here," she said, gesturing at us to hold out our glasses. Once they were filled, she opened her dove-gray clutch and slid out a pack of Camel Blues. Wide-eyed at her audacity, we watched as she lit one and exhaled, long, smoke hovering between us and the arched ceiling far above.

I grinned and lit one, too.

Lindsay reached out a hand, but a quick glance at Daniel—his eyebrow raised—and she withdrew it, slowly.

For a moment, it was just us, sitting in that gilded room.

"So this," Jock said, breaking the silence, "is the kind of thing the three of you were always sneaking off to do, years ago." After so long in New York, he spoke English better than either Margaux or I did, which was saying something. But his accent was far worse; Frenchmen tend to keep their accents as thick as possible. They think it's sexy.

Margaux grinned. "You know girls," she said. "All pillow fights and secrets or dares."

"*Truth* or dare," Lindsay said, laughing. Margaux shrugged.

"What's truth or dare?" Daniel asked.

"Oh my God!" Lindsay cried. "It's the simplest thing ever. Someone asks, *Truth or dare?* and you pick, and then you either have to answer a question or do a dare."

"Seems rather unfair to me," Jock said.

"Who said it was supposed to be fair?" Margaux asked, eyes sparkling.

I smacked her silk-covered thigh. "We take turns," I said with a smile.

"We could always play spin the bottle instead," Lindsay offered with a smirk.

"What's—"

"You first, then, Linds," I cut in. "Truth or dare?"

"Dare," Lindsay said at the same moment that Margaux groaned.

"Delphine!" Margaux cried. "Have you learned nothing? You never let Lindsay do a dare. Don't give her the choice!"

The three of us fell into laughter as Daniel grimaced.

"Why not?" Jock asked.

"Oh—" I said, catching my breath. "Because Lindsay will do anything."

"It's true," Lindsay said with a light sigh and a shrug. "No sense of self-preservation, you know."

"I've got it," Margaux said. "I dare you to tell us who you're most jealous of."

"You don't want to pick something harder?" Lindsay replied.

Was it really that easy for her? It would have taken me days to start narrowing it down. Camille, for having her entire life in front of her. Stella, for having a full life behind her. Lindsay, for—

"Nathalie," she said, rolling her eyes as if it were so obvious. "She was a star! And now, artistic director? She's one of the most powerful women in ballet. Plus, she'll be remembered forever."

"But that awful husband—" I said, then stopped, swallowing my words. Why in the world would I bring up *Louis?* I could feel Margaux's eyes burning into me, and I looked down, face flushed.

But Lindsay only shrugged. "Another star? Seems worth it to me." Beside her, Daniel grunted and we could all see it pass over her face: the realization of what she'd said. She wrapped her arms around him, started murmuring softly.

"Lindsay knows that he fucks everything that moves, right?" Jock whispered to me in low French, his breath tickling my ear. I suppressed the shudder running through me.

"I don't think," I said, trying to keep my voice low, "that she particularly cares."

Across from us, Daniel and Lindsay's conversation had gotten more heated, Lindsay flushed pink with the vehemence permeating her every word. With a quick roll of her eyes, Margaux pulled out her phone in indifferent amusement.

"Whose turn is it now?" Jock asked, staring at me with charming bafflement contorting his perfect features.

"Our games always had a way of deteriorating quickly," I said. Although I'd never seen one deteriorate quite the way this one had.

"Then I guess it's our turn," he said.

His leg pressed gently against mine. Through the fabric of his suit, my dress, I imagined the feeling of flesh against flesh.

"Truth or dare," I said softly.

"Truth," he said.

And there were a million things I wanted to ask him. *Are you in love with anyone? Why didn't you ever come see me? What happened between us?*

"What are you most ashamed of?"

And he looked at me straight with those ocean-bright eyes. "My parents," he said.

It took me a second to remember them from our school days: Fleurine and Félix, a bouncing couple from Normandy with a passion for the ballet that was second only to their passion for their child.

"They're proud of me, but they're—provincial. It's all I can do to keep them away from these things," he said, cheekbones flushing prettily. "I always wondered if I was adopted, you know."

"No," I said slowly. "No, there's something of them in you. They're really lovely, you know. Their energy. Their movement."

"I guess," he said. Our eyes met, and for a moment we sat there, staring at each other as Margaux's and Lindsay's voices bounced off the walls around us.

"I know your mother was tall and dark and elegant," he said, wincing on the past tense. "What is your father like? I've never heard much about him."

I don't like telling men about my father. It's too easy for them to invalidate the whole thing by assuming I have *daddy issues*. It's an accepted form of erasure to say: *You're screwed up about men because one guy treated you like shit when you were five.*

But one is plenty. One is enough to prove that we live in a world where terrible things can happen.

"My father had another family," I said. "Or I guess technically, we were his other family. He moved to California to be with them when I was five."

"Christ." He sounded genuinely appalled. "I didn't think that sort of thing happened nowadays."

"Yes, well. The internet has made it harder for assholes like him to get away with it, but this was still the eighties."

He downed the rest of his champagne. "Okay, your turn. Truth or—"

"I just told you a deep, dark secret! No way. No fair. Tell me *your* deepest, darkest secret."

Tell me you want me. Tell me now.

His cheeks were pink again. "I've been wanting to ask you out since you came back."

I blinked, stunned that my telepathy had worked.

"No, you haven't." What a reflex I had.

He turned even pinker. "I have too. But you—"

"Just what the *genuine fuck* do you think you're doing?" A rich female voice bled through our whispers and our giggles, and the five of us were united as a group once again as we looked up and saw Nathalie's elegant figure, backlit in the door on the balcony, distant and brutal as a goddess.

My heart thrummed with the shock and fear of being discovered, the anxious delight of *oh shit now what* that I hadn't felt since I was a teenager.

"Get the fuck back to the party. You think I'm doing this for my own pleasure? This is our job. Not to mention the disrespect that you—" Nathalie waved a hand in front of her face, though the smoke would have dissipated long before reaching the balcony. "Well, if you don't have some respect for this place at your age, nothing I could possibly say is going to instill it in you. You are contractually obligated to attend the gala. So get the fuck back in there."

She stared at us, frozen in place except for Margaux, who was holding her sides in her silent laughter.

"Well?"

We scrambled to our feet, tossing our lit cigarettes in the dregs of Margaux's champagne. Nathalie didn't wait for us to follow her; she knew we would. She knew our training would take over.

And yet, I thought, Lindsay's arm wrapped around my waist, shoes in hand as our low, worried giggles bounced off of the walls and as Daniel trailed hangdog behind us, there was a strange pleasure in being caught, too. There was still someone watching over us; someone who cared about our actions; someone to approve when we did well, smack our noses when we messed up. Someone whose glance would pin us to our place in the world, ground us, tether us to the earth.

There was still somebody who cared.

CHAPTER 11

— March 2000 —

Spring break had begun an hour ago, and yet I couldn't bring my-self to leave. After setting my bags in the foyer with Michelle, the school's receptionist, I'd wandered down through the woods to the lake. Though it was March, there'd been a late frost and the dusting of snow crunched satisfyingly underfoot. As I broke out on the other side of the forest, the rising wind screeched in my ears, momentarily stealing my breath.

Beyond the lake, the buildings of Nanterre rose up, modern and ugly, the type you find only in the suburbs. The city proper had forbidden their construction after the horrid appearance of the Montparnasse Tower in the 1970s. But there was a layer of trees between the skyscrapers and the lake, and a flock of geese flapped overhead, obscuring them further.

Poor geese. Returned home too soon, coming back to where they'd been born to find everything still frozen over, everyone else still hibernating.

Wrapping my too-thin hoodie closer around me, I made my way to a bench overlooking the water, shuddering as the metal chill soaked through my jeans.

"Delphine?"

My eyes watering in the wind, I whipped around to find him a few meters behind me. Hands in pockets, casual as ever—except for that re-version to my real name.

"Jock," I said. I couldn't help it, that emphasis on the flat *o*, the nick-name he'd brought back with him from his summer in New York. It was too ridiculous. He was too ridiculous.

"Can I sit?"

I raised one shoulder. "Sure."

He lowered himself tentatively onto the other side of the bench. But it was a performed tentativeness that just made me madder. Like *I* was the ridiculous one, like I was so sensitive that I demanded he handle me like a porcelain doll.

We'd never spoken of what had happened at Margaux's party the previous summer. In Pas de Deux class, we went through the motions without ever making eye contact. And while I could still feel his gaze seek me out when we were all together, especially at the end of a long night, especially when we'd all been drinking, I never returned it. I'd been such a fucking idiot. All of that time thinking he wanted *me*, when all of the time he'd only been wanting . . . *that*.

"You haven't left yet," he said.

"Neither have you." The water rippled, pulled into tidal patterns by the wind. The sideways gray light shone so brightly that for a moment, my eyes ached, and I had to close them.

"The boys' Technique midterm ran long. I missed my train."

Looking over at him, I was struck by the pathos of his posture: back curled, forearms resting on his thighs, head down. He knew how to use his body. He knew what every angle and line would communicate.

"What's wrong?" I asked, and hated myself.

He turned, and his eyes were so bright blue they seemed like the only color in the world.

"What happened to us, Dolphin? We used to be . . . you know. Buddies."

"Buddies?" I said, an edge creeping into my voice. "I don't remember that."

"Well, we used to be something, anyway," he said, trailing off. "I wish—"

I waited for what would follow. *I wish I hadn't hurt you. I wish I hadn't hooked up with Talitha. I wish we could be together again.*

I pressed my lips together. "Yeah," I said shortly. "Me too."

His eyes almost disappeared as the wind rose again and he squinted at me.

"I'm glad I caught you," he said. *Yeah, I'll just bet you are, I'm a treat.* "I got an email from New York City Ballet today," he added.

My heart started hammering against my rib cage like a hummingbird; my stomach had turned into a pit. I already knew what he was going to say. Everybody in our world knew what those words meant.

"The apprenticeship?" I said. He nodded. "So, you're going to take it?"

He turned his palm to the sky. Feigned helplessness. It was New York City *Ballet*, what was he going to do, say no?

"They'll *ruin* your dancing!" I cried. "Don't you care about what will happen to your repertory? Fuck, Jacques, you're not even going to audition for POB?"

"It's the music," he said simply. "They treat music differently there. They—they *become* it. And if you're a male dancer, that means more opportunities to prove yourself."

The thought of him leaving hurt like a corkscrew twisting through me. But even as I understood that his absence would feel intolerable, I also understood that my response in this moment would dictate what came next.

I could stay mad. I could keep that anger, grasp it close to my chest like a burning coal and refuse to let go. I could have it—but it would be all I had. I would lose him, forever.

Or: I could kiss him on the cheek, wrap my arm in his, make false noises of excitement and pride. *They're lucky to have you. You'll be amazing! But you have to come back to us. Promise you'll come back!* And there would be goodbyes, and later phone calls and emails; maybe a visit here or there to each other's cities. There would still be him. There could still be us.

I could hold on to my anger or I could hold on to him, but I couldn't do both.

A future without Jock. A future in which Jock wasn't dating me, wasn't dating anyone, was just—*gone*, as though he'd never been there. I could see the contours of my life contort around his absence. I could see all possible futures playing out.

I was so mad at him. I was still so, so mad. But without him around to ignore every day, without him around to punish again and again . . . I would just, what? Fan the coals of my anger alone, guarding it in my chest like my own little treasure?

I couldn't be one of those girls. I didn't want to be like my mother, hating men.

I forced my face into a smile.

"That is amazing, though. But you have to come back to us. Promise you'll come back!"

Something flickered behind his eyes. A warmth, a light I hadn't seen in years.

He grinned. "Maybe one day. But in the meantime, Dolphin—" He tilted his head. "Could we just be buddies again?"

When were we ever "buddies"? The words were right there.

But it was anger, or him. And as he stretched out his arm toward me, I paused for only a moment before I leaned in, let the warmth of his body envelop me once more.

— September 2018 —

I awoke the next Monday to the smell of coffee, strong and bitter and close.

"Delphine?" Stella's voice said gently.

"Stella? Is everything okay?" I said, sitting up.

Stella was standing next to my bed, her French press in one hand and her I ♥ NEW YORK mug in the other.

"You overslept, dear. I'm sorry to intrude, but I did wonder—"

I grabbed my phone. Ten twenty. "Fuck," I muttered. Time was up. I had to tell Lindsay she was out of *Tsarina* today. And as much as I envied the beautiful bubble she lived in—the bubble where her actions didn't have consequences, where she could do whatever the fuck she wanted—I was sick of it, too. It was time for me to burst it.

My plan had been to grab Lindsay for an early coffee before company class, then hide in a studio for the rest of the morning while she sulked and work out the wedding sequence that Camille would dance instead. Now, I'd be lucky if I even had enough time to track Lindsay down before she showed up for rehearsal.

But now that I'd lost my morning, what would I do this afternoon, with the dancers who were still left? We could always improvise, but I hated it. Improvising always felt like I was showing my hand too clearly. I might as well have been shouting at the dancers: *My job's so easy, I just make it all up as I go along!* I couldn't risk anything anymore, especially not with Nathalie breathing down my neck. I was one misstep away from losing the ballet altogether.

Pulling a sweater over my head, I saw Stella standing there, still holding the coffee and staring straight ahead.

"What on earth is wrong with that wall?" she asked.

My mother never cared what the apartment looked like. She'd bought the place after she was named a star, when the proceeds from her first modeling campaigns started coming in. She'd wanted the perfect packaging for her perfect life, and she'd gotten it. But then dance took over again, consumed every second of every waking day; and then I did; and the motley, college-student furnishings inside the apartment remained a shock to anyone who had only ever seen the perfect exterior of our pale redbrick building with its seventeenth-century vaulted arcades, its gray slate roof, from the Place des Vosges. Our furniture had been gathered piecemeal, a collection of items from various decades that she'd liked individually and never really considered as a whole. Yellow IKEA curtains, a rummage-sale side table, her aunt's shag rug.

After my mother retired from dancing, she had her enormous, star-based pension—and nothing to do. So, she'd taken to painting obsessively, day and night. There are worse ways to express yourself, but a mural of butterflies on your bedroom wall is a bit extreme. They always had a faintly carnivorous look about them, no matter how many adjustments she made. The vacation rental agency had painted over them years ago, but I could still see them, their outlines bleeding faintly through.

I laughed in surprise, so hard I snorted. "That's where Maman's butterflies were."

"Well, I think you've got an infestation, because they're coming back," she said, a faint smile on her lips.

"I should get someone in to paint over them again," I said. "I always hated butterflies."

"No, you didn't."

"Didn't I? They scare me now."

Her mouth ticked up at the side. "I'm afraid you only have me to blame for that. There was one spring when we had a rash of butterflies in the city. You must have been five or six. Goodness, I'd never been more popular at work, everyone was so fascinated by that infestation. Anyway, I'd taken you up to Buttes-Chaumont to watch them, but all you wanted to do was catch one. I kept telling you and telling you—they're delicate, you can't touch them without hurting them—but you were so little, and you didn't really understand."

"I don't remember that," I said. But suddenly, I was hit with the memory of a sensation like somebody's eyelashes blinking between my palms.

She nodded. "And then you actually caught one in your hands. By the time I got there, I was too late."

My throat tightened. "I killed it?"

"No, I did," she said. "You'd been so gentle, far gentler than I would have expected of a child of your age, but still—there were too many scales missing, too much structural damage, for it to fly anymore. It would have starved to death, you know. I put it out of its misery."

She smiled at me, lips pressed together in sympathy.

"I don't think you should be afraid of butterflies anymore," she said.

"I'm too old for it?"

"No, it's not that," Stella said, turning toward the door. "It's only—it's funny, isn't it? It's completely counter-evolutionary. How we're scared of things that we might break. So much of our focus goes there. Protecting them, caring for them."

"Well, what should we be afraid of instead?"

"Why, the things that might break us, of course," said Stella.

CHAPTER 12

When my mother started with the company back in 1964, some of the costumes had been in use for more than a hundred years.

"My first tutu—well, they'd replaced the top. But the bottom? It was yellow all the way through, completely disintegrating. Count yourself lucky," she told me when I got cast in my first ballet. It was the same as her first: *Swan Lake*. Not unusual for the *quadrilles*, apprentices to the corps, the lowest of the low, to be put on display here; it requires 120 dancers, 60 of whom are swans. The whole company is only about 150 people, but they're not going to stick the stars in the equivalent of a chorus line.

The stars have custom costumes, because that's what people pay to see. The measurements of the principals and even the soloists are kept on file in the big costume atelier. But we were still disposable. And while they had to pin and tuck our costumes a bit (*You have very short shoulders*, a curly-haired costumer told Lindsay, who stared at her, not understanding, both before and after I translated; Margaux was horrified that her dimensions corresponded to the *large* mannequin), it was only a fifteen-minute process. Nothing like the lengthy fittings Maman used to have. Maybe one day.

For our first performance, we arrived at the theater hours before our call time. We weren't nervous—well, just a little. We'd been on the Garnier stage before for the galas, for *A Midsummer Night's Dream* when they'd needed students from the school to play fairies, for *The Nutcracker*.

But this was different.

At a trip to the flea market a week earlier, Lindsay had come across a bronze bust of three girls. Their heads were turned in toward the center, as though their invisible arms were interlaced.

"The one with big eyes looks like you," I told her.

"Yeah. And this one here"—the girl with the triangular eyes on the right—"that's Margaux."

"And the surprised one is Delphine!" Margaux said.

The girl in the center didn't look particularly surprised. Her eyebrows were raised, yes. Her mouth formed a slight O. But I thought it looked more like she was listening to the others, hearing something they weren't supposed to know. She was the counselor, the adviser: the one who paid attention.

We bought the bust, constructing a plan to share it evenly. It would live with each of us for four months of the year; we agreed to rotate it religiously for things to be fair.

"It's a sign," Lindsay said, swinging her end of the bag as we headed back to the Métro. "I know it is. It's a sign."

The three of us, on the path to becoming stars. Together.

For that first performance, our makeup calls were scheduled two and a half hours before curtain. The makeup room had ten technicians going for hours before each show, but there were so many of us that the lower ranks were forced into absurdly early call times.

"So fucking unfair," Margaux said.

"You won't think it's so unfair when you're a star," Lindsay said, swinging the door open. Ten minutes later, we emerged, still in our sweats and warm-ups but with faces ready for the stage.

"I don't like that color lipstick on you," Lindsay told me a few minutes later as we stretched out with Diet Cokes and Camel Blues on the roof.

I pressed my lips together. The makeup artist had told me we'd go for "a nice coral," but I'd ended up with a clownish orange.

"Yeah. I thought we'd all have the same one," I said. Lindsay's mouth was a pretty petal color, Margaux's a vibrant red.

Lindsay reached over and wiped my mouth with the back of her hand.

"Shit," Margaux said, bursting into laughter.

Lindsay winced. "It's all over your face."

"Lindsay! Fuck, what did you—"

"It's okay, it's okay." She started rummaging through her bag, pulling out Max Factor and a tube of L'Oréal something. "Look," she said, twisting up the soft pink. "It's even called Ballerina Slippers. Better, right?"

She painted my face back into place.

An hour later, we'd gotten our costumes on—court dresses for Act I, the tutus would come later—and stood in the wings waiting for our entrance.

Nathalie walked by, her assistant—Léonie something? I could never remember—trailing her. It was her farewell performance: she'd be turning forty-two in December and retiring. She was playing Odette/Odile, the starring role. A classic.

Even my mother, a diva if there ever was one, didn't have *an assistant.* I felt myself glaring at Léonie as she stopped in front of us. She rustled in a plastic bag, then pressed a Ferrero Rocher chocolate in each of our palms.

"*Merde,*" she said. A tradition at the ballet. Like actors, we'd never say *Good luck*—but *Break a leg* tempts fate a little too much. So we just say: *Shit.* Like: *Shit, it's just* dancing, *after all.* "From Nathalie."

We were so baffled at this outsourcing of affection that we forgot to thank her, and she trotted off.

"I'm going to go look at the audience," Lindsay said, and started heading onstage. We pulled her back, one of us on either side of her.

"We'll see them soon enough," I told her. "Listen."

A moment of silence, with just the clicking of the conductor's baton; then the music swelled.

"We have to remember this, you guys," Lindsay whispered over the Tchaikovsky.

"We will," I whispered.

"Shhh," Margaux hissed.

"Right now," Lindsay said, ignoring her. "This is the moment when our real life starts."

We took our places.

— *September 2018* —

"What the fuck do you mean, *I've been cut?*" Lindsay said.

She had gone entirely pale except for the bright spots of pink on her cheeks. "That's *my* role. How the hell could you give it away?" Her voice echoed around the high-ceilinged costume studio; the dozens of dancers being pinned into tutus looked studiously away from us.

Breathless after my run from the Métro to the Opéra, I'd found Lindsay in the hallway just as company class was letting out. But she had a fitting scheduled and didn't have time for a coffee. If I didn't want her showing up to that afternoon's rehearsal, I had no choice but to follow her to the *atelier flou*, where everyone and their mother seemed to be gathered for fittings.

I put a hand on her shoulder. "Like I said, I really think we should talk about this somewhere—"

Her hands were on her waist, above the half-pinned tutu, like an angry Degas sculpture. "No, we're going to talk about it here. What the fuck did I do?"

I stared at her. "You kicked your understudy in the face."

Her gaze slipped away. "That was an accident."

"Was it?" I said. She blinked at me. I knew that expression so well: blank, angelic, *who, me?* She used it whenever someone was mad at her and she was trying to get off the hook.

"But we're friends. You and me."

I sighed, sharper than I meant to. "Yeah, but come on. Even I can only carry that so far. I mean, you did it in front of everyone, Lindsay! What did you think was going to happen?"

"I wasn't thinking!" she said in a rush. "But can't you fix it? What's the point of you being here if you can't?"

Ouch. I knew I deserved far worse than that from her. But that didn't stop it from sticking in my throat like a hunk of meat.

Across the room, I saw Louis glance over at us, his dark eyes appraising. How was he even still in the company? His expiration date had to be coming up soon. He'd been—what, twenty-three when he'd first gotten with Nathalie? It had made waves throughout the company, their eighteen-year age difference. Forty-one, that made him. Well, he'd be gone soon enough. I scowled at him, and he raised thick brows, turned away.

Lindsay hadn't stopped talking. "Do you know what my dad used to tell me when I was little? *You can be whatever you set your mind to.* And every day, that's all I focus on. Want it. Try harder. Keep going. And then I get cut from *my friend's ballet*? Am I really that bad?"

I reached out and clutched her wrist.

"It's not about your dancing," I said. "It's about your behavior."

"That's bullshit," she said, blinking at me. "*Nobody* could set her mind to this role more than I have. Nobody works harder. This whole place is bullshit."

"Listen to me," I said so fiercely that her eyes cleared and I think she actually was listening, for once. "You're a great dancer. A really great dancer."

Lindsay shook her head. "If that was true, you wouldn't be cutting me. No matter how shitty I acted in rehearsal. I'm never going to have another chance like this, Delphine. You know how much Nathalie hates me. She'll never put me in anything good ever again."

Don't provoke Lindsay. Don't make her mad. Those had been my internal refrains throughout adolescence—and now, I brushed them aside.

She had to understand. I had to make her understand.

"All right," I said slowly. "You really want to know why you lost the part? You really want to know what's going on here?"

"Yes," she said, snapping to attention.

I rubbed my eyes. "It's your partnering."

"What?" Her forehead wrinkled.

"You're great as a soloist, but in a pas de deux . . . you go all stiff. It's not the bloody nose. God knows you're not helping yourself with that shit, but that's not the biggest problem."

I watched her face carefully, half regretting the words even as I said them. She tilted her head to the side.

"The problem," I said, "is that the second you're dancing with somebody else . . . you change."

I swallowed, waiting for her to erupt.

But something had lit up behind her eyes.

"That's all?"

Had she heard me? You need to be able to dance with partners to become a principal. And you need to do it better than almost anyone else on earth.

"I can fix that," she said.

Could she? Even if she could, it was immaterial. "I just think that in the time frame we have for this ballet—"

"It won't even be on the schedule until next season at the earliest."

I hesitated. "Look. You're forgetting that there are two things going on here. The partnering was never the main issue for me." It should have been, but it wasn't. "But if I keep you in the piece, I'm effectively saying to the rest of the cast that I don't care how they behave—or, worse, that I'm prioritizing your feelings over the actual production."

She made a face. "Why is that worse?"

I scraped my fingers back through my hair. If she couldn't see why, I couldn't explain it to her. I shook my head in defeat.

She grinned. "You'll change your mind. I know what's wrong with me, now. And I'm going to get so good you can't say no," she said.

"Lindsay!" I cried. "I cannot, *will not* put you back in it. What part of that don't you understand?"

She was silent for a long time, then shook her head like a wet dog. "Then for your next piece. And the one after that, and the one after that. Partnering is fixable. I just have to get it right, that's all."

There was no way to say, *This isn't a fixable problem.*

"Well," I said. "Maybe."

"I'll need someone to practice with. Who do you think is the best partner in the company?"

My heart thumped. "Jock, probably."

"Yeah, I think so too," she said, and made a face. "What about somebody younger? Somebody with something to prove? Someone who really wants it?"

"I . . ." I trailed off. They all wanted it. That was the problem.

"What do *you* even want?" she said, as if the question were occurring to her for the first time.

I laughed. "What do *I* want?"

"When I heard you were coming back, I thought, Okay, so she's making her name. But then this ballet—" She shook her head. "It's what you'd expect some committee of white guys to come up with. It's not something Pina Bausch does." Pina Bausch, the German choreographer who blended dance and theater into something entirely new with her crazy, laughing dancers, her fantastic sets. No, she wouldn't have done *Tsarina*.

"I'm not Pina Bausch," I said weakly.

"I know. So: Who *are* you, then? What do you want?"

I thought for a moment.

"I want to make a ballet that really means something to me. Something that's not just about being decorative—something that shows the world what it's like to . . . I don't know, to fall in love, to have this experience that's supposed to be the epitome of a woman's life and have it be the best thing that ever happened to you—and then to have it become your downfall." *Too much. You went too far.* I stopped.

Lindsay drew back, nose wrinkling.

"I wonder if Claude would be up for practicing," she said.

I shrugged. Though they were still the same rank, she had a decade of experience on him, and he might be willing to help her out. Despite her reputation as a difficult partner—maybe even because of it. As a twenty-one-year-old *sujet*, he had two decades to make it to principal, then star; Lindsay wouldn't be the last tricky ballerina he had to dance with if he wanted to get to the top.

"I bet he would," I said. "Why don't you ask?"

She had to leave for class soon and I watched her go, relieved and queasy at once. It was over. I'd cut her. And we were still friends—weren't we?

It was okay to enforce boundaries. It was healthy.

But suddenly, I felt very alone.

The eyes of everyone in costuming were studiously avoiding mine as I gathered up my things.

And then I saw it. In my peripheral vision: a spark of movement from the changing area. The curtain on the right was bobbing back and forth as though it had just been moved—but when I pushed it aside, nobody was there.

CHAPTER 13

"Would you eat something, Maman?" We were sitting on red stools across from each other at the little table in the kitchen, just like we had when I was five. Except I wasn't five anymore; I was twenty-one, and if I could have afforded an apartment that was as centrally located as hers, I would have been out of there the very next day. But I wasn't on a star's salary—not *yet*, as she kept telling me—and moving made no sense. For the moment.

My mother set her fork down against the checkered oilcloth. She only ever ate half of any meal set before her (*The secret of my success*, she used to say, scraping the leftovers into the garbage can), but this was ridiculous.

"Can we talk?" she said.

I'd done something bad. Was it that teeny bit of cocaine at Marisol's party the month before? It was so small and I'd hated the taste of it and I'd made *sure* none of the older dancers were there, nobody who could tell on me—

She put a cool hand over my fingers, which were gripping the table.

"It's okay. Nothing terrible."

Only terrible things ever follow those words.

"I didn't want to bother you when you've been doing so well this season. I wouldn't be surprised if you get named a soloist next year, you know—"

Marc had probably been talking to her. I needed to be more respectful in class, was that it?

Or. Or she was going to sell the apartment, finally move back to Nice.

Or. She knew something about the company, something about the promotion cycle, and was trying to break it to me gently? But my mother had never broken professional news gently in her life.

Unlimited tragedies opened up before me. And yet—while we were still in this space between, this moment before she said what was actually wrong, part of me relished running through the possibilities. They were all true—which meant none of them were.

"Delphine, don't look so terrified," she said, and took a deep breath. "It's just a small cancer, that's all."

The words made no sense.

Had I been speaking English for too long?

Just. Just didn't go with the word *cancer. Small* didn't, either.

"A—*cancer?*" I said. "No, it's not."

"It is, I'm afraid. A small stomach cancer."

"That doesn't make any sense. You never *put* anything into your stomach."

Her face contorted into the grimace she made when I was being silly.

"No, I mean it. Isn't it just Americans who get that kind of thing? Like, eating fast food for three meals a day."

"Apparently, that makes very little difference. Or in my case, it didn't."

"I really think—it can't be right, can it? You need to see another doctor."

"Delphine, I have stage three stomach cancer." She said it with a strange emphasis, like it was the name of a ballet. "It's through the lining and into two lymph nodes. They're right about it. Okay?"

"But—but—" The objections were draining out of me. I felt like I was deflating, like all of my organs were being vacuum-packed; soon, I'd just be a little package of meat and bones.

She had cancer. Stage three. That sounded bad. How many stages were there? I didn't know. At that point in my life, I knew nothing about cancer, I knew nothing about lymph nodes, I didn't even know the difference between radiation and chemotherapy.

But I was about to find out.

"What can they do?"

She shrugged her tiny shoulders. She had to have lost four kilos since the previous summer. I should have seen it, I'd been blind. If I'd been watching, this wouldn't have happened. If I'd made her go to a doctor sooner, she'd be fine now. I was all she had and I was useless, I was nothing.

"I started radiation last month."

"Last month!" A month, she'd been going through this. A month, I'd been happily prancing through the halls of the Opéra, taking class and performing and going out for drinks and all the time she'd been here, right under my nose, going through this alone.

"Stella's been going with me," she added. "She's been wonderful. She's been through this all before, with her husband, you know."

"But he died!"

I was trying not to cry. If I were her, I wouldn't want me to cry. But then sharp sobs escaped from high in my chest, and she was coming over to me. *She* was coming over to *me*.

"Delphine," she whispered, holding my head against her body. "Delphine, baby. Hush. Hush now. It's going to be okay."

And although I knew nothing yet, although I was still swaddled in the cotton wool of my ignorance, I did know this: It wouldn't be okay. Maybe not ever again.

⌐ October 2018 ⌐

As much as I loved her—as much as I'd fought for her—once Lindsay was out of *Tsarina*, everything started to come together. Over that next week, I focused the rehearsals on Jock, Camille, and Claude alone. If I was going to fuck up again, I didn't want an audience spreading my failures through the company. Besides, this was where I ruled; this was my domain; and I didn't need anyone taking the focus off of me at my best. Especially not in front of Jock.

The dancers did what I said, and they did it with grace. That week, we were working on more of the Rasputin scenes. After Alix's arrival in a country that saw her as nothing more than a curse, there was one thing she could do to make the Russian people love her: give them a son and heir. And she tried—Christ, she tried. The letters between her and Nicky turned embarrassingly erotic in the first years after their marriage. And, in a sense, their prodigious lovemaking was successful, as they had four children in six years. But they were all girls.

When I'd first conceived of the ballet, I thought the births of the daughters should take up all of Act II, creating that sense of excruciating anticipation she must have felt with each conception, not knowing whether she had finally succeeded; whether this time would be the one that gave her husband, her country, a boy.

Camille and Claude and Jock danced long into the evening for me, jumping and lifting and balancing. Through the windows behind them, the Paris sky burst into night: bright blue twilight to neon violet to silver, shivery dark. If I craned my neck just right, I could see the Eiffel Tower lit up in gold like a Christmas tree from one window; through another, Sacré-Coeur perched above the city, a corpulent grandmother.

It was a delight to run my own studio. Even once I had my own pieces to work on in St. Petersburg, even once I'd found my fire, I was still always and forever *the great choreographer's girlfriend*. No matter how long I spent in the Mariinsky archives, poring over image after image of long-dead dancers; no matter how many hours I put into my Rosetta Stone Russian; no matter how many books I studied, trying to prove to myself that I wasn't just that little girl who barely passed history anymore—somehow, I'd never earned their respect.

But here, for the first time, I was eager to show up and confront the dancers with what I had invented. What I had imagined for their bodies. I was starting to feel that anything could happen. That I could *make* anything happen.

"How long can you hold an arabesque?" I asked Camille one night after five hours together.

She shook her head, blond hair cascading around her shoulders.

"I never timed it."

"Let's try." I started the timer on my phone and watched her strike the pose, on one pointe with the other leg lifted behind her as high as it would go. Ten seconds passed. Twenty. She didn't start shaking until forty. "Hold—" I whispered as her back foot started to shake. Fifty. "Hold, Camille!" Louder.

She stayed for a minute and ten seconds before I let her come down.

"Keep practicing that," I said. "I want a solid minute with the others dancing around you, when you first meet Rasputin and he sparks this new hope in you."

The more I saw what Camille could do, the more I wanted to show her off to the world: Watch this beauty. Watch the precocity. Watch my creation. And there was something more than that, too, though it was hard to admit even to myself. Camille was only nineteen. She had the flawless technical foundations for a leading role, but none of the bad habits or stylistic quirks the older dancers did. She was perfect, moldable clay.

And maybe if I'd kept that focus on her, it would have worked out differently. But the more I worked with the men, the more I became intrigued with what they could do, too. The more I needed to use them.

As the lights along the river exploded into life each night, Claude proved his worth, as well. In everyday life, there was nothing shy or retiring about him, but he was able to put on the Tsar's discomfort with leadership like a costume for hours at a time. He was hapless and dignified at once. With every step, he became this man who would rather have been tending his garden or out riding horses than playing at statecraft. He was tender and tragic at the same time. There are fewer really great male roles than female ones in ballet, and every time I watched him, I thought: I was right to give him this. He deserved it.

And Jock.

For the past thirteen years, Jock had been like a national monument in my mind—like the Arc de Triomphe. Grand, imposing, unmovable. And I'd thought: He can't possibly be that impressive in real life. I'm remembering him wrong. Of course, when I see him dance again, he'll return to life-size. Some of his appeal, after all, was that he was the perfect antidote to Dmitri. Jock's elegant lines against Dmitri's solid bulk. Jock's rolling waves of laughter against Dmitri's low snorts. Jock's way of tilting his head when he was listening, against Dmitri's dark, penetrating gaze.

And yet knowing this didn't shrink him back down in my mind. He was still, always, forever, the one who'd gotten away, and now, seeing him at his best gave me a vertiginous ache at the back of my neck.

Put aside the fact that he hadn't made a single move since the gala. Or that he smiled and chatted up Camille as much as he did me. I still couldn't put my finger on exactly what was wrong. Something in his bearing, something in his aura. Jock's technique was impeccable—and yet the role I had created for him brought out the worst in him. Every time I watched him slip on Rasputin's sly, devious manner, it made me shiver. It was my job to push him into that, to make him lean into the creepiness; and yet—I didn't want to see it. Didn't want to see him twisting the anonymous women of the corps, the courtiers, around his little finger, didn't want to see him charming the Tsarina into forgetting everything but him.

It wasn't fair to him. He was astonishing, his talent and his presence. But I found it unwatchable.

Rasputin, though. They said he could hypnotize you with his eyes.

As much as I hated it, as I watched Jock slinking dangerously around the studio, I thought: I should compress the timeline, make all of the daughters arrive in a single scene, so that we could finally get to the son. Alexei, the boy with hemophilia, the royal curse, the condition that had already killed Alix's brother and uncle. And thus, the arrival of the mystical healer. The arrival of Rasputin.

Once Rasputin came into Alix's life, everything really went to hell. The man was disgusting: a disgraced monk with a prodigious sexual appetite (if you believed the rumors, which I did), no table manners to speak of, and a wife and children he'd left behind in Siberia to play at Tsarskoe Selo with the nobles. The Russian people already hated the influence German Alix had over her husband; they hated the influence this "mad monk" had over her even more. All kinds of gossip spread through St. Petersburg about their relationship, with some truly filthy cartoons of Rasputin and Alix out there. And yet Rasputin was the only one who could stop the baby's bleeding, and so he was the only one she trusted with this most precious of creations. Her legacy.

The more I imagined Rasputin, the more I watched Jock, the more another nagging thought emerged: Maybe it was a love story, after all. But a different kind of love story. One about power.

Isn't that what all love stories are about, anyway?

If only Jock weren't so—conniving, as he danced. If only he would lighten up just a little, let some boyish charm slip through his furious façade.

But he was a star and had been one for years. He was a pro. And he never did.

On our fifth day of rehearsal, he was spinning, jumping like nothing I'd ever seen before. The speed. The power. The rage. It was pure Rasputin, and I couldn't bear it. My ballet was becoming all about him, and it was magnificent, and yet it was like I was driving a stake into my own heart with every step.

"Let's stop for today," I said, turning off the music. Jock came to a halt abruptly between Camille and Claude; the three of them were drenched in sweat, spotting the backs and fronts and underarms of their leotards. "Go home. Take a shower. You did good work this week."

As Claude and Camille left the studio, Jock approached, clear eyes pinning me in place.

My whole body felt hot and pink.

"It's really good, Dolphin," he said. "It's really coming together."

I couldn't help flushing at the praise. I didn't need him to tell me it was good. That *I* was good. And still, it was the only thing I'd wanted to hear.

CHAPTER 14

*D*mitri Sokalov came to Paris when I was twenty-two. Rumors preceded him; the *Russian choreographer* was arriving. His dark, mystical works were coming to Paris—coming to us. When we were growing up, his name had been regularly splattered through the dance magazines: he was a genius, a boy wonder who'd never trained as a dancer himself yet had created his first ballet (*The Golden Slipper*) at seventeen. As the years passed, he expanded his repertoire, but always in the same direction: Russian folklore, the stories of the people, mixing folk dances with classical ballet. And now he would be at POB for four months, creating a short piece on no more than three or four dancers for a special spring performance.

"Who knows? Maybe we'll be in it," I said to Lindsay and Margaux.

"Get your head out of the clouds," Margaux said. Her obvious pleasure at finding the right English idiom undercut its meanness. "We're in the corps. He'd never."

"He might," said Lindsay.

And when he arrived, all fierce brows and wild black hair, it took him only one class to pick me. Me, two soloists, and a principal.

"You bitch," Lindsay said when she saw the call sheet, but she was smiling.

The day of our first rehearsal, I took a deep breath before pushing through the studio doors. I smiled at Laure and Charlotte, the two soloists, and tried to keep my face just as open and wide for Sophie, the principal.

They had to be wondering what the hell I was doing there: they'd climbed the ladder, worked hard to make it this far, put in their time. Who the hell was I? I scampered over to the barre and stretched out, trying to keep my muscles warm.

Twenty minutes later, I couldn't think of any more stretches to do, so I was just bent over my legs, face turned to the wall, when Dmitri came in.

"Good," he said, looking around. "Yes, good. We start."

His French was rudimentary, but we didn't need language: we had bodies. The piece was set to odd, modern music. Not my favorite, but I was always getting cast in stuff like this. The weird stuff. At a particularly discordant twang, I started.

"Russian guitar," Dmitri said with satisfaction.

I'd never worked directly with a choreographer before. Normally, we learned the classic repertory from the ballet masters and mistresses, who learned it when they were dancers from the ballet masters and mistresses before them. To watch someone actually making up the steps . . . well, in other companies, it might be normal. At POB, it's normal if you're already a star. But for a new dancer, it's a revelation.

And I caught something in his dark, flashing eyes. Something the other dancers didn't see. Soon, I was helping him explain sequences to the others, translating motion to speech for them, watching them turn it back into action. I didn't have any Russian; he had hardly any French and even less English; and yet I could see "take your hip out of alignment" from the simple curve of his fingers.

"He wants you to spin, twist around on the ground, do a giant push upstage on your right leg, and then—" I looked back at him. He twirled a finger around a bent hand. "Do a pirouette? But while you're crouched down still. Kind of . . . kind of pushing your way around?"

Sophie nodded. The music started; when she got to the pirouette, Dmitri opened his mouth. Stopped as he watched her.

"It's not what I wanted," he said to me.

"Oh. I'm sorry."

He cuffed me on the chin—a strange, old-fashioned gesture.

"It's better," he said.

It was the first time anyone had ever complimented me on my mind. I was twenty-two years old.

— *October 2018* —

In the grimy café, I tried to catch Margaux's eye, but she'd managed to drape herself over her chair so that her face was twisted up toward the ceiling, eyes half-closed in a classic Hollywood smolder. Next to her, Lindsay stared at her hands in her lap, tearing up her cuticles with her index finger.

At the gala, I'd childishly believed that the cozy fort of our friendship would engulf us again, setting us apart from the rest of the world. But it had been a temporary illusion. Firing Lindsay had proven as much.

I had to fix things.

After a week of working with just the stars, I'd brought in the full cast earlier that afternoon. Margaux was professional. Competent. Distant. As rehearsal ended, I'd grabbed her wrist.

"Come out with me?"

She pulled away. "I'm busy."

"We ended early. Come on—" I twisted my arm through hers. "Let's find Linds."

Without the smoke that had permeated the Cordial Café when we were teens, everything felt too bright, too real. Cordial had always been our place between rehearsals. Almost everything near the Opéra is some kind of historical monument—Hemingway drank here, Zola wrote there—and we couldn't afford the ensuing nine-euro coffees. So, we ran to Cordial: a few blocks behind the Palais Garnier, back toward the Hard Rock Cafe and the movie theaters and the outside world.

"So, what's new? How's *Swan Lake* going?"

Lindsay opened her mouth to answer, not before Margaux groaned deep in her throat.

"It's the same, Delphine. The same eternity frozen onstage. The same living scenery we've always been. That same hell."

"Sorry I asked," I said, my voice quiet and defensive.

Margaux sat up straight. "Let's just finish our coffees and go," she said, wrapping her hands around what was, in fact, a glass of wine. I tried to catch Lindsay's eye, but she was gazing down at her mug. When I'd fired her the previous week, Lindsay had seemed galvanized to change, to improve. What had happened since?

In the mirrors, we all looked so tired. I studied our reflections as Margaux raised an arm to summon the waiter for our check; Lindsay kept her eyes on the black-and-white-tiled floor.

A flock of teenagers came rushing in. I knew who they were at a glance. Little rats—dance students—in the city for an evening, killing a few hours before that night's performance at the Opéra. It wasn't anything they were wearing, or even anything they said, that gave them away. It was the way they carried themselves: they were proud of being watched, confident that their days would continue to unspool before them, full of adventure and mystery and excitement.

For a second, the mirrors became a window to fifteen years ago. If I could find a way through—if I could break the glass—

I wanted to say: *One day a lot sooner than you think, you're going to wake up and you're going to be exactly like us.*

"Come *on*, you guys," I said once the waiter had placed the check on our table. "Is there any gossip I've missed? No one tells the choreographer anything," I added playfully.

Margaux made a disgusted noise. "*She's* the gossip," she said, thrusting her sharp chin at Lindsay. "Her and you."

For a second, my heart stopped: Had Margaux finally told Lindsay what we did, all those years ago? How we'd ruined everything? Did Lindsay now know that you could love someone and they could still betray you, that you could give everything you had and still not be enough?

I stared searchingly at Margaux, memories thick between us.

Finally, she rolled her eyes.

"Everyone thinks you're ridiculous," she said. "This ballet, Delphine? This ballet." And then she raced off in French. "Coming back in your little derivative bubble of nineteenth-century misogynist fuckery—who the hell knows what you like about this story except the sheer *tragedy* of it—and then betraying us? Betraying *Lindsay*? Making her a laughingstock?"

My lips were parted, my body ready to respond though my mind was stuck. Lindsay just stared at the floor, rubbing the toe of her foot in the cracks between the tiles.

"You may call it *Tsarina*, but it's not even a ballet about a woman, Delphine. Not really, not anymore. It's about some fucking charlatan, when it should be about how an entire society, how an entire world order, was set up to fucking *erase her existence*, making her into nothing more than some—defective womb. And if you could make the ballet actually about that erasure . . . well, *that* might be something. But you've totally bought into these patriarchal structures and you don't even see it anymore." Margaux tilted her face up to the ceiling. "I thought you were better than that. You *were* better than that. But you're not anymore."

Lindsay had gone parchment white. "I liked it," she said softly, and simply, in French.

Margaux reached out and grabbed her hand.

"Well. I'm sorry that you feel that way, but—fuck, Margaux, you're dancing in *Swan Lake*. Patriarchal structures?" The small flicker of annoyance deep below my skin had quickly sparked into full-blown rage. "And you didn't have a problem with the ballet until I had to make some really hard artistic choices—choices which, by the way, you'd actually agree with if what you were thinking about was POB."

"Are you joking? You have a nineteen-year-old with no life experience trying to embody a lonely, desperate mother of four. I'm not sure any of us can trust your *artistic choices* anymore."

The warmth of my anger rippled over my skin. "Fine. If you don't see Camille's talent by now, then you're the one who's missing the point. Still, did I think Lindsay should have the role?" Lindsay looked down. "Yeah. I did. And she—" I cut myself off. It wasn't worth it. "Well, there's fuck-all I can do about it now."

"Bullshit."

"Oh, fuck you! So, what you're saying is, you're embarrassed to be dancing a role I created for you. It's such a *humiliation* to originate the role of Queen Victoria?"

Margaux's face had fallen strangely calm. "You want the wrong things," she said slowly. "I stopped caring about that shit ages ago. I started looking for a fucking escape instead. But you would know that if you'd actually been part of my life over the past decade."

"And where have you been, then? There are flights to St. Petersburg every day, Margaux. You could have come to *me*. At least I was busy doing *something*—making a new life, becoming a choreographer. I thought you were doing the same thing, but it's all too clear now that you were just—unraveling. And it's such a fucking waste, because once you could have been a star." I let it sink in. "Once."

As I pushed my way through the mass of teenage limbs cluttering up the pathway between us and the door, I felt the righteousness of my anger pulsing through my skin like heat. I was the wronged party. It was my chance to be mad now.

And it felt really, really good.

CHAPTER 15

Applause, lights down, rib cages heaving; we lined up for our curtsies. Dmitri came onstage then, alien against our nude bodysuits in his black jeans and turtleneck. He'd let his scruff grow out since coming to Paris, covering his jaw in black fur, and except for the enormous bundles of roses splotched red in his arms, he seemed almost entirely colorless.

He handed bouquets to each of us before the curtain went down. We stood for a moment, turning to each other to smile at our success.

Except for Dmitri, whose face was intent, dark, his gaze piercing mine. Had I messed up? He grabbed my waist and before I could think, he kissed me, his beard softer than I would have thought but still rough as a steel-wool brush all the same.

The other dancers were hooting and whistling. I pulled away, breathless. And he grinned.

For weeks, we'd been working on the ballet together. For weeks, I had thought of him only as the genius who was pushing us further than we knew we could go. I could make him smile when I twisted his steps into something new. I'd caught his eyes on my body, day after day. But he was my boss, and I was a ballerina. That was normal. Wasn't it?

The dancers around us dispersed, chattering and giggling at this new gossip, but I couldn't move. From the wings, I saw Margaux raise her eyebrows at me. *Are you okay?*

This whole time I'd thought our relationship was one thing, and this whole time he'd been thinking of it as something else. Thinking of me as something else.

Wanting me.

The next morning, Jock's email was at the top of my in-box.

Congratulations, Dolphin. Do I see a promotion in the near future? You have to watch out for that guy, though.

Hahaha, I wrote back, wondering how he already knew about the performance, if he also knew about the kiss. *Maybe he should watch out for me.*

It took less than five minutes for his email to come pinging back. *No, but seriously. Lucy worked with him a few years ago at ABT, and she says he's a real piece of work.*

I retitled the email *Who the fuck is Lucy?????* and forwarded it to Lindsay and Margaux.

A few minutes later, Margaux's response arrived. Just a link to Jock's MySpace page. There she was: dark haired, small boned. Nestled under his arm at a New York party, his drunken eyes gleaming joy into the camera as she whispered secrets into his ear. Her page showed she was already a principal, had had a spread in *Vanity Fair* the summer before. The better version of me.

"How did he even hear about the performance, anyway?" I asked Margaux and Lindsay in class that morning.

"I . . . may have told him," Margaux muttered.

"I didn't know you even kept in touch," Lindsay said, looking at her. "*We* don't," she added for my benefit.

Margaux's skin burned pink. "I just thought . . . well, he fucking deserves it, doesn't he? He should know that Delphine is doing better than ever without him. Fuck that guy." And she turned away.

Now, as I walked hand in hand with Dmitri along the Seine, the first week of performances didn't so much blur together as fracture into thousands of separate moments. He hadn't tried that kissing stunt again, had reverted to polite, professional nods whenever I saw him in the halls. But the more I thought about him, the more I wanted him. Or rather, the more I thought about his talent, the more I wanted him. Out of everyone—even Sophie, our gorgeous principal—he'd wanted me. He'd seen something in me.

He'd wanted something in me.

And whatever spark lived inside him caught in me, blew itself into flames. Finally, later that week, catching him alone between rehearsals, I'd grabbed his wrist and pulled him around the corner, pressing him up against the wall in a kiss of my own.

I was no virgin anymore. By nineteen, I'd gotten over my qualms and slept with Arthur. Arthur was nothing like Jock, but he was attractive enough, and he was a good guy. I knew that. Sex with him felt like an experiment: *How interesting, that I can get him to twitch like that, to make those faces, those noises;* but *interesting* was about as exciting as it ever got for me. In the three years since then, sex had satisfied more intellectual curiosities than physical ones. Even though we'd never actually had sex, it was like Jock was the only one who'd ever known my password. Everyone else was simply locked out.

But Dmitri was different.

He was a great man. But he wasn't a particularly good one. I knew that already, yes. I also knew that I couldn't help but feel his touch pulsing over my skin every time I thought of him. He had none of Jock's delicate strokes. If Jock was air, Dmitri was earth; and that was what I wanted. Wanted it so much it reverberated deep within me, somewhere behind my navel. To be made solid beneath his compact body, the bulk and the muscle of it. To cover myself in his strange musk.

The first time, Dmitri grasped my wrists with heavy hands and pinned me to the bed. No tentative touches with him; no (God forbid) *caressing.* It was like he could hear inside my head: *Push me down, make me small beneath you.* He shoved his knee between my thighs to open them. *Yes, do it now.* I think we were both a little surprised when I came.

It hurt, with Dmitri. And yet I needed the weight of his torso against mine, my smooth legs entwined around his rough, hairy ones. I wanted it to hurt. Inside me, on top of me, anchoring me to the earth. *Don't mess around. Skip the foreplay:* Now. Here. Yes, *like that; why are you even asking?*

It was strange, as Dmitri and I walked together in the fragile morning light, to feel his hand, thick and almost hammy, in mine. Not like Jock's surgeon's fingers, nothing like that. It was strange to have him wrap his arm around my waist and notice that he wasn't any taller than me, that I'd never fit into the nook of his arm the way I had Jock's. The way Lucy did. It was strange that I took more pleasure in the whispers that were reverberating through the dancers than I did in his whispers to me.

I was the chosen one, now. I was nobody's secret adolescent crush. I was the muse.

It was strange. But it was different, and so it was good.

— October 2018 —

I've always wondered what kinds of idols normal people have. Do bank tellers grow up dreaming of Rockefeller, do pilots long to be like Saint-Exupéry, do soldiers model themselves on . . . I don't know who. Napoleon? Robespierre? De Gaulle? At least they're usually spared the uncomfortable ordeal of facing their heroes on a daily basis. On managing the fierce emotions of their gods—who are only humans, after all.

If meeting your hero can be both a blessing and a curse, working for them is most definitely the latter.

The next day, I sat in the plushy silence of Nathalie's office for our monthly check-in. All of my anger at Margaux had been wrung out of me by the mounting anxiety. When I'd entered, Nathalie had moved past me, quick and light on her feet as ever, and taken a seat behind her desk. So much for chatting on her pristine white couch like peers. I had no choice but to sit opposite her, like a misbehaving child before the headmistress.

For a long moment, we sat in silence.

"The period after the gala, for me," Nathalie finally said, "is primarily a moment of reflection. After the celebration, after we say to the world, *This is the company. This is who we are.* And this year, in particular—the three hundred and fiftieth anniversary—is an important time for me, as artistic director, to think about a different question: *Who are we going to be?*"

She looked at me, green eyes half-closed. She clearly expected some response.

"Yes," I said.

"Over the past few days, I've thought quite a bit about the program for the 2019 to 2020 season. The dancers I will feature. Who might be worthy of being named a star. The pieces that will best show their talents."

Now, this was the way you fired somebody. The way I'd handled the conversation with Lindsay suddenly felt crude and cruel. But—I had a contract. Nathalie couldn't legally fire me.

She *could* just stop using me, though.

She could refuse to show anything I created. Meanwhile, anything I choreographed this year would belong to her, to POB, regardless of whether it ever made it to the stage.

Nathalie closed her eyes fully. "I don't think your ballet is going to work, Delphine."

So. Here it was. The moment I'd been dreading, emerging into reality. Maybe there was something to anxiety, after all. I felt oddly prepared.

I tried to channel the mindset of my first day back, the persona of the successful negotiator. If I could show her that I understood my power—if I showed that I was willing to use it—

"I fired Lindsay," I began.

"Thank you. Nevertheless. I have to say, I've not been . . . impressed with what I've seen in rehearsals."

I hadn't even known she'd been watching. Common courtesy would have demanded that she at least ask permission—or if not ask permission, let me know—or if not let me know, at least be in the fucking room instead of hovering outside, invisible—

I pushed the fury down. "But it's such early days. You know better than anyone that you can't judge a ballet based on the first few weeks of choreography!"

Nathalie opened her eyes, pressed her thin lips together.

"How much stage time would you say the Tsar gets?" she said. "Relative to the Tsarina."

This was . . . about *Claude*? She'd really threaten to cut the whole piece because I wasn't focusing enough on him?

"An equal amount," I said quickly. "He's in every scene the Tsarina is."

"Mm. And Rasputin?"

"But Nathalie, I've actually made a lot of changes. In fact, I'm working on restructuring the whole thing right now. The more I learn about Rasputin, the more I think that maybe the ballet should be about him. But we still call it *Tsarina*, you know, to show that actually she was the reason for his downfall, for his murder. I'm thinking, Greek tragedy. Hubris, the fatal flaw—" But she was wincing.

"Yes, exactly. That's why I wanted to talk to you today. For a ballet about a powerful woman," she interrupted, tapping her fingers against her thigh, "that's certainly a lot of time given over to the men."

I blinked.

"Well, the Tsarina wasn't really powerful, was she?" I said slowly. "I mean, that's the thing. That was the problem. She was trapped by all of these institutions—the monarchy, the church, even the revolution, eventually. Of course the ballet's going to feature men heavily. It has to."

It should be about how an entire society, how an entire world order, was set up to fucking erase her existence, making her into nothing more than some—defective womb.

Shut up, Margaux. I shook my head.

Nathalie was staring at me hard. *"Right,"* she said, lifting her index finger to point straight at me. "And that is why I think this is no longer the right ballet for us."

Her words poured into me, sank right to the pit of my gut. Without *Tsarina*, POB didn't need me at all. And if POB didn't need me . . . well, where the fuck else was I supposed to go?

I gripped the arm of my chair, trying to yank myself back to reality. *You can still save this. This is still salvageable.*

In fact, the more Nathalie talked, the more arguments I found for my arsenal. I could get rid of the men. Well, some of the men. I could give Camille more solos. I could make the four daughters more important— had there been a ballet about Anastasia before? Should I make a ballet about Anastasia instead—?

I was fooling myself. Nathalie hadn't called me in there to defend my case.

"Do you know why I brought you back to Paris?" she said. "I brought you because of *Medusa.*"

The one piece of mine that everyone had loved: Gorgons spinning about, paralyzing and trapping all the men who crossed them. *The start of a new kind of ballet,* the papers had raved. They'd been wrong about that. It—like apparently everything else I was capable of creating—was pure nineteenth century. Driven by narrative, based on existing stories, made pretty and decorative to be palatable to a larger audience. *Medusa* had to be that way, to be as popular as it had been. How many incredible, smaller dances get shown for a season and then never go anywhere at all? Almost all of them. Particularly those with *messages.* You cannot let yourself get put in that box, as a female choreographer. The second you do, the trap snaps shut around you and you'll never be anything else.

Medusa was the one good thing I'd ever done.

I smiled tightly. "I'm glad you enjoyed it."

She sighed and waved a hand. "Whether I enjoyed it or not is beside the point. Oh, I liked it"—seeing my face—"but I like most of your work. That's not why you're here."

I stared at her blankly.

"There are very few feminist choreographers in classical ballet at the moment," she said, twisting sideways so she was half staring out the window.

Ballet doesn't tend to produce activists; we're trained too much, too early, in this art form that is the pinnacle of traditional femininity. If you're any good at it, that means you've already bought into the system. Feminist choreographers come to dance later and flourish in different forms: modern, contemporary.

Nathalie was staring at me. "The board thought it was time for a feminist choreographer," she said. "What they—what *I'd* really like to see is something that highlights all of the amazing women in this company. At first, I'd thought that could be *Tsarina*, but—well. A series of shorts, I'm thinking now. Maybe something with people of color?"

I bit my lip in frustration.

"So do you want me to highlight *this* company, or do you want me to work with women of color?" It came out angrier than I'd intended, but come on; I could count our Black and brown dancers on one hand.

She groaned. "Fine. Point taken. It's just that after that *Vogue* spread of the male stars over the summer, it's starting to look like the men are getting all the glory. We'd like to draw the focus back where it belongs. What is the ballet, after all, if not the ballerinas?"

My phone buzzed. It was Jock.

I'm biting the bullet. Dinner Friday?

"Am I interrupting you?" she said sarcastically.

"I was interested in Christopher Rouse's music," I said, dropping my phone and turning my attention back to her. "With *Medusa*. But I'm not interested in promoting your agenda."

She turned back to me, animated once again. "I'm sure, Delphine, that we have the same agenda. Supporting women in dance. I just need a ballet from you, something that, you know—" She waved her hand. "Celebrates the female form or something."

"The female form?" I said. "Are you kidding me? There's an inherent indignity in being in a woman's body. It's an exercise in constant humiliation. I might not—" I took a deep breath. "Nathalie, I might not be what you're looking for."

Nathalie's forehead wrinkled. "Please don't let the irrelevant *whys* of the thing stop you," she said. "We still want your work. If only you could just . . . make us some nice, short feministy thing."

Off to her side, the sun had risen higher, brighter, and the windows seemed to glow.

What was I going to do, quit? I was thirty-six and I had nothing but this place.

And if I left—what would happen with Margaux and Lindsay? Leaving now would mean that our fragile friendships shattered into a thousand pieces, gone for good.

Then again, besides the ballet, what else did I have to offer them?

Everything I'd felt before leaving the first time—the disgust at the sweaty ambition, everyone else's agendas scrubbing at you until your skin started to blister—suddenly hovered around me, thick and uncomfortable.

"Delphine? Will you stay?" Nathalie said, and her voice had gone soft, even as her face twisted with having to ask. "We do want your work. We want it—very much." This last, as though it pained her.

Well, they did and they didn't. They wanted me to give them a *message*, a progressive *message*, that they could then take and sell.

I closed my eyes, took a deep breath. So, this wasn't going to be the big leap forward I'd imagined. This was just another small, incremental step toward the future that I wanted.

This was what it had to be.

I opened my eyes.

"I'm not unwilling to do something like that," I said softly.

Nathalie smiled. In the sideways light, her eyes were almost transparent, exactly like a cat's.

"Good," she said. "I thought so."

CHAPTER 16

— April 2004 —

It took me all of thirty seconds to spot Stella at the Marché d'Aligre. There was something medieval about the outdoor market, the fruit and vegetable stalls clustered around the flat central building with its Mediterranean shingles and arched windows. Something that made my Parisian soul purr.

Going there had been our Saturday afternoon routine for the first eight years of my life. When I'd joined the company and moved back home, I'd had performances on Saturdays, but Stella had shifted her shopping to Sundays so we could start the tradition again. Over the past few years, the colorful market had become my weekly refuge from the insular world of POB.

In the hot stream of people shuffling through the fruit stands, Stella's bright pink hair immediately stood out. I put a hand on her shoulder, breathlessly kissed her cheeks.

"Sorry I'm late, Stel."

She patted my hand and turned back to the tomatoes, which she gave a soft squeeze. "Slow start this morning?" She nodded at the seller, handed him a five-euro bill, waited for her change.

"I—" My cheeks flushed as she shoved a bunch into her oversize wicker bag. The market was an easy twenty-minute walk from home, and normally I'd have been up at eight to meet Stella. But though Dmitri's apartment was even closer, he'd grumbled when my alarm had gone off. Grabbed my wrist as I'd risen from bed. And then—"Yeah, I guess. Crazy traffic jam at Bastille."

"Mmm-hmm." I could feel her eyes smiling at me behind her dark glasses. "I see."

"Thanks for taking Maman to chemo yesterday, by the way. I couldn't get out of rehearsal." The radiation had been followed by a grueling schedule of chemotherapy, and the truth was that I couldn't stand the sweet smell of the chemicals oozing through my mother's veins. Or the way she sat, folding into herself in the chair as though collapsing in defeat after a battle. All those years of *lead from the sternum, darling* falling away as her spine bent in exhaustion.

Stella put a hand on my shoulder.

"It's no problem, hon. Look, I went through this with Roger, you know. It's not such an easy thing."

She'd always been able to read straight through my bullshit.

"Anyway," she said, dropping her hand and hopping to the next stall. "How were the performances this week?"

I seized on her change of subject. "Amazing. I can't *wait* for you to see it. Have you read the reviews? Dmitri is such a genius."

"Uh-huh." She rolled a fig over her palm, set it back. "And how long have you been sleeping with him?"

My heart fluttered, even as my face burned and I looked down. "*Stella.*"

Her eyebrows leapt up over the tops of the sunglasses. "You're forgetting that I've known you since you were born. And that I have forty-odd years of life experience on you. I'll tell you, Delphine, the Americans have a good expression for this precise situation. *Don't shit where you eat.*"

I winced. "Gross."

She poked at another basket of figs, lifted them to her bag. "But you take my point."

"You *know* how the ballet world is. If I didn't date there . . . well, I wouldn't date at all."

"I imagine you could if you wanted to. Have you looked in a mirror lately?" I followed her to the next stall, where clusters of green grapes glistened in the sun.

I blushed. "I really do like him, though."

"The thing about men like that, dear"—she tossed a bunch of grapes into her bag—"if you want their approval, you're never going to get it by fucking them."

"How do I get it, then?"

She gave me a small smile. "I'll let you know when I figure it out."

— *October 2018* —

I burst through the glass doors of the Opéra, out into a damp, raw autumn day. A young dancer, showing her badge to security, blinked at me, taken aback. She smiled tentatively. My expression was closer to a grimace as I exited through the gates and descended into the Métro.

The longer I sat with Nathalie's words, the more the facts started to dissolve, leaving me only with the awful, inescapable emotions like a greasy film coating my skin.

I had failed.

The single most important ballet of my career—what I'd seen as the glorious jumping-off point to the life I really wanted—was gone. It had taken five minutes to destroy. And now, what was I left with?

This was what circled through my head as I went back to my mother's apartment. *My* apartment. Shut the curtains. Curled up in bed with my laptop, sent an email to Antoine, who managed the jigsaw puzzle of the company's rehearsal schedules, canceling my sessions that day and for the foreseeable future.

And then, I closed my eyes and slept for a day and a half.

In the end, it was Stella who pulled me out of my stupor. If I missed our morning coffee—well, something could happen to her, couldn't it? She needed someone to check in on her. And if I didn't show up, she'd be here anyway, standing over me with her French press.

Still in my pajamas, I padded barefoot across the hall.

"Oh, no," Stella said the second I came in. "Delphine. What now?"

Nathalie cut my ballet. Put into words, the tragedy seemed so—banal. Unremarkable. I tried to situate it in Stella's world: *Imagine if you'd been working on a butterfly exhibition for a year and the Natural History Museum shut it down.* But it wasn't the same thing. Nathalie wasn't just saying I was a bad storyteller, she was implying that I was a bad feminist. That I was the wrong kind of woman.

"Mundane tragedies," I said.

Stella shook her head, hair like dandelion fuzz in the sun.

"No tragedy is mundane. Not while we're living it." She nodded at the chair across from her, and I sat down. In the few weeks that I'd been back, the wicker had already molded itself to my form again and I settled in, inhaling the bitter, familiar smell of Stella's coffee.

It was a long moment before she spoke again.

"Did you know that Roger and I couldn't have children?"

"Stella—no, I never knew that. Shit. I'm really sorry," I said. "Obviously, this isn't anything like that. Not even close."

Stella shrugged. "I got over the disappointment long ago. But your mother was very supportive, and I think you should know that. It's our friends who save us in times like these."

"My *mother*?" I said, shaking my head. "I find that hard to believe."

"Why do you say that?"

"She always regretted having me," I replied. "For most of my childhood, she seemed bitter. Resentful. Those aren't exactly helpful traits in a friend."

"Delphine. Your mother had a lot of reasons to be mad, but you were never one of them." Stella's words echoed funnily in my mind. They were familiar, pulling me back to a time that hurt too much to even touch.

"Do you think—did people judge you for it? Not having kids, I mean?" I said finally.

"People were very kind. Women and men both," she said, pressing her lips together. "I always thought it's because children are the one acceptable thing for a woman to want."

"Love," I said. "We can want love."

Stella shook her head. "Not too publicly. Not too much. Then we're a joke."

I let my head fall to my forearms.

"I don't think I have very many friends left right now," I said, my voice breaking into a sob. "And on top of it, I do, I want love too much. Oh—fuck it—I sound like a teenager. Shouldn't I start feeling like a fucking grown-up one of these days?"

Stella's hand slid into mine. After a second, I sat up.

"Sometimes," she said, squeezing my fingers and letting them go, "I think the real tragedy of life is that we're always the people we were, and it's only our outsides that change. And then one day we wake up to find we're the only adults left in the room—but inside, we're all just children pretending."

My throat tightened. "So what are we supposed to do?"

She smiled. "You rise to the occasion. You step up. You take responsibility for your actions, you do your best to be a force for good in the world.

And you keep close to the people who have known you through both the highs and lows of your life. They see the person you are at your core. The one you've always been."

The wind outside rose, rattling the kitchen window in its frame.

"I'm not sure I'm up to it," I said.

Her voice hardened, just slightly. "But you don't have any choice. Maybe things haven't worked out the way you thought they would, Delphine. That's part of living."

I wiped my hot cheeks with the palms of my hands. "You're right. I know. Let's change the subject. How are you feeling? Isn't your surgery coming up soon? The tenth?"

She made a face. "The fifth."

"Are you nervous?"

She twisted her mug between her palms, staring out the window at the waving tree branches.

"Darling," she said finally, "it is what it is."

I knew that tone. It was the tone Stella used when she meant, *Drop it.* When she meant, *Let's not talk about this now, maybe not ever.* When she meant, *None of your goddamn business.*

She put a hand on my arm. "Go see your friends, dear. You won't always have the chance to make up with the people who knew you when you were young."

But she didn't know my friends. And she didn't know what I'd done. Back when I was still young.

CHAPTER 17

F our months was all the time that Dmitri and I had together in Paris. One morning in early June, I stood on his balcony smoking a cigarette. Behind me, the shopkeepers were manning their crowded bookstalls along the quay, the teenagers with their cloves and their coffees were dangling their legs over the river, the Bateaux-Mouches, the tourist boats, were needling under the bridges. But my back was to Paris as Dmitri dragged his beaten, Soviet-era leather suitcase from beneath the bed and clicked its metal clasps open. I thought it made him mysterious, enigmatic, like he was a spy readying himself for a return to headquarters. It should have just made him seem old.

I stubbed my cigarette out on the wrought-iron railing and went inside, wrapping my arms around his waist.

"Don't go," I whispered, because it was the kind of thing one should say to a lover on the verge of departure. To tell the truth, it had grown exhausting having him there. Sure, our nights together were dizzying spectacles. But while he was able to sleep late, I still had to be at the Opéra at nine thirty for morning class, leaving me stumbling drunk with fatigue by the end of the day—even when there wasn't a performance in the evening.

He patted my hands, pried them off. "I have to." His verbs had gotten astonishingly better since he'd arrived. I was sure it was because of me. "Besides, you'll come to Russia soon."

I laughed. "Right." But his face darkened as he held up a finger.

"I'm serious. Come train with me at Mariinsky."

I made a face. "I get enough training here, thanks." And I wasn't about to let some crazy Russian ballet master mess up my perfect pirouettes with their "aristocratic" gestures. POB is the guardian of an important legacy: the purity of dancing. Quality, not quantity; precision, not virtuosity. I wasn't going to let him fuck it all up with his Russian flourishes.

"Not as dancer. As choreographer."

I blew out my lips. "I'm no choreographer."

"Not yet."

I grinned at his persistence. "Not at all." The last of my mother's cadre had retired from the company the year before, and though their pensions were generous, their newfound lack of structure had instilled a disturbing restlessness in them. Two had recently tried choreographing to lackluster results, and watching them, at black box theaters in the far corners of the city, had made me embarrassed on their behalf. Couldn't they see how derivative their work was? Couldn't they understand that there were so many new ways of using the same steps?

But Dmitri was shaking his head. He pointed at his eyes.

"I watch you, you know. You have talent."

I smiled, shook my head, my hair falling out of its loose bun. "No. Not really."

He grabbed my chin. "Listen. As a dancer . . . you are soloist, maybe. At best. As a choreographer? You could be anything you want."

I felt like I was falling through a deep, twisted hole. Yet I forced a laugh and pulled away. Walked him down to the cab. Kissed him goodbye. Then I sat alone in his apartment, paid up through the end of the month, watching the spring leaves tremble along the Seine.

Soloist. The best I would ever be . . . was a soloist?

At POB, everyone is always watching you. Judging you, assessing you. And yet—nobody ever actually tells you what they think.

My mother always said I had it in me, to be a star. But she had her own reasons for wanting to believe that. And hadn't I always, on some level, known she was fooling herself?

Besides, I had never wanted to coast along on my mother's legacy, I had wanted to succeed on my own merits. Yes, I was good. I was strong, and I was meticulous, and above all, I was a worker. You could put me in front of a new ballet and I'd have my part memorized in one viewing. I showed up for class every day, I was on time for every rehearsal.

But that made me a workhorse, it didn't make me a star.

Lindsay did the same things I did, but somehow you never realized it was a job for her. When she stayed in the studio after dark, there was a bright joy in her limbs, no matter how late it was or how tired she should have been.

Lindsay was a star. Not me.

I might be one of the best dancers in the world. But I would never be *the* best.

Still. It never once occurred to me to ask Dmitri what made him so certain.

— October 2018 —

I woke up in the middle of the night to find two things: I'd gotten my period, and there were a series of texts from Jock on my phone. They stuck in my throat like a challenge. Here was somebody who'd known me when I was young.

We agreed to drinks, not dinner, the following night.

We were meeting at Le Très Particulier in Montmartre, which he picked. It was a forty-minute subway ride from my apartment, with a change along the way. If he'd asked me where I wanted to go, I would have suggested the Hôtel Costes, the Bar Hemingway, the Bar Kléber. My anxiety's better when I don't have too long to change my mind while in transit. But he didn't ask.

Belly in knots, I got out of bed.

On autopilot, I put on a red satin dress with a short flared skirt, heels, eyeliner, red lipstick. It was my standard date look, one I'd adopted for the handful of failed first dates I'd attempted over the last few months in Russia.

When I was seventeen, I never could have imagined this situation: I'd been accepted into the company. I'd been promoted twice in five years. I'd quit. I'd become a choreographer. I'd moved to Russia. I'd come back. Jock had asked me out.

Jock had asked me out.

I still liked his stupid face so much.

Good things could still happen. My life could still surprise me.

As I got off of the train and stopped to reapply my lipstick, I stared at my reflection. *Get your shit together, Delphine. Do not mention* Tsarina. *Do not mention POB. Okay, you probably can't avoid that one. Mention POB as little as possible.*

As I ascended to the street, I checked my phone, only to find three missed calls from Stella. She'd left a message; I'd get to it later.

Sorry, Stella. I just can't deal with another voice in my head right now.

Jock was already at the bar when I got there, lounging in his elegant way in a red velvet corner chair. It was still early enough that the dying light shone through the greenhouse-like windows onto the black-and-white marble floor, illuminating the leafy plants all around us.

He kissed my cheeks; I was sweaty from the rambling walk up Montmartre's hills in heels. He was cool and dry.

His nose twitched as he pulled away. "You're not wearing Polo anymore."

"I haven't worn that since I was seventeen. And even then only when my mother wouldn't catch me."

"This is . . . Mademoiselle?"

"Yes," I said, blushing. "I'm probably getting too old for it, but I can't help it. I love it so much."

"I do, too."

Jock's drink arrived, smelling strongly of whiskey. Slightly surprised he'd ordered before I'd arrived, I quickly scanned the menu and ordered *l'air de panache*, with blueberry, lemon, honey, Madeira, and something called "Elixir of the Lady."

Jock smiled at me from across the table. Here. I was here with him. He'd invited me on a date. I was here with Jock Gerard, and I was finally getting what I wanted.

And then we sat there for a moment: him staring assuredly at me, me trying to think of something to say.

The waiter set down my drink.

"Nathalie cut *Tsarina*," I blurted out.

He winced. "Fuck. Seriously?"

I nodded.

"Damn," he said. "We spent a lot of time on that. She's sure?"

Those evenings in the studio, night falling over Paris as I played with his virtuosity, as I built up an entire body of dancers around him. As I sacrificed the story I had planned to tell for his dancing. *It's really good, Dolphin. It's really coming together.*

All of that, and he was worried about wasted time.

"You don't seem . . . surprised," I said instead.

He hesitated, then shrugged. "I guess I'm not. Or not particularly. It's not really Nathalie's cup of tea, is it?"

"Clearly, it's not."

"Please. Contemporary Danish choreographers with strange haircuts—that's the way to her heart."

Some nice, short feministy thing. Yeah.

"Maybe it's time to go modern," I said.

"Or Greek," he said.

"Like *Medusa*? Yeah. I know."

"Nobody choreographs for men better than you. Perseus? I'd kill to dance that role."

I rubbed my eyes. "Maybe you will. If I can't come up with anything better."

"Is it such a bad thing to have people love something you've made?" He studied my face.

"No, not at all. It's not that. It's just—do you ever feel like your best years are behind you?"

It was the inescapable thought that had been echoing in my head since the day in Nathalie's office—the big, unspeakable thing I didn't dare say out loud to anyone else.

"Dolphin, I'm a thirty-six-year-old dancer. What do you think?"

I laughed, electric jolts running from my belly down through my hips. "Fair enough."

"So, what will you do next? Or instead, rather?" he asked.

I shrugged. "Something short," I said.

His gaze fell to the table. "You don't like your drink."

"It's the coriander."

He gestured to the waiter. "Could you bring my companion—"

"A gin and tonic," I finished.

He turned back to me. "Is it . . . something of a relief? Not to have to do *Tsarina*."

"In a way, yes," I said after a moment. "Three hours is enormous. And, of course, the expectations would have been astronomical." I stopped, considering how to say the next part. *But I wanted to illustrate the illusions we have of love. I wanted to show how even your wildest expectations—the handsome prince, the fairy-tale romance—they can all come true. And they can still ruin your life.* But in what world could I have ever said those words? "Anyway, now Nathalie wants something stupid and feministy," I

said without thinking. Then my eyes went wide and I looked at him. "Shit.
I never said that, okay?"

His face didn't break from that open friendliness.

"Something feminist?"

I bit my lip. "Yeah. No roles for you, unfortunately."

Jock pried my cold, damp hands from my drink and held them again.
When he spoke, his voice was soft and gentle.

"Why don't you come over to this side of the table?"

"What?"

He smiled softly.

"Why don't you come over here?" he repeated.

My skirt had gotten twisted under me, slightly damp, and I shifted,
looking down and trying to untangle it without standing up again completely—

I frowned. "You come over here."

He smiled. Got up. Sat down far too close—no, just close enough—
and put a hand under my chin, soft and dry.

I looked up into his face. His eyes were dark and his lashes long, and
he looked down at me.

"Delphine," he said softly. And then his lips grazed mine. His hand
tightened around my jaw as I leaned into him, as he pressed his mouth
harder, harder.

He ran his tongue over the seam of my lips and I opened for him. I
reached a hand to the taut back of his neck as I bit him, gently, and he
smiled against me.

Hours later, he left me at the Métro station, although not without a
slightly imploring invitation back to his place. That pleading in his voice
satisfied something deep inside me. I wanted to draw that out, to keep him
in that state of suspended desire.

My lips felt swollen and bruised as I got on the train, the skin on my
cheeks and chin rough from his stubble. He'd pulled me back into my
body, and I was grateful.

My phone buzzed. Him: *I have to see you again.*

The train was coming out of a tunnel into an elevated position over
the city, and the sudden reception seemed like a blessing from the universe. Until I remembered Stella's voice mail.

Her tone sobered me immediately.

"Delphine, I've been waiting for you for the past hour. You're not answering your door. It took me six months to get this surgery, so I have to be going." There was a long pause and, throat tight, I checked the phone to see if the message was over. There was another thirty seconds left.

After a strange, muffled noise, there she was. "You know, I really believed you when you said you wanted to come."

I dialed her as quickly as I could. It was late. Fuck. *Fuck.* Okay, no. This could be fine. I could explain what had happened with the ballet, with Nathalie—but the excuses were tinny, even rattling around my brain.

Her phone went right to voice mail.

"Stella, it's me. Christ, I'm so sorry. I got the dates mixed up, and I've been dealing with a few crises—" Crises. What was I saying? She'd been in surgery. Alone. Because of me. The lights of Paris began to dim as we descended into another tunnel. "Stella, I'm so sorry. I'm so, so sorry. I'm going to be there for you when you get up. I'll stock up your cupboards with all of your favorite foods first thing tomorrow. I swear, whatever you need—"

The silence on the other end was deafening.

By the time I looked at my phone, saw that I'd lost service, I'd been talking to myself for a long time.

CHAPTER 18

The day of my mother's funeral, the sunshine was breaking my heart. I wanted it to be pouring rain; I wanted the heavens to open and for water to come falling out of the sky; I wanted a Greek chorus to lament.

I had nothing to wear, so Lindsay picked a black dress out of Maman's closet for me.

"I can't," I said.

"What?"

"Wear her own dress to her funeral."

Margaux opened her mouth, probably to say something horribly inappropriate, but Lindsay cut her off.

"You borrow her clothes all the time, yes?"

I nodded.

"Then once more won't make a difference."

In the end, it felt fitting. She was everywhere, after all: omnipresent in death. Photos of her dancing lined the walls of the apartment, now forever unmovable. Her legacy in the lines of my body, my face: I saw her there, now, in the curve of my neck, in the muscles of my legs. Her words, echoing always through my mind, making my brief flirtation with choreography seem like an unforgivable infidelity: *Of course you'll be a star someday, darling. You're just like me.*

Dmitri must have seen the papers, because he called and emailed several times that week. Since he had left Paris, he cropped up about as often as Jock did, once every few weeks, but he was the last person I wanted to talk to. It was because of Dmitri that I'd betrayed her, left her bedside for his bed. It was because of him that I'd considered the ultimate, final betrayal of leaving the company.

The service was at the Saint-Gervais church. Closed casket; she knew she was too skinny, by the end, for beauty, even by a ballerina's standards. It had been the last thing she'd said to me: *Close the coffin.*

I hadn't been there in years and I didn't know the priest. In the meeting a few days earlier, I'd told him to go ahead and do whatever he wanted, I didn't want to speak, and though he'd had a faintly shocked look on his face, he'd been gentle when telling me that traditionally, Catholics don't have eulogies anyway.

A traditional Catholic my mother was not, but you'd never have known it from her will. No cremation; she planned to await the resurrection in the family crypt at Père Lachaise. After the never-ending mass in the vaulted interior, we stood at the front of the church, cars whizzing by, trying to catch taxis for the interment. Other than the POB contingent and Stella, I didn't know anybody who showed up; some of them must have been the distant relations I'd been emailing all week, but I couldn't have said which ones were which. Not my father, that was for damn sure. I'd hovered over the send button for nearly an hour after writing out just one line to let him know. Every minute that he didn't write back felt like another personal attack.

Marc was there, kissing my cheeks with a quick squeeze of my shoulders. He was always so generous. Since my mother died, something had fizzled out of me in the studio. *I want to keep going—it's what she'd have wanted,* I said. I said it over and over and over, and yet something in me had died with her. I was an automaton, pulling myself through a series of poses. But ballet isn't just about positions: it's about the movements between those positions. I was dull, I was wooden, I knew it in my brain and I felt it in my body, and when Marc had insisted once again that I take a month off with pay, I'd finally agreed.

Once we were at the cemetery, it took a little while to climb up the many pathways, around the numerous graves, to get to the mausoleum some prosperous merchant of an ancestor had staked out for us centuries ago. More tourists come to Père Lachaise than any other cemetery in the world—to them, it's the place where they can find Oscar Wilde and Jim Morrison and Colette (or what's left of them, at least). A place with gently hanging trees and high, narrow stone staircases, weeping stone angels and picture-perfect death masks.

They didn't understand that it was also the place where I was burying my mother.

Finally, finally, it was over.

Stella kissed my head and asked me if I wanted to come home with her, but I didn't. I didn't want anything at the moment; it was hard to imagine wanting anything ever again.

"Tell me," I said to Lindsay and Margaux, nodding at the mausoleum, "that you'll never bury me in there."

Margaux looked shocked. "Never. All three of us will be buried in flames at sea, like Vikings."

"Sounds good to me."

We were silent for a long moment. "This way," Margaux finally said, marshaling us forward among the graves. Lindsay brought up the rear, a gentle hand on my back. So many bodies here. So many they have to dig some up to make room for the new ones. Like everything else, it depends on how much you've paid, how recently you've paid it. Even the necropolis is for rent.

Margaux stopped in front of a sculpture of a green-tinged man lying prone on a slab of marble. *Félix Faure*, I read.

"Now," she said, "do we know the story of Faure?"

"Félix Faure. He was president of the republic," Lindsay said, startling us both into staring at her. She clicked her tongue, pointing. "It says so, right there."

"Yes, he was president. But do you know how he died?"

I shook my head.

"His mistress wanted to try something new on him. Fellatio. And when she did, he was so . . ." She searched for the word.

"Blissed out?" Lindsay offered.

"Yes, okay. Blissed out, that he died right then and there."

"But—why on earth does the statue show him *in bed*?" Lindsay said. "Bad taste, if you ask me."

"I think that's the flag," Margaux said, squinting at it.

"They still didn't need to show him all . . . reclined like that."

I started laughing, so hard that then I was crying, and it was all okay.

"Do you know what I really liked about your mother?" Margaux said as my sobs began to taper off.

I shook my head.

"She never lied. She never sugarcoated anything. After our first *soutenance*, I ran into her in the hall. Did I ever tell you?"

I shook my head. She had, but I liked the story.

"And she kissed my cheeks, and we made small talk, and then she said: *They're going to promote all three of you, you know, but you don't really deserve it.*"

I laughed, my grief made bearable for a split second. "She knew the company better than anyone."

"What I always liked about her," Lindsay said meditatively, "is that she never gave us all of that bullshit about leading a balanced life." Lindsay's parents were always on her about *work-life balance,* and it was a constant source of friction. "Focus on the dancing! Get your style in place! Make sure nobody else can replace you!"

"And *do* not *get pregnant,*" Margaux added. "She always said that, too."

"Right," Lindsay said. "Do *not* get pregnant."

A heavy silence fell. Margaux avoided my eyes.

"How many men," she said finally, "do you think have died from blow jobs?"

— *October 2018* —

I came home—half-drunk and half in love, but full of burning guilt—to find Margaux sprawled out against my door.

"Marg," I said, and it came out strangled, "I'm not interested in fighting tonight, okay?"

She ran a hand through her tangled hair. "Fuck, Delphine. Neither am I." She squinted up at me in the dim hallway light, legs spread long over the checkered floor. "Look—I'm sorry about the other day at Cordial, okay? I just—could I come in?"

Margaux hadn't been to my apartment since I'd moved back to Paris. But before I'd left, she and Lindsay had gathered here regularly: after my mother died, whenever the three of us weren't on the schedule, we'd grab a couple bottles of wine and cluster around the windows, smoking and drinking and talking, endlessly talking.

"Is everything okay?" I asked. The looseness of her limbs, her unfocused vision. Clearly, everything was not okay.

Margaux's face broke into a grin as she started to giggle—a high-pitched, rolling sound that bounced off the stone walls, the marble floors, the ancient steps.

A door opened downstairs. "*Be quiet!*" hissed a voice I didn't recognize.

I bent down to grab Margaux's wrist. "Come on," I said, twisting her around as I shakily put the key in the lock and slammed my shoulder into it. She came stumbling behind me on her long legs, blinking at the apartment as I flipped the lights on.

"Huh," she said, taking in the decor. "Look who got all bougie."

I fought the instinct to drag her into my bedroom and show her the butterflies.

"The vacation rental people redid it. But Margaux, what the fuck is going on? Ever since I got back, you're like . . . yourself but not yourself. What is this? What's *happening* with you?"

She spun around. Little hairs were stuck to her face, and she looked wild-eyed in the golden glow coming in through the windows.

"It's not happening, it's already *happened*," she said. "I like a drink, Delphine. Get used to it."

She was just drunk. I started toward the kitchen. "Want some water?" I called. "Or a coffee, maybe?"

Her voice was so faint, I barely heard her. "You broke her," she said hoarsely.

Lindsay. Always Lindsay. We'd grown up, and yet here we were again: just like we'd always been. Obsessing over Lindsay. Obsessing over what we had done.

"Come on, Margaux, she kicked Camille in the *face.* She gave her a bloody nose!"

"Then change the choreography! Or were you too busy protecting your own career and your own reputation to worry about what this would do to her?"

"You do see that I can't have that shit in the studio, right? You understand that I have to draw a line somewhere before she, I don't know, throws Camille down the stairs or something?"

"Do what you promised to do when you came back. Help her get promoted," Margaux said. "Help make her a star."

I shook my head. "They won't promote her. Not under Nathalie."

"And do you know why they won't promote her?"

"Yeah. Because of her partnering," I said.

"And why is her partnering so fucked up?" Margaux stared at me, eyes wild. I shrugged. "It's because of *us.* She couldn't stand to have anybody touch her ribs after they were broken. Don't you understand? It's our fault. *We* did that."

The full force of it—the impact of our actions, the years they'd spiraled across—took a minute to hit me. How had I not seen it? Partnering relies on that touch, the man holding the woman's rib cage between his hands for spins, for lifts, for turns. For just about everything that would make you want to watch the ballet in the first place. My recent time in the studio with Lindsay flashed before my eyes: her ferocity as she danced alone, her wince and brace when Claude went to lift her. It was right there in front of me, and I hadn't seen a thing.

"But . . ." I grasped for something, anything. "We both know she wouldn't have gotten this far if it hadn't been for us, either. Right?"

Margaux rubbed her fists against her eyes like a child, smearing her eyeliner. "No, we don't know that. We were so fucking arrogant. We made that choice for her. And it's poisoning me from the inside out."

"You can't let it," I said, attempting to be cavalier. But I realized it was the wrong approach when she lifted her gaze. She looked so lost, so defeated.

After a long moment, she spoke. "I was in recovery, you know," she said.

I frowned. "When were you injured?"

Margaux blinked, focusing harder and harder on me.

"No," she said finally. "I'm an alcoholic, Delphine. Or a *functional alcoholic*, rather. That's what they say in group. Did you really need me to tell you that?"

I had, and I immediately flushed with guilt. "But . . . I haven't seen you drunk in years," I said feebly. "Not really drunk."

She looked away.

"Yeah, you have," she said. "Almost every day since you've been back. Just because you haven't noticed it doesn't mean it isn't true."

It hurt. It was fair.

"Every night," Margaux said softly, "I wake up covered in sweat. Like, soaked all the way through. There are three bars on my block alone that I can't go back to. You've been gone forever, Delphine, and yet when you ask what's happened, I don't know what to tell you. I can't even remember half of the nights from the past decade."

It was like she was telling me a story about someone else. It was awful. Everything she said was terrible. And it didn't fit in with the narrative of Margaux's life as I knew it.

"We've been trying for kids. Did you know?" She shook her head at her own words. "We didn't tell anyone—at work, can you imagine? Everyone thinks I've had these amazing vacations in Madrid, and the whole time, we're just there for the hormones, the procedures, because we can't even get them here. Anyway. I've had two miscarriages," she said, her gaze firmly on the window.

Margaux had been there for me when my mother died. When my hair was matted to my face with tears and sweat, she'd pulled it back and braided it. Brought me a wet towel for my cheeks. Made me tea. Said the sweetest little inconsequential things—*come to the window, look at the snow; wear that black jacket, it makes you look like Charlotte Gainsbourg*—that were the only words I'd wanted to hear.

I got up and wrapped my arms around her. I hadn't seen her crying, but her face was wet as she pushed it into my shoulder, sharp and soft simultaneously.

"I mean it, it's poisoning me from the inside out. And I think it's done the same for you, too. We have to tell her, Delphine. We have to tell her what we did."

I stepped back toward the window, my damp dress cooling in the air.

"Absolutely not," I said.

She was crumpled and flushed, and yet it took all of a second for the mask to descend again, for her to become hard and cold and polished. Despite the makeup still smeared down her cheeks, despite her swollen face.

"I see you," Margaux said, eyes fixed on me. "I see you all eaten up just like I am. You thought you could move home and we'd just go back to being a happy threesome, like we were before. But what we did, Delphine, it ruined everything." She paused, letting her words sink in. "There's nothing we can do to change her past, but we could still change her future."

"But what good would it do for her, apologizing? It would just be for us. How in the world would it change her *future*? And anyway, I don't think . . ." I didn't have the words; maybe I didn't understand what I thought well enough to say it. "I don't think we can keep blaming ourselves for what happened, can we? It was thirty seconds, fourteen years ago. She's made her own choices since then. Haven't we paid enough?"

Margaux shook her head. "We can pay and pay and pay. It doesn't matter how much we pay unless by paying, we fix things."

"But I don't know how to fix her," I said. And there it was: the truest, clearest thing I'd said that night, and I was surprised to find how much I meant it.

"Neither do I," Margaux said sadly. "Not really."

I grabbed her hand. "Maybe we don't focus on that for the moment. Let's focus on you. You getting better? You said you have a group? What does that mean?"

"A *support group*," Margaux said, and rolled her eyes—for a second, I saw the girl she used to be. My best friend since I was eight. "A twelve-step program."

"Can you start going back?"

She snorted. I raised my eyebrows, and she gestured wildly, running her hand up and down the length of her body.

"Like *this*?"

I winced. "I think they'd probably understand."

She closed her eyes briefly.

"Maybe," she said after a minute. "When I'm ready. Can we just go to sleep, now? I'm exhausted."

There we were: the two of us, together again. And everything was still wrong, everything was still broken. After all this time, we still hadn't gotten beyond the fact of what we'd done to Lindsay. When I left Paris, I'd thought that it would get smaller and smaller, recede beyond the horizon—and yet that night was here again. Looming large. Ever-present.

I looked at Margaux, her disarray, her despair. I was a dark mass in our triangle, the kind that appears overnight and metastasizes to everything in sight. Ever since I returned, I'd focused on fixing Lindsay's life. I had been acting like Margaux was fine, like nothing could possibly be wrong with her. Like I hadn't done anything to her, either.

"Go to bed, Delphine," Margaux said finally, closing her smudged eyes. "It's long past bedtime."

When I woke up the next day, pale light was streaming through the cracks in the curtains. It was already noon. And on my phone was a message from Stella, telling me not to come by. She didn't want to see me. It was curt; she was polite. Still, I couldn't help hearing the subtext: *maybe not ever again.*

The blanket was crumpled in a ball on the sofa, and Margaux was gone.

CHAPTER 19

— August 2004 —

Lindsay was running ahead, toward the sound of the gulls and the smell of salt on rock. Her hair fell out of its ponytail, bouncing against the small of her back, blond and half-frizzed in the humidity. The road curved sharply down, but her legs kept going, and her voice rose in a laughing war cry.

An elbow in my ribs: Margaux surged beside me.

"Move," she gasped. "She's going to win!"

But who cared? Lindsay had challenged us to the race and we'd played along; when we followed her crazy fairy-ideas, nights turned out better. She had a rough magic about her, a charm that made things just *work*. But winning didn't truly matter to me. The sun was dying on our faces, we were twenty-two years old, and our legs were fast and free as we plummeted down to the sand.

Margaux and I collapsed onto the beach seconds after Lindsay, who was already stripping down. We wore our swimsuits under our dresses. If we'd been normal girls, we'd have been wearing sandals, too, but who wants to risk it? We wore sneakers. We were bony in bikinis, but we wore them anyway, because one-pieces were too much like leotards. The undressing itself didn't faze us; it was a familiar act, down to the perfunctory dressing room looks at the others, the glancing comparison to your own body parts.

When you dance with somebody enough, you learn her body as well as your own. Perhaps even better: because while you only glimpse yourself in the mirror, stolen glances between turns and *tendus*, she's always in front of you, beside you, behind you. I still remember the curve of Lindsay's foot, how the arch was so high she could almost grasp it like a fist. If I close my eyes now, I can still count the bones on Margaux's sternum, from her clavicles down to her stomach.

Thirty seconds in the gut-chilling water was enough before we ran back out shrieking.

"Make a fire," Margaux said, her teeth bashing together as she chattered. Her dark hair was otter-sleek from the water. "We need to make a fire."

We always did what Margaux said; I think deep down, we were just too scared of her not to. You never knew what was beneath the surface with Margaux. Delight? Rage? A kind of existential pain? When she'd offered to host us at her grandmother's Normandy house for the weekend to celebrate her birthday, it hadn't taken much to convince us. Margaux said we were going, so we went. Margaux said to bring our bathing suits, so we did. Margaux said to make a fire, so we started scavenging the beach for branches.

It took us a while to find enough dry wood, towels wrapped around our goose-pimpled shoulders as we pounced around the sand. Once we had enough, Margaux crumpled up pages of the *Elle* she hadn't read yet for kindling and lit it. We watched the unseen fashions crumple and burn, and soon our faces were illuminated by the flames.

I lay back against the day-warmed sand. It was only twilight, but the stars were coming out.

"Four years," Margaux said after a long moment.

"Until—" I said.

"Not *until*, Delphine. *Since*," she said with a laugh. "Our fourth season."

Four years in the company. Nine since we'd met Lindsay, fourteen since Margaux and I had met each other. Taken as a proportion of our lives to that point, it was astonishing.

"Doesn't it seem to you," Lindsay said slowly, "that it's taking a long time to advance?"

I'd never thought about it like that before. The idea pinned me in place for a second. Were we moving fast enough? We were young; there was time. But not that much. Not forever. Four years *since*. How long *until*? We could reasonably expect another ten years onstage. Fifteen if we were extraordinarily lucky. Twenty if the hand of God reached out and touched us.

We were twenty-two, and for the first time I saw my life not as an endless series of seasons cycling around but instead as a finite resource that I was spending down, even now, as I watched the smoke spiraling upward.

Lindsay started humming the variation from *La Esmeralda*, her audition piece from the previous autumn. Then she was on her feet, and despite the unsteady ground, the darkness, her motions were perfect. Sharp, carved with a knife, and yet coy and wild at once.

Her leg flew up over the fire and hit the imaginary tambourine in her hand. Her eyes had gone bright in the flames and it was like she saw us sitting there, but she saw beyond us, too. The smoke made the air wavy, lengthened her limbs into something supernatural.

Still humming, she threw her leg up to her ear and kept it there, propelling herself forward, forward. She whipped around, hair falling over her face. She slid. She reached. She twisted her hip seductively and we laughed. It was our twenty-second summer; the sky was full of stars.

And then a gurgling cry came from the back of her throat.

Lindsay held her foot out in front of her, not pointed, not flexed. For a second, I couldn't tell what had happened. Pinching her fingers together, she plucked glass from her skin. Then the blood welled up, beading along the jagged cut down to her heel.

"Oh my God," I said.

She looked at me, blinking round, blank eyes.

"Give me my bag," she whispered.

Margaux scrambled for it and brought it with shaking hands. I swallowed as Lindsay cradled her foot.

The blood ran dark into Lindsay's footprints compressed in the sand, staining them black in the falling night.

We weren't free. That moment was enough to ruin her forever.

She reached down and clutched her foot between her hands.

How many days, weeks, months, would it be before she could dance again?

Blood tacky on her fingers, she pushed the skin together.

You spent it and then it was gone.

Her mouth puckered. I thought she trembled, but it might have been a trick of the light.

Five. Ten. Fifteen. At some point, we would run out of years.

And then what?

Crumpling to the ground, Lindsay held her bag open so that its contents tumbled out onto the beach. Sunglasses, a portable CD player, her cell phone. She grabbed a pair of pointe shoes from where they'd fallen. Her entire foot and both her hands had turned reddish black now.

They were perfectly new, the ribbons still separate, the toes still stiff. She must have meant to sew them over the weekend, because the ribbons were pinned to the back of the shoe with a needle.

Lindsay removed it. Then she took out a roll of pale pink thread and threaded it.

She held the needle in the fire until it glowed luminous red and her fingers shook pink. I stared at the sticky wet mess of her foot as she put it in her lap, feeling around for the spray bottle of alcohol and water she kept to soften the toes of her shoes. Liquid hit the wound. Her teeth shone as she grimaced.

I cried out as the needle punctured her skin; Lindsay's noise was more like an animal's.

With every yank, as she pulled the thread tight, she gave a sickened grunt from the base of her stomach. The thread turned dark as we listened to the whispery pull of it through her skin.

She didn't scream. Not once.

She was back at work two weeks later.

— *October 2018* —

I stared at the butterflies coming through my wall as the voices in my mind ran around me, jabbering until they sounded like music. *You're the worst person in the world. You're old; you are not that talented. You are awful to the people who love you. You have to manipulate men to keep them interested.*

As Monday morning dawned, the realization that I had to go back to POB crept up on me. How long can you fool yourself about the purpose of your life if you're not actually doing what defines you? An insurance salesman who doesn't sell insurance is just a man. A lifeguard away from the pool is just a person.

Dance is what I do. It was as simple, and as messed up, as that.

I went back to the ballet.

I didn't have any dancers scheduled, only a studio booked and my iPad to record the half-completed motions I was still capable of. This time, the well truly was dry. I'd spent so many months now thinking about *Tsarina* that everything else had been crowded out. What had once interested me in Greek myths? They were full of the same old characters drinking and fucking each other senseless. Where were the pieces of music that I'd once found inspiring? They were all mundane and flat now—or worse, had already been used by other, better creators to create other, better pieces.

I'd have to figure it out through trial and error. I checked the schedule to see where they'd put me, then made my way down to the end of the hall.

In the first studio I passed, Nathalie was rehearsing Jock and Camille in something classical: Nureyev, it looked like. I didn't bother to take out my earphones, and Janis Joplin wailed in my ears as I watched. Camille was all perfect flutters, Jock a gallant prince. I waited for him to look up and see me watching through the window, but he was intensely focused on his work.

The music stopped and he dropped to the floor, all of the quick exhales he'd been fighting back expanding his chest as he fought to catch his breath.

Although he'd texted right after our date, I hadn't heard a word from him since. I'd been waiting for the phone to buzz, sure he would follow up—any moment now.

He still hadn't.

But he would, I was sure of it.

I was almost sure of it.

The door of the second studio nearly hit me as Claude stomped out in a rage—or as much of a rage as he was capable of. His cheeks were flushed like a sunset, ragged pink around the edges, and his eyes were lit up from inside.

"Whoa, what's going on?" I said, pulling my earphones around my neck, suddenly the senior prefect.

"She"—he thrust his arm, pointing back to the studio—"is impossible. I come here to help her out, and what does she do? Fifty times, she must have had us repeat the same damn combination. And then when I tell her I want a break, maybe we try something else, she has the nerve to call me *lazy*."

I moved toward the window, but I already knew whom he was talking about. Lindsay.

"You're not lazy," I said half-heartedly as I watched her climb back onto her pointes, testing the strength of her shoes. They were already in that half-floppy stage, but she must have decided they were good enough to continue, because she began preparing herself for another set of pirou-ettes. "Don't let her get to you." But he was already gone, storming off down the hall.

Lindsay's face was determined as she began to turn. Single, double, tri-ple, and down. We're not ones for the showy turns at POB; better to stick a double than push for a sloppy quadruple. But Lindsay could manage a perfect triple, every time.

Now, she tried it with a different expression. All of a sudden she was eager, inviting, a fairy-tale princess. I looked around and saw the iPhone that she was using to record herself, propped against the mirror. Mean-while, Janis buzzed around my neck: *cryyyyyyyyy—baby*. She'd been my mother's favorite singer, which had never made sense to me. All that howling, that lack of restraint, when Maman was the epitome of female beauty, grace, privilege. But I could hear it, now, for the first time. How the roughness of Janis's voice was the point.

Maybe she has a lot to be mad about, Stella had said.

Again: Lindsay started the traditional preparation, but this time she put her hands on her ribs so that her elbows stuck out. Partnering herself. A double, wobbling at the end.

Oh honey, welcome back home.

Tensing her jaw, losing that benevolent Princess Diana look, she grabbed her ribs again. She made it two and three-quarters of the way around be-fore falling out of it.

Who'll take all your pain—

Her eyes were on fire as she forced herself right back into position and spun again. She didn't even make it halfway around this time before her ankle gave out.

And that was when she lost it, hair falling down in strands and stick-ing to her face as she started slapping her torso, pulling, grabbing at her camisole leotard and yanking it down around her waist. Her body was still perfect, as perfect as it had ever been, if more carved now. The same bones were there, all of her ribs in an impeccable ladder down her torso, but they looked hewn. The same muscles were there, but now they looked like they were made out of stone, like her breasts did, like they were a natural formation made by the weather.

Come on, come on, come on, come on—

And now, half-naked, she smacked one hand on either side of her ribs and spun. It was better. Not perfect. She looked free. She spun and spun and spun until I lost count of the rotations.

Then, just as she was coming out of the turn, she stopped herself and collapsed onto the floor. Chest bare, she lay on the ground faceup. These weren't the normal heavy breaths that a dancer takes after finishing a tough combination. These were jerky sobs, pulled out from her gut.

And all of a sudden, I knew what my ballet was going to be.

A small, inconvenient voice in my head wondered what was wrong with me. Somebody was suffering right in front of me—*my friend*—and the only thing that I felt was curious. I watched her, struggling for perfection, this woman who had been struggling for perfection for more than twenty years, and I was fascinated.

Because, for the first time in a long time, I saw a way out.

CHAPTER 20

— October 2004 —

The *soutenance*—the yearly audition for promotions—was in two weeks, and there was electricity running through POB. Marc hadn't yet posted how many slots there'd be at each level; most years, it was one or two per rank. This year, it was whispered that there would be three soloist spots open. It was perfect: three spots, three of us.

If, of course, that was right.

Worry about the things you can control. That's what my mother had always said. Meaning: Don't look at the other girls, only watch yourself. Meaning: Don't pay attention to who might get promoted, just do the best that *you* can. Meaning: Don't worry about who's on the jury that will determine your fate.

But I couldn't help it. Out of the constellation of authority figures in this smallest of all possible worlds, there were some who loved the three of us (Marc, the artistic director, who gave us all the plum corps roles), some who hated us (Marie-Cécile, the head of the school, who despaired at never getting us to shut up), and some who stunned us with their total indifference (Nathalie, retired star and recently returned ballet mistress, who'd taken to turning away the second she saw us coming).

Figuring out who was on the jury was like cracking a code: we couldn't know what odds we were up against until we knew who would be judging us.

"I hear Pina Bausch is going to be on the jury," I told Lindsay and Margaux as we waited for class to start. Lindsay was bent upside down, stretching out her hamstrings, while Margaux wrapped a leg behind her head.

"Don't be an idiot, she'd never come after that shit show with Marc in Berlin last spring. They said Suzanne Farrell. But that can't really be right? She's *so* NYCB," Margaux said, muffled by her thigh. "Not Paris at all."

I frowned, studying my toes. "Jock would have told me. I don't think it'll be her." Years after his departure and we were still in regular contact. If only by email. If only once a month.

"Marie-Cécile?"

"What about her?"

"She's not on the jury, is she?"

"I don't think so. That wouldn't be fair, would it?" And particularly not to Lindsay, her pet hatred ever since that first Pointe class.

"Who from the company, then?" Margaux asked, letting her leg fall back down.

"Nathalie Dorival." I tore off a bit of medical tape to wrap around my fourth toe, where a blister had started to form. I knew that one for sure; I'd overheard Marc's secretary talking about it the other day.

"What about her hot husband?" This from Lindsay, knocking her head against the wall as she tried to twist herself out of her pose.

"Louis? No way. Nathalie already pulled every string known to man to get him named star," I said. "There's no way she'd also get him on the jury. Besides, do you really think he's that hot? He wears too much eyeliner onstage."

"I think it's kind of punk. He'd be awesome in bed, don't you think?"

Margaux slapped her arm. "I do not. He's married, first of all. And second of all—you don't need a 'second of all.'"

"It must be weird," I said, not for the first time. "Knowing he owes his entire career to his wife."

Lindsay rolled her eyes. "He keeps his old apartment, you know. Just as a secret rebellion against her."

I frowned. "Why would he do that?"

"To fuck other women in, of course."

Margaux flopped onto her back. "Enough! Christ, I swear to God. I cannot have this conversation again."

That week, they posted the audition notice. The jury announcement stated that among others, our promotions would be decided by both Nathalie and Louis.

The bad news came further down.

Two soloist spots, not three.
Two spots, three of us.

~ October 2018 ~

If I wasn't who I wanted to be, if I had failed myself and others, I had the saving grace of dance. My idea glowed, a golden kernel in my mind.

This was what interested me: Janis's crazy, raw voice. The pain that hovered close to the surface. The beautiful ugliness of her wild femininity. I played around with her entire canon, pacing the studio floor, miming movements with my hands, eventually warming up and trying them myself, watching my iPad recordings with no disgust at my limited movement, only the absolute delight in discovery. *Tsarina* felt like an ex-boyfriend I was only just realizing I'd never liked that much, anyway.

I was on my fifth or sixth repetition of "Me and Bobby McGee" when I saw Jock hovering in the studio door. I froze. I knew I shouldn't be ashamed, but I was. I wasn't an actual dancer anymore; I was creating, and it felt like he'd caught me masturbating.

"Don't let me stop you," he said.

I turned the music off. "That's okay," I said. His tights and shirt were sweaty. He'd probably been rehearsing next door for hours, listening to Janis's howls through the walls.

He leaned against the door frame and crossed one leg over the other, like Steve McQueen. "I was just wondering when you'll finally let me make dinner for you."

"Oh, anytime," I said.

Jock grinned. "Tomorrow?" he said, and just when I was about to agree, he cut himself off. "No, I have rehearsal all day. Friday, then?"

"Friday, then," I said as I began to run through the insane schedule of waxing, trying on everything I owned, scheduling a blowout, and finding a pair of black tights without a run in them, all in the next two days.

And then it was Friday and I was wearing a low-cut black dress and had given up on the tights entirely. I was going to Jock's flat (*Jock's flat!* seventeen-year-old me whispered), and he was cooking me dinner.

Finally.

Jock lived in the seventh. I knew absolutely nobody else who lived in the seventh, an area filled with museums and Napoleon's tomb and wide boulevards that make me shrink a little inside. The arrondissement couldn't be more physically or spiritually different from the Marais.

Actually, something about it reminded me of St. Petersburg. The sterile, embassy-ridden beauty of the wide boulevards. The emptiness of the streets themselves. If I craned my neck a little, I could see the Eiffel Tower down a side street—and I could sympathize, for the first time, with the people of my great-grandparents' generation who'd thought it such an eyesore. The twisted metal tower poking its way up through all of this cool elegance just seemed . . . wrong.

He had to have inherited the flat, I thought as I entered the lobby, glancing at myself in the gilt-trimmed mirror above the rich Turkish carpet. POB paid well, but not that well. In the elevator, I frantically ruffled my hair, trying to give it some volume. I appraised my reflection once again; tried to pretend I was even remotely ready for him to see me naked.

And then the elevator shuddered to a halt. I was at Jock's apartment. I was stepping into my real life, the life I'd always wanted: it had been waiting for me in Paris the whole time. I could take what I wanted.

I took a deep breath and rang his buzzer.

He wore a crisp white shirt and dark jeans and smelled like he'd just come out of the shower. His smiling face was open and wide and any nervousness I felt started to fall away as he kissed my cheeks, then thought better of it and met my lips.

"Hi," I said softly after a minute, pulling away.

"Hi."

"What's for dinner?"

His dimple showed as he took my hand, taking me down the hall and into an enormous white kitchen. "Angel-hair pasta with scallops. I hope you eat seafood."

My mouth watered at the smell of the peppery sauce. How long had he spent cooking this for me? When was the last time someone had cooked for me? Nobody since Dmitri—and I'd always secretly hated Russian food.

Jock turned the dial on the stove up, the boiling water rising with it as he stirred.

"I can't believe you've never been over here before," he said.

"I can't believe you cook. No, I can't believe you eat pasta. There's a lot that I'm having a hard time believing, to tell the truth."

Jock set the spoon down and put his hands around my waist.

"Me, too."

This was right, I thought as his lips met mine. We'd finally gotten to a point where the past didn't matter, where it was just the two of us. Where we could be open with each other about what we wanted and what we were willing to give.

He pulled me against the wall, his face warm and his hair still slightly wet. And then his mouth was grazing my collarbone as he tugged the zipper of my dress down and it slid to an inelegant heap on the floor. He made a noise deep in the back of his throat and I was dizzy, trying not to audibly gasp as he stood up to his full height, hands gently resting on my hips.

"Come with me," he said softly into my ear, turning to remove the pot from the stove. Wearing only my lingerie and heels, I was glad I'd forgone the tights as he took my wrist and pulled me slowly through the hallway into his bedroom.

Then I was unbuttoning his shirt, unable to stop myself from running fingers over the sparse hair on his chest, over his soft skin and hard muscles. He leaned in to kiss me hungrily, and his shirt came off altogether, and I could feel his eagerness through his jeans.

Somehow seconds later, my bra and underwear were off and his mouth was traveling down over my skin, teeth brushing lightly over my nipple as I arched up to meet him. I grabbed him and twisted him over so that I was on top of him. I kissed him long and deep as, with one hand, I popped open the top button of his jeans; his erection was so forceful that the zipper slid down almost on its own. I ran a finger down the length of him, smiling as he twitched, then groaned as I covered the head of it with a firm fist.

"Just how fast do you want me to come?" he said, and then I was on my back and he was moving down my body again, this time with intention. He slid a hand down my leg and I wrapped them around his shoulders as he put his mouth to me.

How American of him.

I could feel him grinning as I moaned, as I moved my hips against him. Perhaps too much, because after a minute he set a hand on either hip, pinning me down. I didn't like that—or rather, I did, definitely too much this time—and pulled one of his hands up to my breast before entwining mine in his hair. His grasp tightened around my nipple, just as he slid a finger of the other hand deep inside me and his lips sucked gently on those nerves at the apex of my thighs—

The room shattered and I cried out, not caring how hard I was yanking his hair. I rode it as it pulsed out over me, gasping and whimpering at the same time.

He came up smiling and I grabbed him and pulled him on top of me. "Do you have a condom?" I whispered.

A faintly annoyed look that I'd have picked apart at any other time crossed his face. "Sorry," he said.

I'd been running the cost-benefit analysis on this type of shit for seventeen years, and if it had been anybody but Jock, that might have been it. But it was Jock, and I'd had a new IUD put in only a few months ago, and (I think this was the most important factor) I was still seeing spots and stars, blinking up at him light-headed.

His breathing shortened. I felt him nudge at me, but I was ready. More than ready. I wrapped my legs around him and took the length of him inside me and he made a noise that was half moan, half choke.

We moved perfectly together. We would have made a great pairing onstage. Except for the panting. I couldn't help the panting; I couldn't quite catch my breath, and it came shorter and shorter as he shifted more weight onto me, as his leg came up beside me and he went even deeper.

Together, I thought vaguely. Here we were, about to come together.

I tightened my muscles around him, watching with half-closed eyes as the wave of pleasure riding through me rode through him, too.

"Oh, fuck," he was saying. "Oh—*fuck*—"

I pushed him off me.

"What's that?" I said.

That was a blinking laptop screen across from us, reflected in one of the room's several mirrors. I hadn't had the chance to evaluate my surroundings on the way in, but it had definitely been dark before. And as some unlucky caller's number flashed on the upper-right-hand side of the screen (idiot—he should never have linked his devices), there I was. Illuminated. An entire video screen full of me naked, approaching the camera, every crease and wrinkle exposed.

"What," I said again, voice shaking as I ran over to it, "is this."

Jock had scrambled onto his knees, his hair flopping over his forehead in what thirty seconds before had been a charming way.

"I don't know," he said tentatively. "I don't know, is it some kind of malware or—"

"No," I said, and a strange calm came over me. I couldn't process what it was, but I knew what it wasn't. It wasn't that. I pressed the record button to stop it, then scrolled back to the start.

What shocked me the most, later, was how much I wanted to watch.

Jock's torso appeared on the screen, somehow more threatening with his head cut off by the camera. I pulled the scroll forward. There I was, now, looking somehow stronger and weaker than I'd ever felt. There he was, against me. In single, frozen images as I scrolled, I watched him slide my underwear down and felt myself become slick, hungry again, even as the back of my mouth watered like I was going to vomit.

"What . . . what do you even do with this?" I couldn't look at his face.

His voice was enough to break me, tender and scared. "I don't—Dolphin. Don't do this."

I let go of the cursor, inadvertently freezing the image of him crawling on top of me. I tried to speak, but my jaw wobbled and I broke.

Then I was crying. Fierce, jagged sobs that ripped through me. Ugly crying. The kind you only ever do in front of other girls.

"Oh, come on," he said, wrapping his arm around me. "No. Don't cry. Calm down. Please don't cry."

For one last moment, I let his arms wrap around me, somehow shutting away the fact that he was both the cause and the comfort in this whole mess as I leaned against his warmth, his solidness, his spicy smell.

His arms tightened. I pulled away.

"I'm not—" I said, looking around for something to wipe my face with. The duvet seemed too undignified, and I settled for the edge of my bra. The tears stuck in its lace, spreading it over my face. I stared at it in frustration.

"You are."

"I'm not—" But I couldn't say what I wasn't. I wasn't crying because I was sad. I was crying because it was so much; it was too much; it was so different from what I'd thought it would be. Pushing my palms over my cheeks to get rid of the tears, I couldn't look at him. I could only look at that image of him. On top of me, inside of me. All around me; I was drowning in him. I reached over to minimize it.

Anne. Alexis. Camille.

"Play" icons next to each, the names in white popping out against the black of the folder.

Christine. Danielle.

The names jumped out at me before I could make any sense of them. He moved cat-fast to slam the screen shut. Not fast enough.

"Those are company members," I said. The blood had rushed to my face, my body processing before my brain did.

He swallowed.

"It's not what you think," he offered.

"What I think is—what do you even do with these? Does someone *pay* you for them? Are you posting them online?" I stopped. Everything hurt. It hurt like a feverish ache, like a sunburn, like an IV drip of acid. I couldn't stand to be in my body anymore; I wanted out.

Jock went pale. "I—they're for me! They're only for me."

"You've been filming—*everyone*."

"Okay, okay," he said, holding his palms up. "I wanted—" Bashful smile. "I wanted to be able to watch us again. Later." He tilted his head. "Can you blame me?"

I could still feel the echoes of him inside me.

"There's no Anne in the company," I said.

And he had the grace—can I even say that?—the *grace* to blush.

"I—Oh, fuck. Fuck, Jock! She's in the *school*?"

He sucked the inside of his cheek.

"Delphine," he said finally, "why don't you say what's really upsetting you?"

If I was somebody else—but no. I didn't have the words.

"You've made us into—into *things*," was the best I could do.

He looked vaguely pitying. "The feminist card? You know, Dolphin, just because you've got a handful of daddy issues . . ." I realized that we were standing there naked. My dress was still in the living room; I grabbed his shirt from the ground and wrapped it around me.

"Oh, *fuck* that. This is—it's so much more than that." I didn't know where to start. It was the videos, it was the number of them, it was being thrown in with everyone else, it was my specialness dissolving all over his bedroom floor.

He opened his mouth, but I had to say it.

"They're—they're *girls*, Jock."

He shrugged, smirking, Steve McQueen once again. "I can't help what I'm attracted to."

I stumbled, grasping on to the edge of the desk. It was like he'd pushed me back by the collarbones. Everything he was saying, everything he didn't have to say. I was old, and I was bitter, and the sex kitten I'd thought myself a few minutes before had just been . . . some disgusting bag, pretending.

Fuck that.

And then: "The age of consent is fifteen." He had the gall to say that. To my face.

I flew at him. I wanted to flay him alive. I wanted to literally peel off his skin. But unlike male dancers, who'd been trained in stage combat and had had actual fights with each other, I'd never hit anybody before. I only got a good thump in on his collarbone, hurting my hand far more than I hurt him, before he'd grabbed my wrists and held me back.

My heart was racing, my hair in my face, as I twisted out of his grip. He gave a snort of amusement.

"You think you sound like James Bond," I said breathlessly, pulling away, "but you actually sound like Humbert Humbert."

"Who?" he said coolly, towering over me.

"You realize that when I left the company, those girls were infants," I said.

"I don't see what that has to do with me," he said. "I'm really sorry, but I don't."

He was bigger than me; he was more experienced than me; he believed he was smarter than me. But there was something deeper than that, too, something else that gave him that cool confidence.

There was no way out of this that had me winning.

And meanwhile, there was *me*, the file of *me*, the video of *me*, on his computer, his own personal pornography, nothing more. Nothing less. Nothing else.

"If the board of directors found out—if Nathalie found out—" I stuttered.

His eyebrows went up. "What makes you so sure they'd do anything at all?"

With a spike of adrenaline, I grabbed the computer. He echoed my movement, grabbing at me, but I was still faster than he was as I ran out of the room, heart beating in my temples, his shirt still wrapped around my body.

"What do you think you're—" he called as he ran after me. Somewhere in the middle of the hallway, he grabbed me around my hips. I kicked out at him, crushing my toes against his shin. Why had nobody ever taught me how to get *away*? Balls. You were supposed to hit them in the balls. But how could I do that with his body pressed directly up against mine, no space between us, his erection flush against my back—his *erection?*—and his arms wrapped around my ribs, pulling me back into him, surrounding me with him, him, him.

I shot an elbow back and up, half by accident, and caught him in the eye.

"Fuck," he muttered, stumbling back. At the same moment I fell forward, dropping the laptop down in front of me. I was so intent on trying to catch it that I failed to catch myself and ended up falling down hard onto my knees, skin smacking painfully against the ground like a full-body slap.

Jock grabbed the computer from where it had fallen. Standing over me, he watched me with dark eyes, the scent of stale sweat coming in waves. And I saw the rage rising in him; I saw it rising in him the same way it had in me. I backed into the living room, his footsteps following after a moment, slippery on the wooden floor.

And then, clothes in my arms, shoes in my hands, Jock's shirt still around my shoulders, I ran out the front door.

CHAPTER 21

Y ou think that once you've gotten into the company, you've made it. It's all over: the struggle and the suffering, the longing and the dreams. Part of it is just the way we treat life, like there's this dividing line between childhood and adulthood that we'll arrive at, pass through. But you never do cross over, because it doesn't actually exist.

Officially entering the company was the greatest achievement of my life—I'd done it. Alone among our classmates, Margaux, Lindsay, and I had realized our dream. Our peers had to put themselves through the grueling, dispiriting process of auditioning for other, lesser countries throughout France and Europe. But after all of that—then I was just *there*, in the company, and I had the lowest-possible rank.

There's always another hoop to jump through, another step to climb. When I was a student, I'd thought I wouldn't care, that just being part of POB would be enough.

Of course it wasn't. I wanted to be the best. So did Lindsay. So did Margaux. We'd been lucky enough to all join the company together. We'd have been idiots to think the universe would keep opening up opportunities like that, three at a time, right up to the very top. What, were we all going to be stars together one day? Unlikely.

We kept going.

The three of us had been bumped up to the corps, as *coryphées*, after our first year. We were happy but not particularly surprised, despite what we pretended to everyone except ourselves. That's right, I remember thinking. This is what's supposed to happen. But then our progress slowed, like somebody had accidentally hit pause on our lives. Each year, there were a few soloist spots open. Each year, they went to other people. Dancers who had been in the company longer; dancers who had paid their dues. That first year, I ranked sixth on the wait list, then fourth, then second; Margaux and Lindsay progressed similarly.

We didn't understand what was happening. It was our turn.

And then that year, the year we were twenty-two, there were two soloist spots open. Three of us. Two spots.

And we couldn't imagine anyone else getting them. We'd been so close to promotion these past few years; everyone better than us had already been moved up.

It was our *turn*.

Well. It was the turn for two of us.

"Here's what has to happen," Lindsay kept saying. "No matter who gets picked, we won't be mad about it."

But she was saying that only because she thought she'd be chosen. I knew—and I know Margaux did, too—that whoever was left out was going to be devastated, as well as gloriously, incandescently, furious.

"Definitely." We nodded. "Of course, we'll all be happy for each other. No matter who gets it."

It was easy to say. It was harder to believe.

Harder for me to believe, anyway.

If the jury had any sense at all, of course they'd pick Lindsay.

Sure, we all had our separate strengths. The few solos we'd had were vastly different—Margaux was always cast in the classical pieces, I was in the contemporary ones, Lindsay was in anything that required character work. But that was just *difference*. That wasn't *better or worse*.

But the way all eyes went to Lindsay the second she took the stage? Her intense dancing that made the rest of us look like automatons in comparison?

That was something else altogether.

That was genius.

Lindsay was exactly the kind of dancer who should be promoted to a position where she'd be alone onstage, the center of everyone's attention. She already *was* that dancer—I was sure it was only her foreignness, her stubborn refusal to adhere to POB's etiquette, that had been holding her back.

And then, one day that October, we were sitting on the roof of the Opéra building, looking out over the gray mansard roofs and monuments of Paris under a bright blue sky.

"Corps members," Lindsay said. "We all dance the same, right? Like it's good that we all dance the same. We're really . . ."

"Uniform!" Margaux said. She loved finding English words when Lindsay couldn't.

"Right, uniform. But the whole point of a soloist is to do something not everyone can do."

"Sure," I said.

"And uniqueness only gets more important from there. Like the principals—you could put sacks over their heads and we'd still know who each one was just by the way that she danced. And to be a star, you have to be totally different."

"Well, special," Margaux said.

"Right," Lindsay said firmly. "You have to do things—that no one else can do."

"Lindsay, what are you thinking?" I asked.

"Men *like* me," Lindsay said. "A lot."

I snorted. I couldn't help it.

"So, you're going to . . . what, get up there and fuck someone?"

Margaux shrugged. "She could always just audition naked."

Lindsay laughed along with us, but her eyes narrowed as it tapered off.

"No," Lindsay said, an unfamiliar tone in her voice. "I was thinking of sleeping with Louis."

My eyes went straight to Margaux's. Both of our faces had gone slack. Lindsay wanted to sleep with one of the jury members, with the company's newest star? She wanted to humiliate Nathalie? Because it would come out—it was POB, of *course* it would come out. She would risk all of that for a slightly better shot at the promotion?

"Linds," I said, "you wouldn't."

It wasn't a real question, though. She made a face at me.

"You can't," Margaux said.

Lindsay shook her curls. "Look at it this way. Nobody likes Nathalie. Or at least, we can all agree she's a bit of a bitch. So even if she finds out, nobody's going to care or rush to her defense. And in the meantime, it's easy enough—I'll just chat him up a little. Get him to invite me to that apartment he keeps on the side."

I shuddered.

"I really don't think you should risk it," I said. "It doesn't seem—fair, somehow. And besides, who's to say he wouldn't just sleep with you and then not vote for you, anyway?"

Lindsay shook her head slowly. "He'd vote for me."

Margaux and I briefly exchanged glances.

"Linds," Margaux said, her accent thickening, "you know that he messes around with a lot of the girls, right? Last year, Adrienne tried to report him to Marc for sexual harassment. And Louis just said she was a liar he'd rejected when *she* tried to use *him* to get ahead."

Lindsay blinked at her, wide-eyed. Her Bambi impression.

"Yeah, I know," she said. "That's why it's perfect! Because I know he'll be open to it. And besides, I'd never be dumb enough to report him. Anyway"—she scooted back until she was face-to-face with us on the rampart—"it seems to me that you have to risk something to get something. Playing it safe gets you nowhere."

Before either one of us could say anything else, she'd hopped to her feet. "Sun's gone. I'm freezing. Let's go."

Lindsay trotted down the stairs, always first, always running ahead. I felt a hand on my shoulder and I turned back, wind in my eyes, to squint at Margaux.

And in Margaux's face, I saw everything that was inside me: Worry about Lindsay, yes. But also annoyance at her plan, which would propel her ahead, leaving one of us behind. Pain at her cavalier disregard for other people's feelings: Nathalie's, Margaux's, mine. Disbelief at the sheer gall she'd shown in even telling us.

More than disbelief: fury. Lindsay should have learned to hide that naked ambition long ago. We could have seen it as a compliment—that she felt she could tell us anything, even when her plans directly threatened us. But Lindsay was never deliberate enough for that. She just hadn't learned the code.

"We cannot let her do this," Margaux said.

— *October 2018* —

The lights were off in the hallway, and I sprinted to the floor below, tripping on the last stone step. I had to calm down. If I kept going like this, I'd kill myself, and then where would we be?

Maybe Jock would get blamed for it. That would be justice, at least.

Well, for him. Not for me.

I dressed with shaking hands, slid my shoes on, and left his shirt draped over the banister.

I paced in front of Jock's building, waiting for my Uber. The car was five minutes away—now six—now it appeared to be hovering indefinitely over the Seine. My phone pinged with a message. Jock.

Dolphin.

It was just my name. No need for the needles of terror shooting through my blood; it was just my name.

But the thing was, it wasn't my name.

Then the phone starting ringing. For a moment, all I could do was stare at the letters running across the screen, insisting on themselves. *Jock. Jock. Jock.*

I had to get out of there. My hands were still shaking as I canceled the car and started walking.

As I made my way through the crowds lining the riverbanks in the Paris night, all I could feel were eyes on my skin. We were in the grasslands and I was an antelope surrounded by lions. We were at the circus and I was a bear stumbling around in an approximation of a dance. We were in the theater—

I rubbed my eyes, then yanked my hands away. I couldn't smear my mascara any further, couldn't erase my eyeliner into oblivion. My mother's voice in my head, still: *Being presentable when you go outside is a public service.*

I saw myself as if from above: the disheveled hair, the wild eyes, the makeup running down my face.

Once, I would have made Margaux and Lindsay come over for an emergency coven meeting—that's what we'd jokingly called them, those late nights with the three of us poring over recent heartbreak. But it seemed to me that I couldn't ask anything of Lindsay right now; and whatever had gone so disastrously wrong with my own life, it paled in comparison with what was happening in Margaux's.

Another text. Hands shaking, I grabbed my phone. I couldn't stop myself from looking, even though I knew nothing good was waiting for me there.

Delphine. Call me.

I couldn't believe I was here again.

Again, Jock had seduced me. Again, he'd hurt me. Again, I'd found myself trapped in a back-and-forth with this same group of people, in this same world. It was so small, so circular, we might as well have been horses pinned in place on that carousel I had once loved.

I'd thought that I'd escaped our shared history by moving to Russia. I thought that I'd separated myself from the ghosts of my past. And yet here we were, pulling apart and coming back together in infinite variations, like a kaleidoscope, a courtly dance that never ended.

Staring out at the bobbing lights on the river, my eyes started to tear up again. I couldn't have the things that the world outside of dance offered because I'd committed to ballet. And it was a lifelong commitment, though I hadn't known it at the time. It had changed the way I saw, the way I felt, the way I moved through the world.

I could never tell a therapist; therapists with their graduate degrees and their theories of attachment could never understand what drove us, who we were. I couldn't tell Stella, even if she were speaking to me, which she still wasn't. The only person I could have told would have been my mother. I was starting to see her anger differently now. Yes, she had been mad all the time. She'd never been able to escape, either. The standards she'd learned and the judgments she'd internalized at POB, the irrevocable choices she had made, had followed her for her entire life.

Again, my phone. I declined the call, then turned off the volume. I didn't have to subject myself to any more of this tonight.

But before I could drop it back into my bag, another message flashed on the screen.

If you want to be a child about this, fine. But I really think it would be in your best interest to just get over it.

And then a video message came through, making me stumble back against the side of the Pont des Arts, a low moan coming from my chest.

I didn't have to play it to know that it was the two of us.

The night, the lights, the river, the bridge: everything condensed around me, whooshing into the space immediately surrounding my phone.

He was telling me to tread carefully. To behave myself. To keep quiet, because he had this. I'd always have to do what he said, because he would *always* have this. I could ruin him with the knowledge of what I'd seen on that laptop. But he could ruin me, too.

As I clutched the railing, my entire body felt twisted upon itself, contorted around what he'd done, what he was capable of. For the moment, he'd gone silent, and all I could do was picture him in his flat, smugly imagining my terror as I watched the footage, as I realized what he was saying by sending it.

Could I bring myself to block his number? Even as I woodenly went into my contacts, I was terrified of accidentally calling him, tapping his name so gently that the info didn't even open the first time.

I couldn't do it.

If he was going to do something awful, I had to know. If he was going to blow up my life, I had to be forewarned.

What if I did as he suggested, if I just forced myself to *get over it*? If I didn't take this knowledge to anyone else. My life could stay the same as it had always been. I took a deep breath and tried to feel the relief of that possibility.

Nothing came.

No matter what, I couldn't go back to what I'd felt a few hours ago. I couldn't have even a cordial relationship with Jock. Seeing him every day at the theater? Knowing he had this power over me, the power to expose me in my most vulnerable, intimate moments—to reveal how my body looked and moved and *sounded*—to the entire world?

I had to see Margaux and Lindsay. No matter what I'd done to them, no matter what they were going through. They were still the only ones I could trust.

My heel caught in the wooden planks of the bridge. I pulled it out and sat down, the only single person amid pairs of lovers gazing at the lights of Notre-Dame.

If anyone could understand, it would be them.

Jock emergency. Come over?

Four words. That's all it took. And they were waiting for me when I got home.

When I finished telling them what happened, I took a deep breath. "What do I do?" They stared at me, wide-eyed. "I'm serious, guys."

"Are you kidding?" Lindsay said.

"Seriously," Margaux said.

"You can't do anything," Lindsay said at the same moment Margaux said:

"You have to tell Nathalie."

They stared at each other blankly for a second before Margaux grabbed my phone. "Pass code?" I told her; she clicked around for a minute. The sound of screenshotting, then an email sending.

My mouth fell open.

"Marg, you *didn't*," Lindsay whispered.

Margaux glared at us.

"Oh, calm down," she said. "I just emailed the video to myself. That way, no matter what Delphine decides now or next week or fifty years from now, she'll always be able to get it if she wants it."

I closed my eyes.

"Delphine," Lindsay said, "you cannot do anything. If that video got out—"

"But if she doesn't, how many more women is he going to do this to?" Margaux cried before I could say anything. "She can't just let him get away with this—" She cut herself off in frustration. "*Shit* isn't even a good enough word for it! I don't even *have* a word for it!"

They kept debating, but I'd already thought of every possible argument. There was nothing I could do that wouldn't hurt me at least as much as it hurt him. And yet I owed it to everyone, including myself, to report him, to show the world—or our world, at least—the kind of person that he really was. You could go around spiraling like that for years and never come to a conclusion.

Except.

"You guys," I said softly.

They didn't hear me, their voices still competing with each other. Lindsay's soft but insistent, Margaux's sharp and cutting.

"You guys!" I said louder.

They turned to me.

"I'm remembering something," I said slowly. "I couldn't quite piece it together before. When Nathalie cut *Tsarina*, she kept going on and on about how she'd brought me here because she needed a *feminist* choreographer."

I waited for their reaction. But Lindsay just tilted her head, while Margaux squinted at me.

"Choreographers have to fight to get commissions," I said. "Think about how crowded the field is already. It's full of people like me, retired dancers, not to mention all the people who came to it early as their primary profession. So, we're all out there, competing for the same limited number of jobs. There's no money in feminist ballet. None. Who actually *needs* a feminist choreographer? Who would rather have a 'short feminist work' instead of something bigger and more commercial?"

Margaux got it before Lindsay did.

"Someone who needs to cover something up," she said, face flushing with anger.

"Yeah," I said. "Someone who knows they have the possibility of a scandal on their hands."

Nathalie. Nathalie already knew. And she'd done nothing.

We were silent for a minute, the realization pulsing through us. It was like learning that Lindsay was a terrible partner: something that I didn't want to hear, that felt like a physical blow to the chest, and yet also something that didn't surprise me in the least. Every institution that employs young women inevitably places those young women at the bottom of the ladder. And every artistic institution deals with people whose outsize ambitions and egos mean they will do anything to get ahead. I'd watched all the Me Too scandals unfold—Weinstein, Cosby, Louis C.K.—with confusion at the shock everyone else had espoused. There was nothing shocking about the ritual degradation of young women.

When Peter Martins had left NYCB among allegations of abusive behavior earlier that year, it had hurt like a dull ache. The golden boy, the beautiful dancer, the carrier of Balanchine's legacy. In the end, he'd been just like the rest of them. POB, though—that was more than an ache; that was a gut punch. Even there, where women both reigned and served, somebody had turned the tables. Twisted the rules against us.

No matter how long we mulled it over, no reasonable explanation presented itself for why Nathalie hadn't done anything about Jock. We were missing something, and we didn't know what we didn't know.

What we *did* know was this: I couldn't go to Nathalie. I probably couldn't even go to the board—after all, they could have been who decided to hire me, to hedge against the possibility that what Jock was doing would come to light.

In the end, we determined, I was left with the newspapers. And even though you could usually count on France's press for nice strong outrage on behalf of its women, there was still, and always, that video. The video I'd have to assume he'd post somewhere. The video I'd have to assume the world could see. That was what paralyzed me. It was the papers or nothing at all, and I had no idea what to choose.

I had to let other people know—but was it really the right thing to do if I ruined myself in the process? And what would I be ruining exactly? My career? My reputation?

My contract with POB was watertight, but as my conversation with Nathalie had reminded me, it didn't guarantee that the company would perform anything I created. If push came to shove, they'd be more likely to keep paying me without actually mounting any of my ballets, while still owning anything I created this year as their intellectual property.

A deeper realization burned like an ember in my stomach. I thought

I'd been invited here to make my name, to show the world what I could do. Only, I hadn't. Not really. I was just there as an insurance policy—all so they could hedge against Jock's bad behavior becoming public.

It was all for Jock.

Back and forth Lindsay and Margaux went. The more they talked about Nathalie and Jock and the video and my contract, the more I knew that even if they loved me, even if they knew me better than anyone, they could never understand what I was feeling.

Jock was part of the company, and I wasn't. Right or wrong, I'd be easier to get rid of than he would.

And this was still their world. Lindsay embraced it, Margaux hated it, but nevertheless, there they were.

And I was on both the outside and the inside, simultaneously, forever.

Lindsay left around three, Margaux slightly after. She always had to have the last word. This time, it was: "You're the only one who can give him what he deserves."

What he deserves. It echoed around the apartment as she closed the door. What did he deserve? What did *I* deserve?

My fury at him was unchained, knocking the wind out of me with every other breath. I was hurt, yes. I'd thought I was special, yes. But there was something beyond that. Something to do with the jealous guarding of us on his hard drive; something about being amalgamated with all of those other women into one unknowing harem. The possibility of being exposed as *the same* to the world.

Part of me, the part that had attended Catholic mass for the first eight years of my life, suspected that this was my punishment. Not for premarital sex; I wasn't Catholic enough for that. But I'd done bad things. I'd hurt people close to me. And then I'd left them all behind.

The only element of Catholicism that had ever really resonated with me was confession. And while there were things I was certain I could never say, not to anybody, the sacrament existed for a reason. Telling was good for the soul; I believed that. Apologizing was even better.

There were amends to be made, and I could make them.

CHAPTER 22

— October 2004 —

It took about thirty seconds for Lindsay to get Louis to ask her out.

That night, Margaux and I sat awake for hours, trying to think of how to stop her. The most obvious thing, I thought, was just to talk to her, but Margaux told me to grow up.

"Have you ever," she said, "and I mean *ever*, seen Lindsay take a piece of advice that she didn't already want to take?"

"No," I said, and slouched down on the sofa. Every time I closed my eyes, all I could see was Lindsay lying in bed next to him.

"Push her down some stairs?" Margaux said.

"You're joking." She wasn't. "We don't want to *murder* her."

She showed a rueful dimple. "Most days, we don't. But I swear to God, listening to her chirp on the other day about how *easy* this was all going to be, about how one of those spots was definitely hers—"

"Tell Nathalie!" I cried. Margaux made a frustrated sound from the back of her throat. "I mean, if anyone could stop him—"

"Nathalie's on the jury, too. We tell on Lindsay and Louis will say we've made it all up. We'll ruin Lindsay's chances completely—not to mention our own."

"When did she say she's meeting him?"

I checked my phone. "Wednesday. The night before the second audition. Wait, though. What about something that would make her cancel? Something that would make her *have* to stand him up?"

Margaux's eyes cleared. She sat up, nodding. "Something like ipecac," she said.

It was a syrup that had been popular among the bulimics in our group for a while: an emetic. You couldn't do anything for a good hour after you'd had it, and you felt like hell for longer.

"We could control the timing—"

"It'll be just long enough to keep her out of his apartment, but not long enough to keep her out of the audition—" We were talking over each other; the idea was burning bright between us.

"She'll be fine like two hours later," Margaux finished.

We stopped, looking at each other, waiting for an objection to come up. There were plenty to make, but nothing that was as bad as what she'd planned. Nothing that had the potential to seriously hurt her, her career, her reputation. Nothing that would take either of us out of the running for those spots.

The longer we sat there, the more it seemed like the only choice we could possibly make.

— *October 2018* —

The next morning, a painfully bright Saturday, I made my way across the river to the Hôpital Cochin. The hospital is located on its own strange little campus, full of multicolored landscaping and an unsettling mixture of nineteenth-century public buildings and brutalist architecture that always makes me think of *1984*. I had a bag over my shoulder with a bottle of prosecco, a bouquet of daylilies, and the chewy Swedish marshmallows that Stella liked.

I traced my way through the convoluted map they'd given me at the gate. I thought: For once I've made the right choice. For once I'm doing the right thing.

Stella is wise. Stella will know what to do. Stella will help me figure this mess out.

She was asleep when I got to her room. It was a double room, but the bed closest to the door was unmade, plastic covering stretched taut and shiny in the sun. My mother's stomach cancer hadn't afforded her the same luxury; she'd had a series of roommates rotating in and out, all with their own disgusting complaints, new family members to avoid, annoying television shows to tune out. But always the same smells.

I took a deep breath, feeling the oxygen buzz through my hands and feet. I could be here. I could do this.

The light streamed directly onto Stella's face. It was hot in there, too hot. I walked over and shut the bright blue curtain, frowning at its cheerfulness.

"Delphine?" she whispered, blinking in the sudden dark. I glanced dubiously at the enormous bandage wrapped around her hip. Pinpricks of blood were coming through the gauze, and the impulse to press the call button twitched through my fingers.

"Stella!" I pulled the institutional armchair over to the side of her bed. "Look at you!"

She pressed her colorless lips together.

"Delphine," she said, "I told you not to come."

"I know!" I said. My voice had risen, absurdly chipper. "I know, but I just brought you a few things, and I had to—I had to. Well. How are you feeling?"

Stella looked at me for a long moment. "I've been better," she finally said.

"No, of course, of course. I brought over some prosecco, do you want some?"

She looked away. "I'm not sure it's such a good idea with the drugs."

How kind of you, dear, but . . . That's how Stella would normally refuse an offer like that. I took a deep, halting breath.

"Oh. That was stupid of me. I'm sorry. I'll keep it in my fridge and we can share it when you get back. How about that?"

"That sounds fine." She closed her eyes, and for a minute, I thought she'd gone back to sleep.

"I also brought you these, um, marshmallow things." I pushed the bag toward her, but she didn't reach her hand out, and after a minute, I set it on the bedside table.

"Stella," I said, my heart dropping into my gut, "I'm so sorry I wasn't there for you. I got the dates wrong, and life kind of exploded. I could have killed myself when I realized, I just—"

Her face was frozen, eyes fixed on a point in the middle of the air.

"I figured something like that happened," she said after a minute, her voice slightly strangled. "I should have remembered how you are."

"I know, I'm such a mess! If only you'd reminded me—"

But I'd misread her tone. She wasn't teasing.

She tilted her head. There was an inch of white roots at her scalp where the purple stood out in sharp relief. She didn't usually go so long without choosing a new color.

"Forgetting galas. Sleeping through rehearsals. It is not," she said, "my job to keep track of your life."

I tried to breathe deeply. "No, no. Of course it's not. I didn't mean—"

"You insisted that you be here for my surgery. And then you didn't come to my surgery. I never expected to be the center of your life, Delphine, but you have to admit. It's a bit galling to be tossed aside so easily."

I looked down at her hand curled lightly against the sheets. It was amazing, given how forceful she was, how little space she took up in the world.

"I never meant to do that," I said. "You're so important to me—"

She smiled, but there was no humor in it. "It's very easy to say that. It's a lot harder to show it. What did I get from you back in St. Petersburg, even? One email a month?"

I knew she was right. I knew it was unforgivable, what I'd done. But I also believed I could make her understand. When I was seven or eight, I'd knocked a priceless vase off of her mantel and tried to blame it on her cat. After a few days, the lie had started to feel like it was burning a hole in my stomach, and I'd woken her up at two in the morning to tell her the truth. She'd wrapped a blanket around my shoulders, made me a cup of cocoa, and hugged me. *There. Now doesn't that feel better?*

"Do you remember Jock?" I said slowly.

She waved a disinterested hand at me.

"You're going to have to remind me."

"He's the one I was so in love with when I was a teenager. And we sort of started to see each other—" I recounted the whole ghastly story for her. She listened intently, though her eyes drifted closed every now and then.

"And Stella, I don't know what the hell I'm supposed to do about all of this. I was so . . . shocked. I still am. But anyway, that's what was happening. That's why I haven't been by."

"You're shocked," she repeated.

"I'm just . . . frozen. I'm not sure what I . . . It might sound strange, but I'm not sure what I owe all of these other women. There's a *video* of me out there. What do I do? What would you do?"

It was a long time before she spoke. When she did, her voice was icy, running through my veins in shards.

"Delphine, get this into your head. I'm not your guru, I'm not your mentor, I'm not the friendly neighborhood witch, all right? I don't have any tea leaves to read for you, tarot cards to flip over, horoscopes to consult."

"Wait," I said, voice shaking. This wasn't how this was supposed to go.

I'd only been trying to make her understand why I had been so distracted, that was all. "Stella. Of course I know that. I'm—Stella, I'm sorry—"

"Delphine!" she cried, and put her hands on her temples. She took a few deep breaths. When she spoke again, her voice was tempered and low.

"I am," she said, "not particularly interested in your excuses. And I'm becoming less interested in your guilt by the minute. So, if you wouldn't mind, dear, could you please leave?"

I started to push the chair back. Hesitated.

This was the woman who'd looked after me while my mother was dancing. The woman who'd listened to me, comforted me, helped me grow up. The woman who'd been more of a mother to me than my own mother had ever been.

"No," she said, seeing right through me as she always had. "That's right. It's time to go."

CHAPTER 23

— November 2004 —

Margaux and I hatched a plan. When Wednesday came, Lindsay brought high heels for her dinner date with Louis, and Margaux and I bought a new bottle of ipecac from the pharmacy by the Louvre. We'd practiced the audition piece all day—and it's the strangest thing, I can't remember what it was now. It was fiendishly difficult, but it was fiendishly difficult all five years I auditioned. It might have been Kitri from *Don Quixote* or *Grand pas classique*, which we had to do two separate years; for a long time, I'd convinced myself it was the Black Swan variation, but Margaux told me later that had never been a set piece.

Anyway, the routine itself is a black hole in my memory. But everything that came after is still, always, there.

We were sitting under the awning at Café de la Paix. We couldn't afford to eat there, but we didn't eat anyway, so we just ordered endless black coffees. Lindsay, a dress and the heels shoved into her dance bag, was counting down the time until she could head over to Louis's apartment; Margaux and I were doing the same, but subtracting half an hour. We thought for sure she'd be drinking wine by six and cast anxious eyes at each other when Lindsay kept ordering espressos; they were so small, she'd be sure to notice the taste of the ipecac.

"Three champagnes," Margaux informed the waiter on our next order. Lindsay screwed up her face. "I hate champagne."

"It'll help you relax."

It arrived just as Lindsay had to go use the bathroom. With a hand that was really too steady (was I secretly a psychopath?), I dissolved a spoonful of the viscous syrup into the middle flute.

"Better double that," Margaux said, and I did.

"How fast does this stuff work?" I asked.

She looked doubtfully at our three chairs, crammed together.

"Be prepared to get out of the way fast."

The sickly smell hung over us for a minute, and I lit a cigarette to cover it. Margaux focused on swirling the syrup through Lindsay's glass and separating it from ours. And then we sat there, with nothing to do but wait for her to come back.

"Who do you think they'll move up from *quadrille* this year?" Lindsay asked, sliding back into her chair. "I think Albertine's looking pretty good, personally. If she would only stop clutching her jaw. It hurts me just watching her." She looked at us. "What's going on?"

Margaux smiled tightly.

"Nerves," I said.

"Oh. Well, it's stupid to be nervous about something like this, you know." She shrugged. "Do the best you can tomorrow. But you'd do your best anyway. It's not like being nervous makes you any better. If anything, it makes you worse."

"And who's nervous now?" I said. She raised an eyebrow. "You always jabber when you're anxious."

"Yeah, well," Lindsay said, picking up her champagne and looking away with a grim smile. "I'll just do the best I can, right?"

She started to raise the glass to her mouth. I swear I could hear Margaux's intake of breath.

The best you can.

It was such an American expression. Here, *the best you can* counted for nothing. Not unless it was also flawless.

Lindsay tried so hard at everything. She was always doing her *best*; sleeping with Louis was part and parcel of that. It made my insides feel all twisted and sick. She thought *this* was the best she could do.

I reached up and batted the flute out of Lindsay's hand. It dropped to the ground, shattering into three even pieces and splashing champagne all over me, smelling sticky sweet and wrong. Lindsay jumped up with a shriek.

"Jesus *Christ*, Delphine! What do you think you're doing?"

"Sorry, sorry," I said, dabbing an ineffectual linen napkin on my jeans. "Sorry, there was a fly—I guess I'm a little nervous, too."

Across the table, Margaux's eyes turned soft and sorry. As Lindsay shook herself off, Margaux gave me a sad little smile. As if to say, *So much for that.*

— October 2018 —

What did justice look like? I sat in the living room, painting my toenails, curtains drawn tight against the day.

I dabbed a smudge of red on my pinkie toe. I wasn't there when my mother found out about my father's California family, only when she threw all of his things out of the window into the Place des Vosges. As awful as it had been to witness, it was a long time before I realized that the punishment didn't come close to fitting the crime. He had another *family*, a little boy and a little girl drawling fluent if bastardized English halfway across the world. The existence of that little girl hurt me the most. She was a year younger: just old enough for him to have gotten to know me and then decide on a replacement. And for that—for that small, hopeless feeling, for whatever humiliation my mother had felt, as well—he'd lost a few shirts?

I cupped my left foot in my hand, contorting my body to pull it straight.

What I really wanted was to steal Jock's life from him. Twist it in the right places so that it was no longer recognizable as his own.

The bottle tipped over, glugging polish over the creamy sofa.

It was so beautiful I just watched it for a moment, hypnotized by its shine, before I jumped up and ran cursing to the bathroom for a towel.

I dabbed furiously at the polish, only spreading it into a wider, blurred circle, and decided that consequences be damned, I had to inflict as much pain as he had. I was going to steal his image the way he'd stolen ours.

And by the time I had fixed the couch, the rug, and my nails, I had realized exactly how I was going to do it.

I arrived at Merci first. Asking for favors always makes me feel tetchy, jumpy, and I'd given myself a quarter hour for what was really a five-minute walk through the tiny streets of the Marais. My mother had always believed that *on time* meant *fifteen minutes late*: anything earlier and you'd make the other person feel bad for making you wait.

I could have taken one of the boulevards, of course, but there was something about their sheer size that made me feel exposed. Days later, I still felt all wrong in my body. Instead, I made my way up the Rue de Béarn, then the Rue Saint-Gilles, the Rue Villehardouin. Through the rain, I barely saw the fairy-tale scenery surrounding me.

I'd only just ordered a tisane when Daniel approached the table, hovering until I jumped up and kissed his cheeks.

He looked around, taking in the library-cum-factory elegance of the café, his eyes scanning the bookshelves to our side with such curiosity that the waitress handed him a menu in English. He didn't correct her as she spoke in halting words in that same language. He only responded, apologetically, in his native French.

"Good to see you, Delphine," he said finally.

My bravado momentarily left me as I realized how hard this was going to be. Telling Lindsay and Margaux—telling Stella, even—had been nothing to telling him. He was kind, yes. Sweet, even. And yet I felt like all of the power, all of my courage, would drain out of me as I told him the story, that I would become nothing right before his eyes.

"I was surprised to get your email," he said, not quite meeting my eyes.

I smiled broadly.

"You're the only journalist I know."

He frowned. "But I'm not a journalist."

"You're not?"

He shook his head. "I'm in public relations."

This was the kind of thing I should know. The kind of thing that shouldn't have to be explained to me as a thirty-six-year-old woman. I stirred my tea studiously, tilting my head down as I removed the strainer to hide the blush spreading over my cheeks.

"What's the difference?"

"In public relations, we work on behalf of companies or individuals. We help them get the attention of the press. And the public." Hence the term "public relations," but he was kind enough not to say it.

"Well, that's even better!" I said. "Except—are you expensive?"

He tilted his head. He really had awfully kind eyes.

"Why don't you tell me what you need, and we can take it from there."

The waitress brought his mocha and chocolate croissant over, and he stirred sugar into the coffee, waiting without expectation.

Promise you won't tell Lindsay what I'm asking you to do, I wanted to say before I started. Her reaction, her complete and utter assurance that I'd be ruining myself . . . But I couldn't say it, couldn't ask that of him. His first loyalty would be to her, not to me.

"You know Jock Gerard?" I said.

Something like a wince slid over his features. Interesting; I'd never seen another man, someone who wasn't also a dancer, reacting to Jock before. I always assumed everyone was as charmed by him as I had been.

Apparently not.

"I know him well enough," he said.

"You don't like him," I said.

"I think," he said, "that a man who is surrounded exclusively by women, without a single male friend, shouldn't be entirely trusted. A man who ignores anybody who can't further his career or whom he doesn't want to sleep with can't be entirely trusted. I think that a thirty-six-year-old man who blames his parents for everything that's currently wrong in his life . . ." He dropped the parallel, paused. "I think he's dangerous. And also," he added, fiercer than I'd ever seen him, "I really hate his hair."

I nodded.

"Then you're going to love this," I said, and told him the whole damn story.

He was wonderful. The perfect audience. I don't know why that surprised me so much, but he met my eyes at the right moments, he looked away at the right moments, and he nodded at the right moments. He let me speak without interrupting once, listening intently.

"That's it," I said finally. "Do you know anyone who might be interested in a story like this?"

He smiled. "Are you kidding me? I can think of three or four reporters right off the top of my head."

We ran through the practicalities. The journalist would talk to me, ask me questions. Then he'd have to look into the matter on his own. That would involve calls to the other women I'd seen on the list, to Nathalie and the board of directors, to Jock himself. I wanted to remain anonymous, or as anonymous as I could, given that Jock would definitely know who'd roped the press in. And as anonymous as possible given that the journalist would most likely, Daniel explained, try to get a magistrate involved so he could access the videos, which were undoubtedly backed up in the cloud somewhere, if not actually online.

I sat with that for a moment. The journalist would see those images of me. See Jock slide my underwear down, unhook my bra—

"Do you know any female journalists?"

He nodded. "Tons. Don't worry, Delphine. I'll find exactly the right one."

"Thank you," I said. The panic that had been building like a bubble beneath my skin burst and tears started dripping down my cheeks. "Just—thank you."

He patted my hand. "Don't be scared," he said.

I pulled my napkin up to my face and tried to breathe. When I put it back down, I wasn't crying anymore.

"It's not that I'm scared," I said. "Or not exactly. Not yet, at least. It's just—overwhelming? And crying is, I don't know, the only way all the emotion can get out. It's a release valve. What don't men get about that?"

We were silent for a minute, staring out the window.

"Delphine," he said in a way that made my head twist to the side, avoid his gaze, "since we're here, I wonder—" The rain was really pounding down now; I'd be damp for the rest of the day if I didn't go home after this and change clothes. Until then, there was a coziness to the gold-lit interior of the café that would be hard to leave. "Could I ask you something? About Lindsay," he clarified quickly.

"Sure."

"Do you think she'll ever want babies?" he said, speaking softly.

A lot of dancers at the very top of the field never have children, given that their career window happens to correspond with peak fertility. A few decide to trade in one of those years for a child—almost never more than one.

My mother had me three months before she turned thirty-seven. When she found out that she was pregnant, she'd done what she always did: weighed the pros and cons. Eventually (although, her telling of the story implied, *just barely*), with only five years left on her contract, she'd decided to sacrifice one so that she'd have someone with her in retirement. What she hadn't accounted for then was that the dreams don't go away. All of the fight that's in you, all of the fight that you used for years to get to the top of the field and then stay there, it doesn't just dissolve when you retire—even if you've become a mother. All of the knowledge that's stored in your head—*straighten your leg here, hold steady, move through the movements*—that doesn't disappear overnight. And eventually, the only place she'd had to put her ambition was on me.

Now Daniel wanted to know if Lindsay would want kids. I sat with the question for a moment, trying to get past my own feelings, my own biases. Lindsay. Children. She didn't even like teaching much, and those were ballet dancers. Those were her people.

Taking a year away from dance? Now? She'd never do it. And honestly, it made me a little angry to think that he wanted her to. Had he ever had a conversation with her about her career? She wouldn't give up until she had to: at forty-two.

I was on the edge of piercing the bubble, of telling him exactly what I thought, when I realized: he didn't want to hear the truth.

I heard Stella: *You can choose to be right, or you can choose to be kind.*

"Probably someday," I muttered. He nodded.

"I've just been waiting for her to want to for years," he said. "I always wanted a big family. Always."

Then you made the wrong choice of wife.

"You know that she's turning thirty-six this year? You know what they call a pregnancy at that age?" he asked.

I tried to keep my face blank. *You mean, at my age. Go ahead. Tell me.*

"A geriatric pregnancy," he said.

It didn't sound good, I'd give him that.

"I don't suppose"—his voice had an almost adolescent squeak to it—"I don't suppose you'd consider talking to her?"

No, thank you. I don't do that kind of thing anymore.

But with that question, he'd implanted the scenario in my head, and I was imagining what it would be like to actually sit Lindsay down, to talk to her about this. Maybe they'd be great parents. Maybe children of her own would actually make her really happy.

And still, imagining that conversation made me cringe. People had been telling her what to do with her body her whole life. I refused to be one more person with an opinion about it.

Whatever I owed him or didn't owe him, this was where I drew the line.

"I think," I said, getting to my feet, digging in my purse for cash, "that you should talk to her yourself."

He nodded. "Of course," he said, standing up. "I'll get in touch with somebody for you. Somebody great."

"How much will it cost?"

He looked like I'd slapped him. In fact, he looked more or less like Jock had looked, watching his computer fall.

"I wouldn't dream of charging you," he said.

I kissed his cheeks. "Thanks for meeting me," I said. "Just—thank you."

Meeting Daniel had occupied the better part of my morning, but I'd managed to squeeze in a lab appointment that afternoon.

"Which STD tests do you need?"

How many women had that file contained? At least twenty. Probably more like thirty. And those were just the ones he'd gotten on tape. All of them dancers; no starlets, none of those B-list celebrities he'd accompanied to galas and gallery openings. Of course not—he wouldn't have risked it with them. Not with women who owed him nothing, who got nothing from him other than the pleasures of his presence and his body. He'd known the limits of his power exactly: the ballet was his hunting ground. And fuck, he'd stuck to it.

I sighed. "Oh, all of them."

After enough swabbing and pinpricking to last me a lifetime (at least enough to have me renounce my IUD and swear that *this* would never happen again), I stormed outside to call an Uber: cursing the technician, cursing Jock, cursing myself.

A long voice mail from a number I didn't know waited on my phone. I ordered the car and listened to it.

It was Daniel's journalist. Already. Everyone loves a ballet story.

She was calm. She was interested. She was in control.

What did justice look like for me? This. This was what justice looked like for me.

I called her back.

I told her to use my name.

CHAPTER 24

~ November 2004 ~

After we cleaned up the spilled champagne, Margaux ordered three glasses of white wine (*Not red*, she told the waiter pointedly, *since some of us are clumsy*). She and I chugged ours down, while Lindsay sipped more slowly, until she finally stood, announcing that she was going to change her clothes and head over to Louis's apartment. My hands light and shaky, I followed her out of the café.

The echo of what I'd failed to do pounded through my bones.

Lindsay was going to ruin our chance for a fair shot, and it would be my fault. If I'd been brave enough, I could have stopped her from going. She was in way over her head with this creep who had absolutely no interest in helping her career. He was going to do God knew what to her, and she was going to let him, and she refused to see the truth of the thing. Only Margaux and I saw it.

And I'd failed us all.

"Lindsay, why don't I come with you for your drink with Louis? That way, if it gets awkward, we're together. Plus, it's a long Métro ride late at night, and we can go home together," I said, playing it off as though I'd forgotten her intention to sleep with him. "Stay over at mine?"

Lindsay looked at me, aghast.

"He didn't invite you. He invited me. He said I was the best young dancer he'd ever seen. An ingénue, he called me."

My anger flared. What were the rest of us, then? The ones who had actually trained at POB since the beginning? We were nothings to him? We were invisible?

And she was going to let him talk about us like that?

The rain relented into a gray mist. We made our way toward the Opéra. And then.

It happened so fast. It was like every decision that we'd needed to make to reach that point had already transpired, so when the universe aligned and provided the right circumstances, we instantly saw our cue. We were ready. Just appear onstage, walk across, take a bow. Applause.

As we stood at the corner waiting for the light to change, Margaux grasped my elbow.

She nodded down, to where the laces of Lindsay's Converse had come undone. The graying shoestring lay half in the gutter, its tip jettisoned about by the wastewater rushing by it.

I didn't get it right away. But Margaux's wide, urgent eyes beseeched me.

Step on it. That's all I had to do. Step on it, and she'd trip. A fall wasn't a sure thing—it wasn't like the vial of ipecac lodged in Margaux's purse. But if it worked, she'd trip onto the dirty road, covering herself in filth. Take her out for the next few hours, force her to go home for a shower. It was our best shot of stopping her from going to Louis. The risks were minor: she could temporarily twist her ankle, cut her knee, sprain her wrist. But probably not.

I stepped forward to wrap my arm around Lindsay's shoulders. As I did, I put my foot in the gutter to hold down the shoelace. She settled into my weight and for a moment the world seemed to come together, perfect and calm and cozy.

The light turned.

"Go, go, go!" Margaux cried, false urgency permeating every word. Like the trained dancer she was, Lindsay took an enormous step forward with her right foot as I held the shoelace down on her left.

It would have worked perfectly if her shoe hadn't come off.

But I had all of my weight on the laces, and she always tied them loosely, and the sneaker remained beneath me as she stepped into the street. She cried out as her sole skimmed the gutter, scraping against the filthy pavement. Even in the fading light, her bare foot was hideous from years of pointe work: missing the smallest nail, the large one bruised purple and black, medical tape only half covering the torn-away patches of inflamed skin on each toe.

And Lindsay, who never lost her balance, was flailing.

Then she was sprawled across the center of the street, arm extended beneath her head as though she'd just lain down for a nap. Above her, lights glistened, echoing onto the pavement below.

Pushing down on her hands in a perverse yoga position, Lindsay slid as her bare foot failed to find purchase on the wet surface. She propelled herself partway up, then thudded to her knees, an injured bear's pose.

I didn't see the taxi coming until it slammed into her.

It broke her ribs in three places.

She was out of the company for six months.

Margaux and I were both promoted to *sujet*. It took Lindsay another five years.

Two spots. Three of us.

— *October 2018* —

By the time I tiptoed back to the Palais Garnier on Monday, my rage was dissipating, replaced by a combination of quiet calm and a regret-tinged fear. Did I want to see Jock? I was half-afraid I would and half-afraid I wouldn't.

As I pushed my way through the halls, his absence surrounded me. They were rehearsing *Don Quixote* in the first studio, which was normally a ballet he excelled in. Yet Jonathan, his understudy, was doing his steps instead.

So, he'd called in sick. How brave.

No. How smart. I wondered how many confrontations he'd avoided this way. If anyone else had found out about his recordings and gone crazy in public, I certainly would have heard about it from Lindsay or Margaux.

Nothing stayed secret here for long.

Almost nothing.

"Here's how it goes," I told Camille about an hour later.

Yes, Camille. This was a new chance, my leap forward into the pantheon of famous choreographers—and this time, I'd be doing it with a piece that was fully mine, that I could feel in my bones. Featuring a nineteen-year-old ingénue in a solo piece at POB was the quickest way I could think of to get the press crawling all over us. Yeah, it'd be good for her—she'd probably get a spread in *Madame Figaro* out of it at the very least, not to mention a promotion at the annual audition in November—but it would also be good for me. For every article beginning, *At nineteen, baby bal-*

lerina Camille d'Ivoire has made a splash at the Paris Opera Ballet, there I'd be, a necessary clause in her sentence: *in* Little Girl Blue *by up-and-coming choreographer Delphine Léger.*

It was time to insist on myself. I wasn't going to let other people determine my life anymore. For so long, I'd been living in the shadow of their decisions: my mother's, Dmitri's, Nathalie's. And this time, I didn't ask permission. I had emailed Nathalie, telling her that I needed a studio for a contemporary piece, and Antoine had sent me back a confirmation. No more than that. If she liked it, she could use it. If she didn't—I had to make it anyway. I'd figure out what to do with it later.

"We start with 'Mercedes Benz.' Fade to 'Cry Baby.' Then 'Piece of My Heart.' 'Little Girl Blue.' End with 'Maybe.'" I'd have liked to avoid "Piece of My Heart"; it was so well-known. But it was also so explosive that I just couldn't help it. It had to be in there.

Camille nodded and it broke my heart. The look on her face was the look you gave when you wanted to please a teacher but had no idea what they were talking about.

"See, it's an emotional arc," I tried to explain. "It starts with a superficial desire. Goes into yearning. Then this furious anger. To mourning, ending with resignation: both of how messed up the longing is and also the awareness that she'll never escape it."

"Why—" She cut herself off.

"No, it's okay," I said. "What is it?"

"Why wouldn't you end with the mourning? Or even the yearning?"

God, she was young.

"Because the inescapability interests me," I said. "Do you know what I mean?"

She looked down, shaking her head.

I sighed. "It's just— Heartbreak is cyclical. It's linear every time it happens, but it's cyclical, too, the very fact that it happens over and over." I paused. "Yes?"

Her eyes were wide and helpless. I was making it worse.

"Don't worry about it right now. Should we get started?"

It was just the two of us. Personal, intimate. And as I walked her through the steps that would accompany the ragged acoustic beat of Janis's voice, I had one of those chills run through me. They happen so rarely: those moments where you think, Yes. I'm getting this just right.

Janis's voice boomed through the studio. And Camille spun off into the dance I'd made.

She was good. There was no doubt that she was good.

But on her body, the fluttering feet and flying arms, shuffling leaps and swinging hips—it all just looked *pretty*. The ballet wasn't based on Janis's life, but I'd read up on her anyway; she'd longed for a traditional feminine beauty, and you could hear her inability to grasp it in the fierce roughness of her singing. Ferocity, roughness: they were both missing from Camille's interpretation.

I stopped the music before the first song was over. She waited for my feedback, gasping with her hands on her hips.

"No. I don't want it delicate. I want it *mad.* Try it again."

She centered herself as I restarted the music. It was worse this time. Manic princess. Coked-up fairy godmother. I shook my head and went to her, leaving the music playing.

"I'm not being great about this. I'm not entirely sure how to put it into words—"

I cut myself off, the back of my neck tingling.

It was Lindsay, waiting in the doorway. I smiled and waved, then returned to Camille, putting all thoughts of guilt and betrayal aside. "Try the first reach for me."

Camille extended her hand like she was offering some medieval knight a handkerchief.

"Stretch farther," I said, guiding her arm so her shoulder was just out of alignment. Not very POB at all; no wonder she was having trouble with it. "You're trying to get something that's just out of reach. You think you have it, but it slips your grasp—there!" I looked at her in triumph. "Now dance the whole thing that way."

But though she got the reach right, nothing else was working. Whatever emotion she was trying for, it was unnatural; it made her forget the steps, trip over her feet, come out of the turns a quarter rotation too soon.

"Here," I said, stopping the music and going back to her, totally unsure of what else I could say. "Why don't—"

And I looked up and caught Lindsay's eye—and there. There it was. All of the yearning and longing and crazed *wanting* I'd been trying to get out of this nineteen-year-old.

"Lindsay, could you come in here?" I called.

The door swung open and Lindsay slunk in as though expecting a reprimand.

"Did you get those steps?" I asked. I saw something in her face light up. Understudy; she'd take it. She nodded. "Will you try them for us?" I asked, and she nodded again.

With my hand on Camille's shoulder, I walked her back to the mirrors with me.

And then I hit play.

Lindsay didn't have all of the steps right, but she *was* the emotion. She was nothing but the emotion. Every extension of her leg was full of desire and hunger. Every leap was furious and ugly and perfect. Every turn was precise and crazy at the same time.

I let the music play into the next song. Lindsay stood panting in the center of the room, not having seen the choreography for the second part.

Camille looked up at me, eyes wide.

"Camille," I said, "could we talk for a minute?"

She smiled. "You want her to do it," she said.

"I—"

"That's okay," Camille cut me off. "I would, too."

I looked back to Lindsay standing there, totally exposed to our gaze, our judgment. I thought about everything she wanted. Everything she'd lost. Everything that was just out of her reach.

"Lindsay," I said, "are you in?"

Her eyes were so bright I was afraid she was going to start crying. I wasn't sure I could take that again. But she caught hold of herself with the shuddering remnants of her pride.

"Absolutely," she said.

I ran through the arc I'd just described to Camille, and Lindsay's face melted into an enormous smile.

"I love it," she said. "Delphine. I love it so much."

We clarified the steps of the first piece. I wouldn't normally have run through so much with her in one session, but I wanted to see it. I wasn't worried about her remembering the exact choreography; I wasn't even worried about the steps themselves, which were sketchy anyway. I just genuinely wanted to see her embody the music. I wanted to see these emotions on her—these emotions that women are not supposed to have, much less project into the world—spun into something beautiful.

"Little Girl Blue" started: strings twanging, bass thumping.

Lindsay was long, languid, anguished. Her movements were tentative, like she expected to be pushed over, knocked down, pulled offstage at any second.

Janis's voice came in. Wounded, gently mocking.

Lindsay spun around, in the hands of her pain, slid down into the splits. Wouldn't let it keep her down, pulled herself back up. And as she did, you thought: How many times can a woman do this? How many times will she be able to get back up? And you *felt* it.

Janis's words stretched through the yearning. Reaching for something that wasn't there anymore. That maybe never was.

And Lindsay was perfect. Not perfect in the traditional POB sense; she was raw and right. This was Lindsay at her best. They'd have to promote her after this; she was better than anything I'd ever seen.

Janis howled. *This* was why I loved choreographing. This was why it was better than dancing. Instead of trying to contort myself into someone else's vision, I could take what was already inside me and find the perfect vessel for it.

When it was over, Camille looked up at me.

"Holy shit," she said, and there were tears in her eyes.

I glanced at Lindsay, who was chugging water. And all I could think was, She looks so alive.

CHAPTER 25

I was a soloist.

I was a soloist, and it meant everything and nothing. This was what I had worked for; it should have felt like the natural next step in my ascension to star. But ever since I'd seen the audition results, I hadn't been able to get Dmitri's words out of my head: *Soloist, maybe. At best.*

I'd done everything in my power to get here. Things I never thought I'd do. Slept with a choreographer. Betrayed a friend. Not only could I not push myself any further, I couldn't even imagine what *further* would look like. I was tired deep in my bones, down where I felt the truth of his words.

And I'd done it all to crawl my way—where? To the middle?

Maman would have been breaking out the champagne, inviting all of the older cohort to the apartment for a party. But my mother had been dead for months: months in which the color and life had slowly drained out of Paris. I sat overlooking the Seine, shaking slightly with the damp and the cold as I held a cigarette to my lips and exhaled smoke, the same color as the water, the same color as the sky. This river at the heart of the city, this waterway ten minutes from my front door. My entire life had been lived on this side of it. My mother's flat, the Opéra, the school, were all on the Right Bank. When was the last time I'd even made it down here?

And now. My mother was gone. Lindsay was out for the season, her broken ribs and countless surgeries casting her into a black mood that I couldn't have borne for more than five minutes, even if I hadn't been the direct cause of it. Margaux had conveniently disappeared, as Margaux tended to do, into a new relationship. Jock was still in New York, recently named a soloist at NYCB. Stella was on a field research trip in Africa until the summer.

And I was still here. Mediocre and more broken than ever.

I watched the water rippling gray under an angry sky. Once, Paris had been confined to the two small islands in its center. At the beginning, that's all the city was. And then kings plotted and merchants traded and revolutionaries revolted and here we were. Enormous. Grand. Majestic.

I felt very small.

Because I wasn't any good anymore. I'd known it for a while, but this was the first time I could bring myself to admit it. Even after taking time off when my mother died, I'd never gotten back the spark of joy that dancing had once brought me. The accomplishment that had throbbed in my chest after a perfectly executed adagio had dissolved into a dull relief that it was over, that I'd gotten through it. The ballet had once been the only arena that counted for me: a place where my sculpted physical perfection took me soaring to emotional heights or plunged me down into the depths of obsession. But now, it was just one flat plane of gray.

It was all too clear to me: even if I achieved the absolute most I possibly could, even if I succeeded in following exactly in my mother's footsteps— where would it take me? I'd only end up next to her in that same awful crypt. The arc of her life had played out, come to a close. The anger, the fear, the loneliness: that was the legacy ballet had given her.

I wanted something else. Anything else. A story I didn't already know the end of.

My phone rang, startling me. I grasped it between my hands, Dmitri's name shining up at me. Suddenly, he was the only person I wanted to talk to. He was the only one who'd ever seen me for who I really was and wanted me anyway.

"Dmitri," I said, half laughing, half gasping.

"Darling." I wasn't *darling* to him, of course—at least not the only one. I wasn't naive enough, not even then, to believe that he'd kept an empty bed in the seven months that he'd been gone. But his voice was a low growl, familiar and exciting all at once, and I relaxed into the word. "Have you been practicing your Russian?"

"Of course." I switched languages, falling back into a simple phrase from the Rosetta Stone CDs I'd gulped down that spring. "How have you been?"

"Today in St. Petersburg . . ." he began, no longer the broken-tongued foreigner but instead a man of wisdom, charisma, charm. I understood only a few words, but I still loved to listen. *Purple sky. Icicles. Snow.* Snow like a cake? I was missing something—no. Snow like *frosting.*

And as he spoke, colors exploded in my mind, hovering like fireworks over the damp gray day, illuminating the truth for the first time.

If this was the best I ever would be, maybe there was something—noble—in admitting it.

It rang through my head like verb conjugations: I was a soloist. I was only a soloist. I would only ever be a soloist.

I was a soloist, but I didn't have to be a soloist forever.

And maybe the true betrayal of my mother wasn't giving up dance. Maybe the true betrayal would have been to settle for safe mediocrity when I could have been great. Could have found something to truly succeed in. Could have shone as brightly in my own right as she once had.

"Dmitri," I said, my Russian flowing for the first time: broken, yes; but quick, easy, "can I come to St. Petersburg?"

And as his words rolled back at me in his gruff voice, delight fizzing through the line, I thought: For once, I'm doing the right thing. I've made bad choices. I've hurt people. I've betrayed myself.

But I don't have to be that person anymore.

Once, I was a soloist. But I wasn't a soloist for long.

— *October 2018* —

Thirty-six hours. That's how long it took, after I spoke with the journalist, to get called into Nathalie's office.

Not even two days. Thirty-six hours.

The more I thought about her role in all of this, the angrier I became, until it was burning a hole through my skin.

What I'd really like to see is something that highlights all of the amazing women in this company.

Jock was a star. He was famous, as far as the limited fame available to dancers went. He got prime roles in every major production; his poster was pinned up in every dorm room at the academy; he'd been featured in glossy magazine spreads that were supposedly about his favorite cafés but were really about his abs, his hair, his eyes.

It's starting to look like the men are getting all the glory.

Nathalie wanted *some nice, short feministy thing* as a counterpoint to his bad behavior, in case what he'd done ever got out.

We'd like to draw the focus back where it belongs.

She'd wanted me to protect him, and I'd taken the bait.

And while some of my anger spiraled inward (I'd been too much of a coward to ask Nathalie about her sudden interest in celebrating women; I should have at least hesitated and considered her motives), it was nothing next to the betrayal I felt.

What is the ballet, after all, if not the ballerinas?

I had to remember that what I had uncovered, what I had subsequently brought to light, was much bigger than myself.

Full of righteous anger for my audience, I marched in.

"Oh, Delphine," Nathalie said, standing. "Thank you for coming in. You must be getting sick of my face."

"No, not at all," I said, taken aback by her calm; hating myself for immediately falling under her spell.

She collapsed in her chair, rubbing a hand over her temples.

"Sorry," she said as she pulled an elegant black leather bag from the floor to her lap and rummaged through it. "This job—"

Nathalie downed a handful of painkillers without using water, then smiled tightly at me as she nodded toward the chair. I shook my head. I'd stay standing. She sighed.

"Let's keep this brief," she said, standing, too, with what seemed like great effort.

"I think that's probably best."

She wandered over to the windows, her arms folded across her chest.

"Look, I know you're friends with Lindsay, but at a certain point, you have to consider what's best for the ballet."

The bright daylight made my eyes ache as I squinted at her.

"I like the Janis Joplin thing. Do the Janis Joplin thing!" she added quickly, mistaking my bafflement for anger. "But please. Just leave her out of it."

This was an argument I hadn't prepared for. But this was my ballet: mine. She could take it or leave it as she wanted, but I wasn't going to twist myself into knots trying to please anyone else anymore.

"I need her in it."

"Use Camille."

"Lindsay is the only one who can do it."

Nathalie let her hands fall. "I repeat: Use Camille." She closed her eyes briefly, then turned and picked up a copper watering can with a studied casualness. She tipped its spout into one of her orchids. "Camille is ready for it."

"Camille is a wonderful dancer, but she doesn't have half the life experience a dancer needs for this role."

The watering can clanged back to the table. "Well, none of them have *life experience*, Delphine! They're dancers!" she cried. "Their life experience is this—" Gesturing around wildly, she looked like a red-haired Mrs. Rochester, and I'd never liked her more. "The four walls of this theater. And that's the same whether they're twenty or forty. So, could you please just use the dancers I'd like you to use."

"I can't," I said firmly. "I'd like to. I tried, with Camille. She was my first choice. But the fact is, Lindsay is the better dancer for this part."

"Nobody wants to see *some old lady dancing on her own!*" she cried. "Nobody wants to see any woman dancing on her own. It's a hard-enough sell—"

I tilted my head to the side, ready to make the argument I'd come prepared to defend. "Unfortunately, that's what you asked me to create." She raised her eyebrows. "Some nice, little feministy piece. So that's what I'm doing." I shrugged. "You could have had the imperial family instead, you know."

Nathalie's face was so full of barely contained fury that I jumped when she gave a sharp little laugh.

"And so I could." She gestured to the sofa, and I sat. To my surprise, she lowered herself next to me.

"Believe me, Delphine," she said, and her eyes were clear green and tired, "I'm not your enemy. I'm just trying to run a company. I've had to put one of my best dancers on leave." So that was where Jock was. So sorry, Nathalie. I mentally braced myself, reaching back down for the fury that had propelled me only minutes earlier. "I have an absurd pension roll to deal with. I have four principals out with injuries. I have twenty-five students to keep an eye on this year, knowing that I'm going to break twenty-four of their hearts come July. And that's not to mention the enormous list of stars, principals, *sujets*—hell, even *quadrilles*—all clamoring for better parts. I'm just trying to run a company here," she repeated, and I wasn't sure if it was for effect or because she really was that tired.

I stared at her. *Take it or leave it*, I wanted to say. But after all, this was POB. The place was in my blood, and I wasn't going to give up that easily. Not anymore.

"I understand that," I said slowly. "But I really think you're creating a problem where there is none. Wait until you see this before you decide. Because I'm telling you—Lindsay's amazing. She'll be another star, just wait and see."

Nathalie groaned and let her head fall back on the couch.

"Don't you want a company of stars?" I asked, and she sat back up, looking me full in the face.

"We can't *have* a company of stars," she said. "Don't you get that? Somebody has to be in the background. Somebody has to do the pretty little thirty-second dances. Somebody has to dress up in those idiotic costumes for *The Nutcracker*." I snorted laughter at that, and she gave half a smile. "I don't need sixty Sugar Plum Fairies. Surely you can understand."

Show her, my invisible audience cajoled. *Show her what you can do. Show her what you have done.*

"Look," I said, pulling my iPad out of my bag. "Watch Lindsay for thirty seconds. You still think she's wrong for it, I'll pull her today." Although, Christ, if I had to cut Lindsay one more time, I could forget about what she'd do to me; Margaux would be first in line to gut me, knife in hand.

A brief nod. I hit play.

"Little Girl Blue" came out tinny and too loud, but it didn't obscure what Lindsay was doing. It didn't obscure the clean, emotional purity of her movements, her utter embodiment of the music. Nathalie let me play it for the full minute and a half, through to the end of the song.

She opened her mouth. Closed it. Bent her head to the side, massaging her neck.

And then: a brief nod.

"All right," she said, and stood back up. "All right."

I hadn't been fooling myself. I hadn't been swept away by Camille's reaction. I'd been right. It was good.

I put my iPad back in my bag as she went back to her desk.

And as I watched her shuffle papers around, as she sat down and the glow of her computer lit up her face, the sheer normality of her actions made me light up with rage again. I was waiting for the news to break, for my entire life to change, and here she was. Just going about her day.

The accusations were screaming in my head. *You brought me here to cover up what he did. You knew about this and you tried to make me into your show pony, your smoke screen. You used me as much as he did, in an entirely different kind of way.*

I wanted to hurt her. I wanted to see her eyes water with pain.

I turned back to face her full-on.

"Nathalie?" I said.

She looked up.

"I know why you brought me here. I know that you've been covering up for Jock for months, if not years. And I also want you to know that I went to the papers, and the news is about to come out, and everyone is going to know exactly what you did." I couldn't stop a smile spreading over my face as I spoke.

He wasn't the only one who'd made bad choices. And he wasn't the only one who was going to pay.

But Nathalie just looked back at me coolly.

"Yes, I know," she said. "You wouldn't believe the number of calls I've gotten about it. I think you can probably expect to see it in the papers tomorrow."

An involuntary grunt of surprise escaped me.

She raised her pale eyebrows.

"Is that not what you wanted?" she said.

Yes and no. Yes, I wanted it to go public. No, I wanted it to hurt you a lot more than this. I wanted it to fucking tear you apart.

"When—a young dancer—came to me last summer," she said, bending forward to lean on her desk, interlacing her fingers, "I wanted to fire him. I went to the board immediately. I fought to fire him," she said, her face twisting. "I really did. I threatened to resign myself."

After all of those years as a star, after all of these years as director. She'd been ready to give it all up.

Because of him.

"And I tried to minimize his work with us, this past year. I tried to keep him out of *Tsarina*, if you remember—the casting just felt . . . too on the nose. So I did do something."

"Not enough," I muttered.

She nodded. "No, not enough. He's—well, the board called him a *lynch-pin* of the company. Our Peter Martins, likely a future artistic director. And after that Gucci campaign last year, the GQ cover? *His brand helps our brand*," she said with a dry laugh. "Meaning that, first of all, we need him, and second of all, he wouldn't go quietly. And when they decided that he was more valuable to the company than I was, I had to decide whether it was truly worth leaving over. Eventually, I decided: no. It was more important to keep a woman in this position as long as possible than to make a statement nobody would even hear."

"People would have listened," I said.

She shrugged. "Maybe. But either way, I was a fucking coward."

In spite of myself, the rage was evaporating like steam off of my body. She wasn't apologizing. She wasn't trying to make me feel better. She was just offering me her own, honest appraisal of what she'd done.

"I did yell at him," she added. "I yelled a lot."

I had to laugh at that.

She sighed and looked at me. "As I said, I was a coward. But don't worry. I'm leaving at the end of the season."

We stood there for a moment in silence. Dust motes danced in the light streaming in from the round windows.

"Well," I said finally. "I am sorry to hear that."

Because despite everything—somehow—I *was*.

What is the ballet, after all, if not the ballerinas?

Nathalie smirked.

"I'm not," she said. "And for the record? I'm glad you did it. I wish I'd had the balls to do it myself."

CHAPTER 26

— June 2005 —

The gift-wrapped box was big enough to fit a person in, yet perfectly to scale inside Dmitri's strangely high-ceilinged apartment. St. Petersburg was the opposite of a dollhouse; we were the small ones in this grandiose cityscape, shrunk down like Alice in Wonderland into the playthings of gods.

"Dmitri—" I protested. "What is this?"

He grinned. "Welcome present."

After those final, interminable months of being forced to serve out the rest of the season under my POB contract, I was finally in St. Petersburg. My new life was starting. Dmitri had picked me up from the airport earlier and taken me directly to the mint-green Mariinsky Theatre. I'd smiled and greeted dancer after dancer, all of whom stared back with unapologetic judgment.

Yeah, well. We'd fucking judge you, too, Lindsay's voice rang inside my head.

Fair enough.

My suitcase, he'd given to a stagehand.

"Dmitri?" I'd whispered.

He'd wrapped a heavy arm around my shoulder. "Sign of respect. You are my assistant now. This comes with . . . ah, привилегии. With privileges," he corrected himself in French.

And then he'd spent the rest of the day taking me through St. Petersburg. It wasn't pretty, not in the same way that Paris is pretty; it was lovely in a way that scraped at my insides with a scalpel. History's vicious, pitiless actions permeated the salty cold air. Everywhere I went with Dmitri, he tilted my chin up and there was another historical site towering vertiginously over us. Here is where the people rioted. This is where assassins threw a bomb into the tsar's lap. Over there is where Rasputin died.

"I love you," I whispered to him on the banks of the sparkling Neva, as we stared up at the gold domes of the city. And he kissed me fiercely, hungrily, until I could almost forget he didn't say it, too.

But as we meandered through the streets, I kept composing emails in my mind. Shaking them off. Starting again. *The air smells so salty, it's like a nosebleed,* I wanted to tell Margaux. *It's like Paris meets Venice, magnified to ten times its size,* I wanted to tell Lindsay.

I told Dmitri instead.

And then, in the falling Technicolor dark, he'd taken me back to his apartment. *Our* apartment. In an old pink-and-white palace a few streets back from the Moyka, a wedding cake that had been sliced up during the Soviet era into flats that were taller than they were wide. My mouth hung open as we stumbled up the musty servants' staircase to the three rooms with their original wooden floors, their crumbling plaster moldings, their enormous drafty windows looking out over the crowded canals.

His dark eyes glittered as I hesitated over the box. "Go on, then."

With one hand, I tugged the thick scarlet ribbon so that the bow fell apart, crumpled into nothing. Lifted the cover off of the box—

"Oh!" I said, pulling back involuntarily.

In front of me was the biggest fur coat I'd ever seen, straining at the box's sides like it still had a pulse.

Ew.

I heard Lindsay's voice so clearly that I almost looked for her.

Dmitri's face was open, excited.

"Fox!" he said. "Silver fox."

A tremor ran through me as I grinned wide. He was forty-one. It was natural that I'd have to make some adjustments. He'd grown up in a different time, one where elegant women had had closets full of furs—I fought the urge to wince. Had he ever even seen a girl my age wearing fur? I'd have been surprised.

Classy, Margaux's voice mocked. *Bringing you animal carcasses like a loyal wolf.*

Dmitri raised his eyebrows. "Try it on?"

My hand hovered over the box. Unwilling to descend, to feel the hair—the skin—against my palm.

"It's summer," I said.

He held up a finger. "Ah," he said in Russian. "But it will be winter soon enough."

He definitely bought that for someone else. Someone he broke up with . . . oh, I'm guessing, right around Christmas last year?

Lindsay, shut the fuck up.

But her voice was etched indelibly into my brain.

Who was this girl he'd bought the fox for? Who was the kind of girl who would wear a fur coat in the twenty-first century?

Someone merciless. Someone hungry. Someone—else.

I stared at him, holding his gaze as I reached to the back of my neck, pulled the zipper of my dress down, shimmied it down around my hips. Kept his eyes on mine as I undid my bra, stepped out of my underwear.

All right, then. I could be this girl.

Isn't that what I'd found out, this past year? You go through your whole life thinking you're a good person, and then it turns out you're someone else.

I plunged my hands into the fur, heaving it up around my shoulders. It was surprisingly heavy, but the silk lining fell cool and rippling down my back.

For a moment, he just watched me. Then my blood pulsed fast as he crossed the room, skin trapped hot under the dead animal until I felt feverish.

In my mind, Lindsay and Margaux glared disapprovingly across the room. *Delphine, don't take his scraps. Delphine, this is not who you are.*

He grabbed my hips and ground me against his body.

Yes, it is, I thought.

Behind him, the sky was on fire, electrified orange fading into bloody red.

Yes.

What did they know?

I'd been somebody else this whole time.

— *October 2018* —

The Jock story didn't so much hit the press as explode it. Every day, I scanned the newspapers and gossip sites for my pictures, or even—on some of the trashier sites—the video itself. But the internet was a black hole, and eventually I just set up news alerts so I could read the headlines, keep monitoring mentions of my name for links to the horrifying, almost inevitable, footage.

But I wasn't there. Or rather, I was—but not my video, only my testimony. Only my story. First it was *Le Monde*, with a picture of Jock and me drinking champagne at the gala front and center. I did a double take in front of the newsstand, then turned it over before buying it. I hadn't even known that there were any pictures of us from that night, and it made me queasy. Even more so when I looked at the photo credit: *Courtesy of Camille d'Ivoire*. Reading the story, I found out that she'd been the first one to find the videos and go to Nathalie, three months earlier. I wondered, fleetingly, if Nathalie had been pushing Camille on me in some desperate attempt to right her own wrongs.

Le Monde. My father read *Le Monde*—or, he had when he was still in Paris. Had he kept the habit up over the years, gotten it delivered to him in Santa Barbara? But though the thought of him seeing the story was enough to make me cringe, I had no sense of what his reaction would be. Anger at what Jock had done? Pride that I'd held him accountable? Whatever connection we'd once had, it had been severed when he hadn't replied to my email about Maman's death. Like he'd died along with her.

Jock resigned from his position immediately, but not before the POB board issued a press release stating that Jacques Gerard had been suspended pending their investigation.

And yet it all rang hollow to me.

I wanted more.

I wanted to fracture his image the same way he'd fractured ours.

I wanted to delete him from existence.

Meanwhile, I waited. For the video to appear on some skeevy site, for the unfiltered image of my body to be out there for the world to see. If revenge was all that was left, I believed he would take it. He'd lost his job and his reputation. It was only a matter of time.

Part of me wished he would just post it already; then this excruciating limbo would be over. Then, I could deal with it: hire a lawyer, contact the host site, rally people around me—or simply curl up in the fetal position and refuse to leave the house.

It occurred to me that perhaps Jock was cruel enough to wait until this all settled down, until I'd met somebody and my life was perfect, and *then* spring it. Or, equally cruel, that he'd already posted it to some amateur porn site without my name, but with my face, my body, there for everyone to see.

The latter option was most likely, I told myself. To keep the video for a later date would suggest that he cared about me still, in some sick way. But no, I was just another file on his computer. That's what haunted me most of all.

I scrolled through my Google news feed and saw that more stories had come out in which I was the good guy. *Yes, you are*, the voice in my head whispered. *You are the good guy in these stories. But how many anonymous men are jerking off to your image right this minute? How many people you know will see you naked? How many people will take pleasure in it without ever, ever, telling you?*

I knew I should be seeing a therapist or going to a yoga class or at the very least walking around naked at home in the hope that it would lead to bodily acceptance. But I was already so exposed. I didn't want to talk to a stranger. I had a horror of seeing myself in the mirror. I couldn't stand being naked.

I'd told the journalist what had happened to set myself free, and unwittingly, I'd built another cage.

No, not me—Jock. Jock had built it. And somehow, he'd managed to do it inside my head.

Once the story was public, I braced for Lindsay's resigned disapproval, Margaux's grim satisfaction. The rest of the company's giggles and tsks.

But that's not what they gave me.

After pushing my way through the crowds of photographers around the Opéra's gates the morning after the news broke, I found Camille waiting outside the studio I'd reserved. Pacing, frenetically wringing her hands, she looked up sharp as I approached.

"Delphine," she said, breathless, "I—"

I looked into her golden eyes, squinting at me in fear. And all of a sudden, everything that I had hated about her—her youth, her beauty, her potential—everything that I had fetishized about her—that same youth, beauty, potential—it all dissolved. She was young and she'd been out of her depth, and she'd been trying, the same way we all tried.

"Camille," I said, "it's okay."

Her eyes filled with tears. "I just—I know you went to the papers. And I don't want you to think any less of me just because I—because I was with him, too—"

I wrapped my arms around her as she cried. She felt startlingly like Lindsay, the delicacy of her bones, the softness of her skin. She blamed herself, this girl, when her only mistake had been buying into the same illusion all the rest of us had bought into. It wasn't even about her youth. I was almost twice her age and the same promises had seduced me: that I would be loved, that I would be seen.

"It's not about you," I whispered into her hair. She pulled back, startled at the sound. "It's the hardest lesson to learn, because we want to believe so much that we were the special one, we were the one who made him fall in love, finally and for good. But that's the trap, do you see? And it's cruel precisely because it works on everyone. He hurt us, and we have to own that pain, you know? But we also can't blame ourselves for feeling it, or for feeling the emotions that led to it in the first place. Just—care for yourself, Camille. Be careful, yeah?"

She gulped, shuddering.

"Thank you," she said, and smiled. Her mouth was still quivering a little, but her face was open, calm. And then she walked away.

Inside the studio, Lindsay was ready and waiting for me, eyes feverishly bright.

"You turned off your phone," she said accusingly.

I sighed, rubbed the tight spot between my eyebrows. "Yeah. Look, Linds—I know it's not what you thought I should do, but I went to the press—actually, Daniel helped me. I didn't know what to do and he was the only person I could think of who—who could actually help. I knew you wouldn't approve of it, but I hope you can forgive me—"

Her hands went to my shoulders, warm and steady. "I read the articles," she said in a low voice. "I read it all. And I changed my mind. Let's destroy him."

"Yeah?" I said, setting a shaky hand on hers.

Lindsay's face broadened into a grin. "Yeah."

"But what more can we even do? Beyond—" I waved a hand vaguely at the window, at the reporters outside. "I mean, he'll never dance here again. But beyond that? Everyone was of age, everyone consented. To the sex, at least. And in the meantime, there's this video, just hanging over my head, just—" My voice trembled. "Just there."

I wrapped my arms around myself and stood there, trying not to cry.

And then, Janis wailing: *Cry—baby.*

I whirled around.

"Succeed," Lindsay said, nodding at the music. "Do your work. That's how you win. That's the *only* way you win. You work. He doesn't."

I wiped my cheeks with the backs of my hands.

"Yeah," I said. "Yes. Let's go. Here's what I've been thinking about. The whole piece is a baring of the soul, right?"

She smiled. "Right."

"So, we start out with you fully costumed. I don't know in what, but some dress, probably. And in each piece, we have you shed something partway through, onstage. So by the time we get here, you're just in a bunch of long, layered beaded necklaces and a pair of nude briefs." I looked at her. "What do you think?"

Lindsay saw the worry on my face and laughed. "I love it," she said. "Why the briefs, though? Get rid of those, too."

I bit my lip. "I'm not sure they'll let us," I said.

"Well, keep it in your back pocket," she said. "What do I take off here?"

"I think in this one, you'll do the big reveal. The top. Right when she gets to the *come on, come on, come on* part." Lindsay nodded again and started rolling down the top of her leotard.

"You don't have to do it *now*," I said, laughing.

She frowned. "But my tits will move totally differently without the leotard versus with it on," she said. She glanced down doubtfully at them. "That is, if they move at all." We laughed; I started showing her the new turn sequence I'd come up with. She watched closely and seemed to have mastered it before I was even done demonstrating.

As we finished that day, we went out into the hall together. At the bulletin board, Antoine was just pinning up a notice. He closed the glass over it and smiled at Lindsay. I knew that formatting almost as well as Lindsay did: it was the announcement of the company positions open for audition the first week of November.

She ran to it, and I followed.

Lindsay's eyes were bright as she scanned the paper. Three corps members. Two soloists. One principal.

She turned to me, grinning. "It's mine," she said. "I'm going to do the 'Cry Baby' section for them."

Would Lindsay dance it topless? I wouldn't put it past her. I opened my mouth—then closed it.

What did she have going for her that other company members didn't? She was fearless. She'd have a ballet made for her. And if she believed my choreography would help get her the position—who was I to say differently?

I caught Lindsay watching me, amusement covering her face.

"You're worried," she said.

"Yes—no," I said. "I don't know. It's just risky, isn't it?"

Her face spread into a broad smile. "Everything good is risky," she said. "The thing that you have to remember is that if you *don't* risk anything, you risk everything."

And the fundamental rightness of her words thrummed through me. Maybe we could make a place for her at the top ranks of the ballet. Alone; without a partner. Show them all what a woman on her own could do.

I grabbed her hand.

"Let's do it," I said, and the words came out fierce. "Let's make you a principal."

Margaux, meanwhile, didn't show up at the Palais Garnier that day. When I finally brought myself to turn on my phone after rehearsal, I scrolled through the dozens of voice mail notifications from unknown numbers, the paragraphs-long messages of support and derision from various company members, only to find that she'd sent me a single sentence.

Good for you.

In the glass foyer behind the artists' entrance, I paused, staring at it, before pulling up my hood to brave the crowd again. Approval or contempt? With Margaux, the line was always blurred.

And the more the voices swelled around me, echoing through my head, the more it seemed like a benediction. A blessing. *Good. I wish nothing but good for you.*

She could have meant anything. So why not that?

CHAPTER 27

— February 2011 —

The night of my twenty-ninth birthday, Dmitri finally met Stella. "I'm going to dine with two old ladies today," Dmitri said, kissing me that morning. He was forty-seven. But it was okay; it was a joke, and besides, I didn't feel it. Russia was time outside of time. Nothing that happened there, including aging, could possibly count.

We were having my birthday dinner with Stella, that night at her hotel (*Sleep on a sofa? You must be joking, darling, with these bones?*). She'd stopped in the city on her way back from the eastern forests, where, to hear her tell it, the most exciting insects lived. And for the last two weeks, we'd had long, intense nights: dropping into hookah bars and visiting jazz clubs, trying every cuisine St. Petersburg had to offer, from Siberian to Persian.

There was one fact that festered, though: Dmitri showed no interest in Stella, despite all of the color she brought into my life. He had a performance, he was tired, he wanted to watch a football match—anything and everything seemed more important than meeting the woman who had practically raised me.

Finally, I'd roped him into her last dinner in town—he couldn't exactly turn me down on my birthday—and we showed up at the Four Seasons in our finery: me in cocktail-length red silk, him in a gray suit he'd had made in England on tour the previous year.

Stella, resplendent in vintage pink Pucci that clashed wonderfully with her blue hair, ran an approving gaze over him as we said our hellos. A flush of pride ran through me: *Isn't he beautiful, this man?* But the gaze he turned to her held none of the same appreciation. His expression was flatly incurious. Dull. Resigned.

Stella and I dove into our normal chatter as though he weren't there.

"Delphine, the *nails* on these women—"

"I know! Have you seen mine—"

The whole time, Dmitri sat, chain-smoking beside us, occasionally emitting a small, barely audible sigh.

It wasn't until we started talking about dancing that he perked up. One of our best performers, Marina, was out that season, pregnant, and we were doing our best to choreograph around the space she'd left in our latest work. *His* latest work.

"I'm always shocked when dancers get pregnant," Stella said, raising her eyebrows. "You're all so *skinny*. When your mother told me she was having you, you could have knocked me over with a feather!"

I raised a shoulder. "I mean, we're still women, after all. I imagine abortions are a lot more common than you'd think."

Dmitri grunted. "Tell that to Marina."

Shock rippled across Stella's face; I suppressed the same expression on my own.

"It's amazing, the stigma that we still attach to abortion. As a society. You know I was a *salope?*" Stella said.

My mouth fell open. The 343 *salopes*, bitches, were prominent French-women who publicly claimed to have had abortions, signing a statement written by Simone de Beauvoir back in 1971. Abortion was still illegal in France then, and they opened themselves up to all kinds of legal troubles. The procedure was finally legalized a few years later.

"Stella, that's—that's incredible! I had no idea."

"So, did you have one?" After his silence, Dmitri's voice seemed to shake the table like thunder.

"Dmitri!"

But Stella just stared at him steadily, like she knew she was smarter than him.

She *was* smarter than him, I realized with a shock. I was so accustomed to the idea of him as a genius that it felt like a punch to my solar plexus. In half an hour, she'd seen right through him. In all the years we'd spent together, I hadn't even realized there was anything to see through.

It was a long minute before she spoke.

"Does it matter?"

He just looked at her, his dark eyes half-closed.

I hadn't realized, until that moment, just how much I'd counted on Stella liking him. How much I'd wanted to see the two of them bent over the table in passionate discussion—the way Stella and I did in her kitchen, the way Dmitri and I did in ours. I had the sudden urge to name all the things I liked about Dmitri. *Aren't his hands gorgeous?* I wanted to say, grabbing his wrist and holding it up to her. *Look at how strong and sexy they are.*

But he just sat there with his half-hooded glare, and it was all too clear that my castles in the air had been entirely made of sand. And the tide was coming in.

"Well," she said, and her tone was one that she'd used when I was little and being particularly obstinate about something stupid. "Agree to disagree, in that case. Tell me more about this *Baba Yaga* ballet you're doing."

But as Dmitri plunged enthusiastically into a description of our—his— latest piece, modern music and ancient witches, neither one of us was listening. We ended dinner by eleven.

As Dmitri went outside to take a call, Stella threw her arms around me. "When are you coming back to Paris, dear? The parade of tourists in and out of your apartment is just depressing."

For a moment, the possibility flickered, seductive, behind my eyes. But the three grand I made from the vacation rental every month was what I lived on (*You get exposure,* Dmitri had said when I'd asked him, tentatively, what my salary would be—*and you get to work with me*), and besides: Dmitri was in St. Petersburg, not Paris.

"I'm—I'm not, Stel. I live here now."

She pulled back, searching my face. After a long moment, she nodded. "All right, dear. Happy birthday. But I do hope you'll remember: there's a difference between getting older and growing up."

The next morning, Dmitri and I walked to the Mariinsky like nothing had happened, but inside, I was still fuming. Stella's words echoed as I stared at the dancers in the studio. Their flat stomachs, the elegant curves of their spines. Couldn't he have made more of an effort with Stella? After all this time. After everything I'd told him. He couldn't have just—I don't know, faked it?

"Two groups," Dmitri announced. His voice hadn't even fully formed the words before the corps members had encircled him, waiting for their orders. I sighed and grabbed the two principals: Irina and Alexei. He'd finalized their pas de deux earlier that week, and now it was up to me to do what I always did—run through the steps with them, bring them from competent to perfect.

I was good, in the studio. I wasn't great. The language thing, which I hadn't thought twice about when moving to Russia (I'd picked up fluent English from Lindsay almost by osmosis, hadn't I?), was no small thing—I wasn't thirteen anymore and the cases and constructions of Russian still escaped me. But although I'd settled into English with the dancers (they could understand, even when they pretended not to), I couldn't stop the ends of my sentences from rising into semi-questions even when I was giving orders. I had nothing like the natural authority he had—in part, because I wasn't the author. There was a feeling of becoming furniture when I took my group aside to rehearse. Of being just an object in the room that they had to move around.

I hated what he'd done for Irina and Alexei. The music was his favorite, that twanging Russian guitar, but everything he'd created was just a little too on the beat, a little too perfect. And this scene, where Baba Yaga meets and seduces the young prince, felt wrong as I watched them run through it. It was choreography for rescuing a damsel from a tower. It wasn't a dance about a witch.

So I started tweaking.

I did this sometimes. Extend a step an extra beat, put a hand gesture in, raise a leg a few centimeters. Dmitri never called me out on it—whether he didn't notice, thinking those were his original steps, or he noticed but was all too happy to take credit, I never knew. I'd gotten away with tiny things in the past, but that day I just grabbed Irina by her shoulders and spun her into a series of steps that could generously be said to have been *inspired* by Dmitri's.

By the time we regrouped to run through the piece as a whole, Irina was grinning at me. I smiled back. It was better; she knew it was better. Sly and twisted and just—witchy.

But as Dmitri watched her, his face took on the exact same expression he'd worn at dinner the night before. Removed, distant. Judging.

"What did you do," he said to me in low, accented French.

"A couple of things," I said, fast—he never completely understood me in French, particularly if I went quickly, though he was too proud to admit it. Most of the time, I found this charming. "If we do a single pirouette instead of a triple there, she'll hit the ground just a second sooner and can spin back up into an *échappée—*"

"No." Back to Russian now, stalking over to turn the music off. "No, no, no. You've missed the entire point, Delphine. As usual."

Again, the dancers cast their glances down to the ground. Again, I faded from the professional I knew I could be into the role of incompetent assistant and girlfriend. Again, I was furniture.

He rehearsed the principals for the rest of the afternoon. But the next day, my steps were still in the piece.

It's still performed that way today.

⁓ October 2018 ⁓

There were photographers outside my building by the time I came home from the Opéra. Luckily, there was a servants' staircase off of the Rue de Birague, though it didn't prevent my in-box and my DMs from filling up with requests from writers of all nationalities. Nothing from my father. Nothing from Stella. Apparently, I would be in both *The New York Times* and the Комсомо́льская пра́вда that week. A quick text to Daniel settled all of these problems: I referred everyone to him for comment and sent him a headshot of me from five years ago to distribute. I didn't want to see Camille's photograph of Jock and me again.

Through it all, Daniel wouldn't accept any money. I took him out to breakfast the following week to thank him; fittingly, he chose Merci again.

When I arrived, he was already sitting there, catlike, staring at the table without seeming to actually see it.

"Everything okay?" I asked, taking the seat across from him.

Daniel smiled. "Absolutely! You've made me the most popular guy at the office. Not," he added quickly, "that that's the point."

"No, it's okay. I'm glad this turned out to be . . . mutually beneficial."

"You know Lindsay's birthday is coming up?" he added.

Of course I knew Lindsay's birthday: October 31. You never forget the birthdays you learned as a child; I knew it as well as I knew my own.

"Right. Well, I've been thinking—she never lets me celebrate it, but since you're back this year, I thought maybe we could do a surprise party? You could take her out for the day, shopping or something, and then bring her back home? I thought November first, so she won't expect it."

I lifted my eyebrows, trying to soften my expression.

"You know, she really does hate her birthday." And always had, at least since she'd turned nineteen and was no longer the youngest dancer in the company.

He gave a crooked smile. "Well, she's not the only one in this marriage, and she'll just have to accept that. Will you bring her by or not?"

I felt knocked back by the anger in his words, the barely masked contempt in his tone. Okay, I'd have to tread lightly. This was apparently about a lot more than just a party. And in the grand scheme of things, it wasn't that big of a deal—she'd have a party, she wouldn't love it, it would be over. I could always tell her about it ahead of time.

"Sure," I said slowly. "But if I were you, I wouldn't invite anybody other than her closest friends. You never know how she'll react to—surprises. Besides, I think she's going to have a lot on her mind with the *soutenance* coming up."

"True enough. Speaking of which—I was really glad to get your email," Daniel said, his tone shifting so that he sounded more pleasant, almost sycophantic.

Oh, God—did he want to talk about kids again? *Please don't. I am nowhere near mentally well enough to handle your emotions right now.*

"I just—did you have to cast her in that ballet?" he said, voice gone raw.

This? I was going to have to talk about this again? Why couldn't he just trust his wife and me to do our jobs, to take care of ourselves?

"She's good, Daniel. She's really good. Don't worry . . ." I leaned forward, trying to get some reaction other than sulkiness. "She's not going to embarrass herself—she's going to astonish everyone. I wouldn't be surprised if she even got named principal this year. Because she deserves that, you know. She's always had that in her."

He met my eyes, now. "Yes, I know," he said. "I saw her run through some of it at home. She's fantastic. You think I don't know that about her? It's what I first loved about her, that quality. You just can't stop watching her, you know? You can't look away."

It was a long moment before he went on. Back in the kitchen, somebody dropped a load of dishes, and they clattered to the ground, a shattering sound ringing out as the tiny café fell silent. Then gradually, somebody spoke, and the low murmur around us returned.

"Do you want children, Delphine?"

I opened my mouth, about to give my standard answer—*Someday, maybe, with the right man*—when the audacity of the question registered, exploding inside me. Blonde or brunette. Spit or swallow. Virgin or whore.

Men are always trying to get us to pick a camp, to declare our allegiance, to reveal what kind of woman we are so that they can judge whether we're doing it right. Why can't they just let us be people?

But before I could formulate the words to politely tell him it was none of his business, he'd gone on.

"I have three little sisters, did you know that?" I shook my head, trying to follow his logic. "They're all back in Bordeaux, and I don't get to see them half as much as I'd like to, but I basically raised them when our mother got remarried. And none of the other shit—stuff," he corrected himself (although really, whom did he think he was talking to?), "none of that mattered to me, because I always thought, Okay, this is what I'll be good at. I'll have lots of children, and that's what I'll be the best at. I'll be the best *dad*."

I grimaced. I really wasn't the best audience for a man espousing the joys of fatherhood. But Daniel missed my reaction entirely and continued staring at me with those broad, appealing eyes.

"I thought that in her thirties, she'd realize what she was asking me to give up—what *she* was giving up—by not wanting kids. And the past few years, I've thought, Well, she has to realize eventually, right? She has to figure out that the ballet thing is just going to turn into a dead end, and then she'll look for something else."

The ballet thing. I tried to keep the disgust off of my face, but I could still feel my upper lip curling slightly.

Commands rang out around me, the commands we'd been following forever. *Straighten your leg. Turn your head. Don't look at her, look out at the audience.*

"But if she gets this promotion—we're going to miss our window for a family," he said, and put his face in his hands.

She's been performing her entire life, I wanted to scream. *Why does she have to perform motherhood just to give meaning to yours?*

"Can't you do something?" he said finally. "Cast someone else? Someone younger? If that happens again, she'll quit. I know she will. She couldn't take it. But as long as she's the lead, she won't give it up. And I'm worried I'll miss my chance to be a father." He paused. "I'm asking you to give me that chance."

"I keep going back and forth," I said finally, "between thinking you're a coward and thinking you're an idiot. But really, you're a little bit of both. If you had any bravery whatsoever, you'd be telling this to Lindsay. Not her friend whom you've known for half a second."

His fingers curled into the skin of his palm.

"And if you had any intelligence whatsoever," I continued, "then you'd know that what you're asking me to do would not only seriously harm my career, but it would also jeopardize one of my oldest friendships. With a woman whose choices I happen to respect. If you had any compassion, you'd realize that Lindsay's been working toward this her entire life, and that if she wanted to be your walking uterus and au pair, she'd have volunteered for the task years ago. If you had any artistic sense, you'd realize that she deserves to be seen by as many people as we can cram into one theater. And if you had any social sense, you'd realize that I did my utmost to try to avoid saying all of this to your face the last time we met. But you don't, and so I'm forced to say it to you now."

He slapped his palms down on the table and raised a tortured face.

"I thought you were different from them," he said, and his voice had gone quiet and mean. "I thought you were the nice one."

I shook my head, getting my purse. "People always think that. It's not true."

His face glowed red, sweat appearing on his forehead. His hands twisted around the table edge and he gave a slow, bitter smile.

"No, it isn't, is it. You're as much of a cunt as the rest of them."

I slid ten euros across the table.

"And you know what?" I said, standing up. "I'm absolutely fine with that."

CHAPTER 28

*C*hoose your own identity, drop the old one on the floor like a fur coat. Shape-shift into someone else. Someone who knows more about life than just the inside of a ballet studio. That person's gone forever. You've left her behind for good.

How easy it is.

Seven years into my life in St. Petersburg, I looked like a new person. At the very least, I was a more polished version of the person I'd once been. The Russian women I knew saw the upkeep of their bodies as both a public service and a point of excruciating pride. When I'd first arrived, I was more interested in libraries, in language, in history, than in anything else. Inside the ancient, dusty, abandoned archives at the Mariinsky, I wasn't a soloist anymore; I was a choreographer in training, apprenticed to one of the great artists of our time, and I was going to show everybody exactly what I was worth.

As it turned out, though, nobody wanted to listen to me that much. To them, I was an alien commodity, always trailing behind Dmitri and watching them too closely with intense eyes. It took me about a year to realize that my air-dried hair and my hangnails weren't helping matters. Our literature teacher had told us, when we were pretending to read *War and Peace* for her class, that the Russians had always admired French style. Turned out she was right—only they admired the French style of the nineteenth century. My scuffed sneakers and torn jeans weren't getting me anywhere.

And so, I'd adapted my own regimen of upkeep, trying to keep myself seventeen forever: at first begrudgingly, then with increasing panic as the years began to carve lines into my face, loosen my skin. It started with a weekly manicure, which took an astonishing two hours. Much longer than it did in France, as the Russian technicians used tiny motor tools to carve away any trace of cuticle, rather than half-heartedly shoving them back with an orange stick. Add to that a monthly waxing appointment—eyebrows, upper lip, underarms, bikini line, legs—from which I invariably returned oiled and pink and cranky. When I was twenty-eight, I conceded to Botox, a quick crunch of needle against bone between my eyebrows that I couldn't stop hearing for days afterward. The lasers, I think, began at thirty, zapping the broken blood vessels around my nose, tightening the falling cheeks. The makeup went from a quick swipe of mascara to a full face of foundation, concealer, eyeliner, that took me forty-five minutes. My air-dried hair was subjected to a weekly blowout, then a twice weekly one, which was when I finally understood the point of shower caps.

They never did get me to spray-tan, though. I remain proud of that.

I'm not sure the dancers ever saw me any differently, though. Even as I physically metamorphosed into somebody who looked more like them on the surface, my weight rose incrementally each year until my bones were softened, the lines of my body increasingly obscured, and a leotard became unthinkable. Even as my days went from hours of studying alone, trying to catch up on the education I should have gotten, to running between the café and the salon and the studio—my own studio. Still they turned away just before I'd finished speaking. Not blatantly enough to reprimand them for it. Just enough for it to sting.

My St. Petersburg life.

How easy it was. Until it wasn't.

"Let me get this straight." We'd defaulted to English a long time ago. "You're breaking up with me because of *Baryshnikov*?"

Dmitri sighed. "I'm not breaking up with you." His low-thunder voice rolled through the carved marble entryway to the Yusupov Palace, bigger than our entire apartment. I winced and looked to see if anybody had heard—but our tour guide hadn't arrived yet. We were alone. "Why do you have to be so dramatic always? All I'm saying is that *White Nights* was some bullshit capitalist propaganda."

That line between my eyebrows would have shown if I hadn't frozen it with toxins on a regular basis. *White Nights*? The Baryshnikov movie where he tap-danced with Gregory Hines? Where Helen Mirren put on pearls and a Russian accent? "And all I'm saying is that I loved it as a girl,"

I said. "I used to watch it on Stella's old VCR about once a month. I didn't mean anything political by the statement."

He ticked his tongue. "Everything is political. Especially here. When will you get that into your head?" He tapped my forehead lightly with a fist; I tried not to duck away.

No kidding. Seven years, and we'd never been inside the goldenrod palace where Felix Yusupov had murdered Rasputin a century earlier, even though it was just around the corner from us. *I'm no communist, but that doesn't mean I'm a monarchist either,* Dmitri had said furiously when I'd proposed going my first week in the city, then hovered over my shoulder as I frantically flipped through my French-Russian dictionary for *monarchist.*

But when I asked why, Dmitri had gone so quiet, so bored, that I dropped it. He'd been in his twenties when the Cold War had ended; I'd been eight. He'd been in the USSR; I'd been in France. He had the right to his feelings about the Romanovs. He knew far better than I who they'd been.

"Pursuing *Tsarina* is only going to bring trouble," Dmitri said, words echoing around that cold, austere room. "Nobody wants to see some pro-Romanov bullshit. Nobody ever really did, even *before* they died."

"Maybe," I said, wrapping my arms around myself. "But—I don't know. It's interesting to me. The interplay of bodies and institutions. Don't you think?"

His bushy brows drew together. "I still think you'd do better doing *Rasputin. Tsarina*—she's a dangerous figure, you know. Even now." Why the tsarina more than anybody else? More than the crazy-eyed Rasputin? Even now? I imagined Margaux rolling her eyes as he spoke, tried to shake off the feeling that she was hovering over my shoulder, observing with that critical gleam in her eye. Not that I'd ever tell her about the conversations I had with Dmitri; our group emails had tapered off into fact-based updates years ago.

Dmitri had been famous for so long now; he'd forgotten how it felt to be the assistant, the one in the shadows. If he'd ever known. Ever felt what it was like as the months passed, then the years, and you were *still* trying to get his dancers to just fucking listen to you for once, *can't you just fucking listen?* And they did, a little, because you were the boss's girlfriend, but they didn't listen well and they didn't listen without whispering all sorts of Russian shit that you still couldn't understand.

"I want to do something big," I said quietly. *Speak up,* the Lindsay in my mind said with a quick elbow to the ribs. I raised my voice. "For my first full-length ballet. I want to—make noise. She wasn't even Russian, you know. The tsarina. She was German, and that's—"

Dmitri's eyes flashed dark. "Your *noise* is somebody else's history. My history."

"I know that—" I raised my hands, gesturing around us. "Why do you think we're here? I want to learn, Dmitri. I want to make art that's—you know, *about* something. Something bigger than just myself. Something bigger than art about art itself. Something that's—"

But I broke off as he started shaking his head.

"This was a mistake," he said, turning toward the huge entryway arching behind us.

I watched him, baffled. "I don't get it. Is the problem that it's not my history? Or that it's yours?"

"A mistake!" And then he was going off in Russian, too fast, too much slang for me to understand. *Stick to your fucking fairy tales.* That much I understood as the heavy door swung open, letting in the sounds of the Neva lapping gently in the canal.

"Madame Léger?" I snapped back around to find a middle-aged man with glasses scuttling down the red-carpeted staircase toward me. "I'm so sorry that I'm late. Should we start the tour? Or are you waiting for somebody else?"

My brain reeled and halted, grasping for the Russian word for *alone*.

"No," I said finally. "I am lonely."

We didn't break up for another six years.

— *October 2018* —

It happened.

The video finally appeared.

Jock had, in fact, posted it on an amateur porn site—by itself, thank God, none of the other dancers' videos were up—and a trashy Italian magazine had picked out some stills and run with them. That was what popped up in my Google alerts: *Porno amatoriale di Delphine Léger, ex ballerina del balletto nazionale di Parigi.* No other site was reposting them, though one, then five, then twenty, were covering the Italian publication's article—an endless loop of my worst nightmares.

I wanted to go through and evaluate every movement I'd made, every action and reaction. Wanted to know how he came off looking. Wanted to analyze every wrinkle and pore and pouch.

I had to watch it. I couldn't watch it. I had to know. I already knew.

I sat in front of my computer for what could have been minutes, hours, days. I was shaking, I was crying, and I didn't even realize either of those things until I went to the bathroom to vomit and caught sight of myself in the mirror.

This wasn't me.

I closed the browser window and opened another. Started looking up lawyers. And by the time I had made an appointment with a woman specializing in sexual harassment and revenge porn, I was back in my body enough that I could make myself get up and take a shower. All of a sudden, all I wanted was the heat of the water: scalding all of this off of me, letting me shed my skin like a snake so I could replace it with a new one.

But I was in there for a long, long time, and I still didn't feel clean.

Once the video was out there, I felt fundamentally changed on a cellular level, and yet the details of my daily life all looked the same. How was that possible? When I came into the studio the next day and found Lindsay waiting for me, warmed up and ready to go, she paused as I threw down my bags.

Had she seen the site? Watched the footage? Surely she'd be disgusted by me if she had.

A second later, her arms were around me.

"Do you want to talk about it?" she whispered.

"I . . ." How to translate the dark recesses of your mind into words? "No."

She nodded, and for a second, I just let myself stand there, head against her shoulder. This was all I needed, right now. This was enough.

As I pulled away from her, I was so tense, I was vibrating like a string. But then I looked at her: shadows beneath her eyes, crease between her eyebrows, mouth drooping. Her face was drawn; in the harsh overhead light of the studio, it looked almost gaunt, skeletal. Something was wrong, something beyond me. Why is it that trauma is written so easily on women's bodies? It's so readable if you know how to look. Maybe it is on all of us, men and women both; only I'd spent my life in a world full of women and I'd never learned to truly see men's pain.

Still, I didn't think that was it. We were simply more legible.

"Linds—is there something else going on?"

She sighed exaggeratedly: a deliberate shorthand to cover up the depth of . . . whatever it was, going on inside her.

"Daniel," she said simply, and shrugged.

I winced. I had debated telling her what had transpired at Merci, ultimately deciding it wasn't my place to meddle in her marriage. "Ah, fuck. I'm sorry. Our discussion . . . it just totally devolved. I lost—I lost control. He asked me to take you out of the ballet, but I didn't want to get involved—and I'd *never* take you out of this part, but . . ."

She shook her head. "It's been going on for years, this kid business. I'm running out of ways to tell him we're just not going to have any, but no matter what I say, he just—doesn't hear me. I can't be that person for him. I told him we should get a divorce." Her voice was tired, and I *knew* that tiredness, knew that exhaustion in my bones. *After all this time. Here we are.*

I swallowed. "What did he say?"

"Couples counseling. Again. As if any therapist would be capable of understanding—" She waved her hand around the studio. For a moment, she stared at it almost longingly, as though she were nostalgic for a moment she was currently living. Then she slapped her hand down to her thigh. "Well, we're doing it, and it is what it is. So, what have you got for me today?"

"I've been sketching in some of the iffy spots. It's a bit intense, are you ready to start?"

Lindsay was always ready. She nodded.

"The more I think about this, the more we need to show what you can do. You, not Camille, not the other soloists—or the other principals, even."

Her tired mouth twisted into a mischievous grin.

"So, every single movement you make—Linds, I want you to think back to all of the corrections you've ever gotten and disregard them completely. I want your hips out of alignment. I want your shoulders arched back. I want those big hand flourishes in there. You know what I mean?"

Her face was bright. "Yeah," she said. "You want *me*."

Throughout the afternoon, we had her strip down more for each additional section. I gave her my scarf and sweater to give her more layers; I'd have to bring up some really long necklaces from wardrobe for the next rehearsal. No matter what I threw at her, she assimilated it in seconds and mirrored it back to me just as I'd imagined. No—better. Off the leash of POB style, Lindsay was limned with some desperate elegant wildness that I'd never pictured but that showed each sequence off to perfection.

"Try it again," I called out around six, right when we were running through "Maybe" for what I'd promised would be the last time. "This time without clutching your torso like that."

"Like what?" Lindsay asked. I searched her face for sarcasm—she always seemed to know what her body had been doing at any given moment—but didn't find any.

"In the last part. You were doing this . . ." I demonstrated the way she'd grasped her rib cage with white knuckles on the last run-through. "It's looser than that. Not as controlled."

"Oh." A shadow flitted across her eyes. "Sorry."

"It's okay. Just go again."

Halfway through, I had to stop the music.

"No, see, there—" But I was cut off as she ran over to her dance bag and vomited. She heaved into it as dramatically as she did everything else—I could actually see the violent contractions of her rib cage. Just watching her made saliva rise in the back of my mouth with sympathetic nausea. I ran over to her, put a hand on her back.

"Oh my God. Are you all right?"

She wiped her mouth, standing back up. Her eyes were glittering and fierce. "Yeah," she croaked. "Sorry. Let's go again."

"What? No."

She smiled weakly.

"It's not the flu. I must have eaten something. You won't get sick. Let's finish here."

"Well," I said doubtfully, "if you're sure—"

And that was when she bent over and threw up on my feet.

Lindsay said she didn't need a doctor (her actual words were, *You must have lost your mind*), but I insisted on taking her home.

I kept a hand on her back as we walked down to the Métro. What if it was something serious? You have to be really sick to vomit in public instead of holding it in and rushing to a bathroom. Especially if you're a dancer; your body doesn't just lose control like that. What if this wasn't just a bad oyster? What if it was the first sign of the kind of illness that eats you up inside, the kind that wastes you away and owns you, the kind that turns you inside out with fear and laughs about it? I'd seen it happen before. It happens so often that everyone has a story about it. You listen to enough of them and tragedy starts to turn mundane. We're all going to die. And yet each time somebody does, there it is again: A new world is born. A world without that person.

As we stood on the platform, the heat from her warm muscles pulsed familiarly beside me. I could smell the drying sweat on her skin, the sour odor of vomit.

I clutched her shoulder.

"You'll feel better tomorrow," I said. "And then, Linds—you're going to make it. This time, I really think you are. Nathalie won't have any choice but to make you a principal."

She grinned, but there was something wobbly behind it. I tightened my grip on her as she tilted her head, studying my face.

"Yeah," she said. "But what about you?"

I took a step back. "What about me?"

"I think you've avoided asking yourself an important question," she said. "Maybe you've never even thought about it. But I really think it could change your life."

"What's that?" I said.

"Someone has to be in the next generation of famous choreographers. *So why not you?*" she said with emphasis. "Why not you, Delphine? You could be known everywhere. You could charge whatever you wanted for companies to put on your shows. You're good enough; so why not?"

And for just a moment, I saw it again. Since Nathalie had cut *Tsarina*, I hadn't let myself think about it: fame. But here it was again. My name with Balanchine's. With Nureyev's. With Petipa's.

"It's a good story," I said finally.

"Story?"

I shrugged. "I mean, who knows what's going to happen? Anything could, right?"

Lindsay snorted.

"All I'm saying, Delphine," she said, "is that somebody's going to go down in history. Why not you?"

By the time I had a response for her, warm air was blowing through the tunnel as the train came toward us.

"I think it's just—dance is the only thing that interests me. The only thing that I'm really good at. The only thing I've ever done that matters. So, I have to keep going. Regardless of how famous or obscure I end up . . . I can't stop doing it. I could try, but there'd be no point. It's who I am. You know?"

Her porcelain face was on fire as she stared straight ahead, down into the tracks.

"Yes," she said finally. "I know."

"And thinking about being famous, or becoming rich because of dance—I want it so much it hurts. I want to leave a legacy, and dance is the only way for me to achieve that, so all I can do is just . . . not think about it too much. Try not to want it too bad. Because if I let myself want it and then I failed, the failure might destroy me."

She didn't say anything for a long moment.

"What if not wanting it can destroy us, too?" she said, staring right at me. "Living our lives as though we expect to be forgotten. As though now is all that matters. It might be easier on the mind to live like that, but it's harder on the soul." She widened her eyes. "I really think you should remember that."

CHAPTER 29

— April 2018 —

"An . . . English story for children? Never heard of it. A centaur and . . . Santa Claus? No, I don't think so. What else?" I couldn't take my eyes off of Olga's expertly manicured red nails, shining around her teacup. They weren't red the way that a Frenchwoman would have done them, short and matte; instead, they were perfect glossy ovals, glittering in the Mariinsky's office lights.

"Oh, okay. Well—" I'd been banking on the fact that she'd want to do *The Lion, the Witch, and the Wardrobe.* With the potential international audience, the strange creatures, the virtuosity of the Mariinsky's dancers—but she didn't, and my plan B was a weak one. I already knew it was weak. "I know we'd talked about maybe returning to *Tsarina—*"

The artistic director's thin lips stretched thinner under their bright red lipstick. "No," Olga said. "*You* talked about returning to it. As I recall, I said—"

"*No way in hell,*" I muttered. "Yeah."

She laughed. "Look, Delphine, we'd love to feature your work again. After the success of *Medusa,* upper management's really starting to pay attention. Any chance you want to do a series of shorts in that vein? Twenty, thirty minutes?"

Twenty minutes. Thirty. I'd been thinking in these segments for nearly a decade. And while at first I'd been desperate to get started, to pay my dues, to make my name—I couldn't stay here forever, spiraling around the patchwork routine I'd made when I was twenty-three. Roll out of bed by ten to observe the dancers taking class. Watch Dmitri's rehearsals, help him work through the harder bits, the parts where he got stuck. Gather my dancers for a brief rehearsal of my own at the end of the day, their muscles sore and trembling, their bodies unwilling to give a hundred percent when they'd be onstage in just a few hours, their faces full of barely concealed annoyance at having to work with *me*.

At least I was finally getting paid. It was a small consolation, though.

When I'd poured out my frustrations to Margaux and Lindsay in our monthly email, cracking myself open to them after years of gradually hardening up, it had taken only a few hours for the responses to come barreling back. *You're better than that, Delphine. You need to stand up for yourself. Don't let them make you small!*

I bit the inside of my cheek. "The thing is, Olga, that I really think it's time I started work on a longer piece. As you say, *Medusa* did really well last year. And if it's not *Lion*, if it's not *Tsarina*, I get that, but we've known each other for ten years. Can't you trust me enough to give me the space?"

Her dark eyebrows arched higher than I'd realized they could go. "A blank check?"

"In essence. Yes."

Those red nails drummed against the shiny wood of her desk. "And you'd really risk it all for that?"

"Risk . . . all what?"

"Him. Dmitri. Your relationship."

"Why . . . what does this have to do with him?"

Every feature on her face seemed to have rounded into a perfect O. "You really don't know?" Wrapping her hands together into a single fist, she bent forward across the desk. "He was sick with jealousy after the Gorgon piece, Delphine. Of course, he never actually said as much, but he barged in here, demanding to know why *Medusa* was getting press that *Baba Yaga* never had. If we gave you a full-length ballet . . ."

My mouth was dry, and I tried to swallow. The months of sulkiness, the hunched shoulders, the passive-aggression in his eyes. Well, at least now I knew what had provoked it all.

"You are very good. I wouldn't be opposed to cutting you loose," Olga said, shrugging. "But. Up to you, I suppose. You want to risk it?"

He'd resented my success. He wanted me to know my place.

"No," I said hoarsely. "Or—not now, I think. Not yet. I'll expand on the Gorgons, then, I guess?"

Her helmet of black hair was bobbing in agreement as I got up to leave. "Yes," she said. "I think that's probably wise."

— *October 2018* —

That afternoon, I spotted Margaux approaching the Palais Garnier from the opposite direction, and I ran up to her.

"Margaux! Where have you been? I've been calling and texting." I looked at her more closely. "Shit, are you okay?"

Her hair was limp and greasy, hanging around her shoulders instead of pinned back in a work-ready bun. Her skin had broken out around her chin and nose, and she hadn't bothered to cover it up. Her eyes were red rimmed, puffy, so purple underneath it was like a child had used a marker to color them in.

"Yeah, I heard, you got him," she said dully. "That's great."

"But it's not just that," I said. There was so much I wanted to tell her. "Look, do you have some time to get lunch?"

She looked me straight in the eyes.

"I really don't," she said, and started to walk past me.

I reached out and grabbed her shoulder. "Hey, wait! What are you doing?"

She sighed. "I'm going to rehearsal, Delphine. What does it look like I'm doing?"

When Margaux got mad, she usually just screamed at me. It was a small price to pay for getting things dealt with quickly. I didn't know how to handle this Margaux, the one giving me the silent treatment.

The last time we'd seen each other—I stopped. When was the last time we'd seen each other? When she and Lindsay had been at the apartment to talk about Jock. I took a step back. A few weeks ago, she'd come to me with a million serious problems, cracking open her chest to show me her damaged heart: the drinking, the miscarriages, the Lindsay stuff, all of it.

And I hadn't done anything since. All I'd done was ask her to be there for me when I hadn't been there for her. To pick up the pieces of my life when she'd actually needed my help. Shame flowed through me, flushing me.

I saw our friendship ending, saw how it had been ending for a long time. Since I'd returned, certainly, but even before that. And I knew I'd do whatever I had to in order to save it.

"This isn't us!" I cried, and my voice for once held all of the urgency, all of the fear, I truly felt. "We don't do this sulky shit other girls do. Something's wrong, you say it to me, and then we work through it."

She stared at me. "Maybe we can't, this time," she said, turning away.

After all of our shit with Lindsay, *Margaux* was going to be the one to implode? She had the right to. But if she was going down, I'd be at her side the whole time.

"Do you remember," I said quickly, before I could even think, "the first time we met?"

She paused, turning back. Her eyes had softened, almost imperceptibly.

"Yeah," she said.

"You said, *Hi, I'm Margaux. I'm one hundred thirty-two centimeters tall and I weigh twenty-eight kilos.*"

She frowned. "No, I didn't. They never would have let me in if I'd been that fat. You said, *Hi, I'm Delphine. Do you know about sex?*"

"I didn't!"

"You most certainly did."

And then we were both laughing. Laughing hard, almost bent double.

"Oh, come on," she said, and grabbed my elbow. "Let's get a coffee."

We sat down on the Café de la Paix terrace. Even if we'd end up paying nine euros for our coffees, it would be worth it. At least we were talking.

"Marg," I said as she pulled out her phone, "what's going on?"

A line appeared between her eyebrows, and she pressed her lips together. "Do you ever feel like you've been playing out the same stories, over and over again, your entire life?"

I reached out and grabbed her hand. "All the time," I said. "Every single day."

She raised her eyes to meet my gaze. "After this whole Lindsay thing, then the Jock thing, I got to thinking—I'm just so sick of it," she said. "This world. These crazy dramas we bring on ourselves. More than that. We *create* them."

I wrapped my arms over my chest.

"I understand, but Margaux, things are changing. Lindsay's in my ballet now! But you knew that. And Jock did get fired—" I stopped myself.

She shrugged. "Yeah, okay. The players might change, but the fundamental dynamics are the same. And I'm just along for the ride. Nothing

I say or do matters." Her eyes were bright with tears. "Meanwhile, every day, it's the same damn thing for me. I wake up sick. I start shaking. I drink to feel normal, you know? The place where everyone else starts from, I need a drink to get there."

I cupped my hand around her chin. "It must be so hard. Have you started going back to meetings?"

She smiled furiously, twisting away from me.

"I've been in recovery for the past two weeks!" she said. "And nobody except Julie has even noticed." She stopped for a moment. "You know, when you told me you were coming back, all I could think was how wonderful it was going to be. I fell for your lines, you know. *Everything is going to be just like before.* That's the problem, though. It is. It's *exactly* like before. All this shit is going on with me and the two of you, it's like, Oh, what opportunities are *we* going to grasp today? How are Lindsay and Delphine going to become stars? And I'm just supposed to be the sidekick and happy about everything good that happens to you and be sad about whatever bad shit happens to you. But that's not me. What about when bad things happen to me? Or good things," she added defensively, as though I'd been the one to leave them out.

I was too stunned to respond.

"I have my own problems, you know. You know that Julie's going through IVF now? Yeah," she said as I blinked in surprise. "She's in Madrid this week. Alone, because I have performances. She's forty, so it's been tough, but she doesn't trust me to stay sober for nine months anymore. Not after I lost the first two."

How had I not realized how much this meant to her? Those miscarriages hadn't been accidents she'd taken in stride, hadn't been the end to unwanted pregnancies. They hadn't been examples she'd been using to prove that she really was an alcoholic. They'd been tragedies in their own right. Tragedies I hadn't been there for. Tragedies I hadn't even *acknowledged*.

"You always did want lots of kids," I said.

She turned those flashing green eyes on me.

"I can't believe you remember that," she said.

Did she think I paid attention only to myself? Of course she thought that. Because that's what I had done and fiercely fought to keep doing. That's what got us here.

"I'm sorry, Margaux. I'm so, so sorry. What can I do to help?"

She showed a dimple. "Well. Being here is a start. Forcing me to be here with you is even better."

My heart ached at her smile. It had taken so little on my part to make her happy; the little I'd been withholding from her for—how long? Maybe forever. And all she'd needed was a simple acknowledgment of her pain.

I'd failed her in so many ways.

"I'm not saying this because I need you to have any particular reaction," I said slowly. "Maybe you need time to forgive me. Maybe you never can. And I would understand that. But I want you to know how really, truly sorry I am. How furious I am at myself for—letting myself be so willfully ignorant of what was happening with you. For not listening, for not seeing you. And you're right, it's not just now, it's always been that way. You deserve to know how angry I am at myself about that, and how deeply sorry I am. But you don't have to do anything with that," I added quickly. "It's not your responsibility to forgive me or make me feel better. Just—I'm sorry."

Her face, which had been in her familiar Margaux-mask as I spoke, softened slightly.

"The thing I keep coming back to," she said finally, "is *why* didn't you notice? Why didn't you do anything when I asked for your help?"

Because I wanted to believe it wasn't real.

Because I wanted to keep my teenage image of you alive in my head forever.

Because a million things, none of which reflect particularly well on me.

"I just—" I shook my head. "Too wrapped up in myself, I guess."

Her face darkened. "That's an easy answer," she said. "Besides, it's one I just gave you. This isn't an open-book test."

"No, you're right." I thought a moment. "I made what I wanted to believe more important than what was actually happening. I wanted things to be like they were before—before everything we did to Lindsay, before my mother died, before Dmitri—because then maybe I'd have the chance to get my own life right. I wanted that so badly, Margaux."

She nodded, leaning back and folding her arms across her chest. "I'm going to tell Lindsay what we did," she said. A challenge. "I have to. It's time for me to make a break with the person I used to be."

Pleas danced through my mind. *Wait a month. Two. Wait until after the ballet premieres. Wait until I leave.*

"I get that," I said finally. "Will you tell me before you do it?"

"Sure," she said.

And as she got up to go, there were no invitations to brunch, no tearful hugs or promises of forgiveness to come, no mention of the future or the past. But as she was halfway down the street, a gust of wind came by, blowing up her skirt and exposing the leotard underneath to the world. She turned back to me, as though by instinct, and winked.

And it felt like I was seeing her for the very first time.

CHAPTER 30

— April 2018 —

When a relationship falls apart, it's like a building crumbling: slow at first, then all at once.

Would it have made a difference if I'd told Margaux and Lindsay about it all? If I'd said: *I was in costuming at the Mariinsky, furious about Dmitri's insistence on keeping me in my place, when I discovered something to be even more furious about.*

"You look mad," my friend Galina, a costumer, said. No emotional weight to her words; just pure observation.

"Yeah, well. I am," I muttered. "Dmitri—" But I didn't have the Russian words for why I was so upset. Not that I had them in French, either.

He made me small. That was it, in part.

He liked me small. Better. But still not all of it.

He kept me small, and he liked it, and the whole time he had me convinced it was my own failings preventing me from moving forward.

Galina's face went shaded, concerned, and she grabbed my arm, making me stumble into a group of mannequins and knock them over like bowling pins.

If I'd said to Margaux and Lindsay: *It was April but it was still freezing and dark by five in the afternoon, and there was something wrong with the electricity that day, so the lights were flickering overhead like a horror movie as she whispered.*

"You poor thing," she said. Half-sorry and, somehow, half-delighted. "All those other women—we were sure you had to know."

I stared at her square, polished face, certain I'd misunderstood.

"All those—?"

Her mouth rounded as she dropped my arm.

What would Margaux and Lindsay have done? They would have been outraged on my behalf—but I was too tired for their outrage. They would have tried to be kind and soothing, never a natural look on Margaux—but I couldn't have taken their pity.

Because how do you describe what that kind of betrayal is like to someone who's never experienced it? I'd spent decades witnessing my mother trying and failing to show the world what she'd been through. I could have told them: *It's like discovering that he has a terrible illness, except, somehow, he's managed to transfer all of the symptoms over to you. It's like being sprayed with a fire hose, except instead of water, what comes at you is everything bad you've ever believed about yourself. It's like discovering that all of the women you thought were crazy were actually normal, that their actions were a logical response to the conditions of their lives, and oh yeah—now you're one of them.*

Now you're the kind of woman that men call crazy, too.

True, our relationship took shape at a moment when I was vulnerable. When I was too scared to go on, when I was willing to let the nearest man shelter me from the falling wreckage of my life. But I wasn't that person anymore. I'd grown into someone else before his very eyes, and he didn't like it.

I no longer cared what he thought about me. I wasn't going to be small anymore.

I walked out of the costume workshop and realized that there were only three people in the world who had never made me feel small: Margaux. Lindsay. And Stella.

I emailed Nathalie from the hallway, and I had my POB contract for the 2018–2019 season within the week.

— *October 2018* —

As it turned out, I didn't have to worry about when I would see Margaux again. That Saturday, Lindsay texted both of us to meet her for brunch.

It was colder now, real autumn weather. Autumn always made me a bit sad. The summer ending, everything dying, smearing memories on the ground alongside the leaves. I had on a scarf and coat, and so did Margaux. Lindsay appeared wearing only a long-sleeved T-shirt, unprepared for the actual temperature and yet completely unwilling to sit inside.

I kissed Lindsay's cheek, and she seemed to flinch.

That sensitivity to being touched—it was a symptom of cancer, right? Her face was as pale as my mother's had been in the days leading up to her death.

She sat with her arms around herself, glaring fiercely at the general vicinity.

I glanced at Margaux, who raised her eyebrows and gave a brief nod, like we were police officers about to go in on a bad guy.

But she hadn't seen Lindsay vomiting. She hadn't seen her pale and shaky and sweating.

Oh my God. She was going to tell her.

I shook my head frantically. Margaux sighed and looked away.

"Did you see," Lindsay said finally, "that I put a clip of the rehearsal footage up on Instagram?"

"I haven't been on Instagram in days," Margaux said.

"A hundred thousand views," Lindsay said.

I frowned as I took out my phone and pulled up Lindsay's page. "I really wish you wouldn't do that," I said reflexively. "It's getting so close to its final form now; we want people to actually come and see the show."

"They'll still come," Lindsay said.

"Not if they can see it all online."

"It's just a clip, Delphine," she said. "Besides, they'll want the chance to see it live. And eventually, they'll start coming just to see *me*."

Margaux snorted. She looked like she hadn't slept in a week.

"Awfully sure of yourself," she said.

"I'm sure of this," Lindsay said, her voice turning fierce.

"It's that good?"

"Yes, and I'm that good in it." She shrugged. "Watch it. You'll see."

Nathalie would lose her mind over this. "You need to take it down," I said.

"It's fine."

"It's not."

Lindsay's eyes, bruised and tired, flicked away from me.

"Lindsay," Margaux said, breaking the silence, "I need—"

"Should we order?" I said. "What do you feel like?"

Margaux's eyes narrowed. She tried again. "I've been wanting to—"

"Oh, hello!" I said to the waiter. He hesitated a minute at my maniacal smile. "We were just figuring out our order. I'm not sure what everyone else feels like, but I think I'd like—"

"A bottle of pinot grigio," Margaux said, glaring at me.

"You can't!" I said.

She sighed, rolling her eyes. "I can. Please," she added to the waiter, who nodded and took off.

"Margaux—"

She held up a hand. "I don't want to hear it."

The waiter came back with a bottle of wine, condensation beading on its green glass despite the cold. He set three glasses in front of us, crystal ringing as it hit the metal table.

"Margaux, don't drink it. Please," I said as she swished the few centimeters the waiter had poured around in her glass, brought it to her nose, nodded.

"If you're so determined to escape reality, why can't I?" she said. The wine glugged out of the bottle into our glasses. Lindsay stared at it, the faint nausea on her face pinging at my heart.

"Oh, that's rich. Just because I think there's a time and a place—"

"You guys," Lindsay said.

"Fuck your time. Fuck your place."

"You guys!" Lindsay said. She held the glass of wine with an outstretched arm, before letting it smash gloriously onto the cobblestones.

"I'm pregnant," she said dully as the café sprang into action around her.

— *April 2018* —

Cinderella knew what would happen, you know. I think we forget that when recounting her story. The fairy godmother told her right up front: *At midnight, all of this disappears.* But we never believe the things older women tell us, do we? We have to live them for ourselves. And so, awful as it must have been to see the coach collapse back into a pumpkin, the horses shrink into mice—she can't say she wasn't warned. Instead of surprise, Cinderella must have felt something else, something more like resignation and disappointment. *Oh, this. Well, of course, this.*

And what woman hasn't felt that, more times than she can count?

On my way home from the theater, I was once again Cinderella. I had moved quickly through the first hot shock of the knowledge, the cold throb of betrayal, and settled into a painfully familiar, bone-deep exhaustion. Again, my life had blown up. Again.

And yet there was still the itch of an idea in the back of my brain: a woman, dancing alone to Peggy Lee's "Is That All There Is?"

The first few notes pinging out of the piano. Her husky voice talking as a ballerina walked out to the center of the stage. Or not the center—no, just off center, stage left. And then the swooping of her voice, the leg coming around, mirroring it—

I stopped still in the middle of the Ulitsa Glinki, people rushing around me, nothing but extraneous movement my brain quickly filtered out. I knew it then. I wasn't just a fairy-tale princess in rags, staring at a pumpkin. No matter what had gone wrong with Dmitri, the past thirteen years had transformed me in other ways.

I was a choreographer now, through and through.

But I was never going to truly be one here, where my role was defined entirely by my relationship with Dmitri. This was never going to be my place; it was always going to be his. I couldn't stand on my own here. He would always overshadow me.

Which was why my immediate instinct had been to email Nathalie.

I thought of the tsarina. Stranded thousands of miles from her home among people who hated her. Determined to prove her worth by producing a son, she was betrayed time and again by her own body, giving the nation daughter after unnecessary daughter. At least she'd had true love, whatever that was. If she hadn't been royalty, would she have stayed? Would love have been enough to carry her through the bear traps littering her Russian existence?

I no longer had love. But unlike her, I could go home.

My mother had been dead for more than a decade now. Paris seemed, for the first time, a canvas upon which I could create my own life. I'd spent my time in St. Petersburg getting older, yes; but now, finally, it was time to grow up.

Thirteen years, though. Thirteen years gone, in a flash—the daily construction of a love story that now seemed like nothing more than a wasted experiment, a period that would make me cringe when I thought of it, later.

I stood in front of our ancient, battered door for a few minutes before I could bring myself to go inside. I don't know what it was—the bittersweet knowledge that these were the last moments that the apartment belonged to the both of us, I think. A kind of goodbye.

And there he was: at the dining room table where he always worked, his dark head bent childlike over his notebook. He used markers to write out the steps, liking the smoothness of the ink gliding across the paper—it helped him go faster, he told me when I awoke once, in the middle of a bright St. Petersburg night, to find him inspiration-struck, his hand flying across the page. I'd wrapped my arms around him from behind, rested my head on his. He'd made me feel so safe, then.

But I had never really been safe.

He didn't look up as I came into the room.

The humiliation still burned in me, but the thing I felt more than anything was defeat. I was done trying to get him to be the person I wanted him to be. Finished with pretending to myself that that person even existed, buried under layers of arrogance and indifference. Tired of contorting myself into various positions, trying to find a single one that would please him.

"Dmitri," I said, "we're over."

He looked up, confused. "Over?"

"You've been fucking everything on two legs. And I just can't keep trying anymore."

I saw the look cross his face before he spoke. The trapped animal, the caged boar.

"For fuck's sake, Delphine. You're French. Does it even really bother you?"

I saw him then as he truly was. His graying hair, his thickening waist. The promise that the company had seen in his youth, the mediocrity that had emerged from the seeds of his talent. I imagined a Russian woman, all long sleek hair and long sleek limbs, in his arms—and the only thing that flickered in me was sadness. For her, and for the girl who'd fled Paris for him thirteen years before.

"No, it doesn't really bother me. Not anymore," I said. "That's why this is over."

He rubbed his face with those enormous hands. "So, what are you trying to say? You're leaving me?"

I looked around at the home my mother's apartment had allowed us to have: a version of the flat Dmitri had when I'd arrived, one floor up in the same building, one room bigger. It had felt almost bare at first, his belongings diluted over the larger area, mine contained in a single suitcase. Now, all these years later, my life with Dmitri was etched in every object, my existence slowly insisting on itself until the space had become mine as well. The poster of Isabelle Durand as Nikiya. The fern I'd bought from the pushy florist on a sweltering June day. The ancient bedspread I'd found at the back of a closet, hand-embroidered by Dmitri's mother, which I'd spent days washing and rewashing by hand before its pinks and greens emerged fresh and we could use it on our bed.

"No," I said slowly. "I'm not leaving." I let that sink in for a moment, let the hope spark in his heart. I relished my cruelty before I took a breath and went on. "You are. Come back in five months, if you can afford it. But I'll already be gone."

— October 2018 —

A minute—an hour?—later, Margaux opened her mouth. My heart was a trapped animal in my chest, and I had no thoughts, only instincts. I should have felt relief that Lindsay wasn't sick, and I did. But I was overcome by this vibrating sense of wrongness in every part of my body. Everything that she'd worked for, suddenly in jeopardy. Just like it had been when we were twenty-two, except now, she wouldn't have the time to come back from it.

See how fast your body could turn against you? It could happen in a single instant.

Don't congratulate her. Don't ask her about her career. Let her speak first.

"What are you going to do about it?" Margaux said.

Lindsay's eyes bulged.

"What do you mean, *what am I going to do?* I'm going to get rid of it."

Say something, Delphine. Something supportive, something helpful.

Softer now, Lindsay, you're a fairy princess and he's your prince.

"Is that . . . wise?" Margaux said carefully. Not carefully enough; she was translating badly. In French, the sentence sounds like a true question: Is that a good decision? In English, it's more of a statement, a judgment: That's not a good decision.

Go to him, go to him—smile.

"Would keeping it be wise?"

Margaux bit her lip. "You're thirty-five. Almost thirty-six."

Smile more.

"And?" Lindsay's tone was pure ice.

Margaux ignored the provocation, lifting her palms up. "How many more chances will there be?"

Smile like you mean it.

"Margaux." Lindsay's face had turned red—not with shame but with frustration. "I'm sure of one thing. And it's that I didn't come this far to only come this far."

"Meaning . . ."

Lindsay's fingers curled around the edge of the table, grasping it like she was about to flip it over. "Meaning that I'm on the verge of—of everything. It's all happening. How can I let—a little growth—take that away from me?"

"A growth?" Margaux said, almost spitting it at her. "It's a baby."

"Not yet, it's not." Her jaw was set.

"It is," Margaux said. "You're creating life."

"That's an easy answer. Too easy."

She shrugged. "It means a lot to some women."

Lindsay's eyes blazed. "I am not *some women*."

"I thought you had cancer," I managed to choke out.

"Well. It's not that different, is it," Lindsay said.

"Lindsay!" said Margaux, looking genuinely shocked—rare for her.

"Cut out all this Catholic shit. There's something growing in my body that I don't want."

"Yeah, except you can have it out in nine months," Margaux said. "And it's a human being."

"I'm going to have it out a lot sooner than that," Lindsay said grimly.

"How can you listen to this shit?" Margaux exclaimed, turning to me. "It's a baby! It's not like she's living on welfare or has an abusive husband or her life would be in any danger. It's not like anything's at stake here!"

"Yes," I said slowly. "I'm listening. And it seems to me—" I glanced at Margaux. Nothing I said was going to convince her. I knew that. And yet . . . "It seems to me that what we're talking about is the potentiality of a life versus an actual life." Lindsay was doing exactly what I'd been trying to do for myself: taking charge of what happened to her life. How, after everything, could we deny her that?

"We don't live anything like actual lives," Margaux said, her lips pulled back in a hideous smile. "And you know it."

I tried another tactic. "Lindsay, how far along are you?"

Lindsay shook her head. "About seven weeks. It's still early. I could miscarry." But she wouldn't meet my eyes. We all knew that lucky miscarriages didn't exist outside of the movies. Only unlucky ones.

"Do you want children?" I asked her. I'd been with Dmitri long enough to recognize the trapped, resigned look that immediately appeared on Lindsay's face. *This question again. Seriously?* This *question again?*

"Maybe someday," she said. "But . . . I don't know. Not with Daniel. And not because I feel like I have to."

Margaux shook her head, hair fanning out around her face. "There's no someday. There's only now."

"Did you read that on a bumper sticker?"

"If it's a question of raising a child," Margaux said, and there was an edge of hope in her voice, "I could take it. Julie and me."

"Yeah, I can't see that ending in total catastrophe," I muttered in French, before switching back to English. "If it's a question of the ballet, Linds— you *could* have it and come back. You'd still have a few years left. You're young." The lie tasted like copper.

"No, *you're* young," Lindsay said. "I'm not. Not anymore."

"I'm older than you."

She squinted in frustration. "Thirty-six is nothing for a choreographer. Thirty-five—okay, almost thirty-six—for a dancer is . . . it's my last chance to advance. I'll never get beyond *sujet* if I leave now. Worse, I'll never know if I could have. It'll just have been decided for me."

It wasn't untrue.

"Here's what I think," Margaux said, and I winced at what I knew was coming. "I think you're in love with your pain. I think you've been waiting for a promotion for so long that you've decided it's going to fix your life when you get it, that everything that's wrong is because of your job title. And now you're about to get it and you don't even realize that it isn't going to make anything better. It's actually going to make things so much worse. Because what happens when you get to principal? When you get there and everything is exactly the same as it's always been?"

Lindsay shook her head. "It wouldn't be. Won't be."

"This baby? I think it's a gift," Margaux said finally.

Lindsay stared at her, uncomprehending. Turned to me.

"I think . . ." I hesitated. *I think if you have it, you'll hate yourself forever, and you'll hate Daniel more. I think you'll come to hate the baby, too. I think you'll always regret not finishing the ballet. I think if you do this, you'll ruin the ballet.*

But it wasn't just *the* ballet. It was *my* ballet. I had to stay the hell out of this.

"I think you already know what you want to do," I finished lamely.

Lindsay scrunched up her face. "Well, of course I already know what I want to do. I just—" She swallowed. "I didn't want to do it alone."

Margaux sat back, crossing her arms over her chest.

"You're not alone," I said.

A sad smile crossed her face, then quickly faded.

"Do you need somebody to go with you?" I asked.

"One of you," Lindsay said softly. "Maybe."

Yeah, and I was pretty sure I knew which one.

"Margaux," Lindsay said, and her face had gone wide and open, "I know that you and Julie have been trying. I know it might be hard for you to see me do this. But you're also a dancer. You've been right next to me as I've clawed my way up here. I thought you'd understand."

"I don't. I don't understand how you fail to see that real life is so much more than what we're living. Life can be . . ." Margaux closed her eyes, found the words. "So much bigger."

Lindsay's face fell. She loved me, but she looked up to Margaux.

"It's okay," I said to Lindsay. "I'll take you."

"Can you help me set up the appointments?"

Anything. "I—sure."

"You let her get away with too much," Margaux said to me in grim French. "It's only going to hurt you."

"Stop being the Oracle of Delphi. It's her fucking life."

It was only after I said it that I realized I'd replied in English. But Lindsay had shrunk back into herself, and I don't think she even heard.

CHAPTER 31

"You fucking cunt!"

The words echoed through the Place des Vosges walkway and before I could identify the voice, footsteps pounded up behind me.

I turned. There he was: Jock, looking like he wanted to slam my head against the medieval bricks. Adrenaline rushed through me. Adrenaline and the smallest bit of regret.

No. It wasn't my fault. *You can't go around taking responsibility for bad men, Delphine.*

"I want to talk to you," he said.

"I'm busy," I said. Lindsay was going to the second of her two legally mandated medical consultations; I'd promised to join her.

It doesn't matter, she'd said absently when I asked her if she wanted me to go to the first one. *I can tune out French pretty easily.*

She'd called the day of the appointment, in a panic about some metal thing. After I'd finally convinced her to pass me to the doctor, I'd explained that it was a speculum. How had she made it this far without encountering a speculum? But no mother had been around to hound her about pap smears and checkups when she was a teenager; she'd never had anyone looking out for her. Anyone but us.

This time, I'd be there for her.

"I don't care how busy you are," Jock said. He looked awful: hair lank, eyes red. "I want to talk to you. This is my *life*."

"And it's not my life, too? My body?" I shot back, venom in my voice.

For a moment, he seemed to recoil, shocked that I had it in me.

"I need you to get out of here. I think I've been pretty clear that I don't want to talk to you. I blocked your number," I said.

"You ruined my career."

"No," I said. "No. *You* ruined your career."

His arm shot out. I braced for a black eye, then watched as he yanked his bloodied fist back from the stone wall.

It went with his wounded, hard-done-by air. The bleeding, the crumpled hand. The self-inflicted damage.

"What do you even know about me?" he cried. "I was in love with those women. Fuck, I was in love with you! Why the fuck do I have to suffer for the rest of my life because I was in *love?*"

Here was a scene seventeen-year-old me could not have imagined: Jock Gerard could tell me he loved me and it would only make me feel contempt. He was swearing and sweating and contorting himself into strange shapes to try to prove that he was right—and he would never, ever, see why he was wrong.

"You made those videos without our consent. You couldn't possibly love anyone you'd do that to. You aren't capable of loving women at all. You love *collecting* women."

He looked away.

"So what if I do? So what if I love collecting them?"

I felt my lips curl. "Because we're people—" I started.

But then I stopped myself. I refused to try to convince him of my basic humanity.

Like so many men before him, Jock had wanted something, so he'd simply taken it. Over and over and over again. Women were disposable to him. *I* was disposable.

For a moment, I saw myself wrapping my hands around his neck until his pulse weakened, then petered out. He'd never believe I was actually capable of it until it had already happened. He was bigger than me, which was why he'd never see it coming.

My hand tightened into a fist.

But *even then*, I was never going to convince him. In no version of his world would I ever be in the right.

That would just have to be okay.

The desire to change him began to flow out of me—years of wanting to change him, I suddenly realized—leaving wide-open space inside. And just like that, I was free. I didn't want to hear what he had to say in his defense; I didn't even want to yell at him anymore.

I didn't have to make him see that I was worth something.

I didn't have to be responsible for his feelings.

"We're *people*," I finally said as he stared at me, wild-eyed and furious. The simple revelation stunned me. I had never really believed it until now. I still couldn't believe that I'd never seen it before. How little he'd thought of me. How little he'd thought of us.

For so long, he'd been the one who got away.

Well, I'd done one thing right since coming back to Paris. I hadn't let Jock get away.

Later that week, I heard bustling in our hallway, the roll of a suitcase over the old marble floors, and the three-legged gait that told me Stella was back. My initial instinct was to jump up, lean on her buzzer until she opened the door to me, and throw myself into her arms, full of apologies and promises.

Something was stopping me, though. I didn't want to play that part again: the errant pupil, the narcissistic teenager. Nor should she have to be the forever understanding, patiently forgiving teacher. But I did miss talking to her every day. I missed the warmth of the sun on my shoulders as we sat in her kitchen, coffee mugs in hand. And I missed something bigger, too. Something that had never been part of our relationship: a true recognition of who she was. I was an adult now, and she was a person I wanted to know—on her terms.

We are all stuck in our own stories. And it is so easy to see someone through only one lens: the role they play in yours. Stella had been right. I'd only ever seen her as a guru, a mentor, *the friendly neighborhood witch*. Who was Stella in her own story?

When I finally went over to Stella's later that day, I didn't bring any peace offerings, didn't prepare any speeches. I just went across the hall and rang her buzzer.

In the moments before the door opened, I tried to remember everything I'd realized when Margaux had confronted me. That I had caused her pain; that it was my responsibility to offer the apology and then leave her alone. Everyone had their own timetable, and she was not responsible for managing my feelings.

Stella pulled the door open and stared me down with her powerful eyes, so blue they were almost neon in the dark late-afternoon apartment. I took a deep breath and began.

"I'm so happy you're home, Stella. I have just a few things that I think need to be said, and then I'll leave."

Stella froze in surprise, then nodded.

I followed her down the hall to her kitchen. Her movements were more abrupt as we walked, and I wondered how long it would be until she was better, back to the Stella that she used to be.

Or maybe she was someone different now. I had to leave room for that, too.

"You know how when you're a child," I said as we sat down at her table, "parents are these absolute figures? They're not real, three-dimensional beings to us. We treat them like robots, like their only function in life is to serve our needs, whether that's something simple like giving us food or something way more complicated."

After a long moment, she nodded.

"I guess what I'm trying to say," I went on, "is that you've been telling me who you are for a long time, but I was refusing to see it. It was easier for me to keep you separate in my mind as this mother figure, because that's what I needed. But that's only what *I* needed. It wasn't doing you any good. And, as it turned out, it's actually done you a great deal of harm."

As I spoke, I watched her changing face in the dim light, her hands folded together on the table. I was trembly, ungainly. I felt like I'd stripped my skin off and was just waiting for her to stick a fingernail into my tender muscles.

I took a deep breath and went on.

"I'm so sorry for that, Stella. And you don't have to tell me it's okay or that you forgive me or anything, because it's not and I don't even forgive myself. I don't know that I ever can. But I do want you to know that—that I am truly sorry, and that if you feel like we can have some kind of relationship in the future, I'll go forward in it with much more—respect. A lot has happened lately that's made me rethink—well, everything. I'm working on my attitudes and my relationships. This one is really important to me."

For a moment, we just sat there looking at each other. I was, I realized with an uncomfortable jolt, still waiting for her to comfort me. "I'm sorry," I said, standing up so suddenly that my chair screeched behind me. "I should go."

Stella reached out a hand.

"Not yet," she said. "It's my turn now."

Gently, like a hostage negotiator, I lowered myself back down.

"I appreciate you saying all of that," Stella started. Her voice was gravelly, hoarser than usual. "I appreciate your thinking about it more than anything. I think you're right. We really do need to set better boundaries with each other going forward.

"I've been sitting with some news for some time and wondering if and how I was going to broach it with you," she went on. "But there's one thing that you're right about, and it's that we can't go through a friendship constantly worried about managing each other's reactions. So, I'm going to tell you, and then I'm going to give you a hug, and then I'm going to ask that you go home and spend some time with the information on your own. And then come back for brunch on Sunday and we'll see what this new friendship could look like. Okay?"

My heart had already been hammering so loudly I wouldn't have thought it could get any louder, but by the time she finished, I was almost twitching in time with its pounding.

I nodded.

"They weren't able to do the hip replacement," Stella said. "When they went in, they found that the bone had deteriorated too severely. It turns out that I have a condition called multiple myeloma, in which cancer cells gather in the bone marrow."

Stella was watching my face attentively. I squeezed her hand and nodded for her to go on.

"It's stage three. At my age, that gives me about two to three years with treatment. And, as you know, I've been through that kind of treatment, both with my husband and your mother, and I've seen the kind of effects it can have on our last days. That's not something I want for myself. And so," Stella said, taking a deep and unsteady breath, "I've decided not to treat it."

My chest was so tight I thought I'd cough up my heart right there on the table. But I couldn't process this here; I could react later. I clenched my jaw to hold the tears back. All I had to do was keep it together for a few more minutes.

"I . . . understand," I said, barely in a whisper. "I understand your choice."

Already, I was imagining what my life would look like without her. I bit my tongue hard to keep from crying out: *How can you do this to me? Why would you do this to me?*

But the answer to both of those question was the same. She wasn't doing anything *to me.* She was doing it to herself. Not *doing* it. Letting it happen. Letting it go. It wasn't about me.

Everyone had changed since I'd returned to Paris. The sketches of the people we'd been in my memories were now shaded with levels of chiaroscuro. Everyone was more than I remembered: more complex, more complicated. More than they'd been before.

Or, at least, more than I'd ever known.

In the moment it took for Stella to come over and wrap her arms around me, the futility of having any emotions about the people you love changing before your eyes washed over me. And what was death but the ultimate change?

I held Stella tight, waiting for her to pull away. As she did, my brain grasped for something rational to say. I had to take my place as one of the adults in the room.

"Do you have all the information you need?" I managed.

She smiled. "Yes, dear," she said.

Behind her, the Place des Vosges floodlights went on, lighting up the trees and their full, colorful branches. For a moment, I seemed to be living in every October I'd ever known. I was five, I was twenty-two, I was seventeen, I was thirty-six: all here, all at the same time, the days and years collapsing around my feet like a skeleton's bones after the wires have been pulled out.

"I think you should go home now," Stella said gently.

This was it. As images of this empty apartment pushed their way into my mind, I reminded myself that all I could do was show up. Bear witness. Be here.

I nodded.

"Brunch on Sunday, then," I said.

Stella tilted her head to the side. "Don't make promises you can't keep," she said.

"No," I said. "I don't do that anymore."

CHAPTER 32

I n France, we used to punish abortion with the death penalty, and a lot more recently than you'd think. We guillotined the last woman in 1943.

Four years into World War II, and the government decided to spend time, money, and energy condemning the morals of one woman. A woman who'd provided free abortions to prostitutes.

Her name was Marie-Louise Giraud. She was thirty-nine years old. She'd been known as a *faiseuse d'anges*. A maker of angels.

The government prosecuted her not because of any moral argument but because they were still trying to build up the population after World War I. Technically, she was executed for "crimes against the nation."

I was so sick of men.

Lindsay was sitting in the waiting room, her eyes closed. It was a standard waiting room; it was every waiting room I'd ever been in. I sat down next to her, but she didn't open her eyes until I touched her arm.

"Oh, hey," she said.

"Hi. How are you doing?"

She shrugged. "It's not how I'd normally choose to spend an afternoon, but . . . you know."

"Yeah."

Closing her eyes again, she tilted her head back against the wall.

"Tell me some good gossip," she said.

"Oh. Well—"

At that moment, a short, pale nurse came out and called her name. I swiveled my head around at the handful of women surrounding us. Surely they couldn't just identify you like that in public?

Lindsay laughed at my expression as she stood.

"You're such a prude. Sometimes I think you're more American than I am," she said. "Let's go."

The procedure room was cheerful and, from the Lacan and Eva Hesse posters framed on the walls, weirdly leftist. Red curtains and ferns by the window only added to the seventies vibe. It actually reminded me of my mother's living room as it used to be. All it needed was a barre under the window and ashtrays on the side tables.

The nurse did some basic examinations and set up some injections as Lindsay stripped down and I pulled a chair up beside the table.

"Are you weird about shots?" I asked in a whisper as the nurse dabbed her arm.

"Why would I be weird about shots?"

"Some people are."

"Nothing hurts this one," the nurse said to me in French as she stuck the syringe in.

"No, that's true," Lindsay said.

I laughed. "It's hard to remember that you speak French," I said.

She gave a languid smile.

"That's because it's humiliating when I get things wrong," she said. "And I'm so tired of being humililiated—humili—looked down on."

"That stuff works fast," I said to the nurse.

"Yeah," she said. "It's really good." She turned to Lindsay. "The doctor will be right in."

"Where do you think it is?" Lindsay said as the nurse left the room.

"Where what is?"

"The abortionator."

"The—"

She made a frustrated noise at the back of her throat, but slow. "The—you know, the machine."

I looked around. "I don't know. Are you scared?"

"I don't get scared," she said. "But yeah, a little."

I reached out and squeezed her hand. "They say some people don't feel much at all," I said.

She scrunched up her face. "Not *that*. I really don't mind pain, you know. It's the judgment that gets me."

"But nobody—" I stopped. "Daniel. You didn't tell him?"

"Not going to, either. No, I meant Margaux."

"Oh, Lindsay. You know she doesn't mean half of what she says."

"She meant everything she said."

Yes. She had.

"It's the right thing. I don't know why she doesn't see that. I don't know how to make her see that." Her eyes widened at me almost comically. "The right thing."

"I don't know that there is one right thing."

"Of course there is. Don't be silly. It's just—" Her head lolled to the side and she grinned at me. It was a grotesquely inappropriate expression.

"Just what?"

"They tell you that you can grow up to be anybody you want. Do anything you set your mind to. Just hang in there, aim for the moon, and you'll hit a star—what's that saying?" She saw the expression on my face. "Whatever, it's a thing in America. There's just this idea that you can do whatever you want. But no one ever tells you there's going to be so much judgment."

"You can't take it to heart. It's all wrapped up in Margaux's own . . . well, her own life, really. What she wants. What she thinks she can and can't have."

"But isn't everything wrapped up in all that stuff for everyone?" she asked. "The only part of this I'm upset about is that there's going to be this *thing* about me for the rest of my life that people are allowed to have opinions on, you know? Which means I can't ever tell anyone what I've done, and I'm not even *ashamed* of it."

"Well, yeah," I said, shifting in my chair. "But everyone has opinions about our bodies anyway."

"Not like this. Not ones they get to say. Anyway, I always assumed that friendship would override all that," she said, slurring her words slightly.

I grabbed her hand, which was hard and cold. She was so high, a little sentimentality wouldn't hurt her.

"It does," I said.

She squeezed my fingers, her eyelids dropping. "Not really," she said. "But in the end, it will."

"That's pretty grim, Lindsay."

She widened her eyes. "Don't you ever think about it?" she said. "I think about it all the time. I imagine you at my funeral, you know. It makes me feel less alone."

It hurt my heart. "But you won't even be there," I said.

"Of course I will," she said, and that was when the doctor came in.

— *August 2018* —

Walking through an airport is the only way to be somewhere and nowhere at the same time. And the between-space of Pulkovo soothed me: it was a place for people bound together in a pocket of waiting. As I rolled my suitcase to my gate, I realized that only a few weeks earlier, Dmitri had been here. His feet had paced these same slick floors, covered the same nowhere-country, as he'd made his way home to St. Petersburg from his world tour.

Part of me had wanted to fly to Paris the moment I received Nathalie's email. After all, I didn't owe Dmitri anything, anymore. And yet I owed it to myself to confront him in person, to deliver the triple blow: *I know you've tried to limit my career. I know you've cheated on me for years. Now, I'm leaving you for the best ballet company in the world.*

That was five months ago. And every morning since, I'd awoken in the apartment I'd thrown him out of, feeling a seemingly impossible mix of absolute certainty and complete anxiety. The day of my flight could not have come fast enough.

It took a moment to orient myself in front of the departures board. The airport's renovations made it look eerily like Charles de Gaulle: the open space of the terminals, the high vaulted ceilings with tiny, recessed lights like stars. The only difference, really, is that in Paris, the airport's ceilings are rounded, soaring, cathedral-like. In St. Petersburg, everything is angular. Sharp.

My chest tightened as I approached the gate. A few passengers dotted the rows of seats in the waiting area, but most had clustered around the Air France desk. Above the dozens—hundreds—of anxious people, an LED screen blinked. CURRENT TIME: 7:42. FLIGHT SCHEDULED: 11:00 [DE-LAYED]. BOARDING: 12:30.

Five hours. Five hours here?

I took a deep breath. I'd get out eventually.

I claimed a seat by the window, dropping my tote bag down around my feet. Thirteen years in Russia, and I'd ended up with two big suitcases, a carry-on, and a tote bag full of junk. Worst game show ever.

BOARDING: 13:25, the screen flashed. A groan went up around me. For a moment, the anticipation was like an itch under my skin: didn't they know I was going *home*? How could they keep me suspended, paused in the present moment, for so long? The dusty smell of my mother's apartment—Stella's rich coffee—Lindsay's and Margaux's smoke rising pungent through the air—they were all waiting for me.

As I had wrapped up the season at the Mariinsky, as I'd waited for my POB contract to come through, as I'd plotted my withering final speech to Dmitri, I'd also plunged back into my email correspondence with Lindsay and Margaux. Tentatively, at first, then with increasing joy as I remembered just how great my days with them had been.

"Oh, fuck *you!*" a man called out, and I swiveled around in my chair to see him yelling at the Air France screen, which now read, BOARDING:—

Those dashes flashed insistent yellow. I couldn't be stuck here any longer. On the other side of this nothingness, people were waiting for me. My real life was about to start again. I rose to my feet, ready to storm the desk with two hundred Russians. Until I heard a deep tearing sound; for a second, I thought my jeans had split. Instead, my belongings were tumbling out of my tote bag, scattering around me, as I stared at the torn bottom seam, threads flapping in the artificial airport ventilation.

I picked up a hair clip, my wallet, my phone. Jammed them into my pockets. Grabbed everything else and ran to take my place at the back of the line.

And then for half an hour—an hour—two—I stood waiting, shifting from foot to foot, my arms full of possessions that had seemed so vital to me only a few hours earlier. Now they pressed into my skin, cutting my arms, making me sweat. The Gogol book I'd bought for my Russian class a decade ago. A mink wrap I'd found hanging in the back of my closet long after my suitcases had been packed and set by the door. An empty metal water bottle I'd bought after reading about PET and had meant to fill on my way to the gate.

My phone buzzed twice in quick succession in my pocket. An email. It doesn't seem right that something as insubstantial, as intangible, as email should have the power to change our lives. And yet after Olga—and then Galina—had told me the truth about Dmitri, twin strands of disgust and shame pounding through my blood, there in my in-box, beckoning like the title of a play: *An Invitation*, by Nathalie Dorival.

As long as I stayed in Russia, I was still the object in Dmitri's sentence. He was the subject: Guess what *he* did to *her*. As long as I stayed there, that's all I would ever be.

And what about my home? The place where they'd known me since I was small, the place with all of my memories, the place that was *always a good idea*?

I had made mistakes there. I knew that. But it had been so long—I'd gone so far—and Lindsay had never found out. Was it enough? I knew I couldn't rewrite the past. I knew that my last days in Paris, back in 2004, would always be a gaping wound on the skin of my life.

But if it came down to being the villain or the victim—I knew which one I'd rather be.

My mind cleared. I was going home. That was all that mattered.

"Save my place?" I asked the frizzy-haired woman behind me. She raised her eyebrows—just a centimeter, but I saw. "I'll be right back. I promise."

Almost imperceptibly, she nodded.

At the nearest trash can, I let everything I was holding tumble out of my arms. My St. Petersburg life, taking its place among McDonald's wrappers and day-old newspapers. Arms covered in red welts, I ran back to my spot.

Then I grabbed my phone and opened my in-box.

Air France.

Please evaluate your flight from St. Petersburg to Paris.

For a second, I wondered if I'd taken the flight already, if this was all a fever dream. But a quick glance around at the Cyrillic signs brought me back to reality.

The second email: *Please evaluate your flight from St. Petersburg to Paris.*

The LED screen flashed with the persistent buzzing of a mosquito. BOARDING: CANCELED.

And a third time: *Please evaluate your flight from St. Petersburg to Paris.*

Suddenly, the oblivion of the airport was intolerable. The lights around me whined through the brightness of my tears. The frizzy-haired woman, now at my side, looked at me in muted alarm.

"I'm sorry"—wiping my cheeks, muttering apologetically—"it's just, I need to get on that plane." She tilted a gray head, uncomprehending, as my words echoed back to me: I'd spoken in French, not Russian.

And then I really was crying. "I'm sorry—" I sputtered as she shuffled her feet uncomfortably. It was the only Russian phrase I could remember. "I'm sorry, I'm sorry—"

Her palm, cool and steady, went to my back as she pushed me through the remaining people up to the desk. Two flight attendants with perfect, stage-ready makeup, looked up at me.

"French," the woman said roughly.

"I need to get home," I said in a small voice.

The brunette spread on a wide, pink smile.

"Madam," she said, and her Russian accent was thick as grease, "we apologize for any inconvenience—"

I choked back a sob. "You don't understand. I need to get back to Paris!"

The flight attendants exchanged worried glances. I felt the eyes on me then: The woman behind me. The old man and little girl off to the side. The security guard by the gate. I shuddered, but there they still were: gazes like insects on my skin.

"Please," I said. "Just let me onto the plane. Can't you just let me onto the plane?"

Watching. Everyone, watching. The people waiting behind me, the people passing through, the strangers sifting through my appearance, my actions, my words, like Cinderella tweezing lentils from ashes, weighing my virtues and my failures like Anubis with his feather, like the gilded audience at the Palais Garnier in their red velvet seats, leaning forward to gasp—

"Just let me go home!" I cried.

— *October 2018* —

"I can't make it to rehearsal today," Lindsay said drowsily as we left the doctor's office. "I seem to be bleeding from my vagina."

I wrapped my arm around her. "I know, honey. I hadn't planned on it."

"Don't you go teaching it to that little girl, though," she said, pulling away with unexpected force. "That's *my* dance."

"Lindsay, is Daniel home?" I asked her.

"I told you. Daniel doesn't know."

"Yes, and it's just—seeing you like this. He might figure it out." An understatement. At best, he might think she'd been day drinking.

"Shit," she said, and stopped, blinking in the bright cold sun. "I didn't think it would be like this. I thought it'd be more like . . ." She trailed off for so long I thought she had lost her train of thought. "Getting a mole removed!" she said triumphantly.

"Well, it wasn't."

"Too fucking right."

"Here, give me your phone," I said. She plucked it out of her purse and handed it to me.

"Why?" she said about thirty seconds later.

"I'm telling Daniel you're staying over with me tonight," I replied, typing. "I'm pretending to be you or he'll think something's strange. How should I word it?"

"Say, *Staying over at Delphine's tonight*," she said.

I stopped. "That's it? No *See you tomorrow*?"

She shook her head.

"No *xoxo*?"

She made a face.

I sighed. "Okay," I said, and hit send. "You're all set." I tried to hand the phone back to her, but her palm was pressed against her mouth. "Are you okay? Let's go by the pharmacy—"

"Ugh, it's not that," she said. "It's just—it's my birthday."

"Oh my God," I said before thinking. I couldn't believe that she'd done it on her *birthday*. And that I'd forgotten.

And oh, fuck. The party.

"Lindsay . . ." I said tentatively. "Um. I forgot to tell you, but I think—shit. Daniel's throwing you a surprise dinner tomorrow, okay? I couldn't stop him."

She made a face. "Are you kidding?" she said in the drawling, annoyed tone of a teenager. "I don't want to go. Ugh, he'd be so *mad* if I didn't show up, though."

"We'll get you there on time," I said, sliding her phone into my pocket and getting out my own. "I think it's just going to be Margaux and me. I hope. That's what I told him to do."

"Oh, like he *listens*," she said, her hand drifting to her stomach.

Lindsay slept for thirteen hours straight. I woke up to the sound of her creeping into my room, door whining and balls of her feet light against the wood floor.

"Delphine?" she stage-whispered.

"Yeah," I said, my eyes still closed. "How are you doing?"

"Fine." She sat on the foot of the bed. "I mean, I feel like I've been hit by a bus. Other than that, though . . ."

"I left the painkillers by your bed."

"Did you? Thanks."

She didn't move for a long time. My mind began to fight its way back to sleep.

"I'm worried about Daniel," she said finally, her voice cutting through like she was on a loudspeaker. "He hasn't written back to your message."

I opened my eyes. Sat up.

"Is that normal?"

She rolled her eyes. "He sends about a message an hour. He must be really mad."

"But you didn't tell him."

"No, and before you ask, there's no way he guessed on his own. It's like—he watches me all the time, you know? He watches me constantly, but he never *sees* me. Not the real me. Not like you and Margaux do." She looked at me, wild-eyed. "You don't think—"

"Margaux? Margaux wouldn't tell." I only half believed it; I could see from Lindsay's face that she didn't believe it at all.

"Let's face it. Neither of us knows what Margaux would or wouldn't do at this point," she finally said.

I rubbed my eyes. "I think that if he knew, he'd be banging down the door. Screaming like that guy in *The Godfather*."

She gave a humorless laugh. "No, it'd be more like a month of him crying and us having these *deep talks*."

"Not the silent treatment, though?"

She shook her head. "He's not stubborn enough."

"That's good. I always thought that was the worst."

She frowned. "That's what you do when you get mad."

I laughed. "I know. That's why it's my chosen form of punishment." I pulled down the bedclothes on the other side of the bed. "Get in. Go back to sleep. He doesn't know, Lindsay. Whether he should or not is up to you. But I think you're okay."

She shuffled up to the top of the bed on all fours. It was a long time before she spoke, and I was falling over the border between sleeping and waking when she finally said, very softly, "Yeah. Maybe."

CHAPTER 33

"I can't believe," I said to Lindsay as I got out of the taxi, "that I've never seen your house before."

Lindsay climbed out and stood next to me, staring at the gray stone building. We were smack in the middle of the Batignolles district, an area I've never really understood. It's a mixture of these weird little shops, superspecialized in things like sex toys for skaters, boho hangouts, seedy train stations, and nineteenth-century museums. I had no idea why anyone would choose to live there. You'd never know what to expect on any given day, in any given moment.

She shrugged. In one of my black dresses and a pair of my heels, she looked as classy and nervy as a racehorse. I could almost feel her skin rippling as she stood next to me.

"It's not that special," she said.

"I think we have to go in at some point," I said finally.

"Fuck it. Yeah," she said, and moved toward the door.

Upstairs, Margaux was sitting on the sofa, across from Daniel in an armchair. He was bending toward her, making her look like an unwilling therapy patient. The second we walked in the door, he jumped up.

"Surprise!" he said.

It was all I could do not to giggle as I watched Lindsay, looking back and forth between him and Margaux.

"Where is everyone?" she said finally.

"I didn't think you'd want anyone else."

"I don't." Her eyebrows drew together as she turned to me. "So the surprise is—"

"Dinner?" I said weakly.

"Oh," she said, and turned back to him. "Thanks. That's perfect."

"You're late," Margaux hissed at me as I kissed her hello, grasping my shoulder with her nails. I could smell the wine, strong on her breath, even as I pulled away. "We've been like this for *half an hour.*"

Daniel and I watched each other.

I can't believe what you said the other day.

I meant it, and I'd say it again.

It never happened, okay? For tonight. For tonight, it never happened.

It took me a minute, but I nodded and kissed his cheeks.

"Excuse me, ladies. Lindsay, can I see you in the kitchen quickly?" Daniel asked.

Lindsay bent up from kissing Margaux. "Sure," she said, and followed him there, turning around to roll her eyes at me.

"I can't believe you left me here alone with him," Margaux whispered as Lindsay disappeared. "Does he even know?"

"No," I said softly. "And it better stay that way."

Margaux twisted around, knocking into something on the record cabinet next to her.

It was a bronze bust of three girls.

"Oh my God," I said, looking at the sculpture. "The flea market." She smiled wide as I ran up to it. "We were—what, eighteen?"

"Nineteen. Lindsay was eighteen. And we thought it looked so much like us—"

"Do you remember who's who?" I asked her.

She was staring at the faces. "It was so obvious that day."

"I think Lindsay was on the left," I said.

"No, Lindsay was in the middle."

"But the middle one's just a little bit taller—that would have been me—"

We sat there for a minute, studying it. Were the girls we'd been actually interchangeable? Regardless, it was creepier than I remembered. The staring, for one thing. Had they always stared like that?

"Do their eyes look weird to you?" I asked after a minute.

Margaux frowned, as voices rose from the kitchen.

"Did you have fun, at least?" Daniel was talking in French.

"Oh, yeah, it was a *ball*." Lindsay was having none of it, shooting back in broad, loud English.

Margaux and I stood for a moment in silence, staring at the sculpture. Those eyes. They were huge, grotesque, compelling.

They wouldn't stop *looking*.

Daniel came out of the kitchen, an enormous smile stuck across his face.

"Well!" he said. "Shall we all sit down to dinner?"

"Wonderful Bordeaux, Daniel," Margaux said, reaching to pour herself another glass as the rest of us sat down at the table. I felt her gaze land on me, challenging, and I looked away.

"Thank you," Daniel said with genuine pleasure, and launched into a monologue about the wine shop down the road.

"And when the Beaujolais actually came—" he was saying, when Lindsay smacked her hand lightly on the table.

"Oh, enough of that," she said. "Let's talk about something we all care about."

"So," Margaux said, downing the last of her glass. "Thirty-six, huh?" Her words were slushy, like she had bread in her mouth.

"Should we do something?" Lindsay mouthed at me. I shrugged, then noticed Margaux's thin gaze pinned on us.

"Whisper, whisper, whisper," she said. "Everyone just has so much to whisper about tonight."

"In English, would you?" Lindsay said.

"I said," Margaux said, her accent pronounced, "that we all have so much to *whisper* about tonight. Don't we?"

Daniel filled my wineglass and we sat there in echoing silence.

"The chicken is lovely," I said to Daniel.

"It's pheasant," he said, but his eyes hadn't left Lindsay.

"What was the first birthday we spent together?" Lindsay asked, swallowing. "I don't remember." *Look at you, Linds. Trying.*

I looked at Margaux, trying to make myself as bright and shallow as her eyes. "I don't know. What was it, Marg?"

"My ninth," she said. "We went to see *Giselle*."

"The whole class, wasn't it? And your father showed up in a gorilla suit?" She cracked purpling lips into a smile.

"But that would have been just the two of us. Lindsay, we were thirteen when you came—"

"No, I was twelve," she said. "It was that October when I turned thirteen. You'd saved up and bought me an ice-cream cake, but you couldn't find a way to get it in and out of the kitchen."

"Yes!" I cried. "And so we kept it on Margaux's window ledge because it was so cold that year—"

Lindsay was nodding. "But it melted all the same."

"It did make the loveliest splash," Margaux said. "When we finally dropped it."

Mellowed considerably by the wine and the memories, we moved back to the living room after dinner. Daniel pulled another bottle out of somewhere and refilled our glasses.

Lindsay shook her head as he got to her. "I have to dance tomorrow."

I raised my eyebrows. "Lindsay, you're not—" I cut myself off just in time.

"Not what?" Daniel said.

Lindsay was staring at me so hard that her eyes seemed to glow. I shook my head.

"Linds, are you all right?" he asked, turning to her. She gave a wide smile: a total miscalculation. I'd never seen Lindsay smile like that when she was actually happy.

"I'm fine," she said.

"Are you sure?"

"I'm *fine*," turning those ember eyes on him.

"We're just putting rehearsal on hold this week while—um, I figure out the next section," I said.

Lindsay turned to me, her gratitude a little too visible for discretion. She might as well have been winking at me. *Protect yourself better*, I wanted to say to her. *You're not taking care of yourself.*

"Oh!" Daniel said. "Linds, maybe this is a good week for us to take off, then. You've got all that vacation time, after all."

Lindsay waved her hand. "I still have class."

"What's the point of all of the vacation days in your contract if you never take them? We could go down to the south for a while. See my sisters."

Lindsay wrinkled her nose.

"Or go out to the Pyrenees. Get some hiking in before it snows?"

"When have I ever liked hiking?"

A shadow crossed his face.

"Daniel—" I said, watching the color rise in Lindsay's cheeks.

He didn't look at me. "Or Switzerland. We could go to that spa you like—what's it called?"

Go to him, Lindsay, go to him—smile.

"I don't feel like a long train journey, okay?"

"Daniel," Margaux said, "Julie and I are planning Christmas at our place this year. I wonder if you have some wine recommendations—"

But he held up his index finger. *Just a minute.*

"You don't want to see my sisters. You don't want to go to the Pyrenees. You don't want to go to Switzerland. So, what do you want, Linds?"

Smile more.

She pressed her lips together, looked down at the floor.

"Should we—should we go?" I asked.

"Stay," Lindsay whispered. "Please."

Daniel shook his head. "Oh, right. So they can be on your side, I guess? So I can be the bad guy, so you can team up on me—"

"Daniel," Margaux said, putting a hand on his arm. Remarkably controlled.

"—so I'm just this asshole trying to force his wife to take a fucking *vacation.*" He held up his hands. "Yeah, I'm so awful, aren't I? I'm the fucking worst, I know."

Smile like you mean it.

"Daniel," I said.

He whipped around, staring at me. "And you. Don't tell me you're not fucking enjoying every last second—"

"Oh, for fuck's sake, Daniel!" Margaux screamed in French. "She had a fucking abortion, all right?"

There was a silence like I'd never heard before.

His voice, when he spoke, was strangled.

"Lindsay, is that true?"

She looked him right in the face. "Yes," she said.

And I waited for the explosion, for the excuses. I waited for him to hit her or scream at her or something; I waited for her to tell him about the audition, the ballet, the one hundred thousand views on *Little Girl Blue.*

I didn't expect him to crumple down on the couch, his eyes watering.

"Why?" he whispered, hoarse.

Margaux and I were frozen in place.

But Lindsay became more fluid than ever. She was by his side, running fingers through his hair.

"Hey, it's okay," she said softly. "It's all right."

I couldn't watch it. And I couldn't look at Margaux, who had to be as uncomfortable as I was. All I wanted to do was close my eyes; but I didn't seem capable of that, either.

Lindsay kept on whispering to him. "It's going to be fine. And maybe, you know, maybe this was a good thing—"

Shaking all over, he got to his feet.

"A good thing?" he said.

With his hands down from his face, he looked like an old man. His reddened eyes might just have been rheumy, his haggard, splotchy face just sun damaged. He turned toward the windows, his hand absently patting the side of his head. All three of us watched as he wandered back and forth as though he'd gone senile, just patting the side of his head.

He's drunk, I told myself. He's just drunk.

"My God," he muttered over and over again. "My God, my God."

Lindsay grabbed his arm. "You understand why I had to, don't you?" she said. He let his hand fall and watched her, eyes wide in disbelief. "I didn't say anything, because it wasn't even a decision, really—"

"Of course it wasn't even a decision," he said, gesticulating madly toward her. "Of course it wasn't. There have to be conflicting desires for there to be a decision and Lindsay, when have you ever let my desires conflict with yours?"

"That's not what I meant."

"It would be if you thought about it. It would be if you had the capacity for—I don't know, Lindsay, what? Self-reflection? Compassion? Love?"

She reached for his wrist. "If you could just think about it from my perspective for half a—"

"Your perspective." He snorted and stepped back. "Your perspective? We live our entire goddamn lives from your perspective. What about mine? What about—" And he waved his arm and knocked into the bronze bust, and before I even saw it move there was a sound like breaking open a chicken carcass and it wasn't there anymore.

A deep, animal groan came from Lindsay, who'd fallen to the floor.

She was cradling her foot.

Her foot, like a bloody, broken bird, sat shaking in her hands.

She was too stunned to cry. Margaux's face had the same blank horror on it that I felt on my own.

No needle and thread could fix it. Not this time.

He fell to his knees.

"Oh my God," he said. "Oh my God."

But as he crouched down, I saw it happen. The way his eyes lifted, the look in them, the way he couldn't stop the softening of his mouth's edges as he watched her.

He was *glad*. He was *smiling*.

People show you who they are.

Lindsay saw it, too, and her face went cold. She was somewhere deep inside, now. Somewhere beyond us; the world had narrowed to the two of them.

"You never saw me," she said in a tone so cool and measured it made my skin tingle. Daniel wasn't listening. He was just looking at her foot, rocking back and forth, all sorts of Catholic expressions tumbling out of his mouth, and the whole time he was barely containing both joy and relief. He was performing concern, and not that well.

She used her hands and her good leg to scoot back, away from him, her legs trembling wildly as she stood.

"You never did," she said. Her tone had turned curious, questioning.

I didn't want to look at Daniel's face and yet I couldn't look away. Everyone has an opinion about our bodies. Everyone always does. They think about and talk about our bodies like we belong to anybody and everyone but ourselves.

"How long have you been pretending, I wonder," she said, half to herself, "that I'd grow up and settle down. That this was some phase. That this was anything but who I am."

"Lindsay, get off your feet," he said sharply. Like her foot belonged to *him*.

She was shaking her head. "Well, you got it now, didn't you. Oh, Daniel. If only you'd been a day earlier."

"Lindsay . . ." He stood up shakily. "Lindsay, you shouldn't—"

"Oh, what the hell?" she said with a hysterical giggle, waving down at the bloody purple thing, hideously swollen, that had been her foot seconds before. "I'm already fucked, right?"

"Maybe not," he said. "Maybe we can fix it—"

I turned to Margaux, but she was clutching the back of a dining chair looking nauseated.

"Call an ambulance," I said. But neither of us moved.

"Fix it," Lindsay said, giggle rising. "Fix *this*? How many bones do you think are broken, Daniel? Should we start taking bets? I'm going to say twelve or thirteen. No, thirteen. I'll give you twelve, if you want it. Anybody want twelve?"

"You need to get off your feet," he said, reaching for her wrist.

She stared at him taking her hand. *It's not your foot, Daniel, it's hers.* As she watched him, her face started to transform. *She doesn't belong to you, Daniel, she belongs to herself.* One minute, she was Lindsay; the next, her lips had curled back, her teeth were showing, her face had flushed almost as red as her foot. *It's not your body, you motherfucking asshole, it's hers.*

"You never saw me," she said again, except this time, it was a scream.

And then she flew at him. Arms flailing, clawing at his eyes, her fists making a sickening thumping sound that was quickly drowned out by the scrambling as they ricocheted off of the sideboard and sofa, as he tried to get a grip on her flashing hands.

He'd humiliated her. He'd broken her, and he'd taken pleasure in the breaking. But her balance was so off, her hands so slippery with blood, that she tripped and crashed against the wall. She didn't have the strength anymore.

I felt it coursing through my veins. Rage at his inability to recognize the gulf between their bodies. At the prospect of her as nothing but a beautiful, broken thing. He had only ever seen her as a means to an end, a vessel for his ego. And now, her fading strength as he towered over her fragile form. The strength that he'd taken away.

Lindsay, crumpled on the floor, watched my feet as I moved toward them. Then she tilted up her face, like a child taking communion, to meet my eyes.

Something shuddered through me as we watched each other. The past, the future. The girls we were and the women we'd become.

I slammed my hands into his chest.

My invisible audience shut their eyes, pleasure pulsing through them like a purr.

He stared at Lindsay as he hit the window. It wasn't until his back smashed against it, almost bouncing off the surface, that he looked at me.

I thought you were the nice one.

But people, Daniel. People show you who they fucking are.

Then the glass cracked, and he fell through.

CHAPTER 34

— November 2018 —

Wordlessly, we gathered in front of the window. I wrapped my arm around Lindsay's waist, and she leaned into me, taking the weight off of her foot.

Below us, he was just a dark mass. His falling body hadn't set off any security lights in the seventeenth-century courtyard. All I could see were vague outlines: Bushes. Stairs. Lanterns.

Daniel.

A breeze blew by, rustling leaves like a whisper, and Margaux grabbed my hand. Hers was hot. Her hands were never hot; her blood always seemed to have its own inherent chill.

We were six floors up. He was dead.

But as I stared down at him, all I could think about was my mother.

Everyone goes on about daddy issues, but no one ever talks about "mommy issues." My father was nothing more than a blank slate, a void from which I'd somehow extrapolated ideas about who I was, about my place in the world. My mother, on the other hand—she was omnipresent, inescapable. Her half meals and her tight dresses, her image and her reality. All of it sculpted to please an audience of men who watched her through half-closed eyes from a dark auditorium of indifference.

Be better.

How?

You figure it out.

Perpetually hungry, she spent her life frantically adapting to what she imagined their desires to be.

The room pulsed with Daniel's absence. Thirty seconds ago, he'd been here with us. Thirty seconds ago, he'd been a person.

He wasn't anymore.

As ballerinas, we grew up training with other girls, overseen by women. But the men loomed over us always: their presences and their absences. Marc, Dmitri, Phillippe, Jacques—I'm not sure it even mattered who they were, in the end. Just their existence was enough to bring us to our knees. Always, we were striving to make ourselves better for them. Trying to meet their silent expectations for us, studying their faces relentlessly for reactions, correcting ourselves, waiting for that constantly withheld approval. A slight wince at our thighs and we reshaped our bodies with hunger, carved for their pleasure. Pursed lips at our trembling arms and we stayed in the studio late into the night, whittling ourselves into their ideal form. Drawn eyebrows at our stomachs and we were on our backs, grunting out crunches until we were wrung out like damp washcloths.

And as the three of us gathered around the dark window, arms around each other, all I could think of was how proud my mother would be.

For the first time, I'd changed a man's body. Truly changed it. Permanently. And I'd done it all on my own.

The high ran through me. I'd taken an action and right here, immediately, seen the consequences form before my eyes. Right here in the real world.

He'd made me mad.

I'd made him disappear.

Lindsay started shaking. I held her tighter, and she wrapped her hand over mine as she whispered something.

"What did you say?" My voice rang out over the courtyard, bouncing off of the old stone walls, louder and stronger than I'd intended.

"*Thank you,*" she repeated, her voice rough.

And with perfect stage direction, a square of light flicked on, casting his horrible, broken body into relief. The blood lay in a pool beneath his head, somehow static and spreading at the same time.

His face was illuminated, and he'd gone pale except for the blood on his lips, where he must have bitten them during the fight. He was a teenage girl's dream of a vampire. He was a Romantic poet dying of consumption in Venice. He was an indie rock star who never saw the sun.

"We have to do something," Margaux said, her eyes almost black in the shadows, staring at him.

But what were we going to do, hide the body? Lindsay was injured, and besides, someone else, the source of that light, might already have seen.

We squinted down at his form. I couldn't tell if Lindsay's trembling was rumbling through all three of us, but I was shaking, too. With adrenaline. With power.

"No," I said. "We don't."

This wasn't the movies, and our lives didn't work that way. Someone was always, always, watching us, and it was too late. It had been too late since I'd pushed him through the window. It had been too late long before then.

Besides, I didn't want to cover this up. Monstrous and horrible as his body had become, as horrified as I was that I'd actually killed somebody, I also felt like I was watching the stage at the end of the best dance I'd ever made.

In the darkness, I felt my mother beside me. Smiling.

Maybe, after everything, this was her legacy. She'd spent her life performing for the void. But two hands on Daniel's chest and I'd flipped the script, made the only ballet that could truly be for us and about us at the same time. I'd achieved what she never could: we had become the spectators, for once. We had been the ones to please.

And he was the one who'd failed.

His death was my masterpiece. Because that's all ballet is, in the end. Just bodies moving through time and space.

CHAPTER 35

The fear didn't set in until we reached the police station. Under the fluorescent lights, the open-floor office had an aquatic, neon-blue tinge. And as I sat on the public school plastic chair, I figured out exactly what the nearly empty space reminded me of. The Planet Neptune Oceanarium, back in St. Petersburg. The mazes of backlit, aquamarine tunnels filled with fish captives of all sizes, unable to comprehend the human faces staring from behind the glass.

I'd killed a man.

I rolled the Styrofoam coffee cup between my hands. The last thing I needed was caffeine. The anxiety in my blood already felt chemical. Why hadn't I asked for a lawyer earlier? Half an hour ago, I could have done it casually, back when the ambulance had come for Lindsay, when police had asked Margaux and me to come account for what had happened: *I should probably just give my lawyer a quick ring. . . .* It would make me look far too guilty now that I was alone with the cop.

On the drive through a dark Paris, the police car had felt familiar, pedestrian without its sirens: as long as Margaux and I didn't try to open the doors, it might as well have been a taxi. Still riding the adrenaline high, I'd been hypnotized by the façade of normality. But then Margaux had been shuffled off to a back room, and the cluster of police had winnowed down to two officers: the man sitting with preternatural stillness across from me, and another, at the far end of the desk, leaning back to flirt with the woman manning the telephones.

I was on my own.

The officer in front of me—Kevin Granget, the nameplate on his desk read—had these beautiful eyes: large and brown, like a cow's. I couldn't let them fool me; he would never understand what I'd done. There was no chance I could convince him I had been right.

"So, Mademoiselle Léger." His voice was calm, plush. Distracting; I barely noticed as he hit a button on his computer to start recording me. You couldn't train that kind of stealth into someone. And he was young, too—younger than me by at least a decade. Some kind of prodigy; had the other cadets envied his precocious talent? "Tell me your story."

All I could see was my shaking hands, jostling the coffee cup almost imperceptibly. Why couldn't I control my body now, in the only moment that mattered?

"He fell," I said, and my voice was as unsteady as the waves at the Planet Neptune dolphin show. "He fell out the window."

"And how did he fall?"

If you'd ever asked, I would have cavalierly said that it'd be pretty easy to lie to the police. Not easy like first position is easy. But easy nonetheless. Just stick to your story, right? They're just words.

The coffee splashed, burning the back of my hand. I winced, shaking the boiling liquid off my skin, bringing it to my mouth.

My story relied on more than words. It relied on movement, on physics. And what was physics but the description of an objective, measurable reality? My hand moved the cup, which stirred the liquid, which fell onto my hand. My hand hit his chest, which hit the window before he hit the ground. It wouldn't take a genius to figure that out if they studied the scene. Bodies told their own stories, after all.

"I pushed him." My words were muffled by my hand, and a wrinkle appeared on his forehead. Maybe he was older than I'd thought.

"I'm sorry, I didn't hear that."

I laid my wet hand flat on the table.

"I said—"

And then I looked at him.

His eyes were wide, his gaze intent. Not a scary kind of intent. Something else.

I recognized that look. Not from Dmitri or Jock or Daniel, even. It was older, deeper than that. Like some ancestral DNA deep within me hesitated at his urging. It tugged at the part of me I'd just overcome: that desire to be a good girl for him. To make him happy. To perform.

"I pushed him," I said again, loudly. "He dropped a statue on Lindsay's foot."

Alarm shot through his face.

"I'm not sure I see your point."

"It's her foot! She's a dancer."

"Oh, she's a dancer."

"Yes, we all are. And if he could do that to her . . . well. And then I was trying to get him off her—"

"Was physical violence in character for him?"

Wouldn't that be a tidy ending to the story? Nice and neat, all smoothed over. The abuser gets pushed out the window, saved by *female friendship* and *camaraderie* and the indelible bonds that men like to think bind women together. They never see the places where those bonds fray; they don't care enough to look.

"No," I said, surprised at the defiance in my voice. "I was shocked."

"Hmm. Why do you think it shocked you?"

"Because—" The question took me back to that second meeting at Merci, to the tone of his voice as he called me a cunt. Maybe I shouldn't have been so shocked. "Because he seemed like a gentle guy. I don't know what it is about that, but . . . you grow up thinking that you just have to meet the right man, the one who adores you and idolizes you and talks about how he respects women and all of that shit, and then you'll be safe. But the truth is, if you're a woman, you're never safe, are you? Not really."

Scribbling furiously, he flicked a glance at me. "And why's that?"

The daily humiliations, the way that we served as *object lessons* for the men in our lives—

"You're bigger than us. After everything's said and done, we depend on your goodwill. Not just to make things easier. For *survival*. If you want to, you can kill us, and we know it."

"And so you believed that Monsieur Faidherbe intended to hurt you? Or Madame Faidherbe?"

I had forgotten that was his last name. Faidherbe had been some general of the empire, right? A relative of Daniel's, maybe? I was so fucking tired of famous men.

"I think he did. Do I think he meant to knock that bronze onto her foot? No, not entirely. Do I think he was glad it happened? Yes. Do I think he liked seeing her hurt? Yeah, I really fucking do." I swallowed. "And it's Mademoiselle Price. Not Madame Faidherbe."

He licked his lips, recording what I'd said.

He hadn't understood. If he'd really understood, he wouldn't be able to flip over the page with such disinterest.

How could I make him see?

"He just—he was *glad*."

"And that . . ." He stared at me, intent. "Scared you?"

"It made me furious. He broke her foot because he was angry at her. And he was angry because she'd made a decision about herself, about her body and her life, and he negated it entirely by being *bigger* than her. But he was so much less than her. Do you see that? He was a *nothing*. So, fine. You want to know what happened? Here's what happened. I pushed him."

"You pushed him."

"Yes, I pushed him."

His cow eyes met mine.

"Just one moment, Mademoiselle Léger," he said smoothly. "We seem to be having a problem with the recording equipment." He stood up in front of the computer, clicking a few buttons. "Pichard?" he said, calling out to the older cop, still flirting with the young receptionist. "Pichard," my policeman said again, and he finally looked over at us. "Can you call IT? This idiotic machine—"

Pichard sighed, clumsily making his way through the maze of desks before disappearing into a back room. Granget stayed in front of the monitor, clicking, tapping.

As we waited, my mind began to whirl. After all of it, after the hunger and the striving and the sweat, what had kept my mother going? Putting her makeup on at her dressing table, showing up for first dates? She'd gotten kicked in the face over and over and over again—forced to leave the ballet, betrayed by the father of her only child, wretched and alone behind the closed door to her bedroom after Phillippe—and yet, each and every time, the façade would slip back into place. The ballerina mask would fall over her features. Her beauty would return, austere and icy, smoothing out the raw emotion.

I couldn't perform for the void as she had. She'd believed it held potential—for love, approval, acceptance. I knew now that it was a false promise. The audience was never going to give you what you weren't willing, or able, to give yourself.

But knowing how to perform—that was still a tool. There was power there, power I could use. Just as she had.

I was going to hold this fury inside of me, like she did; it was inevitable. And maybe sometimes, I'd even act on it. But all of the circumstances of my life—the money, my appearance, the work I did—all of them combined to give me plausible deniability. It was its own kind of curse.

But it was also its own kind of blessing.

Granget had stopped clicking around on the screen and had put his palms on the desk, bending himself toward me.

"I'm not entirely sure," he said in a low voice, "why you won't let me help you."

I started, head snapping back. At the same moment, Pichard came stomping out from the back room.

"They said it should be working fine," he said, raising heavy shoulders. "Try again."

Granget hit a button and sat back down. "So sorry about that, Mademoiselle Léger. I didn't quite get your answer to a previous question." And his voice was velvet again. "Was this kind of behavior usual for Monsieur Faidherbe?"

My eyebrows drew together. He held my gaze.

When he looked at me, what did he see? A pretty face. Tutus and pointe shoes and pink everywhere. Everything about dancers is always overlaid with a filter: softening us, making us palatable for general consumption.

"I have to say," I began slowly, "that he was the kind of man who seems harmless. But it really wasn't unusual behavior. He was—an angry guy. At his core."

Sometimes a truth and a dare sound the same.

Granget was scribbling again. When he looked up, I realized I'd been wrong about his eyes. They weren't like a cow's at all. They were a deeper brown, almost black. Night eyes.

"And did you have a reasonable fear that Lindsay Price's life was in imminent danger?"

I widened my gaze.

"You know," I said, and in the underwater emptiness of the room, my voice had a strange ring to it. Girlish. Coy. "I really did."

The corner of his mouth twitched.

"All right. Let me just print out the transcript here and get you to review it—well, what there is of it. Again, I apologize for our technical difficulties." He hit a button and a printer ground to life across the room. "I expect a *juge d'instruction* will contact you in the coming months to verify the facts of the case. We request that you do not leave the country while this investigation is ongoing and that you refrain from discussing this case with any press or members of the public."

Pichard came over and shoved the transcript into my hand. It was still warm, smelling of fresh toner.

"If you could just read and initial—what you just said," Granget went on, a delicate emphasis on that word, *just*, "and sign at the bottom, please."

I blinked at him as he pushed a pen across the table.

"I'm not a murderer?" I whispered.

He raised his bushy brows. "As you know, that's primarily up to the magistrate. On the whole, though, I rather think not. What you've confessed to is assault. Manslaughter at worst. Or it would be, had Monsieur Faidherbe not been in the midst of attacking Mademoiselle Price. As it is, *defense of others* seems to cover it quite well. One only has to look at Mademoiselle Price's foot to ascertain that." He continued speaking as he shoved his chair back, stood up. "Please be aware that you have the right to retain legal counsel for any future meetings, and honestly, I'd highly recommend that you do so. Why didn't you tonight?"

"I don't know."

"I suggest you be more careful in the future." I blinked up at him, and he patted my hand. "It's the innocent people who need lawyers, Mademoiselle Léger. After all, there are only so many arguments one can make for the guilty."

CHAPTER 36

— November 2018 —

As soon as Granget released me, I went directly to the hospital, pushing my way through the press already gathered at the sign-in desk on the ground floor. Wanting, wanting. To get a slice of Lindsay, to capture her image on camera. *We're not yours,* I thought, covering my head as a photographer recognized me and the flashes started. *We don't belong to you.*

Lindsay lay on her back, and I caught my breath, unable to stifle the sharp sound of my inhale. They'd suspended her foot in a sling hung from the ceiling. At my footsteps, she tried to shift, to see who it was. The plastic covering on the bed squeaked. She was like an injured animal in a cardboard box; there was nowhere for her to go and the fight was fruitless, but either she didn't realize it or she didn't believe it, because still she struggled to rise.

"Hey," I said, hurrying to her side. "Hey."

Her face had sunk in on itself, eyes shaded purple-blue in tired rings that seemed to envelop them. I put a hand on hers and she collapsed again.

Her eyes flashed at me.

"If you say you're sorry, I'll kill you," she said.

I swallowed.

"Because if you hadn't done it, I would have," she continued. "My whole life. Literally everything I've ever worked for. Gone, that fast. You saw it, too? That smile?"

"I saw it," I said hoarsely.

She nodded sharply. "So you were doing it for me. You were like—an extension of my body. So don't you dare go blaming yourself."

With weak hands, I pulled a chair next to her bed. She twisted her neck so she could keep looking at me with that fierce, blazing gaze.

"I'm not sure about that," I said after a minute. "I never would have thought I'd be capable of this. Of killing anyone. Especially not—well. I'm not sure who that makes me. I'm not sure what kind of monster I am."

Her eyebrows jumped up her forehead.

"You're the same person you've always been," she said.

"Am I?"

"Always."

What had she seen in me before? What murderous rage that I hadn't seen myself?

"I didn't know that's who I was. The anger, and then the . . ." *The joy,* I wanted to say. The joy, but also the shock, the fear at the power inside of me: that I was capable of this. That I was capable of murder. "I killed— your husband," I said. "I took him away from you."

Her features drew together. "This is exactly the conversation I didn't want to have," she said. "In that moment, I would have done it if I could have, but I couldn't, so you did, and I'm glad he's dead. Yeah," she said, pinning me down with her eyes. "I really am."

And then she started to cry.

I made myself watch her. I owed it to her, to bear witness to her grief. "You're allowed to hate him and mourn him at the same time, you know."

"It's not that," she said, choking a little, then catching her breath. "Or not exactly. It's just—I'm still trying to make sense of a world without him in it."

He was her family. Her only family, really, besides me and Margaux. She hadn't seen her parents in years. They hated to fly; she never took time off. Daniel was her only life outside POB. And now—

Even as I told myself not to ask, I found myself asking, "When was the first moment you fell in love with him?"

"I don't know. Did I ever really love him?" She pressed dry lips together. "No, that's not fair. I think it was on our second date. He hadn't even kissed me on the first, so I sort of assumed he was a gay fan. But he was nice to spend time with. He was a good listener, you know," she said, challenging.

"I know he was."

"Yeah. Well. To a point. Anyway, we were walking along the river and all of a sudden, he stopped. And he said, *I've been wanting to kiss you forever, but I've just been so scared.* And I laughed and said, *Why on earth would you be scared of me?* And he said, *Because you're so alive.* And I thought then and there, This man sees me. He understands what drives me."

The tears were sliding down the side of her face now, spreading in dark little pools of damp on her pillow.

"Oh, fuck him," she said. "I was wrong, obviously. Once we were married, everything became about the things I couldn't give him, the things I wanted that scared him, the ways in which I was fucking everything up. When you gave me the Janis role, he was so mad he pulled our bookshelf over. It was so *loud*, I nearly jumped out of my skin. One minute we're fighting like grown-ups and the next he's punching a fist through the wall like an adolescent boy. He couldn't stand—he couldn't *understand*. He never saw me. All he ever wanted to do was just *look* at me. I'm so sick—was so sick," she corrected herself with surprise, "of contorting myself for him."

I'd been wrong. I didn't owe her roles, I didn't owe her an audience. All I owed her was precisely what she had just given me: the truth.

"I'm not sure I can explain it, but . . . that's exactly what I've been feeling. That there are these men who just do not see us as real people. Who see us only as characters in their life stories. It's been building and building in me, and then, what he did? The way he looked at you?" I closed my eyes. "I wanted to kill him. But I also just wanted to kill somebody."

It was a long time before she said anything; when she finally turned back to me, her face was hungry.

"I'm sorry it wasn't me who did it. I really mean that."

I squinted; outside, the day had turned bright. We were above the trees, in her private room, and I could see each individual branch below us, stretching toward the sky.

"So, when are you going to get out of here?"

"Sometime next week. They want to do the first surgery later today."

"The first?"

"I'll need two or three, eventually."

"But you can go home in the meantime."

She blew out her lips. "For all the good that'll do me. Six months from now"—nodding at her foot—"you won't be able to tell that I was ever a dancer."

I'd been avoiding looking at it. As she moved, I caught a glimpse of the dark brown-purple bruise, the sickening green rings, the strange, bear-claw shape.

"People will always be able to tell. Trust me."

"I just mean from my feet. Even my normal foot. The toenails will grow back, the blisters will heal."

Dancing strips off your skin. You cover the raw patches with gauze and tights and satin. But the damage underneath never stops rubbing, never stops festering—not until *you* stop.

"Where's your makeup?" she said finally.

"I—" My laugh surprised me. "All rubbed off, I guess."

"Remember when I taught you how to do it?"

It had been our second gala together. When we were really little, none of the girls had bothered putting on anything beyond a bit of powder to keep us from shining too much under the lights. But the year I was fourteen, we'd decided that we were old enough to get away with more.

In the crowded dressing room with the wooden cubbies and the lights framing our faces, Lindsay had pulled out a bag of makeup. Not just any makeup: *American* makeup. Maybelline and Bobbi Brown and CoverGirl. With an expression as studious as I'd ever seen it, she'd rimmed my eyes with black.

I remember how astonished I'd been when I saw what she'd done.

Lindsay smiled. "I loved those dressing rooms. Before I was corralled into them as a *quadrille*, that is. I used to come in before anybody else just so I could have a minute alone in them, pretend I was an *étoile*. Although, of course, the *étoiles* have their own dressing rooms. I didn't even know that then. I used to sit there and think, This is what it'll be like when I'm famous."

Well, we're pretty fucking famous now.

"Linds," I said, a choked sob in the back of my throat, "you were so good."

"But I don't—didn't—just want to be good. I wanted to be the best," she said, and her face drew into itself again. She turned her head toward the window.

"You'll feel better when you get out of the hospital." She looked at me skeptically. "No, really. This is the worst place in the world."

She smiled slightly, though tears were still running down her cheeks. "Yeah, I know. Speaking of, I've always wondered . . . was it all this"—she gestured at the room, the beeping machines—"and your mom dying, that made you leave Paris?" She paused. "Or was it me?"

Here it was. The question I'd been running from for thirteen years.

And here she was. The woman I'd been running from. A woman who felt everything, stifled nothing. Showed her love and her rage to all of us and fuck anybody who couldn't take it.

It was—unworthy of her—to pretend I didn't know what she was talking about.

"It was you," I said.

She nodded. "I thought it might have been."

The only thing worse than telling was not telling.

The words lodged in my throat and I took a breath to shake them free. "It was my fault, Lindsay. Your accident. I made you trip. I didn't see the cab coming, I swear that I never meant for that to happen, I only meant for you to fall."

My pulse roared in my ears, but she simply tilted her head.

"Yeah. I know," she said.

"You—you know?"

Her gaze was clear and direct. "I've always known. I saw you step on the laces. And you held on for too long for it to be an accident. I'm not that dumb."

"But—you never said—"

"What was I going to say? At first, I honestly thought I might kill you. But then—" She grimaced. "I mean, we all do fucked-up things. Not to say that wasn't really fucked-up. But what I was planning—well, that was really fucked-up, too. It took me a while to recognize that, how it must have felt to you and Margaux. And then, I guess I just convinced myself that in some twisted way, you were trying to protect me?"

I looked down at our hands—practically middle-aged, veins straining as they sat clasped on the sheets. Mine was sweaty and shaking, but still she held it.

"I don't know that I was."

"Maybe not," she said. "But you did."

My heart broke open.

Everything was forgiven in advance. Everything I could ever do.

Lindsay grinned. "I mean it, though. I really did think I'd kill you. I was furious. The whole time I was in the hospital, I just thought about all of the things I'd do as revenge. Shove you in front of a bus. Push you down some stairs. I don't know, I've never been much of a planner. It took me weeks to get over. But it helped that I didn't have to see you because I wasn't at the studio, and then by the time I came back, I realized I had to let it go."

I laughed, my body trembling. "You've never let go of anything in your life. Do I still have a target on my back?"

She rolled her eyes. "Like I haven't had the chance? Okay, fine, I'm definitely not the best at letting things go, but I did then. Part of me knew I could hold on to it, but if I did, it would have meant giving you up. Either way." She closed her eyes. "I think I only realized how much I'd fight for that—for you—when you told us you were leaving for Russia. I just knew I never wanted to live in a world where you weren't my friend."

I could only nod, crying too hard to speak. I was crying for all of the wrong choices I had made: for abandoning Lindsay and Margaux for Dmitri; for all of the grief I still hadn't let myself feel—for Daniel, for Jock, for Stella. For my mother.

But I was crying because I was happy, too.

I saw them around us, then. The girls we'd been.

They were scared and uncertain and fascinated. Unmoving. Pure potential energy: poised at the top of a hill. Not knowing what that energy would turn into; not even aware yet that it would morph, change, someday. Only knowing that the future was in front of them, wide-open possibility.

A perfect, empty stage.

"I think you're kind of heroic," I finally said.

"Yeah, I'm a fucking knight in shining armor." But she was smiling.

Slowly, the girls disappeared.

"Lindsay," I said after a long minute, "are you going to be okay?"

Outside, the trees waved their branches at the sky.

"I don't know. It's like—there's nothing next, you know? It's just this big blank." She sighed. "I guess the good thing about being in here is that I'll have bottles and bottles of painkillers at my disposal. Cheap ticket out if things get too bad, eh?"

I shook her shoulder. "Shut up about that. There is something next. You just don't see it yet."

She winced. "If there is, I've got no clue what it could be."

"You'll figure it out. You'll just need time and space to do it in."

Her eyes were watery and watered-down as she met my gaze and held it for a long moment.

"You know the one lesson I never learned?" she started, before swallowing and pressing her lips together.

I waited for her to finish, but her lips were wavering despite how tight she was trying to hold them.

"How to leave," she finally said. "How to walk away."

I put a tissue to her cheeks and she let me, lying still this time.

"That was never my problem," I said.

She let her eyes close. "I'll think about what to do next, okay?"

In the hallway, Margaux was waiting. "She knows," I said, wrapping my arms around her. "She already knew." I felt Margaux stiffen in my embrace. "And it's fine. We're fine."

Margaux pulled back, setting her hands on my shoulders. "Not yet," she said, meeting my eyes. "But we will be."

I nodded and let her go. It was what we needed, each and every one of us: to say our piece. To be visible.

And, at least among ourselves, we finally were.

EPILOGUE

"Come *on*," Margaux called to Lindsay.

Huffing up the hill, Lindsay turned a pink-cheeked face up to us.

"I'm *trying*," she said, sticking out her tongue. "Broken foot, remember?"

The breeze waved our hair around us, Medusas in the wind. I stood between two trees, clutching Stella's urn to my chest, and for a moment, I could feel her there with us.

Watching. Listening. Smiling.

Stella had died in spring, her favorite season. *Everything's being reborn,* she always said. I'd come over one morning in April and found her sitting in the kitchen, head gently resting on the table, coffee mug steaming in front of her, and I'd known. I hadn't had to take her pulse, hadn't had to feel her skin, to understand what had happened.

She'd achieved exactly what she'd wanted; this part of her story was over, on her terms.

Stella was gone; and Stella was everywhere.

In the months after Daniel's accident, as her condition slowly worsened, the four of us had eked out a friendship of our own. Having Stella there with Lindsay and Margaux reminded me that these both were and weren't the people I'd known half a life ago. The memories, the shared experiences: they'd never go away. And yet as the three of them told the stories of their lives to each other, I was constantly astonished at how little I knew, how much there was to learn about these women who had shaped me.

It could take a lifetime to find out.

Stella had already had her public memorial service at Saint-Sulpice, where hundreds of her friends from around the world had shown up to pay tribute. They would take her ashes with them to scatter around the globe. The three of us had offered to take the part of her that would remain in Paris.

We stood at the top of the hill in Buttes-Chaumont, the closest thing we have to wilderness in this city, with the Temple de la Sybille arching above, open to the elements on every side. Below us was a murky lake, running shallow and slow around the island; on its banks, trees were exploding into life, wildflowers in bloom.

Beyond it all, the Paris skyline.

Only a few months earlier, there was so much I would have said about Stella. *She taught me how to speak. She showed me what I'm worth. She helped me, after all this time, to grow up.* But I was only a fraction of her story, in the end.

Lindsay went first, launching into a description of her and Stella sword fighting with their crutches. Then Margaux, with a story about the two of them discussing folk remedies for infertility from around the world.

And then it was my turn.

"Right after Stella got her diagnosis," I said, my voice soft in the wind, "I was having breakfast with her in her kitchen. I was making the coffee, which she hated, because she said I always made it too weak. And when I turned around to look over at her, she was sitting, leaning back against the wall, the sun on her face."

I swallowed, took a deep breath, and went on. "And I said, *What are you doing?* She didn't open her eyes, she just kept sitting there in the light, but she told me. She said, *I'm practicing dying.*"

Lindsay gasped and Margaux raised her eyebrows; I smiled.

"She said, *I've always thought that dying will be a little bit like dissolving into the sun. We'll leave our little frames behind and see the whole picture for the first time. The entire panorama. I like to feel the sun on my face because I can practice living and practice dying, both at the same time.*"

Without prompting, Lindsay reached down and picked up the urn, loosening the lid and starting to shake it gently.

At this very moment, Stella was becoming a part of everything. Her ashes were being cast into the Grand Canyon, spread into the soil of a Kyoto garden; scattered over the ice at an Antarctic research station, hovering in the air over Mayan ruins, drifting into the Baltic Sea near where she'd been born.

Carried into the Paris wind.

Our lives had all changed since the previous November. We'd been objects of public fascination, Lindsay and Margaux and I. Far more visible than we'd ever been as ballerinas. And if the story told in the press wasn't exactly right, if it made Daniel out to be something of a monster, if it gave us credit for motives we'd never really had, it was a compromise I was willing to accept. It wasn't the whole story. It wasn't the exact story. But we knew the truth, and that was what mattered.

Julie had emailed me at the end of Margaux's second stay in the rehab facility, back in February. We kept running into each other there during visiting hours; maybe, she suggested in delicate, formal tones, Lindsay and I would like to come to dinner to celebrate Margaux's return home? As it turned out, Lindsay was still in the hospital following her second surgery, but I'd gone. Tentative, unsure. When was the last time I'd made a new friend? Ten years ago? Thirteen? Yet somehow, as we stood elbow-deep in puff pastry—chatting about Julie's brothers, her father's stationery shop, her own bakery—it occurred to me how much I liked her. Not just *for Margaux*—but as a person.

"Delphine?" Lindsay had said to me when she got out of the hospital, "what did you do with your St. Petersburg apartment?"

Dmitri had never moved back in, but I hadn't been able to afford to leave it empty. "My apartment? I sublet it, but the lease is up in August. Why?"

"The thing is, my pension is great and all, but it's hard to get by day-to-day without something to do. Some kind of purpose. I've been thinking maybe I'd go abroad for a while."

"What would you do there?"

"Teach English, of course!"

And while Margaux and I had laughed ourselves silly at the idea of hundreds of Russian children learning to speak—and swear—like Lindsay, she'd defied us both by starting a training program a few weeks later in Paris. They were going to send her to Shanghai for three weeks of student teaching in July. If she passed, she could go on to St. Petersburg. She could go anywhere.

I planned to stay in Paris. But in the days after Stella's death, I'd come to terms with the fact that there was nothing left for me in my mother's apartment. It was my inheritance, sure. But so was dance, and I'd given that up, too. Maybe my real inheritance had always been something else: that anger just beneath the skin and the self-preservation to know when to use it.

So, I'd sold the flat. I was looking at one-bedrooms now, on the Left Bank. Life didn't have to be just one thing or the other, didn't have to be only home or not-home. It could be familiar and strange, both at the same time.

The magistrate had ruled Daniel's death "accidental" in January, after two months of endless testimony—with a team of expensive lawyers present, this time. It didn't entirely sit right with me. His death would always live in me, dark and bloody: the best and worst thing I'd ever done. Part of me wished the magistrate had ruled it a suicide—after all, he had been the cause of his own death, when you came down to it. If you squinted at reality a bit. But of course, that would have required a blurring of the facts that stretched credulity just a little too far. In the end, I was legally innocent, and so was he. And yet there was so much that statement didn't take into account: my emotions, for example. And his.

In the meantime, Nathalie's reaction to all of the press we'd gotten had been notable only in how absolutely typical it was.

"You know, I've had two scandals this year, and you've somehow managed to end up at the center of both of them."

"I guess that's true."

"I think it might be better if we were to put this relationship on hold. At least until all this blows over."

It was just the kind of freedom I needed. The money from the flat, combined with what Stella had left me and the damages I was likely to get from the Italian magazine I was still in the process of suing, would be enough to start something entirely new. *Little Girl Blue* would be premiering at a small art-house theater in Amsterdam in November, starring a Swiss dancer I'd always wanted to work with. I didn't know exactly what would come next—lately, I'd allowed myself to imagine running a dance company of my own, composed entirely of women. The idea was terrifying, exhilarating, transfixing. I knew now, finally, that those feelings were hard to come by. You had to pay attention when they showed up.

At the bottom of the hill in Buttes-Chaumont, Margaux was standing perfectly still, staring straight ahead. Margaux, who'd applied for a leave of absence; Margaux, who was still figuring the future out; Margaux, who was healing.

"You guys," she said softly. "Look."

Lindsay and I turned our gazes to the clearing in front of us.

There was a group of little girls—seven or eight, no older—jumping around like errant fairies. Empty juice containers were scattered around them. Their clothes weren't the hot-pink and bright patterns we'd had in the late eighties, but otherwise, they could have been us.

There was music playing, some pop song I didn't know. One of them flung out her arms and careened around the park in time to the beat. Another had a strange, robotic dance in which she moved one part of her body at a time. Another was spinning around on the grass. And one just bounced up and down, her eyes closed.

It was spring in Paris; the air was sweet. Bees buzzed and butterflies floated around the trees.

They had no idea anyone was watching.

And there they were: just dancing.

ACKNOWLEDGMENTS

WITH PROFOUND THANKS:

First and foremost, to the Sarahs! To Sarah Phair, whose passion, drive, and talent found this book its home, even when it meant fast-paced texting on cross-country flights. I'm so grateful to have you on my team. To Sarah Cantin, whose brilliant vision for the novel infused it with new life and whose unparalleled editorial skills shepherded me through this process with grace and insight. I can't imagine a better editor for this book. And to Sallie Lotz (an actual Sarah!), who has a keen and incisive eye, and whose love of France and ballet may outstrip even my own. Your enthusiasm and creativity pulled me through some very tricky edits.

To all the people at St. Martin's Press who brought this book to life. I can't thank Olga Grlic enough for this wonderful cover, which exceeded even my wildest hopes. Sona Vogel's copyediting made the book actually readable, while Devan Norman's design made it beautiful. My deep thanks to those in marketing and publicity who spread the word about the book: Erica Martirano, Katie Bassel, Brant Janeway, and Kejana Ayala. And to everyone else at SMP who supported this book on its path to publication: Thank you so much for your support.

To Jess Pan, who's been my lighthouse for a long time now. Your encouragement kept me going through the darkest times. Without you, this book wouldn't exist; your notes, ideas, and banana jokes kept me from hitting myself in the neck with a ski (and making a ton of equally bad mistakes!). You're an incredible editor and a great friend, and I'm overwhelmed by how lucky I am to have you in my life.

To my family: my father, Steve Kapelke, who provided stellar feedback throughout many drafts; my sister Liana Kapelke-Dale, who gobbled up more than one version of this in record time and shared her keen insights; my mother, Kathleen Dale; my sister Jessi LeClair; my brother-in-law, David LeClair; my nephews, Alden and Alex LeClair; my uncle, Phil Kapelke; and my cousins Paul, Joan, Tom, and Kevin Cushing, all of whom make coming home such a delight. And to Elliot, who I'll miss forever.

To the DWG Writers' Group in Paris for their editorial eyes, their unflinching and insightful critiques, and their friendship: Albert Alla, Peter-Adrian Altini, Peter Brown, Amanda Dennis, Nina-Marie Gardner, Sophie Hardach, Rafael Herrero, Matt Jones, Corinne LaBalme, Samuel Leader, Ferdia Lennon, Reine Arcache Melvin, Spencer Matheson, Mark Mayer, Dina Nayeri, Chris Newens, Helen Cusack O'Keefe, Tasha Ong, Alberto Rigettini, Jonathan Schiffman, and Nafkote Tamirat. Special thanks to Tasha for introducing me to this wonderful group of writers.

To Charles Coustille and Albert Alla (again!) for their insights into the complexities of French names and the French judicial system. Any mistakes are definitely, *definitely* mine.

To the people at my "day jobs," for never making them feel like day jobs. I'm particularly grateful to Kristin Fracchia, Rita Neumann, Naomi Tepper, and of course Bhavin Parikh at Magoosh; and to Sherri Doudt, Jae Osebach, Charissa Raynor, and Chris Hedrick at NextStep.

To Jenna Casey, Colette Cavanagh, and Mia Psorn, the original Montmartroises: so many places here will always make me think of you. Though none of our adventures made it onto the page here, I'll always treasure them—and look forward to the ones yet to come!

To Martine Corbière, without whom I would never have made it through my first few months in France (and without whom my suitcase certainly would never have been seen again!), and who made my return not only possible but the best possible experience. And to Annie Wiart, who helped me through my horrendously awkward early attempts at French and guided me towards comprehensibility.

And to Susanne Hofmarcher, who will always be Paris to me.

1. The novel's structure alternates between Delphine in present-day Paris and Delphine in the past as she progresses through her years in the academy. How did the structure of the novel inform your reading experience and your understanding of the plot and narrative world overall?

2. Consider the significance of the question on page 2: "But how much is *pretty* worth?" How does this question come into play throughout the novel?

3. On page 34, Delphine thinks, "But when you spend that amount of time onstage, being watched just feels right. That sensation—everyone is watching, everyone is waiting—had mostly vanished in Russia, but it was back now." In what ways does the theme of being watched versus being seen appear throughout the novel? What are some other themes that you picked up on as you were reading?

4. Compare and contrast Delphine, Lindsay, and Margaux's characters, and discuss the evolution of their friendship over the years. In what ways are the particular limitations of friendship revealed through this trio? How do the characters' memories of their friends hold them back from becoming the women they want to be?

5. On page 65, Delphine thinks, ". . . compared with St. Petersburg's oversize grandeur, Paris felt like a dollhouse. St. Petersburg's wedding-cake mansions were an oil painting, Paris's *hôtels particuliers* a watercolor. St. Petersburg's skies were Technicolor, Paris's a muted pastel. Petersburgians were hard, unyielding, while Parisians were—something else." Compare and contrast St. Petersburg and Paris and their significance in the novel. What do the two cities mean to Delphine? What does each of them represent in her life?

ST. MARTIN'S GRIFFIN

6. On page 118, Delphine thinks, "Did Lindsay now know that you could love someone and they could still betray you, that you could give everything you had and still not be enough?" Consider the relevance of that thought to the secret that Delphine and Margaux are keeping. How does keeping this secret define their relationship and create tension within the novel?

7. What role do men play in the novel? Consider primary male characters like Jock, Dmitri, and Daniel, and secondary ones like Delphine's father and Louis. In what ways do men in the novel—even the ones who are meant to be "good"—ultimately end up being a disappointment? How does each of these character arcs contribute to the theme of female rage?

8. Consider Delphine's words to Nathalie on page 126: "There's an inherent indignity in being in a woman's body. It's an exercise in constant humiliation." In what ways did you see this sentiment manifest throughout the novel? Does the meaning of this change in the context of her words on page 41, "A ballerina is a perfect woman. Thin. Beautiful. Invisibly strong"?

9. *The Ballerinas* pulls back the curtain on the elite and rarefied world of ballet. Whether or not you are familiar with this world, was there anything new that you learned through reading the novel that surprised or intrigued you?

10. Compare and contrast Delphine's mother and the other maternal figure in her life, Stella. What roles do each of these women play in her life? How do they influence the woman Delphine ultimately becomes? In addition, in what way do the teachers and more senior company members, such as Nathalie in POB, serve as parental and authority figures for Delphine and the rest of the trio?

11. How are Delphine's *Tsarina* and *Cry Baby* ballets significant in the larger context of the novel? In what ways might Delphine be projecting her personal experiences onto each of these ballets? In your opinion, is it possible for an artist to create without projecting these experiences?

12. Consider the epigraph from *Rosencrantz and Guildenstern Are Dead* by Tom Stoppard at the beginning of *The Ballerinas*. After finishing the novel, why do you believe the author chose to open with these lines?

13. Examine the scene of Lindsay's birthday dinner, including the fatal moment at the end. What emotions did this evoke for you? In what ways do you see the entire novel building to this moment? Overall, how did the ending of the novel make you feel? What do you think the future holds for Delphine, Lindsay, and Margaux, beyond what the author tells us?

ST.
MARTIN'S
GRIFFIN

Rachel Kapelke-Dale

RACHEL KAPELKE-DALE is the author of *The Ballerinas* and coauthor of *Graduates in Wonderland,* a memoir about the significance and nuances of female friendships. Kapelke-Dale spent years in intensive ballet training before receiving a B.A. from Brown University, an M.A. from Paris Diderot University (Paris 7), and a Ph.D. from University College London. She currently lives in Paris.